Two Spirits

This novel is more than just an exciting story of Native Americans in the Civil War era. Drawing upon Diné philosophy, it presents a positive way to approach life. It calls for acknowledging and respecting the important role that eroticism plays in a person's existence. It provides a sense of humanity in its recognition that people, who would today be identified as transgendered or gay, were always part of the Diné way of life. Above all, this book—I hope—will provide the means for Americans to look at, if not re-look at, the Native population which has been pushed into the cracks between the pages of American history textbooks.

—Wesley K. Thomas, Ph.D. (Diné), Assistant Professor Anthropology and Gender Studies, Indiana University

With its sweet and triumphal love story, *Two Spirits* is a welcome addition to the literature of the real West and the hidden history of same-sex people. It gives a whole new meaning to "how the west was won."

—Bo Young, Editor, *White Crane Journal*

Two Spirits is a story of compassion, and of love between males—one of them a person of "two-spirits," a berdache. It is a tale of spirituality, injustice, and courage set against the stark tragedy of the Navajo experience of the 1860's.

—Ruth Sims, author, *The Phoenix*

Two Spirits is a spectacular tale based on the 1860s eviction of the Navajo people from their sacred homelands. The reader is transported to an earlier era where little-known spiritual traditions were, until recently, unmentionable outside some Native American cultures. With an obvious love and deep respect for the Navajo, Williams and Johnson expose a clash of cultures that will stun many. *Two Spirits*, a treasure to read, is a rare combination of historical fiction and spiritual wisdom at its absolute finest.

—W. Randy Haynes (Cherokee), author, *Cajun Snuff*

Two Spirits

A Story of Life
With the Navajo

Walter L. Williams & Toby Johnson

Commentary by Wesley K. Thomas

Printed in the United States of America by Lightning Source, Inc. Cover art copyright © 2006 by Sou MacMillan

Published as a trade paperback original
by Lethe Press, 102 Heritage Avenue, Maple Shade, NJ 08052
lethepress@aol.com
LethePress.com

First U.S. edition, 2006

ISBN 1-59021-060-3

Library of Congress Cataloging-in-Publication Data

Williams, Walter L., 1948-
  Two spirits : a story of life with the Navajo / Walter L. Williams &
Toby Johnson ; commentary by Wesley K. Thomas. -- 1st U.S. ed.
     p. cm.
  ISBN 1-59021-060-3
1. Navajo Indians--Fiction. 2. Two-spirit people--Fiction. 3. Indians,
Treatment of--United States--History--19th century--Fiction. I. Johnson,
Edwin Clark. II. Thomas, Wesley, 1954- III. Title.
  PS3623.I5664T89 2006
  813'.6--dc22
                          2006037178

Acknowledgments

With beauty before me, beauty behind me, beauty above me, beauty below me, beauty all around me. In beauty I walk the pollen path. (Navajo/Diné Invocation)

With beauty before me, I give appreciation to Toby Johnson, for applying his writing skills and gift of characterization to transform a tragic history into a fictional plot that is interesting and entertaining while also evocative of a larger philosophical and spiritual message.

With beauty before me, I give appreciation to the Arch and Bruce Brown Foundation for awarding this book an Historical Fiction Prize.

With beauty before me, I give appreciation to the University of Southern California, the UCLA American Indian Studies Center, and the University of Cincinnati for funding my research trips to the Navajo Nation, from the 1970s to the 1990s.

With beauty before me, I give appreciation to Steve Berman of Lethe Press, for having faith in this project, for giving valuable suggestions that made the story more compelling and exciting, and for bringing this book to completion and spreading its message throughout the land.

With beauty before me, I give appreciation to Dr. Wesley Thomas, a professor of anthropology at Indiana University, who through his own Diné upbringing has absorbed a knowledge and a sense of spirituality about Two-Spirit and gender variant people, and whose friendship and advice about the cultural accuracy of this book has been invaluable.

With beauty before me, I give appreciation to all the other Diné people who have been so forthcoming to me, and whose provocative, intriguing, and precedent-setting wisdom about everything that matters—from spirituality to sexuality—has been so transforming in my own life.

In beauty I walk the pollen path.

Walter L. Williams
Los Angeles 2006

Sacred Time

Sa'ah Naagháii Bik'eh Hózhó

"Continuing, Re-occurring Long Life in
an Environment of Beauty and Harmony."

Dream Time

I dreamed in a dream of a city where all men were
   like brothers,
O I saw them tenderly love each other—
   I often saw them, in numbers, walking hand in hand;
I dreamed that was the city of robust friends—
   Nothing was greater there than manly love...
   The manly dear love of comrades.

Historical Time

While the protagonists of this novel and their personal adventures are woven out of the imaginations of the authors, this story is based on indigenous traditions of the Diné or Navajo people and on real historical events that happened to them at Fort Sumner, New Mexico Territory, in the 1860s.

Though the complexity and timeframe of the events have been simplified and compressed, the suffering and the injustice—as well as the ultimate triumph—described in the plot was the actual experience of the Diné.

After the story, the authors discuss the accuracy of this historical anthropological novel and their reasons for collaborating on this project. Following that, Diné anthropologist Wesley Thomas provides a commentary contrasting his culture's ancient wisdom with changing concepts of gender among Diné people today.

Part I

Journey

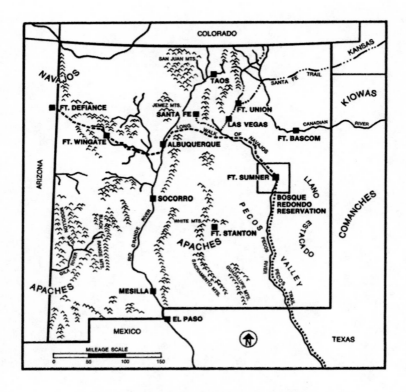

New Mexico Territory, 1860s

1

NEW MEXICO TERRITORY

"Fort Sumner comin' up," the driver called out, and banged his fist against the side of the stagecoach to make sure his sole passenger understood they'd arrived at their final destination.

This is the most arid and desolate place I've ever seen, thought Will Lee, the bewildered and increasingly more disappointed young passenger. *How could Indians live in this god-forsaken desert? This isn't what I expected.*

The clay soil all around was red; what stunted crops or grass struggled to grow through the caked, cracked surface looked pale and desiccated. The sun was so hot ripples of heat radiated from the ground, and so bright just looking out dazzled the eye. As the coach passed by, Will had to squint to make out the series of low-slung buildings of the fort on his left. They appeared to be constructed of rough bricks made from that very red clay. Some of the buildings had overhanging roofs; most were square featureless blocks with few windows. There were trees growing here and there among the buildings, but the leaves were dry and dusty with the same red color.

On the other side of the road, obscured by a screen of brush and sparse-leafed trees—all also dusted with the red clay—was a wide and deeply washed riverbed. Through the trees, Will could occasionally see into the eroded terrain. The land looked dry and hot. There was no river, only a sluggish, shallow creek that wound back and forth across the floor of the riverbed, with a band of pale shrubbery along the water's edge. On the other side there were figures moving around what looked like primitive mud huts. *The Navajo.* Will's heart pounded.

He thought despondently about his dreams of escaping war-ravaged Virginia to find a heaven of peace and loving comradeship in the wide world out West.

Today was May 4, 1867, just two days after Will's twenty-first birthday. He still had the delicate features of an adolescent, his face thin with high cheekbones and naturally pale skin. He had black curly hair and deep emerald-green eyes. The color was said to have come from his father's father whose portrait hung over the homestead hearth. The unusually vivid color of Will's eyes sometimes caused passersby to do a double take. Will never knew how to understand the attention. He wanted to think he was comely. His father, stern and stiff-necked, had once scolded him mercilessly for looking too long at his own reflection in a mirror. "Vain and self-willed," his father, the Reverend Joshua Lee, had called him.

Though slender, Will's physique was solid, his muscles well-defined, his shoulders square and strong from working the family farm. But his father, never satisfied, had always insisted that he slunk from the really hard work. He'd told him this every time he pulled out his whip and beat him on the backside. "To teach you the fear of God," his father would say.

The handsome, but shy and easily intimidated-looking, young man was happy to have escaped his father's authority, though now as he looked out of the stagecoach his idea of starting a fresh new life here seemed to be evaporating in front of his eyes like a pail of water sitting in this blazing sun. *This sure doesn't look like the Promised Land. It's more like the back wasteland of hell.*

He'd been remembering his preacher-father tell the story—with that grand oratorical pomposity Rev. Lee was famous for throughout Lynchburg and the surrounding counties—of Moses and the Israelites in the desert for forty years. Moses never found his own way into the Promised Land. *I don't guess I have any business comparing myself to Moses, but how am I ever going to make it to any promised land anywhere, much less lead anybody else to freedom?*

Will reminded himself he wasn't going to think about his father's religion anymore or judge his own life according to that man's way of thinking. *I burned those bridges behind me.* Now he would see his life the way that poet described in the book Harry Burnside had given him to read on the train. Mr. Burnside had told him to go discover the "wide world out there." He'd said it'd be an adventure. He'd said there'd be loving comrades out there for Will to meet. He'd made it sound so simple.

"Wide world." Those had been the same words his friend Michael used. "Let's escape," Michael had said. "There's a wide world just a'waitin' out there for us." Will's heart ached at the recollection of Michael.

They were going to go on that adventure together. Now Will wondered where Michael was. Had he made it to Norfolk harbor? Was he a seaman now, out sailing the ocean blue, on his way to ports exotic and unknown with comrades by his side? Or had his journey taken as unexpected a turn as Will's?

Will felt as lonesome as he ever had in his life.

This isn't much of a wide world. Has there been a mistake? Mr. Burnside's friend in Washington said Fort Sumner was built to protect the Navajos and give them a home. Who'd want to live in this desolation? What kind of protection could a place like this offer? And from what?

As the stagecoach had approached Fort Sumner and the Bosque Redondo Reservation, in the distance Will had seen Indians tilling the desiccated soil under the supervision of armed soldiers. Closer by, he'd noticed another group making mud bricks, also under the close watch of blue uniforms. That's what had got him thinking of the story of Moses. *Moses freed slaves who were making mud bricks, hadn't he? That's what the blue uniforms are supposed to stand for: freeing slaves.* Will thought contemptuously about the war that had dominated his life back home. *Blue vs. Gray. What a hornswoggle! These Union bluebellies look just like slave overseers.*

The coach pulled up in front of a building that bore a sign in military stenciling: "Sutler's Store." Standing in the shade of the overhanging roof were blue-uniformed soldiers surrounded by a crowd of brown-skinned men and women dressed in rawhide or else in tattered cotton clothes that looked like white men's hand-me-downs.

The young Virginian had expected the Indians to appear fierce and threatening, but these poor wretches who toiled under the soldier's watch or stood around the store looked beaten down and dispirited, less like recipients of the government's altruism and largesse and more like its slaves—though brown-skinned now, not black. *Could this be a prison and not the reservation, after all?* Will had imagined lush mountains and babbling brooks with encampments of clean white tepees that glistened in the sun. That was how his childhood picture books had shown Indian villages. *Maybe the reservation is somewhere else.*

The air was dry and dusty, full of gnats and insects that swarmed in his eyes and nose as he climbed down out of the stagecoach. He wondered where he was supposed to go. *Is this the right place?*

Will's confusion—and hope for some alternative—ended when a uniformed soldier approached. "You the new Injun Agent?"

"Good afternoon. I'm William Lee. I've been appointed apprentice to the Agent at Fort Sumner." He extended his hand. Though wind-beaten and sunburned, this soldier reminded him of the draft officer for the Virginia Militia whom he'd served under back in Lynchburg. That man had been a good soldier, a handsome gentleman and a kindly benefactor to Will. He hoped this fellow would prove to be of the same caliber.

"Sergeant J.F. Peak, aide to General James Carleton." The soldier looked at his hand with disdain and gave a cursory salute. "Welcome to Fort Sumner and the beautiful Bosque Redondo Reservation," he added with obvious sarcasm.

"Is this really the reservation?"

"You got any complaints?"

"I just meant I thought maybe there might be someplace else, well, more hospitable for the Indians."

"Jezzuz," Peak sighed. "Look, Gen'rl Carleton wants to meet you right away. C'mon. Where's your baggage?"

"This is all I've got." Will held out his single carpetbag.

"I ain't no bellboy," Peak sneered. "You want a redskin to carry y'r damn bag?" He turned away without waiting for an answer and headed toward the main group of buildings which Will could see on the other side of a low wall.

"By the way," Peak called over his shoulder, "the last Agent's gone, ain't nobody here for you to apprentice to. You're Agent now. I hope you're gonna be a damn sight better than that last." He said only partly to Will, "You Injun Agents're just a nuisance 'round here," as he walked on.

Gone? What does that mean? Three days ago on the train Will would have imagined that meant the previous Agent had retired a successful man and gone into ranching on the verdant prairie. But as he looked around at the unwelcoming and uncompromising terrain he'd now arrived in, he began to worry that maybe that last Agent died of thirst out there in the desert or, worse, been scalped by Indians. *This isn't what I expected at all.*

On the other hand, of course, he'd just gotten a promotion!

"Gone?" Will called out to Sgt. Peak, but the soldier had strode out of hearing range and did not answer.

As Will hurried to catch up with him, the sergeant pointed out a solitary wooden structure far from the other buildings, "That'll be your quarters out there."

"Want me to take my things over?"

"You deef or somethin'? I said we was goin' to go see Gen'rl Carleton. Ain't you listenin' to nothin'?"

As they entered the compound formed by a short wall of adobe brick, they came upon a commotion. Chained to the wall were five Indians, three of them bare-chested, Will observed with a flutter in his belly. They looked strong, but starved. One of them, with his arms twisted in the chains, appeared to have just fallen or been knocked to the ground; he hung painfully from the shackles.

"God damn it," a soldier standing over the man shouted angrily. "You tryin' to trip me or somethin'?" He punched the Indian in the midsection.

Will felt called upon to exercise his office as Indian Agent. He wondered if this was a test to see how he'd acquit himself in this new job. "What's happening here, soldier?"

The uniformed man looked around, saw Will and flashed a smile, but addressed Sgt. Peak. "Oh, Sarge, it's you. Why this damn Injun stuck his foot out as I was walkin' by. I thought I'd better teach him a lesson." He laughed.

"That's okay, Mac. As you were," Peak said. "I thought you was on scout duty."

As the jaunty young man came toward them, Will spoke up, "I'm the new Indian Agent, soldier. Tell me, how come these Indians are in chains?"

"Bein' punished for tryin' to escape," Peak answered curtly. "This here's Private Timothy McCarrie." He seemed to resent having to make the introduction. "And this is William Lee. Like he said, he's the new Agent."

"Everybody just calls me Mac." Pvt. McCarrie was a rangy redhead. He had a tall feather stuck in the leather strap of his union kepi; he wore the blue wool military cap with black visor pushed back on his head so bright copper curls framed his face, accentuating a splash of freckles, wry grin and sparkling eyes. Though Will was put off by his treatment of the chained Indian, he couldn't help finding the man's features appealing.

The soldier nodded to Will, then began to explain to Sgt. Peak why he wasn't on scout duty. Will was left standing by himself. *This is Army business, none of my concern.*

He noticed a young Indian woman had come over to attend to the men in chains. She wore a long dress woven with complex designs in rich earthen colors. A leather bucket hung from her shoulder. When McCarrie walked over to Peak, the woman rushed to the man who'd been kicked and punched to offer him a drink of water scooped from her bucket with a drinking gourd. She placed a hand tenderly on the back of his neck to comfort him.

Will was entranced. Something about her was just immediately attractive to him. The Indian's oval-shaped face with deep-set eyes was gaunt. She, too, appeared starved. But her complexion was clear, and her rich brown skin glowed. In her eyes Will imagined that untamed wildness he'd been expecting among the Indians. But her gesture seemed so sensitive and considerate. Her long black hair lay over her shoulders and hung, untied, to the middle of her back. She looked to Will to be about his own age, maybe a little older. For a woman, she seemed tall, her shoulders broad and square.

Will stood watching. One of the men in chains, pointing at him, called out "Has-bah" to her.

Alerted, she turned and looked straight at Will. For a moment, her dark brown eyes locked on his. He smiled and nodded, thinking— hoping—she'd return his sign of salutation. But instead a glare of hate struck back at him like a physical blow. He'd been excited that he'd seen the humanity in this Navajo woman. Her reaction made him quail.

Pvt. McCarrie seemed to notice Will's bewilderment. "The Navajos don't much like to be looked at in the eye. They consider it disrespectful. Better watch yourself, sir—" He grinned at Will and winked, "—if you want to make friends with the lady."

"Thanks for the advice," Will said, grateful McCarrie had sensed his hurt feelings and grateful for the knowing wink—whatever it meant. *At least somebody saw I was trying to be friendly.* Will felt a surge of pride that McCarrie thought he wanted to make friends with the lady.

After Peak dismissed the private, Will followed obediently as they passed through the fort. He could see the strength of the Union Army— rifles and cannons and soldiers—all arrayed to control the Indians. *That Indian woman Has-bah doesn't realize I'm not like the rest of them. She doesn't know what brought me out here.*

In the middle of Fort Sumner, framed by buildings on all four sides, was a rectangular parade grounds. At the near end, a flagpole flew the Stars and Stripes. At the far end a gallows stood. The three limp-hanging nooses reminded Will of the incident in front of his father's churchhouse. He shuddered and forcefully pushed the memory away.

2

THE GREAT PLAINS

The first part of Will's journey west, on the recently built Union-Pacific Railroad, had led him into a strange new world far from his Virginia home. This land was so different from where he had grown up near rural Lynchburg just east of the Blue Ridge. Crossing the Great Plains, he had seen the landscape stretch outward in magnificent emptiness as far as the eye could see. At times the only feature was the thin thread of the railroad track, both before and behind, bisecting the unending sea of grass. And stretching out above were skies bigger and bluer than any Will had ever known down-home in Virginia's land of woodsy hills and low-lying mists.

Lulled by the clacking of the wheels and the monotony, Will could not help but relive over and over again that awful week that led up to his fleeing Virginia. Then one afternoon, while caught up in an imagined argument with his father, he spied a dust cloud up ahead and to the left of the tracks. It was clearly moving toward the train.

"Stampede," several passengers gasped in agreement as they crowded to the near side of the coach to watch. The cloud loomed larger. As it neared, he could see at its base a huge herd of dark brown beasts that looked like overgrown and thick-furred bulls with monstrous humps. They were buffalo and there were thousands of them. And they were running right toward the train. The locomotive lurched to a halt; the engineer leaned on the whistle. A shrill scream split the air.

Will turned to a soldier sitting across from him. "Why are they running toward us?"

"The sound of the train prob'ly panicked 'em," the soldier said. "Once they get to stampedin', the stupid animals just run, even toward what's scarin' 'em."

As the herd thundered closer, Will was awestruck by the dusty beauty. For the first time, he felt he was actually in the fabled West.

The soldiers and some of the passengers took up shooting positions at the windows and from the platforms between cars. Will hunkered down in the seat, deafened by the sound of the approaching hoofbeats, frightened that his whole adventure might end right here in the wreckage of the train car trampled by the mighty beasts. That would just confirm his father had been right about his sinfulness and even God was out to get him.

"What'll happen when they reach the train?" he yelled to the soldier who now aimed his rifle out the window.

"Just watch. They'll flow right around us... like water."

"Are we in danger?"

"Oh, no." The soldier looked around with a warm but half-sniggering smile. "Less'n you get a fancy to climb down from the train 'n take a walk through the herd, farmboy." He added that last appellation in a tone both condescending and solicitous.

"Guess that's what I *usta* be," Will said truthfully, glad, under the circumstances, to have the protection of the U.S. Cavalry. "Now I'm gonna be me an Indian Agent."

The soldier guffawed as he turned back to the window. The herd was just starting to swerve outward to part around the train. The soldier drew a bead on one of the lead animals. He fired. The report rang out inside the car, even above the pounding of the hooves. The huge beast fell. The onslaught parted around the body but kept coming.

The buffalo streamed alongside the train now, their huge heads just outside the windows. More shots rang out.

"Why are you shooting them?" Will hollered.

"These devil cows are the Indians' vittles, britches and tepees," the soldier said. "Shootin' buffalo is almost as good as shootin' Injuns."

Will understood. To the settlers moving west and to the workers building the railroads, the Indians were a terrible threat. He wondered if they would be a threat to him personally. *I am, after all, headed right into their world. Would I have the courage to shoot an Indian myself?*

Will hoped that would not be his job. He wasn't going to be a soldier. He was only to be an apprentice to the Government Indian Agent and help the Indians find a place in the civilized world.

The soldier fired his rifle at a buffalo outside the window. The animal turned its head and looked directly into Will's eyes as it fell.

Will knew he didn't fit in the world of men like that soldier who only wanted to kill Indians. His soul trembled at the thought of the anger those men must hold in their hearts. He'd never felt he fit in any world.

By the time the shooting was over, a hundred dead or wounded animals lay in pools of blood soaking the dry prairie sod. The herd moved off into the distance oblivious, the dust churning into the sky above. With one last shriek of the whistle, the train started rolling again—slowly so that the cowcatcher at the front could push aside the great bodies that had fallen on the tracks.

3

FORT SUMNER

As Sgt. Peak led Will through the fort, few of the soldiers seemed to take notice of him. Some nodded civilly, one or two actually smiled, but others scowled and turned away. It just occurred to him that the position of civilian Indian Agent might be hated by both sides, when Peak pointed out a door in a small adobe brick building.

"Gen'rl Carleton's office. You behave proper now, you hear!" Sgt. Peak knocked on the office door and announced, "New Agent's here." Will heard a stern voice inside. "Permission granted. Enter."

He had to stoop slightly to get through the doorway. Heavy burlap curtains hung closed over the window in the far wall, casting the office into tenebrous gloom. His eyes took a moment to adjust.

Sitting formally behind the desk in the middle of the room was General James C. Carleton. He looked to be about fifty years old and all very spit-and-polish in his full dress uniform in spite of the heat. Will noticed how much cooler it felt inside the dark little office. *I see why one might live in a man-made cave out here.*

The general had a dark beard, with a hint of gray shot through it, neatly trimmed away from his chin in the popular style that emphasized the sideburns. His forehead was high. His face was handsome. Will started to like him immediately. But when the general lifted his gaze, Will saw his dark eyes looked piercing and unforgiving. He wasn't sure the general was going to like him in return.

He'd actually known of Gen. James Carleton by reputation. News of the Indian Wars had reached home. He was proud to meet the man in person and wanted Gen. Carleton to like him. He handed over the sealed envelope that contained the documents of his appointment.

The general motioned peremptorily for him to take a chair in front of the desk. He opened the envelope with a silver dagger and looked through the contents. As the general did so, Will noticed that another officer sat silently in a chair by an empty fireplace to the right of the desk. Even though Will's eyes had adjusted, he still couldn't see very well. He glanced back and saw that Sgt. Peak stood blocking the light from the doorway.

"Mr. Lee," the general began abruptly, "This is Lieutenant Bauer, my adjutant and secretary," he indicated the man in the shadows. "You met Peak back there, I guess. Now I understand you were hired as an apprentice to the Indian Agent here at the Fort. Well, that man's gone. And none too soon.

"Given the ridiculous way our government is organized, the civilian Agent from the Indian Office and the military commander are both responsible for the reservation Indians. I hope yours and my relationship will be more successful than what happened with that last scoundrel."

Will could tell this was intended as a command. "I hope so, too, sir."

The general looked at him with an expression of annoyance, apparently perturbed that his patter had been interrupted.

"He was one of the most uncooperative men I have ever had the misfortune to come across. No wonder he ran afoul of the Indians. He seemed to think that in spite of all my years of dealing with the Navajos, *he* should be collecting the rewards for protecting them here, just because he was a friend of the Territorial Superintendent in Santa Fe. My God, man, it was I who defeated the Indians in the first place, devised the whole strategy for their containment and protection, and brought them here to this reservation." He sat back and straightened his uniform jacket.

"Well, no more needs to be said of him. He is gone and I am still in command, and you, Mr. Lee, are the Agent now. I trust there will be no such problems between you and me." Then a hint of a smile flickered across the general's face. "Let's work together to demonstrate the success of our little experiment here in Indian management." He added with forced joviality, "Then we can both be proud." Apparently satisfied with his speech, the general struck the top of the desk lightly with the heel of his fist like a gavel. "Now, you may speak."

Will marshaled his words. He wanted to know how come he'd gotten the promotion so easily. And he wanted to know what had happened to his predecessor. *Had the last Agent been killed by the Indians?* he'd been questioning. *Now it sounds more like he was fired for embezzling — or competing with the General.*

Will sensed all this was a delicate subject. The general hadn't volunteered that information. He knew his job would depend on Carleton's good opinion of him. Now that he was thousands of miles from home, he felt at the mercy of the military officials. He had nowhere else to go, and he needed Carleton to approve of him.

"General Carleton, this is my first trip west, as you may know, and the first time I've ever seen Indians. I'm grateful for the confidence you show in me in making me the Indian Agent. I intend to do a fine job here."

Will tried to sound earnest but to keep his emotions under strict control in what he understood to be military style. In his most deferential and diplomatic tone, he went on, "I hope you'll give me the benefit of your experience. I want to learn from you, sir. I've read of your campaigns against the Apaches and the Navajos with Kit Carson..."

The general interrupted, "You know Colonel Carson was under my command." His tone suggested resentment that Kit Carson had become more famous back East than James Carleton.

"That was my point, sir," Will added. "Your success is, uh, illustrious..." He had learned tact around his father's parish.

"Well, thank you, but I do realize Colonel Carson has received much of the fame..." His voice trailed off. Then he quickly added with appropriate mock humility, "Rightly due him, of course, you understand. Colonel Carson is a brave man."

"Oh, I understand, sir," Will replied. "But you were in charge of the Navajo War. General, if you can help me learn how to do my job well for the government, I'll be much obliged."

Carleton leaned over his desk and cracked that hint of a smile again. "Well, son, I'll be the first to offer my advice and help. Take your time, get used to things. It's not a hard job. Just leave the problems to me, and everything will go smoothly. I promise." He now seemed confiding, almost protecting.

"Looks like there's a lot that needs to be done." Will sat up straight and spoke with enthusiasm. He wanted Gen. Carleton to see he wasn't afraid of the job. "The Indians seem pretty miserable."

"Well, sir, no, there's really not a lot to be done. You've got to understand savages. Once you've spent some time here, you'll learn. Of course, the Navajos are having a bit of unhappiness as they adjust to the civilized way of doing things. They've been living like wild animals up in the hills, with no discipline. It's inevitable that it's going to take them some time. But we've got that time. This is the Lord's work we're doing here. We will do it in the Lord's time. The Indians will learn to be civilized. That's the responsibility incumbent on us by Christian love.

"I notice in your file," Carleton continued, "that your father's a preacher. So I know you've had a fine religious upbringing."

Will winced. Fortunately, the general was looking at the papers on his desk and did not notice. "You'll understand that saving the souls of these heathens requires us to deal firmly with them. It's the only way civilization and Christianity can spread. You understand this is a job for the military. We know what we're doing. Everything we do here, even when it sometimes doesn't look like it, is for their own good. And for the glory of the Lord."

The religiosity vexed Will. He'd seen firsthand how hollow all his father's pompous talk about the love of God had been.

"Because I defeated the Navajos and removed them here to the reservation, the lands they'd threatened with their savage warparties are now safe." Carleton gestured expansively. "A whole vast territory has been opened for settlement. You don't hear those settlers and ranchers and silver miners complaining about General Carleton, no sir."

The general seemed to need to justify his campaign. Will reminded himself to show forbearance. *Carleton is an officer and a gentleman, and deserves respect.* Nonetheless, the territorial concerns sounded far afield from the concern about Christianizing the Indians, but apparently, at least in Carleton's eyes, the two issues of providing benefits for white settlers and religion for the Indians were definitely connected. "All for the good of civilization and saving souls, of course," Carleton concluded.

"Well, sir, I really want to learn all about this. I'm eager to be of help in every way I can."

"Of course, of course. Now, you must be exhausted." The general turned genteel. "I'm sorry to have wearied you further with all this talk of military strategies. You must be hungry. Supper will be served soon." He looked up at Peak, "Sergeant, you'll show Mr. Lee here to his quarters. And be sure to show him the mess hall and the latrines."

"I showed him his cabin already," Peak said.

"Oh, yes, I can find my own way." Will didn't want to cross Peak. "But I do need directions to the latrine…"

"Excused, Mr. Lee." The general nodded. "Make sure he knows where to go," he said to the sergeant.

Outside the door of the general's office, Sgt. Peak took Will by the arm and half-pushed him around the corner. He pointed to a small shed about a hundred feet away. "Them's the latrines." Jerking Will around so he was facing the opposite direction, Peak pointed again.

"The mess is in that building over yonder. And you can find your own way to your quarters, like I showed ya earlier."

"Thanks very much," Will said. "I'll be fine."

As Peak turned and headed back around the corner of the building, Will let out a sigh and, leaning against the adobe brick wall, reached into his jacket and pulled out a bright red bandana to mop his brow. It was hot. He took off the jacket and started to stuff it into his carpetbag, when he realized he could hear voices. He looked around and saw that he was standing right next to the heavily curtained window behind Gen. Carleton's desk.

"Well, Lieutenant," he could hear Carleton's distinctive voice only slightly muffled by the burlap, "what do you think of our new Agent?"

"Well, sir, he seems a pretty fresh fish. I doubt he'll be of much use round here."

Will sidled toward the window. He wanted to hear this. But he didn't want to get caught eavesdropping.

"Nothing would make me happier than for our little Rebel here to just settle back and enjoy doing nothing," Carleton's voice boomed. "That's why McDonald sent him."

Will reacted to the word "Rebel," and so he didn't attend as closely as he should have to the rest of the sentence, especially the phrase "why McDonald sent him." He had hoped the personnel file would have ignored his military service with the Confederacy—he knew it could make him enemies out here in the middle of this blue-uniformed army—and the documents shouldn't have mentioned it. After all, his service with the Confederacy had never amounted to much of anything.

Will had explained all that to Commissioner McDonald in the Office of Indian Affairs in Washington, D.C. McDonald had told him not to worry about it. He again wondered how he got the job so easily. The Commissioner had said his youthful good looks and sensitive demeanor would assure the military that he was no Rebel threat. McDonald had smiled slyly and said he certainly wasn't threatened.

Then why had he had to report this fact to General Carleton?

"He could be unpredictable." Lt. Bauer was speaking. "What if he finds out and wants to get cut in?"

"We'll deal with that if it happens. What he doesn't know won't hurt him," Carlton replied. "I think I like the lad. Besides, our friend Peak can take care of matters if he has to."

Will heard Sgt. Peak guffaw.

"That will be all," Carleton said, apparently dismissing one or both of the men.

I really am eavesdropping. And Sergeant Peak might be coming around the corner any second. Will's heart started to pound. He grabbed up his carpetbag and started away swiftly. He didn't care what direction he was going in.

In fact, the way to the Indian Agency and Will's quarters was away from the front gate back toward the vast area set aside for the Indians' farms. But his quick exit from the officers' quarters took him right back the way he and Peak had just come.

And so in a moment he again came to the wall and the five chained Indians and the woman he thought must be named Has-bah. *Since I'm returning without Peak,* Will thought, *maybe she'll be more friendly.*

Will was still a good hundred feet away when Has-bah looked up. This time, she didn't scowl, but looked intently. She looked surprised, as though she'd recognized someone long gone. But, of course, that couldn't be.

Once again, Will felt his eyes lock almost uncontrollably on hers. He remembered again what Pvt. McCarrie said. He tried to look away, but couldn't. There was something about the Indian that arrested Will and tore through any volition he might have tried to muster. He felt disoriented. A swell of desire dazed him. A feeling of hollowness seized his midsection.

Suddenly he felt himself sailing up into the air. *Maybe I fainted 'n have fallen over backwards.*

But that's not what happened, and Will knew instead, that the look in Has-bah's eyes triggered something ageless and eternal in him. His soul resonated like a struck bell. It was as though he'd been here before or, perhaps, had seen this all in a dream.

A vision surfaced in his mind. He found himself on the edge of a deep canyon. He was wearing a vest of Indian beadwork and could feel the sun shining warmly on his bare chest between the leather-bound edges of the vest.

A huge hawk soared into his vision, and he was caught up in the bird's flight. He seemed to be flying with the hawk. Below stretched a valley such as he had never seen. The walls, sheer cliffs hundreds of feet high, were of reddish-orange rock burnished smooth by the whistling wind. The canyon seemed to meander in a labyrinth of ravines off into the purplish distance. Through the floor of the canyon, a river formed a bright blue vein down the middle of a band of lush green vegetation.

Then, just as fast as the vision had come, it was gone. Will was back standing a hundred feet or so from the wall. The mysterious and fascinating woman whose gaze sparked the vision had looked away and no longer seemed interested in the new American.

What happened to me?

He decided it had to be the heat. Or maybe it was his nervousness in meeting Gen. Carleton, then the surprise of finding that the man was hiding something from him. He could understand apprehensiveness at starting a new life and a new job. But not strange visions. Unless he had had some kind of real mystical experience, maybe a premonition of things to come…

How long have I been standing here? Embarrassed, Will looked around, as if surveying the whole area. From where he was now, he could see off a ways the wood building Peak had told him was his quarters. He started in that direction.

But he took one look back at Has-bah. And, as he did, to his amazement, a hawk just like the one in his vision rose up from behind the wall. The bird perched on the top of the wall, then spread its wings. They were almost five feet across. Then the bird took flight and soared up and away. Will's eye followed its flight into the brightness of the sky.

When he looked back down at the Indians, Has-bah was gone.

4

Lynchburg, Virginia

Will was nearly sixteen in April 1861 when Virginia seceded from the Union. Though Rev. Lee was a strong supporter of the Confederate States, his sensitive wife became despondent when the fighting began in earnest. She came down with a strange illness, stopped eating, and remained in bed most of the time.

"Son," she said, "I need you here. You're gonna have to nurse me. Now with the war goin' on, I just can't depend on Maudie. Why she might run off with the darkies any day now and leave me all alone, with just your father. I couldn't bear it." She repeated, "I need you here."

Will could not tell if his mother were sick with physical disease or with emotional melancholia because of the possibility of his being called to war. She'd already said many times that she didn't want him joining in the battle.

Her husband could not tell either. Sometimes he would accuse her of malingering, berate her for her sloth, and harangue her with Bible verses about the responsibility of wives to obey their husbands. This sometimes got her up out of bed and to the table for dinner. But it did not make her well.

Reverend Lee was usually very persuasive. He was quite an accomplished orator. He had taken it upon himself to preach the Southerners' insurrection as though it were a religious Crusade. Citing verse from Holy Writ, he proclaimed the God-given right of white men to own slaves and the Constitutional principle of states' rights. He became an important raiser of moneys for the Army of Northern Virginia under the command of the distantly related war hero, Gen. Robert E. Lee. The Reverend traveled throughout the area calling for tithes for the war effort and for volunteers for the fighting.

The draft officer for the Virginia Militia was a member of Reverend Lee's congregation. He understood the importance of the preacher's ministry, especially when it came to collecting funds for the Army. And so he appreciated the Reverend's plight in having a sickly wife and allowed young Will to remain at home to care for her so her husband could be free to carry his message far and wide.

As the bloodshed became ever more evident, Will was thankful that he did not have to join the carnage and that he could serve by helping out in the local draft office and caring for his invalid mother, but he rankled under these privileges because they kept him at home and subject to his father's domination, always treated like a child. He'd always been close to his mother; he'd grown up helping her with her womanly tasks like gardening and knitting and needlepoint. She'd been his best friend. But by 1864, as Virginia's Shenandoah Valley north of

Lynchburg was totally ravaged by Union forces, she had become just an invalid.

Then toward the middle of March 1865, the draft officer Will was assisting announced that the condition of the Confederate Army had grown critical. For nearly a year, the armies of Lee and Grant had been savagely dogging each other in upper Virginia north and east of Richmond. Lee's rag-tag troops were being decimated in a series of bloody battles. Now with Sherman's invasion of Georgia and South Carolina crippling the Confederacy to the south, Lee's army had to be reinforced. All able-bodied men were called to join the fray.

Will was frightened but, even though he had no taste for battle and didn't believe in the cause, he just couldn't stay a homebound child, terrorized by his father's arbitrary rules, any longer. He was, after all, nearly nineteen. *The neighbors must wonder why I haven't enlisted.*

His military adventure was short-lived, however. Along with a small band of boys, most of them younger than himself, he marched off, under the direction of the draft officer, to join his distant cousin's forces west of Petersburg, near the town of Appomattox.

On the way they were caught up in one skirmish. Only a few shots were fired. They came from atop a ridge. The boys all fired back, with lots of noise and gunsmoke billowing about. They didn't know whether they killed the Yankee sniper or if he just climbed back over the ridge and down the other side. When the smoke cleared and things settled down, they discovered one of their number had been shot in the head. It had reminded Will of learning to fire a musket shooting cantaloupes; they just blew apart into pieces. He hadn't known the boy who'd been killed. But he took to heart the haphazardness and deadly seriousness of war. If that's what growing up and becoming a man was about, he didn't want any of it.

The group of boys from the Virginia Militia arrived on April 8, most of them excited and anxious to avenge their compatriot's death. They were shocked that the very next day Gen. Lee surrendered the Army of Northern Virginia to Ulysses S. Grant. The little band turned around and wandered home, a remnant of the devastated forces of the Confederacy.

5

Bosque Redondo

A huge brass bell pealed at intervals throughout the day at Fort Sumner. Will was surprised the first time he heard it. It was so loud he thought it must mean an attack. He rushed to ask one of the soldiers, and was told it rang to tell the Indians the daily schedule: when to start work, when to eat, when to stop work and come in. Will couldn't help noticing the similarity to plantation life in the South.

The great bell had been cast in St. Louis and brought all the way out here by wagon. "The damn thing weighs a thousand pounds," the soldier proudly informed him. "You can hear it for miles out in the desert."

During his first couple of weeks at Fort Sumner, Indian Agent Lee had little to do. The Indians wouldn't talk to him. They looked down at the ground and shuffled off whenever he tried to approach one of them. A few of the soldiers were friendly, but most treated him practically the same way.

He saw Gen. Carleton regularly in the mess hall. A couple of times, he tried to make an appointment to develop plans for how they were going to resolve the Indians' difficulties. Carleton always either dismissed him abruptly or bantered jovially about the weather. The general never invited him to sit at his table.

Will pondered over the eavesdropped comment from Lt. Bauer that first day: "What if he finds out and wants to get cut in?" *Find out what? Cut into what?* Will decided it'd be disrespectful and suspicious to think they were keeping a significant secret from him and that that comment had really been just more of the general's annoyance at his predecessor who had apparently been involved in some kind of competition with Carleton. *This is the military. Matters of protocol and hierarchy would likely be very important to these people.*

Will could see that the general and his officers were accorded better treatment and given better rations than the other men around the fort. From the outset, he had understood himself to be on the level of the enlistees. He simply didn't know what the protocol was; he hadn't had anybody to apprentice to to instruct him in what was proper.

Perhaps all Bauer had meant was that he could have claimed some of the perquisites if he boldly pressed his way into the upper echelons, but where, as a civilian, he didn't really belong. *Well, I don't want to get involved in any kind of competition with Gen. Carleton, especially over anything as unimportant as hierarchy or, even, the food served in the mess. There's bound to be more than enough food.*

Carleton had answered Bauer, "I think I like the lad." Will was pleased with that; it seemed to ameliorate whatever threat he'd imagined. He wanted the general to like him. So far as he could recall, he'd never heard his father say he liked him.

Will told himself he should be much more concerned about the welfare of the Indians than of himself. That was his job. And he was concerned that Gen. Carleton didn't seem to notice—or didn't care about—the obvious hardships the Indians were suffering here in the desert.

Now he needed to know more about conditions on the reservation. He told himself not to get unduly suspicious, but to keep his eyes and ears open.

Will composed a list of questions. At the top of the list was "What happened to my predecessor?" He asked this of Sgt. Peak one day when he found the soldier out near his quarters watching the Indians as though keeping the nearby camp under surveillance.

"None o' your business, Mister Lee," Peak said. "That was 'fore your time here. Don't matter none."

"Oh," Will said, "but if he made mistakes with the Indians, I ought to know."

"Well, then, sir, let's just say he stuck his nose where he shouldn't've." He paused, then added mockingly, "...like into one of them Injun squaws, if you know what I mean."

"I don't understand."

Sgt. Peak waved him away. "You go back to your report writin', Mr. Lee. You write all the reports you want. But don't go botherin' us soldiers out here. We got soldierin' to do."

"Sergeant..."

"That's enough," Peak snapped. "I said that's enough. You go back to your quarters. That's an order."

"I don't think you can order me."

"That's an order," Peak took a step toward Will, clenching his fists.

Will turned and went back to his quarters.

Indeed, he was writing reports, though so far he had little to report about. All he really had was his list of questions.

When he'd asked Gen. Carleton what he was supposed to do about the Indians—they looked so listless, sickly and bedraggled—the general told him to stay away from them. "You'll just get them riled up. And then we'll have to settle things with military force. We're not here for war, Mr. Lee. We're here to protect the Indians and keep them safe and peaceful."

Another of his questions was "What are we protecting them from?"

Will's first report was about the makeup of the fort: number of buildings, number of soldiers, position of the fort in relation to the Indian camp, number of trees in the area—all things he could see and count with his own eyes or with the help of his field glasses.

In the records he inherited from his predecessor, Will found a census of the Indians on the Bosque Redondo Reservation. According to this count made two years before, in January 1865, there were 8,577 Navajos, 465 Mescaleros, and 20 Gila Apaches living in 1,276 lodges, along with 3,038 horses, 6,962 sheep, 2,757 goats and an uncounted number of chicken and domestic pets. He hadn't heard of Mescaleros before, and didn't know the groupings of different kinds of Apaches, but he'd heard of Navajos. The whole country knew the Navajos were one of the most fierce of the Indian tribes. *They hardly seem fierce, now that I've seen them face to face.*

The Indians lived in small settlements scattered over roughly ten square miles, though most of them were encamped close to Fort Sumner since they relied on the military for rations. The creek that ran alongside the Bosque Redondo provided water. Will described this as a small creek because that's what it looked like to him in early summer. It was, in fact, the Pecos River.

Where the river had cut a deep rut through the parched land, the Pecos was a wide dry wash almost a half-mile across. The course of the water wound back and forth across this wash and formed what Will called the creek. Close to Fort Sumner, this creek made a sharp bend that brought it right up to the closer bank.

For a couple of miles stretching north of Fort Sumner, along the east bank of the wide riverbed, were the fields and farmlands of the reservation. The red clay dirt did not look like farmable soil. There was only stunted maize growing in the fields, along with struggling beans and squash vines planted at the base of each stalk.

This was hardly a sufficient food source for the thousands of Indians living huddled along the creek. Will observed, however, that they did not actually depend on the produce of their garden. He kept writing the word "garden" in his report, each time wishing there were some more apt word to capture the desolation of what was supposed to be an agricultural area. The military supply convoy that had arrived a couple of days after he started his job at Fort Sumner, coming from Santa Fe with several wagonloads of goods and produce, had delivered bags and bags of flour and cornmeal, as well as meat and fresh vegetables. Little of the meat and vegetables ever made it to the Indians, only the cornmeal and flour. This was their major food source. But Will did not see how the Navajos could survive on grain alone. The Indians raised chickens, so he figured them to have eggs. But still that did not seem an adequate diet.

At the north end of the reservation, a sluice gate directed some of the water of the Pecos down an irrigation ditch called the *acequia madre* to water the farms. *Where does the water come from?* Apparently at some time in the past there must have been much more water running through here. That would explain the wide deep wash.

A group of Navajos had camped along the riverbank just above the bend in the creek. From his quarters, he could see into this camp. He learned from Mac McCarrie, that soldier who'd befriended him, that the Navajos ordinarily lived in conical-shaped lodges called hogans that were formed of mud and earth packed over an armature of limbs and branches above a shallow excavation. These might have what was called a brush arbor attached to provide shade outside the hogan. Such hogans could be built quite solidly and spaciously. But most of the Indian dwellings around the reservation looked like barely more than piles of brush or heaps of stone and earth. The dry, rocky-hard desert did not offer itself for construction of the Navajos' native habitat.

Ironically, the soldier who instructed Will about Navajo ways, Pvt. McCarrie, was the man who'd punched the shackled Indian the day Will first arrived. For all that Mac McCarrie was sometimes antagonistic toward the Indians, he knew a lot about them and proved a better source of information for Will than Gen. Carleton. Will enjoyed his conversations with the affable redhead.

"We use their Mexican names for the warriors," Mac explained. "That's the influence of the Franciscan missionaries; they gave what the Spaniards thought were proper names to all the Indians. Their own language is so hard to pronounce. You know, in their language they call themselves 'The People.' It's pronounced 'Di-nay.' 'Navajo' is a Spanish word that means 'cultivated fields,' I guess 'cause they were farmers."

"Farmers? I thought they were supposed to be fierce warriors…"

"The Diné aren't nearly as warlike as some other Indian tribes. The nearby Apaches and the Comanches from across the Texas border, for instance," Mac said. "The Diné were mostly sheep and goat herders. They used to live up in the Chuska Mountains to the west and in the Canyon de Chelly at the base of the mountains.

"You should see this canyon," McCarrie said, getting noticeably excited. "The explorers called it 'the Navajo fortress.' It looks like the ruins of a European castle with rock walls and towers and spires, but all of it was carved out of the sandstone by the river. I was up there on a raiding party. Real beautiful scenery, but scary as hell. There are places where you can see ancient cities built into the sides of cliffs, but all mostly abandoned now.

"Got a funny name! It's a Spanish version of a Diné word, but it's spelled like French—D-E-C-H-E-L-L-Y—and it's pronounced 'd'shay,' like a horse-drawn buggy. That's where the Navajos were 'fore General Carleton ran 'em out and made 'em come here."

Mac explained the Navajos lived in small settlements of one or two families rather than in large tribal groupings and seemed to prefer to stick to themselves. *Why are we at war with the Navajo?* Will added a question to his list.

Mac also told him that among the members of this nearby camp were leaders who had power and influence over all the Navajos. *How is the political authority of the Navajo structured? Who is in charge? Is anyone in charge?* More questions for the list.

Scraggly cottonwood trees and now yellow and dry grasses grew all along the riverbed. The name Bosque Redondo, he learned, referred to a grove of cottonwoods at the bend in the river. It was those trees growing on the high ground along the eroded wash that formed the natural screen that separated the Indian camp from the fort.

One large hogan had been constructed on the high ground not far from the quarters for the Indian Agent. At first, Will assumed it must be the home of the chief or the wealthiest man in the camp. But watching the Indian settlement from the stoop of his cabin, he'd seen only ceremonial events, dancing and drumming, thereabouts.

All these observations simply resulted in more questions for Will's list. He hoped his careful accounting of conditions here would bring funding from Mr. McDonald back in Washington to build the Indians decent housing. *Why couldn't wooden cabins, like the one I'm quartered in, be built for them?*

By mid-May, the days were uniformly hot. There'd been no rain at all in the couple of weeks he had been there. Will considered with alarm what might happen if the creek dried up. He presumed Gen. Carleton and his staff had investigated such concerns before choosing this particular location. Though, as he saw the disregard with which the Indians were treated, Will had his doubts. Carleton seemed to ignore a lot of what was going on.

6

BOSQUE REDONDO

One afternoon, Will was drifting in and out of sleep in his quarters out back of Fort Sumner. The day was stifling, and there was nothing to do to escape the heat but sleep or daydream. He'd been thinking longingly about his friend Michael.

Suddenly, Will was awakened by a loud explosion. *Oh my God, it sounds like artillery bombardment.*

He jumped up from his cot and pulled on pants and boots. A flash of light erupted with another explosion. He flung open the wooden door of his cabin, expecting to see plumes of smoke. Instead, what he saw was a sky full of roiling clouds, and then lightning, followed by a clap of thunder. A furious storm was right overhead. He could see the Indians scurrying around in their camp seeking shelter.

Will felt a thrill: relief from the heat, *a blessing from the heavens.*

The wind was downright cold. The air smelled rich of impending rain. As the shower began, Will walked out and stood bare-chested in the coolness. He threw his head back, closed his eyes and opened his mouth to let the raindrops quench his thirst. He stretched his arms and laughed that he'd mistaken the storm for war.

He swallowed the rainwater and bent over to shake his hair, like a dog shaking water out of its fur, when something hard hit him on the back of the head. He startled. *Is somebody throwing rocks?*

A pellet hit the ground next to his feet, throwing up a splatter of red mud. Then another, and another. *It's hailing.* Will darted back inside.

From his cabin, Will could see the Indians huddling in their mud huts. The rain had become a full downpour. *Will the huts just dissolve?* The wind was whistling outside; the hail subsided, but the downpour went on harder than ever. He worried that his own cabin could not withstand the onslaught. Then the rain slowed, and then was gone.

Will went back outside. To his amazement, the sky was clear overhead. The late afternoon sun hung brilliant red near the horizon, shooting out beams of orange-golden light. In the northern sky, the clouds towered high as the storm moved on. Rain showered out of them in sheets onto the parched desert. On the edges of the storm, great plumes of falling rain poured down but never reached ground, evaporating in the desert air and being churned back up into the tempest. Surrounding the blue-black heart of the storm, the clouds were white and billowy, kissed with orange from the setting sun.

Out of the storm, lightning flashed, sometimes jumping from cloud to cloud, sometimes rocketing to earth. Thunder still echoed, though it no longer sounded like artillery. A breeze was blowing. And it was still cool. Will gave thanks. He wondered if the Indians worshipped storms.

Concerned about the Indians, Will clomped his way through the brick red mud toward the camp. The ground had turned to a thick liquid, so it was difficult to keep his footing. He could see some of the soldiers watching the storm pass. A few of them were drenched. Others must have come out after the hail and rain had abated; their uniforms were dry. Along the creek, the Indians were moving around, inspecting for damage from the downpour. He hoped they'd be more friendly to him if they saw he was concerned about what had happened to them.

At the edge of the wash, he could see that the creek had doubled in size. Just then, he heard a dull roar. The sound was increasing in volume. Suddenly, the Indians began screaming. Will saw that one of them just across the wash from him was shouting and gesturing, pointing up the creek bed. Will's eye followed his hand. And his stomach sank.

There were a couple of Indians quite close to him struggling to climb up the muddy side of the wash. He ran to help. He slid in the mud and by the time he got a hand down to help them up was covered in it. On the other side of the wash, more Indians were struggling to get to higher ground. The roar was getting louder.

A wall of water eight feet high was rushing toward them. Will didn't see any more people trying to climb out on his side, and he pulled at the two men he'd helped to get away from the edge. Together, the three of them ran as fast as they could from the oncoming torrent.

Water splashed all around them. The crest of the flash flood was higher than the walls of the creek bed. As the water reached the bend in the creek, it flowed up over the sides and surged against the nearby bank of the wash. Will looked back in horror to see the spot where he'd been standing crumble into the flood.

The two Indians he had helped ran back down to the edge of the swollen river. They pointed at a tree that thrust up from the bottom of the riverbed. An elderly man and an even more elderly looking woman were stranded up in the tree, while several more people were clinging to the trunk in the raging water.

That tree must have survived floods like this in the past. It was such floods, obviously, that had cut the wide deep wash. But how long can it remain standing?

Will noticed the young Indian woman, the one he thought was named Has-bah. He'd seen her from a distance during his observations of the camp, but she'd never paid him any attention. Now she was on the other side of the torrent. She came striding down to the water's edge, obviously in command, with a rope wound round her forearm. The small crowd who were pointing at the tree and shouting quieted down and tried to help.

Will wanted to help, too. The tree with the stranded Indians was much closer to him than to Has-bah. But he didn't have a rope, either with him or in his cabin. It'd take much too long to run back to the fort. *And, anyway, I'd probably have to fill out some damned requisition before they'd give me a rope.* He looked back, hoping to see that the woman had gotten her line to the helpless victims of the flood, but she was nowhere in sight.

Then, a moment later, Will was shocked to see that she stood practically right next to him. Has-bah's woolen dress was drenched, and her long black hair streamed water. She'd swum across to this side to get a better throw. *How had she done that?*

The Indian woman tried to get the rope out to the people in the tree, but to no avail. She could throw it out to them, but none was able to catch it. The people in the limbs were elderly and not spry enough to grab for it, and those in the water didn't dare release their grip on the trunk.

Will remembered something he'd seen done when there'd been a flood near his home in Virginia. He ran back up the slope to his cabin. The door was hinged with leather straps but had a steel doorknob bolted firmly to the wood. He felt in his pockets. Not finding his knife, he ran inside and hurriedly looked around. There it was on his desk. He'd been sharpening the nib of his pen earlier. He snatched up the knife and cut away the three thongs that held the door.

He came running back down the slope, dragging the door behind him. He went straight to the woman with the rope. He didn't try to communicate with her; she was obviously willing to cooperate. He grabbed the rope from her hands and tied a sturdy knot around the knob. He dragged the door upstream a short distance and threw it into the torrent. It immediately washed up against the water's edge. Without thinking, Will clambered down into the river, clinging with one hand to an outcropping of rock that he hoped would be stable enough. One of the Indian men he'd helped up rushed to hold his arm so he could push the door farther out into the flow of the river.

Succeeding, he turned to the Indian and grinned. The man yanked him up out of the water. The Indian joined him in holding firmly to the rope as they watched the door float downstream toward the stranded people.

"Grab hold," he yelled, not knowing if they could hear him or if they could understand English.

Has-bah, now at the edge of the water as close to the tree as possible, also yelled out something to them.

As the door bobbed in the water near the tree, one of the men holding onto the trunk released his hold and lunged out. He threw himself onto the makeshift raft. Now Will and the Indian pulled back on the rope to keep the door from floating on away from the tree. Will struggled to anchor his heels in the slippery mud.

Soon all the people in the tree, including the old ones in the limbs, were clinging to the door. The weight of the people against the force of the water made it difficult to hold. Will feared the raft of people might be washed downstream any minute—the tragic failure of his bright idea. He and his Indian helper began to walk slowly downstream, pulling in on the rope, dragging the raft toward the side. It was hard work. The Indian kept losing his grip and slipping in the mud. Will wasn't sure he could manage alone. He, too, felt he was losing control.

Then he felt someone else grab the rope behind him firmly and solidly. Slowly, surely, the raft with all its passengers safely aboard was pulled in to shore. Several Indians reached out and helped the survivors scramble out of the water. Will relaxed his grip. He turned and, to his surprise, saw that the person who'd joined the emergency tug-o'-war was none other than the mysterious woman, Has-bah. She looked toward him, but without expression.

Then one of the Indians by the riverside called out, catching her attention. She looked away, then grabbed the rope from Will's hand, coiling it round her forearm as she headed over toward the nearly drowned Indians. The old man they'd saved was clutching his chest as if in pain.

Suddenly, Will found himself standing there all alone, half-naked, soaking wet, covered with mud. He wanted somebody to say thanks, but the Indians had abandoned him. He didn't think it wise for him to go over and force his way into the circle around the ailing elder. So he turned and headed up the slope toward his cabin.

He could see a small crowd of soldiers silhouetted in the brilliant orange sunset. They had gathered at the top of the slope to watch. *Why hadn't they helped, for God's sake? And now they'll probably make fun of me when I go in for supper.*

When Will reached his now-doorless cabin, he saw that the water was already subsiding. *I guess I ought to go down to the creek to wash this mud off while the river is still flowing deep. It probably won't be long before everything is back to just the way it was before.*

Will didn't know it yet, but nothing was ever going to be back to just the way it was before.

7

FORT SUMNER

The next morning was sweltering. The beginning of summer heat, combined with the moisture from last evening's rain, drove the humidity to an unbearable level. After breakfast, Will came back to his cabin. He sat on the front stoop to watch the Indians inspect what remained of their shelters and search for belongings that had been swept into the water. They had suffered a terrible devastation. Many of the mud huts looked at least partially damaged by the pelting hail and rain; some of them must have been washed away altogether.

Perhaps he could convince Gen. Carleton to requisition supplies from Fort Defiance or from Santa Fe, where the Territorial Headquarters of the Indian Affairs Office was located. There might be timber and planking available to construct regular housing for the Indians.

I'm not sure the Navajos want me meddling in their affairs. They didn't seem particularly grateful to me for rescuing them from drowning. But I'm going to try. Will decided that in a day or two, when the immediate trauma of the disaster had passed, he would go down to the camp and insist on meeting the chief. There was bound to be a man in charge down there. *I know that's who I need to talk to.*

The troops had also come out to survey the damage. Many of the men had stripped off their uniform tunics and shirts, since the humidity soon had everybody's clothes drenched with sweat. Will wore only a sleeveless muslin undershirt. He found he couldn't pull his eyes away for long from the sight of the men's bare skin. He'd noticed a couple of them before and had been drawn to something about them. He hoped Pvt. McCarrie might appear among the bare-chested soldiers.

One of the young men had an especially striking physique. Every muscle in his chest and torso was clearly defined. He was walking back and forth along the edge of the creek bed. As he moved, the muscles rippled under his skin. He occasionally shouted epithets at the Indians, and Will hated him for that. But he couldn't keep himself from looking.

Sgt. Peak swaggered right toward his cabin. The soldier wore a blue uniform shirt unbuttoned and hanging open. Peak was a big man, his chest well-muscled and hairy. Peak's face was craggy, his features a little too heavy, but he was handsome in a burly, masculine way. His thick hair and beard must have been brassy red in his younger days, but now had turned a dull sandy gray. His face had been rendered leathery by the desert sun. From things he'd heard him say, Will guessed him to be in his early forties, but he looked worn and hardened well beyond that age.

Peak came right up to Will. He took a whisky flask out of his hip pocket, and then sat down uninvited beside Will on the cabin step. The step was short, so Will was crowded right up against him shoulder to shoulder.

"Wanna sip?" Peak slurred. "General's declared it a holiday. 'Cause of the flood last night. The heat and all."

"No," Will said with no effort to be polite. At home, he'd been taught always to say, "No, thank you." Sgt. Peak didn't notice.

"It's always a damn holiday," Peak went on. "Ain't got nothin' to do out here anyway… 'ceptin' wait for a chance to shoot some Injuns. Say, you been here two weeks or so? Had your fill o' Injuns yet?"

Will was furious at Peak for invading his solitude. "I don't feel like I've had time to even begin to understand them," he said, forcing down his bile.

"Well, the only thing ya gotta understand to stay alive is that ya can't trust savages. At every post I been at, all they do is cause trouble."

"They probably feel the same way about us." Will wasn't sure why he defended them. He still worried they'd scalp him along with the rest of the men at Fort Sumner if they had half a chance.

Peak continued, "If I had my way, any time there's trouble I'd shoot a bunch. Right on the spot. It's the only language they understand." He took a swig of whisky. "Only way to show 'em they better not try resistin' us. This is civilized country now."

Will wondered if he could get information out of the obnoxious soldier. Maybe, in his drunken state, he would explain some of the mysteries Will had encountered. "Are they better off here than in their homeland?"

"Damn the damn Injuns." Peak rocked back and forth on the stoop. Will smelled the alcohol fumes. "The white settlers are damn sure better off with them here. Keeps both the Navajos and the Comanches from makin' trouble.

"Besides, we be doin' the Injuns a big favor bringin' 'em here," he added. "Out there in that damn canyon of theirs, they lived like animals. Savage heathens they were—pure 'n simple... good for nothin' but trouble. Here on the reservation, Gen'l Carleton gonna get 'em civilized so that they live in goddamn harmony with the blessed Christians comin' out here to settle the land for the Union."

Peak laughed at his own little speech. "Only good Injun's a dead Injun."

"How come you're so bitter toward the Indians?"

"I been hurt bad... real bad, ya hear... by the damn Injuns. Got a score to settle up. Mebbe I'll tell ya 'bout it. If you're interested..." Peak's voice trailed off as though he'd forgotten what he was talking about.

"Yes, I would be interested," Will said. In an odd way, he felt sorry for the soldier. *That kind of hatred must cause its own pain.*

"Interested in what?" Peak scowled at Will quizzically.

"In why you hate the Indians."

"Who needs a reason to hate Injuns?" Peak stood up, his chest puffed with bluster. He pointed out toward the camp where the Indians were cleaning up the damage done by the flood. "Just look at 'em. Too stupid not to build their houses away from the goddamn river."

"Has it flooded like this before?"

"Goddamn right. Every time it rains, the water rises."

"Well, they have to be near the water," Will said. "It's hot and dry out here."

"Damn right."

"Has a flood ever come through here and washed out the Indians', uh, dwellings before?"

"In winter, the river's full. But no floodin' like last night," Peak chuckled meanly. "Still, it's their own fault. Too high 'n mighty to live like decent folks."

"How come the government hasn't built regular housing for them here?"

"We got better things to do with the goddamn taxpayers' dollars," Peak said. "It'd be a waste o' money. Wouldn't they go buildin' houses right where a flood'd wash 'em away again?" Peak was still standing up waving his arm in the direction of the Navajo settlement. He rocked back and forth on his feet. Will wondered if he were going to fall over, perhaps right into his lap. "Gen'l Carleton's got better things to do with that money than spend it on the Injuns, I tell ya."

"What money?"

In seeming exasperation, Peak answered, "The goddamn money the government sends out here, that's what."

"The government is sending money for the Indians?"

"Now, look here, don't you go stickin' your nose in places it don't belong. That's what happened to the last Agent. Bet he wishes he never stuck his nose into the money."

Is that what Gen. Carleton doesn't want me to find out about? "What *did* happen to the last Agent?"

"He had to run off, ya know." Peak laughed raucously. He pointed into Will's quarters. "An Injun girl got herself killed and raped in there… had her throat cut. Sure angered some Injun braves… Well, it served him right… shouldn't't've asked 'bout the money. And neither should you, you goddamn Reb…"

As Peak's tone turned angry, Will reconsidered his inquisitiveness. *Maybe I'm just creating trouble for myself.* He changed the subject. "What do you know about the Indians', uh, village?" He struggled for a word to describe the group of hogans he could see across the river.

"I know it ain't no village, Mister Southern Gentleman. Navajos call 'em 'outfits.' Least in Christian English… dunno what they call 'em in the heathen tongue o' theirs. Whaddya want to know?'

"Well, who's the chief?"

"God only knows. There's an old man they trot out for Council meetin's whenever a delegation shows up to negotiate a goddamn treaty. But that tall woman ya see now and then seems as much in charge as him. Damn! Can you imagine 'em all bein' run by a woman?"

"I know who you're talkin' about," Will said. Now his curiosity was really piqued. "Who is she?"

"That's her over there," Peak pointed toward the main hogan. Several of the Navajos were gathered there. And, indeed, Has-bah was among them.

"Most o' the Injun women are so goddamn ugly, they ain't good for nothin' but fuckin' and killin'. Hell, only way you can tell the women is by what they call themselves. Usually got a 'bah' in their name. Guess that means woman." Peak took a long swig from his flask. "That one's a different matter. She's quite a looker, ain't she?" His tone had changed from anger to lasciviousness. In a gesture that downright appalled and embarrassed Will, Peak grabbed at his crotch and made a couple of unsteady thrusting motions with his hips. "Bet she could use a good fuckin' by a real man. Get her off her high horse."

"I agree with you, Sergeant, that the woman is attractive and carries herself well," Will said with exaggerated propriety. "But I don't think you—or any of the soldiers—should be having relations with the Indian women. It wouldn't be Christian." He could hear his father's tone in his own voice. It surprised him. It surprised him, as well, that he had felt a surge of lustful excitement from Peak's words.

"Don't you go tellin' me what to do and what not t' do. You ain't some kinda officer out here. Y'r just a bureaucratic nuisance we gotta put up with 'til we manage to get rid o' you."

"I'm the official Indian Agent," Will said sternly.

Peak stepped back and made a display of looking Will up and down. Then he spat on the ground and sneered. "You're just a skinny little boy, playing like a man. Why, I bet you're still a damn virgin."

"I am *not*." Will wondered though if his meager experience would even be counted in Peak's judgment. *I am certainly not going to explain.*

"Well, then, why don't you and me go on down right now and find that squaw and take us a little satisfaction?" Peak said. "It sure would raise my estimation o' you, ya little Rebel grayback."

Grayback was an epithet for soldiers of the Confederacy who wore gray uniform jackets; it was also a term for body lice. Will felt his bile rise at the suggestion—from *this* man out of all of them—that he might be anything less than scrupulous in his personal habits. He made an effort to suppress anger, and to speak calmly but forthrightly.

"I don't think you have any right to talk to me that way. And if you keep this tone of voice with me, mister, I'm going to report you to General Carleton."

Peak laughed scornfully. "You do that." He did a wobbly about-face and, without a word more, staggered down toward the creek bed.

Will felt relieved the man left. He wasn't sure he should have been talking with Peak at all. He'd gotten a little bit of information, but he'd also riled up the man who seemed his major antagonist.

What did I learn? He looked into his cabin and shuddered to think what had happened in there. *Well, if that were so, it's a credit to Gen.*

Carleton that the Agent was dismissed. Will was relieved to surmise that apparently the Indians hadn't murdered the Agent and that the man had just run off.

But about the money? Will had understood that the government wanted and expected the Indians to be self-sufficient. *That's why, I thought, there's so little assistance available to them. But then why were they moved to this harsh environment?*

What was the money Peak talked about? He would have to add that to his growing list of questions for Gen. Carleton. He'd never been shown any disbursement figures or been told how to requisition aid for his charges. *What if there are funds to be had for the Indians' support?*

That's what Carleton and Bauer had been talking about me maybe wanting a cut of, wasn't it?

Will was gratified to have learned that the flash flood was an out-of-the-ordinary occurrence. If the river rose even several feet when it rained, he could see there was still lots of room for the water in the wide creek without endangering the Indians' shelters. It would have disturbed him to think the Indians were so out of touch with the realities of desert life that they had built their homes right where disaster was imminent. Of course, this wasn't their homeland. Maybe they had no choice but to live in hovels because they were not allowed to build decent shelters or were refused the basic materials needed for doing so.

I will have to write Mr. McDonald about this. Some policy changes are needed.

If the previous Agent had been so insensitive as to murder one of the Indian women, it's no wonder he didn't report bad or ineffective policies on the Indians' behalf. Maybe he'd been as crude and mean and narrow-minded as Sgt. Peak. And Carleton had made that veiled reference to the Agent expecting to "collect the rewards" for keeping the Indians here. He had been embezzling, hadn't he?

Will surveyed the camp, the "outfit," he corrected himself. He noticed that the gathering near the central hogan had broken up. He found himself searching for the tall Indian woman. He thought maybe he was right that her name was Has-bah; Peak'd said "bah" is usually a syllable in women's names.

He felt a certain pride in feeling attraction to the woman. Not that he'd do anything like Peak had talked about. It's just that he'd never felt an attraction of that sort to a woman before. He understood enough about human nature to know what men are supposed to want to do with women. If that were done right, it would result in the conception of a child. And that's what God had created the sexual organs for. At least, that's what his father had said.

Will thought about Charlotte Franklin, his former schoolmate and his father's choice for him as a bride. The old man had suggested several times it would make him very happy if Will married that charming Miss Franklin and brought her home to fill the empiness in the Lee household.

Will cringed with embarrassment at the memory of what happened to this suggestion that Sunday morning only a few weeks ago. He certainly hadn't made his father very happy that day. Now he knew his father wouldn't be any happier that the first woman he felt such feelings of attraction for was a Navajo Indian.

She doesn't seem to like me, though. But considering what the previous Agent—an embezzler and a murderer—apparently did, her reaction isn't surprising. I hope I can show her I'm not like that and I respect her.

Unlike other women Will had met, Has-bah seemed self-possessed and strong and authoritative. At the same time, she had a streak of kindness and compassion. Last night, she'd risked her life to swim across the raging torrent to help her comrades. The other Indians were afraid of the water, but this woman had overcome whatever fears she might have had. *I honestly hope I can prove myself to her.*

8

PECOS RIVER

Will scanned the far side of the creek. *Yes, there she is.* He felt a surge of excitement. Has-bah carefully searched the ground, apparently looking for belongings that had been washed into the flood.

She walked farther down the creek on Will's side of the water. His eyes followed. He admired the supple way she moved. Even from as far away as he was, he perceived a certain grace in her movements. *Now,* he told himself, *Has-bah is nothing like Charlotte Franklin. Nobody is expecting me to feel something I don't feel. This is up to me.*

Trying to understand just what it was about her that appealed to him so, he watched the Indian woman intently till she disappeared into a clump of trees that grew close to the water. Lots of debris, including several uprooted trees, had piled up there. That was an obvious place to look for things that had gotten washed into the flood.

A little sorry he'd lost his view of her, Will looked away. His eye darted back to that bare-chested soldier with the muscled physique. He was still out there roaming up and down the near bank of the wash.

Then something else caught his eye. Sgt. Peak was clumsily slipping down the bank into the creek bed near where he'd just seen Has-bah. He remembered what Peak had suggested. *I don't like this. In fact, it was my questioning that brought the soldier's attention to Has-bah. If Peak carries out his lascivious plan, in a way, I'm responsible.*

Will jumped up from the stoop and hurried to the bank. He agilely vaulted down, grabbing at a large rock for balance. He made his way to the pile of debris. He arrived just in time to see that Peak had, as he'd feared, accosted Has-bah while both of them were out of sight in the clump of trees. Neither noticed him.

Peak waved his pistol at her. "Get down on the ground. Up there," he said and pointed towards a flat space farther back in the grove.

Has-bah obeyed without expression. *Does she understand English?* She seemed either cowed by Peak's gun or confident that she could handle him. Perhaps she was playing along with Peak till she had him in a vulnerable position and could turn the odds. *Would the Navajos know about alcohol and its effects?*

Will didn't want to meddle. He should let Has-bah handle things her way. He imagined she could overpower the drunken soldier easily with the strength he'd seen last night. He didn't want to insult her, though he prepared himself to intervene if there was even a chance Peak might hurt her.

"Know how long it's been since I had me a woman?" Peak slurred the words even more than earlier. He seemed to talk to himself as much as to the Indian. "Even if you is an Injun gal, still's better'n nothin'. Hell, last woman was an Injun." He laughed. "But she weren't much fun… just lay there.

"Now you keep still, ya hear, and show a little cooperation. Don't say a word, and there'll be no trouble. I know how you savages are."

He grabbed at his crotch just as he had earlier. "Bet you're wantin' this, ain't ya?"

Has-bah looked up at him blankly. *Maybe she doesn't understand.*

Will didn't know what to do. He'd always avoided confrontations at all costs, but he struggled within himself. He didn't want to surprise Peak and risk getting both himself and Has-bah killed, but he couldn't stand idle and watch her raped.

Still brandishing the pistol, Peak nearly fell to his knees right atop her legs, pinning her feet under him. With his free hand, he unbuckled his belt and then undid the buttons of his fly.

For all Will's horror at what he witnessed, he found himself growing excited. He found himself leaning closer to better see the soldier's erect organ. Peak grabbed himself and wagged it as if a treat for Has-bah. Her face remained strangely calm, which bothered Will all the more.

Peak reached down and caressed Has-bah's slender ankle, then began sliding his hand up her leg, pushing the wool fabric with it.

Will's heart thundered in his chest. *When is it going to be time to stop this?*

Peak's hand reached far under the fabric of the long dress. Suddenly, his expression changed. As if stung, he yanked his hand away. A moment later, he grabbed at the dress, ripping it angrily. The faintest of smiles crossed Has-bah's face. Peak released the pistol's safety.

Now. Will rose from behind the bush. Neither Peak nor the Indian woman noticed him.

Peak still clutched part of the dress. "Y-You're not a goddamned woman at all."

Will looked down at Has-bah. Her lower body lay exposed. The legs and hips were slim, but showed muscle. But what caught his stare was her penis and testicles. Will glanced into that face, so feminine and so in contrast to the lower part of her body. His world reeled.

Peak staggered to his feet, pulling his pants up. He then held the gun with both hands pointing it directly at Has-bah's chest. "You disgusting freak. I'm gonna blow you straight to hell where you belong."

"I don't think that would be a good idea, Sergeant." Will struggled to keep his voice as calm and authoritative as possible. He clasped his hands behind his back to prevent Peak from seeing how they trembled. He hoped it gave the suggestion that he tucked a firearm behind him.

Peak looked around with a wild-eyed expression, "What're you doin' here? Guess ya changed your mind and decided to join me after all? Well, here's a surprise. Look at this," he said. "This here's no woman at all..."

Will looked at Has-bah's face. She seemed frightened, but there was also a look of smug superiority. Maybe she was afraid of Peak's violent reaction, but she wasn't ashamed at all of the truth he'd discovered. In fact, she seemed proud of it, as though in his reaction it were Peak who was peculiar, not she.

None of this made any sense. But Will knew he wasn't going to allow Peak to hurt this person. Has-bah seemed to be a valued and respected member of the tribe. She hadn't done anything to deserve Peak's outrage.

Peak still held the pistol limply in his hand, but he no longer aimed it at Has-bah. Will had stopped him from shooting her. He felt a great relief.

With a firmness that surprised even himself, Will stepped up, reached for the pistol and took it right out of Peak's hand. The sergeant looked at him, flabbergasted.

Feeling confident, Will got an idea. He pointed the gun at Peak and then at Has-bah. "Shooting this Indian might not be such a bad idea. Guess I could shoot you both. But, Sergeant, if I just shoot her, somebody's gonna hear. Your troops are gonna show up and find you with... uh, with *him*." He said the gendered pronoun very distinctly. "I wouldn't need to shoot *you* then, would I? Not that I'm the kind to do somethin' like that, Sergeant. But I just bet you'd be the laughingstock of the whole fort."

Will wasn't sure Peak would understand in his drunken state, but the soldier was obviously panicked.

"Do you want your comrades to know you were demanding sex from another man?"

"Hey, I wasn't demanding sex from another man," Peak shot back.

"Looks like it to me."

"Look, Mr. Lee, I thought we was friends. After all, we had that nice little talk this mornin' on your front porch."

"I'd hardly call that a front porch, Sergeant," Will said, toying with the soldier. He warned himself not to get too cocky. "How about buttonin' yourself up there?" He gestured at Peak's pants fly with the pistol.

"Hey, don't do that. The gun might go off."

"Yes, it might."

"Look, whaddya want me to do?"

Will's emerging plan was all based on a bluff that even he didn't entirely understand. "Well, first off," he said laying out an ultimatum, "leave the Indian alone. In fact, stand up and get over there." He gestured Peak away from Has-bah.

Peak struggled to get his trousers back on straight and his belt buckled.

"And button up your shirt, Sergeant. Look like a soldier, not some goddamned libertine." Will enjoyed using Peak's panic against him.

"Yeah, yeah."

"Then, second, I want your word of honor not to say anything about this today, and I'll offer mine not to mention it either. To anyone. Ever."

Peak limply held up his left hand palm outward. "Promise. But what about that one?" He pointed at Has-bah who had pushed her dress down now and was cautiously coming to her feet.

Will turned to her. Even after what he saw, he could not think of that face belonging to a man. He softened his voice, "What is your name?"

"I am called Hasbaá," she said, pronouncing it a little differently than Will had been imagining, but he was pleased to know he'd figured out that was her name. This made him feel more of a connection with her.

"Hasbaá, do you promise never to mention this to anyone? If you tell, it might not go well for you. You could get killed."

"I promise." She nodded.

"Well, there you have it." Will turned to Peak. "This Indian dead would be nothing but trouble for you. In fact, if you give her any trouble in the future, I'd be bound by my oath of office, you know, Sergeant, to testify to this whole incident. You understand that?"

Peak seemed to have sobered up fast. "Look, Lee, I don't want no trouble. I don't got no loyalty to them Injuns. I don't give a damn what they do to each other. You just keep your mouth shut, and I'll do the same."

"Now, you go on back to the fort, Sergeant. I'll stay here with the Indian so it doesn't look like you've been back here alone with her, uh, him. Oh, and I'll bring you back the pistol later. After you've had a chance to sober up."

Peak wobbled off in dismay. Will and Hasbaá watched as he headed up the creekbed.

"There," Will said, "that seems to have taken care of him." He smiled, feeling a sense of accomplishment and a bond with this Indian.

Hasbaá said nothing.

He stuck the pistol into his belt. "You all right?" he asked. He extended his hand. But she just looked at him. Then she turned and without a word ran toward the Indian settlement.

He wasn't sure what it meant that the Indian woman he'd been so fascinated with turned out to have a male body. That did help explain her surprising strength last night. *But what does it mean that she's a man?*

Whatever it meant, Will still found her fascinating and attractive. *Maybe even more so now.* His heart was pounding, and he was trembling all over. Only some of that was out of relief that nobody had got shot.

Will stood there by himself. His heart was beating so hard he feared his chest might explode. Then, uncontrollably, a wide grin spread across his face.

The rest of that day Will felt both anxiety and excitement. He didn't think he could expect Peak to keep his word not to say anything. But it didn't seem to make much difference. Peak wasn't likely to implicate him in anything he might say lest Will recount the event differently. And Peak wasn't likely to reveal what he'd discovered about Hasbaá, simply because it would suggest he'd been somehow more involved with the Indian than he should have. Will couldn't help laughing every time he remembered the look on Peak's face when he discovered the Indian had male organs.

He wished Hasbaá had whipped the daylights out of ol' Sgt. Peak, just to teach him a lesson. *But maybe that isn't the way of the Indians...*

Will had never thought a man would dress as a woman. In Virginia, such a thing would have gotten a person lynched. He laughed to himself to think that any number of those people back in Lynchburg whom he'd always taken to be fine, genteel ladies might have had more than expected under their voluminous dresses. *After all, I never had a chance to look.*

But what does it mean? Is it just a costume? Or is a man who dresses like a woman inviting sexual congress with other men? Will did not add this to his list of questions for Gen. Carleton, but he certainly held it in his own heart.

Will was swept with emotion. His mind went back again to that Sunday when Charlotte made her questioning accusations...

9

LYNCHBURG

It was the third Sunday in April of 1867. Will had driven in with his father for services. While Reverend Lee went into the church the back way, Will tied up the mule and buggy. Then he slipped into the white clapboard church building. Seeing Michael Halyerd in his usual place, he climbed over a couple of children, crowding them at the end of the pew, so he could get the seat next to his friend.

Will had met Michael, a neighbor boy, when the Halyerd family had moved to Lynchburg in 1864 from western North Carolina after their house was burned by Union raiders. Michael's grandmother had been a Cherokee Indian. Some of the townsfolk shunned the boy because of his darker skin color—even though he was, in fact, three-quarters white. But Will found Michael's thick black hair, rich tan color, and dark liquid eyes and gentle manner fascinating.

Though Michael was several years his junior, Will liked being with him. The two took long walks together, sharing their dreams for the future. Michael wanted to be a sailor and visit exotic places in the Old World. He loved the sounds of words like "Shanghai," "Madagascar," and "The Ivory Coast." His thirst for adventure inspired Will.

For both of them, though, the dreams seemed to be just dreams. Neither knew how they could possibly get away from their lives in Virginia. Will was kept busy farming. Michael also had to work. Often that required his traveling to the next county where his brother managed a timber mill. He'd be gone for weeks at a time. Sometimes, when Will hadn't seen him for some time, he would wonder if Michael had discovered a way to escape their uneventful lives. He always felt excited for Michael when he had those thoughts. But he also felt especially lonesome and sorry for himself. The times of occasional boyish play with Michael were the only bright spots in his life.

Michael had been away for the past two weeks, and Will had missed him. As Will settled into the seat in the crowded pew, Michael turned and gave him one of his funny winks. Will sat with his thigh pressed against Michael's. Each time one or the other moved his arm, their shoulders brushed. He could feel Michael's warmth radiating through his white linen shirt. And when the congregation stood to sing, through the starched white fabric he could just make out the outline of Michael's chest and torso.

After the service ended, Michael and Will bypassed the receiving line at the door where Reverend Lee stood accepting the flattery of his parishioners. "What a great Christian you are, Brother Lee," more than one parishioner gushed. "You know how the devil lurks in the human heart," another added, "and you make him squirm."

When an elderly man stopped Will to tell him how lucky he was to be the son of such a righteous preacher, Michael slipped away.

Will struggled also to get away from the parishioner, but once outside the building, he was caught by Charlotte Franklin.

"Why, William," she said in a dainty voice, "how ever so fine are you today?"

"I'm doing well," he answered with studied indifference. This was not the first time he'd been accosted after church by the very eligible Mistress Franklin. "How's your family?"

"Just the same... Oh, William," Charlotte was not one to waste time with social niceties. "I don't want to talk about family with you. You know what's coming up next Sunday?" she asked. "We young ladies have got all the plannin' done for the church picnic. I'm just getting so thrilled thinkin' about all that good food and all..."

Charlotte let out a little squeal, perfectly timed with the raising of her right shoulder and a drawing back of her lips to show off her white teeth. "It just occurred to me you might be able to give me a ride. Ya' know, we could go there together."

Charlotte was an attractive young lady, with long blonde hair and pretty blue eyes. She dressed stylishly in full skirts of pale yellow organdy with white lace that closed around her neck but allowed the milky white skin of her shoulders and upper chest to show through. A wide-brimmed straw sun hat that tied around her chin with a green satin ribbon topped her church outfit, and she wore matching green satin gloves.

How am I going to get out of this? Not only do I not want to attend the church social because I don't want to get treated like the pastor's son, but I also don't want to get trapped in Charlotte Franklin's clutches. He knew his father and old man Franklin had decided he would make a good match for the girl.

"Gee, Charlotte, thanks for the invitation. That'd be nice, but, uh, I really can't."

Charlotte's cheery mood changed with amazing suddenness. With her hands on her hips and her shoulders hunched forward with indignation, she blurted, "Well, William Lee, I tried. Just like all the other times. But you simply can't be moved. Sometimes I don't know whatever I'm gonna do, with so many of the young men dead from the war, or left with stumps where their arms and legs should be. And here you are, perfect as the day you were born. You are the handsomest man in the whole county, and I can't even get you to turn your head."

Now she was practically pleading, looking at him in a way that made his heart shiver. "It is me? Is there something wrong with me?"

"Oh, no, Charlotte," he said genuinely, but maybe a little too quickly. He knew what it was like to believe people thought there was something wrong with you. But he didn't want to give her any ideas. "It's not you. You're the prettiest girl in these parts."

"Then I can't understand you..." Her small mouth pouted. "You know, people are wonderin' just what's the matter with you." Her voice took on an edge. "Will Lee," she said. With each succeeding word, the volume and timbre of her voice increased and her Virginia country accent broadened. "People... are... beginnin'... ta... talk!"

Oh, God. The world came to a complete halt. Will imagined all the parishioners standing around chatting in the cheery spring sunlight suddenly hushing themselves and turning, like clockwork figures, in his direction.

He wasn't really sure *anybody* had overheard, but he just froze. He didn't have any idea what to say back to Charlotte. He stared at the ground, afraid to raise his eyes. He could see only the hem of Charlotte's yellow skirt on the bright green grass of the church lawn. But he could imagine that her milky white shoulders were now hunched very high and her white teeth gleamed through a tightly drawn smile on clenched jaws.

And so he didn't hear the pounding sound coming toward him until a war whoop right behind his head resounded above the galloping hoofbeats. A rope fell across his right shoulder. He looked up.

"How'ze about a little ride, buddy?" Michael called out. There he was on horseback, high above Will looking strong and powerful, and holding out the rope. Without even thinking, Will grabbed hold with both hands and, with the assist of a quick jerk on the rope from Michael, pulled himself right up behind his friend onto the horse's back.

With another whoop, Michael turned the horse, and off they went at a gallop. With both arms, Will clutched hold of Michael. He was aware of the bony structure of Michael's ribcage. He didn't dare look back. But he could imagine the expressions on the faces of Charlotte and the other churchgoers. He knew his father must have witnessed the whole incident.

Michael had not objected to Will's continuing to hold on to him tightly, as they rode away from the church leaving Charlotte standing bemused, even after the horse slowed to a leisurely pace. After a while, Will became a little self-conscious and relaxed his grip, though he still kept one hand on Michael's shoulder to balance himself.

"You know," Will said in his friend's ear, "Maybe Charlotte's right. I'm now the only guy my age who isn't married? Most of them are already fathers. I can't even imagine myself—"

"I ain't never gettin' married," Michael interrupted. "As soon as I can save up enough money, I'm gonna be off to Norfolk to be a sailor. Why, I've already saved some from haulin' lumber."

"Yeah, me, too. I've got it hidden in the barn."

"How much?" Michael asked. "Let's go count the money. Maybe we got enough 'tween the two of us to run off to Norfolk together…"

"I dunno." Will's emotions were a whirl. This seemed the best offer he'd ever been made. But the truth was he wasn't interested in going to Norfolk Harbor. *He* didn't want to be a sailor. "I get seasick just crossing a wide river on a raft."

"You stay on dry land then. But let's get out of here. Isn't that what you want? There's a wide world out there..."

Will turned serious. "Maybe my dreams of leaving home are just shirking my responsibilities. I know I ought to get married. God knows, Charlotte wouldn't be such a bad wife. Besides, I'm going to have to support and take care of my father in his old age."

"Oh, come now, William," Michael spat back, "you know Reverend Lee'll be preaching 'til the day they put him in the grave and rakin' in the money. He don't need you to support him. He gives the people all the hellfire and damnation they can handle and they always cough up plenty o' money to relieve their guilt."

Will grinned at his friend's critique of the preaching profession.

"Hey, Will, cheer up," he said, "You've got two legs and two arms—complete with all your fingers and toes even." Michael wiggled his own fingers outlandishly. "And the whole assembly looks pretty good to me."

Will wasn't sure what to make of that. Was Michael simply confirming Charlotte's observation that he was practically the only intact and eligible bachelor in these parts? Or was there something more?

"Maybe I should show an interest in Charlotte."

"But she's a girl," Michael interrupted.

"At least that'd get people off my back," Will continued, "...'cause I'd be fulfillin' my responsibilities."

"Why, sure, you could get married and have a whole slew o' young'uns—happy as a pig in a mud waller 'cause you'd fulfilled your re-spon-si-bil-i-tees." He drew the last word out in ridicule.

Michael gestured wildly, and both were liable to lose their balance on the back of the horse. Will could not help but laugh. As they neared the barn, Michael waved one hand in the air and let out another of his whoops and urged the horse on into a canter. They were both bouncing around and laughing when they arrived at their destination.

"You gonna show me your fortune," Michael jibed.

"Well, c'mon then." Will led the way into the dusty barn. He went back to the rear and started digging under a pile of hay.

While Will was getting into his hiding place, Michael spied an old bonnet Will's mother used to wear for going out in the sun. He tied it around his face, mimicking Charlotte. "Oh, William, I just don't know what I'ze gonna do 'bout you. You the only whole white boy in these parts, and you just ain't takin' a shine t' me nohows."

Will was embarrassed, but he was enjoying the playfulness. Michael grabbed him under the arms and pulled him up and swung him around. In the silly Charlotte voice, he screeched, "So c'mon, honey boy, with all your appendages intact. How'ze 'bout givin' me a little re-spon-si-bil-i-tees kiss, so's we can set the date to tromp down that there aisle?"

With that, Michael laughingly gave him a full wet kiss, right on the mouth. Will laughed and played along with the fun. Then he lost his balance and fell backward into the pile of hay behind him, pulling Michael with him. He looked up at this beautiful boy, just a few inches above him, who he could see was looking back at him with the same intensity. Though Michael's face was shadowed under the bonnet, they held each other's gaze. Suddenly, neither was laughing. Again their lips met. Time stood still.

Michael gently pushed the bonnet back off his head, so that his face was no longer hidden. He braced himself with a hand on the post that held up the hayloft above. He slowly released his grip and lowered himself to kneel on one knee, his leg between Will's legs. He kept his eyes locked on Will's as his face grew closer and closer.

Will craned his neck just a little and brought his lips to Michael's. They brushed dryly at first. The touch of Michael's lips sent pleasure through his whole body. He was terrified of what he knew was about to happen. And yet he wanted it to happen with all his soul.

Michael let his full weight down on top of him, and they both settled into the brittle, crackly softness of the hay. They wrapped their arms around each other and pulled close so they could feel each other's muscles. Clumsily they pulled each other's shirts off and clutched tighter, struggling to increase the contact all along their bodies. They kissed deeply and passionately. Excitement burned in Will's body as it had never before. He could feel himself hard against the hardness in Michael's trousers, and he tugged at the waistband, trying to get the clothes out of the way.

Michael stopped them for a moment and took charge. He sat up on his haunches and said to Will to spread his shirt out on the pile to protect their skin from the prickly hay. He lay his own next to Will's and then pulled his boots and trousers off and helped Will with his.

Then at first awkwardly they lay down side and side and wrapped their arms around each other, and pressed their naked groins together. Will had never even seen another boy's erect penis before, let alone felt one press against his belly. They were both trembling, but they were also grinning widely as they pulled each other close. Their mouths met again, and they kissed hungrily. Time seemed to blur into the surge of pleasure and feeling between them.

After a while Will pulled away and struggled to get his breath. He smiled warmly into Michael's eyes, then arched his back away so he could look down at the other's chest and long torso. It amazed him to see their two bodies, almost mirroring one another, but one dark and one light, so close against each other, almost as if grown together somehow from the base of their sex. And it amazed him especially to see their two penises side by side. They playfully squirmed to grind the roots together and watch the heads bob up and down in sync. Michael giggled.

"Thank you," Will whispered.

"You are *most* welcome," Michael replied with mock formality.

Then he rolled over on top of Will and began in earnest to pump himself rhythmically against Will's belly. Will found his loins seemed to know almost by themselves how to respond to the motion, and the two of them seemed to move in unison one against the other, driving the sensations in their bodies higher and hotter.

They rolled over so Will was on top, but kept the rhythm moving smoothly without losing a beat—or a thrust. They moved in so many different ways. Sometimes sliding side to side, sometime humping back to front, always keeping their penises in light contact. Will saw he could lead Michael's motions, sliding long and slow or else fast and hard. Or he could follow; he could let Michael's urge to drive their pleasure higher pump their motion. And they could press their shoulders together and feel the tight muscles of their chests—and their hearts — pressed together.

Michael was back lying on top, but Will had his legs on either side of Michael's with his knees bent so he had leverage, and he was leading their motion as he pushed his pelvis up higher and higher, forcing them tighter and tigher together. Then all of a sudden Will felt the come start moving deep inside him and up into the head of his penis. He bucked against Michael hard one more time. And he heard Michael catch his breath and shudder in his arms, then cry out, then clutch tightly against him. Their mutual spasms rocked their bodies against the prickly hay.

Will felt such a flood of joy and thankfulness for his friend. It was an almost metaphysical emotion he felt, yet it burned in his limbs as a physical urge.

10

Fort Sumner

Now that same physical urge seemed to be building in him again, this time for Hasbaá. Will shook his head, trying to dispel the confusion.

The Indians all seem to treat Hasbaá with utmost respect, he explained to himself, seeking to replace the emotion with rationality. *Surely, they know this person is male. Could it be possible they don't know?* Even in his ignorance of Indian culture, Will doubted that could be so.

If only the Navajos would talk to me. If only I knew enough of the Navajo language to talk to them. But that's not the real problem, is it? The real problem is that the Navajos don't trust me and don't want to trust. And I can't see why in the world they would or should. To them, I'm just another white man.

The next morning after his baffling discovery about Hasbaá, before going up to the mess hall for the usual breakfast of coffee and biscuits, Will poured water into his wash bowl, cleaned his face, brushed his teeth, and shaved. He combed his hair and did his best to make himself look like a gentleman. *Ain't nobody gonna question my personal hygiene.*

After returning from the mess, he got out his field glasses and took his usual position on the stoop of his quarters, now still doorless. So far as he knew, the door had washed away in the flood. He didn't know how to get materials to make another one. He hadn't asked any of the soldiers about it yesterday because, as Peak told him, the general had declared it a holiday. *And I know they'd 've complained if I'd asked for help on a day off.*

None of the soldiers had mentioned his participation in the daring rescue the other evening, though many had watched. The Indians hadn't seemed thankful. It all looked pretty futile. *Maybe coming to Fort*

Sumner hadn't been a very good idea in the first place. Is this government appointment, which I'd thought was going to be my salvation, turning out to be my downfall instead?

I'm twenty-one years old, time for a man to be looking for a wife, taking a steady job and beginning to build a home. When am I going to grow up? How am I going to grow up out here in the West? Going back to Lynchburg is out of the question, but what's going to become of me in this wilderness?

As these vexing questions raced through his mind, a gray-haired old Navajo woman walked up to him. She was short, sun-beaten, and stooped with age, but she walked with dignity. Her eyes sparkled with intensity. She wore a purple satin skirt and red velvet blouse, belted with a silver-decorated leather strap. A necklace of greenish-blue stones hung around her neck. Will recognized the clothes as out-of-style fashions from back East, probably cast-offs brought out here by missionaries or left by army wives or settlers.

Will started to stand up, but she motioned him to remain sitting.

In well-enunciated English, she said, "I come to you today as representative of my people, the Diné. We wish to express our deep appreciation to you for what you did during the flood. And for how you came to protect Hasbaá yesterday from the soldier."

Will was surprised this old woman knew about that incident. Apparently from Hasbaá's point of view, it wasn't a secret to keep.

"All the Diné are talking about it. We cannot figure it out."

"What can't you figure out?" he asked.

"You must forgive our confusion and our failure to express our thanks. We had to have a meeting of our elders to discuss what we believe you did."

"What I did?"

"We have a word in our language which means to give without expecting anything in return." She said a word in the Navajo tongue. "We have never observed a Hairy Face to act so much like a human being to endanger his own life to help the Diné."

Will smiled and rubbed his freshly shaven jaw, "I'm not a Hairy Face."

She remained serious. "Perhaps not. We consulted with Changing Woman this morning, and she has already hinted to us that you are different from the other Hairy Faces. Changing Woman can tell these things.

"We have known good Hairy Faces before, but not since the soldiers in blue uniforms came into our homeland. The Hairy Face man named Kit Carson had been a friend, but then soldiers used him to betray us." She paused solemnly.

"Since you have done that which we have not observed at this place before, we are thankful to you. What we have is yours. If you have needs, let me know. People refer to me as Dezba. I am leader of our community."

Will recognized the female syllable in her name.

"My name's Will, Will Lee. What I really need most is for the Indians to talk to me. I'm supposed to be your advocate. But I need to find out about your needs as well." Will jumped up now, in deference. *This is the chief I've been wanting to meet. But how can that be?* Though he was proud of himself for recognizing her name as that of a woman, Will felt baffled. *The chief's a woman? Well, Hasbaá's a man.*

"Please, why don't you sit down?"

She waved the offer away with a firm hand. Was that custom or an expression of authority—or of humility? "How is it you speak my language so well? I'm sorry to admit I do not know a word of yours."

"Now you will learn," she said. She pointed to the stoop. "You sit down. Listen. This is a story you should know. I will tell you."

"Some years ago," Dezba began, "a Diné hunting party found an Englishman named John Blewer in the hills lost and starving. They brought him back to our camp. He told us he had been hired as a tutor for the sons of a wealthy family. He was trying to go to California, but got lost in our mountains.

"We welcomed him warmly when we saw he came in peace. I decided to place myself, my brother Barboncito, and my sister's child, the one we call Hasbaá, under the Englishman's tutorship. Though Hasbaá was still quite young then, I knew the child would someday be an important person for the Diné. We all knew that an ability to speak English would be a benefit for our people.

"We Diné wanted to establish good relations with the Hairy Faces. The Diné knew we would need to be able to communicate with the strange new people who were coming into our lands. We took the English teacher into our outfit and gave him a home and a place of honor as part of our family. Other Diné people came to learn English from him as well.

"John Blewer lived among us for many years. He died one day from a rattlesnake bite. We mourned his death and have honored his memory since.

"After the soldiers came," Dezba said, "we tried to use the language we'd learned. But we did not understand why the Hairy Faces did not do what they said they would. Had we misunderstood? We wished John Blewer had been with us to explain. Perhaps you will be able to help us understand the Hairy Face ways."

"I hope so," Will answered. "Will you tell me more about the ways of the Diné?"

"That will require consulting Changing Woman. I will talk with Hasbaá, who best knows Changing Woman. Be at the center of our settlement before the sun sets." With that, Dezba turned and walked away.

Will spent the rest of the day in anticipation of meeting this changing woman, whoever she was. *Why was she called "changing"? What would she be like? Apparently, she was also a chief. Dezba, who called herself the leader of the community, had to get her advice or approval.*

Will had admired his own mother's strength and capabilities in running the family household. But he'd never heard of women taking community leadership like Dezba and this changing woman. *By whose authority were these women appointed? Why does Dezba have to consult the other woman about me? And why would Hasbaá, this man in woman's clothing, be closest to the changing woman?*

11

Bosque Redondo

Just before sunset, Will walked over to the Diné settlement. The Indians no longer shunned him. A couple actually spoke to him, though with lowered eyes. Dezba greeted him and motioned him toward an earthen structure near the middle of the settlement.

Outside the low structure, a fire blazed in a pit. Around the fire, stood three Diné men, clad only in blankets thrown casually over one shoulder, their heads bowed in reverent silence. Two other men, fully dressed, stood in the shadows outside the circle; their soot-marked faces and hands showed they were tending the fire. Dezba directed Will to join the circle with her.

He could see large stones in the firepit glowing from the heat. When he looked up, he noticed that one of the men in the blankets was Hasbaá. His heart started to pound. Without the usual women's clothes he had always seen Hasbaá wearing, the Indian looked like a handsome, though delicate, young man, reminiscent of Michael Halyerd. Will couldn't help his gaze being drawn to Hasbaá's naked shoulder.

As Will joined the circle, Hasbaá picked up a blanket and, letting it fall open, handed it to him. Will looked around nervously; he was afraid he was going to start grinning. He held the blanket a moment, then saw that Hasbaá also handed one to Dezba. After taking it, the old woman turned away from the circle, disrobed, placing her clothes in a neat pile, and wrapped herself with the blanket.

Will felt he had no choice, especially not if he truly wanted to gain the Indians' trust and cooperation. Taking a deep breath, he turned around and followed Dezba's example.

Sitting by the entrance to the earthen structure, looking very weak and haggard, was the old man Will helped rescue from the flood, the one who'd clutched at his chest. While Will wrapped the blanket around himself, Hasbaá went over to the old man and gently helped him stand and remove his blanket. Then, chanting in a sing-song rhythm, Hasbaá sprinkled the old man's naked body, using a leafy branch dipped into a bucket of water. Hasbaá helped the old man to get down on all fours and crawl into the earthen structure.

After the old man, the others in the circle went to Hasbaá, one by one, and dropped their blankets. Hasbaá sprinkled each in the same ritual way. Then Dezba stepped up to be sprinkled. She, too, let her blanket drop.

Will tried not to show his shock. He had never seen a woman naked before, especially in public and with men present. The Indians' nonchalance and lack of shame made this all seem quite natural.

After a moment, Hasbaá beckoned Will toward the little opening, then motioned for him to drop his blanket, all the while continuing the prayer-like incantations. Will felt some sort of communication exchanged by the expression in the mysterious Indian's eyes, but he wasn't sure what it was. It was certainly recognition. He hoped it was also gratitude—he had, after all, saved Hasbaá's life. Perhaps it might even be friendship.

He dropped the blanket. As the cool drops of water struck his bare skin and ran down his chest, he watched Hasbaá's eyes peruse his body. He sensed something reverential and yet also definitely erotic, though Will was only just now beginning to understand what that meant. He saw that again Hasbaá looked into his eyes. He remembered McCarrie's comment and averted his gaze.

His own feelings for this strange male-woman were certainly respectful and reverential, yet, too, also somehow erotic. He felt a nervous excitement in his belly. His eyes—and his desires—were drawn to Hasbaá's physical presence: the dark, deep eyes and gauntly handsome face; the dark, rich olive-brown skin; the form of the physique covered teasingly by the blanket; the texture of skin and muscle of bare shoulder.

Will hoped Hasbaá felt towards him the same physical fascination. Uncontrollably, he looked up and sought out the other's eyes. Hasbaá noticed but turned away and motioned for him to get down on his hands and knees and follow the others into the low structure. He worried that he'd embarrassed Hasbaá by his look.

Inside, Will could barely see. Dezba, who'd entered just before him, gestured to him to crawl toward her counterclockwise around a pit dug in the center. She and the others were all sitting cross-legged along the perimeter of the round structure. Will joined them. On the other side of the entrance from him was the little man with the weak heart.

After a moment, Hasbaá entered, first handing in a bucket of water. Will could see in the dim light that now Hasbaá also had discarded the blanket, as he had expected—and hoped. Hasbaá made no attempt to hide his manhood.

A glowing red-hot rock was thrust through the opening and pushed with a piece of timber into the pit in the center by one of the men tending the fire. This was repeated, perhaps as many as twelve times. Will lost count. As the glowing hot rocks accumulated in the center of the circle, the faces of those sitting around became dully illuminated. And the temperature rose steeply.

When the requisite number of rocks had been rolled in, Hasbaá reached out and pulled a leather flap down over the opening. Hasbaá chanted loudly, then turned to Will and spoke softly in accented, but clear, English.

"This ceremony will cleanse and purify your soul. Relax. You are in no danger. If the heat becomes too difficult, lean over and breathe near the ground. Changing Woman will help you."

Will looked around. *Is the changing woman here?* The only woman was Dezba and from the way she'd talked earlier he knew she was not the changing woman. *Could one of these men be? Was that what the "changing" part of the name meant? Could one of these men change into a woman? Is that what Hasbaá did?*

Hasbaá threw leaves onto the rocks, saying, "Sacred herbs purify the breath." The leaves flared quickly and filled the room with fragrant smoke. Hasbaá repeated this three times, each time with a different kind of leaf. At least once the smoke smelled of tobacco, such as Will had known from his childhood.

Then, pouring several handfuls of water onto the rocks, Hasbaá started another chant. The rocks sizzled, and the little chamber filled with steam.

Will's effort to understand what was going on was fruitless. *I certainly can't understand the words Hasbaá is chanting. I don't understand why we're breathing burning herbs. And now I don't know why we're being scalded with steam. It's hot, but not unbearable. Just relax as Hasbaá instructed.* The steam penetrated the pores of Will's skin, and he began to perspire freely.

He had heard about Indian "sweat lodges." He'd always imagined them to be something like the Turkish steam baths advertised by fancy hotels in big cities.

Hasbaá's chanting continued for a long while. Will listened to the droning as one did to a musical instrument, seeking not to understand with the mind but to feel with the spirit.

After a while, the flap was thrown open, and the room cooled down a little. Then soon more rocks were rolled in and the flap closed again. More water was thrown onto the rocks. And again steam billowed in clouds. This time, the others all began to sing in unison.

The rhythm lulled Will into a dream-like state. *Hasbaá had said this ceremony would cleanse and purify me. What,* he wondered, *do I need to be cleansed and purified of?*

12

LYNCHBURG

For months after his mother's death Will had been at a loss for what to do with his life. He was despondent and unable to make any decisions. He felt only an empty place in his heart. And he hated living with his father, who had turned more embittered than ever.

But then something had changed that day Michael snatched him up and carried him away from his father's church. They'd gone to the barn to count the money Will had collected. Then Michael—beautiful Michael with the long torso and the reddish-brown skin under his bright white shirt—was kissing him.

And the kiss became an introduction to another world and a whole 'nother dimension of human experience. Will discovered something he'd been longing for, but had never understood. *Physical affection, that's what it is.* He could feel his whole body alive but relaxed and at peace. Everything seemed perfect. *Maybe this is what love is.* He smiled and nuzzled Michael's face with his chin as they lay against each other, exhausted in blissful torpor. Michael squeezed him back, then they both let out a long deep sigh almost simultaneously and drifted into light sleep.

The slumber lasted only a minute or two. Will felt a chill and realized he'd awakened. And he was still lying there in the barn, his clothes along with Michael's laid out under their bodies. *I didn't dream it* he said to himself whimsically. He had no doubt at all that it had happened. Not yet opening his eyes, Will pressed tighter against Michael to absorb the warmth of the other's body.

Then, suddenly, as if out of nowhere, a roar erupted in the air above them. Will opened his eyes just in time to see his father coming down full force across Michael's bare chest with a horsewhip. Reverend Lee's face was contorted in a bellow of disapproval and rage. The sharpness of the blow literally knocked Michael out of his arms.

Will rolled over on top of him to protect Michael, so that his father's second blow fell on his own shoulders. And though the whip hurt like hell, he felt an exhilaration in knowing he'd protected his friend. Now Will bellowed. He scrambled to his feet and turned to face his father.

The whip rose again. His father was still going after Michael as if by blaming the mixed-breed Indian, Reverend Lee could distance himself and his own blood from what he was seeing. As the whip came down, Will grabbed his father's arm and deflected the blow.

The man's face was livid. "Sinner," he shouted. Then more viciously from between clenched teeth: "Abomination." He hurled the whip aside and turned on Will, grabbing him by the shoulders and shaking him violently.

"Get your clothes on, boy," Reverend Lee hissed at the dark-skinned young man who by now had gotten up and was cowering in the shadows of the barn.

Michael grabbed the clothes from the haypile and struggled to pull his shirt and trousers on as fast as he could. Will was left standing stark naked while his father held him tight with a hand on his upper arm.

"Leave this place, you vile reprobate," Reverend Lee shouted. "Keep your perverted hands off my son."

Ignoring his father, Will looked beyond to where his friend now stood looking hapless. "Michael," he shouted. "Get out of here."

"I can't leave you like this." Michael's voice was hoarse with tears.

Will shouted, "I'll be all right."

Reverend Lee spat out, "You are not all right," as though responding to a different meaning for his words. "You are a god-forsaken sinner who deserves…"

"Michael, save yourself. Get away from here and don't come back."

"But, Will," Michael stammered, "you were going to come with me to Norfolk."

"I can't, god damn it."

Reverend Lee released his claw-like grip on Will's arm, drew back his hand, and slapped him hard across the face.

Michael turned and, looking back over his shoulder, ran out the door. In a few seconds, the hoof beats of his horse echoed in the hollow barn.

"Good riddance," the old man whispered.

"You don't know. You just don't know," Will pulled away from his father before another slap could be delivered.

13

BOSQUE REDONDO

The sound of water sizzling on hot rocks of the sweat lodge interrupted Will's troubled recollections. Hasbaá spoke in Diné, then turned to Will and explained in English, "Each person will now give a prayer to our main spirit, Changing Woman. Your prayer can be a prayer of thanks or a wish for yourself or for others."

So Changing Woman is not a person, after all! I'm sure glad I never asked any stupid questions about who the changing woman was.

The old man sitting next to Hasbaá chanted a prayer in Diné. When he finished, Hasbaá spoke something in answer, and then everybody said a short phrase in unison. Hasbaá threw more herbs onto the rocks and then another splash of water. The heat felt intense and Will worried he might faint.

Remembering Hasbaá's earlier instructions, he leaned down and breathed the air nearest the ground, which seemed cooler. His knee inadvertently touched Hasbaá's leg. Hasbaá did not flinch or move away, and Will let his knee stay. He didn't know whether this was a sign of Hasbaá's acceptance of him or merely an indication of a different attitude among the Diné about body contact. Nonetheless, he was grateful for this touch.

When it came to Dezba's turn, she prayed first in Diné and then briefly, for Will's benefit, in English. "I pray that the cleansing power of the sweat lodge ceremony make this young man strong and faithful to the ways of our ancestors. He has come among us and shown himself more like one of your own people, Changing Woman, than like his. We welcome his good will. And we are grateful to him for helping us in the flood. We are thankful to you and to all nature for all that happens to us, pleasant and unpleasant. Out of the devastation of the flood, this young man has revealed himself as our friend."

It amazed Will that these people saw such goodness in him. His father had preached to observe only the worst in body and soul. As the other Diné prayed, Will thought of all the pain and terror he'd experienced from his father's religion.

14

LYNCHBURG

For the next week after Reverend Lee had caught him and Michael, not a word was spoken in the Lee house. Will rose early every morning and went to work before dawn. His garden was bursting with life; he could spend the day weeding, tilling and watering—and, above all else, avoiding his father.

Mid-morning, Reverend Lee would take the buggy into town. He always walked around the barn the long way along the edge of the garden to get the mule. Will thought it was obvious Reverend Lee was checking to see if he were out there working. He wondered if his father suspected he might have run off in the night or if he were making sure he was seen leaving so he *would* run off during the day.

He didn't know what to do. He thought seriously about leaving. *Maybe that's what my father really wants me to do. It would save us both the embarrassment of having to finally face each other. But where would I go? How would I support myself? The money I've stashed away won't last long. I'd have to get a job. What could I do?*

He kept hoping that Michael would show up and tell him. But then he'd remember that he clearly told Michael not to come back. What had happened to his friend? He wanted to go over to the Halyerd place to see if he could find him, but he was afraid of being seen by Michael's parents. The Halyerds had always been friendly to him, but maybe now they would have changed their minds.

Had his father told them what he had seen? Or had he kept the secret to himself? If the latter were so, it would not have been to protect Will, but to protect the preacher from any suggestion he'd failed to bring the boy up right. Or had he told everybody in the parish to assure them all he had no soft spots for sinners even in his own family?

In the evenings, as was his duty, Will prepared supper. He served his father in the dining room. Neither said a word. Will ate his meal in the kitchen. He'd become like a slave; he felt what it must have been like for old Maudie to have to eat by herself in back.

Maudie and her family had been the Lees' slaves. She was the midwife who'd bought Will into the world, the granddaughter of the midwife who'd brought his granddaddy into the world, passed down like family possessions. Now they were gone, freed by President Lincoln's Proclamation. But they were not forgotten. Will occasionally saw them around town; they were always friendly with him. But the Lees' treatment of their slaves had marked all their lives.

Thinking of himself like Maudie back in the kitchen, Will recalled the ordeals she and her two sons, Calvin and Japhet, had endured under Reverend Lee's ownership. Their father, 'Zekial, had died before Will was born. An intoxicated brawl had broke out among the stable-hands back behind the church one hot summer night after a parish supper. When Reverend Lee, who was then just an assistant pastor, tried to break up the fight, his own slave 'Zekial punched another slave who'd been cowed by Lee's intervention, and knocked him into a coma. When the slave, who belonged to one of the leading parishioners, died two days later, Reverend Lee, in his stern and juridical way, insisted 'Zekial be prosecuted for murder. During the trial, he appealed to the court for the penalty of death in keeping with the Biblical injunction "an eye for an eye." Reverend Lee demonstrated his personal and professional righteousness by offering his *own* property for sacrifice to the intransigence of the written Word. "Let the slave's blood be poured out onto *my* fields," he proclaimed rhetorically, "as a sign of propitiation to God's bitter justice." It was not long after that that Reverend Lee was elevated to full pastorship.

After supper each evening, Reverend Lee retired religiously to the desk in the front room where he sat to write his sermons. Lee usually planned out and drafted his sermons in a couple of hours on Saturday morning. But that week he sat at the desk, under the light of a kerosene lamp, night after night. He was writing and rewriting and poring through his theological texts and studying his Bible every evening even after his son went to bed.

Will decided the only way to survive was to ignore the old man, stick to his routine and not panic. He didn't know what he'd do if he panicked. He got up in the morning, did his work, fed and bathed himself, and went to bed at night just like always. And so on Sunday morning, as always, he got ready to go to church.

He figured there was a good chance Michael would be there, and they could at least see that each other was all right. Will set out on foot and took the shortcut across the meadow and over the creek, reversing the route they'd come last week on horseback. It was a long walk; it took him an extra hour. But he didn't want to ride in with his father in the buggy. And there was always the chance he'd run into Michael riding in on his horse to the Sunday service.

As he walked along through the spring morning, he occasionally stopped to look at wildflowers or to listen to the birds in the trees up above. He kept reminding himself to treat this Sunday just like every Sunday. But between reminders, he worried what Reverend Lee had thought when he saw he wasn't there to ride in with him. *Will he be surprised when I show up at the service?*

And if Michael is there, what am I going to do? Should I take my seat beside him as usual? Will decided he'd sit elsewhere so as not to offend his father openly. But, surely, that will start tongues wagging. Well, I'll arrive a little late, and that'll be an excuse to take one of the last open seats. Then it won't look like I intentionally avoided the usual place next to my friend.

Will cursed himself for worrying so much about what other people would think. He'd considered not attending the service at all, but he was certain that would have been noticed. *And then what will people think?* He scolded himself for always going along with whatever *they* wanted. What about what *he* wanted?

Just as he reached the edge of the clearing around the churchhouse, he heard the congregation singing what he recognized as the regular opening hymn. He started to sprint when suddenly his foot came down almost dead center on the head of a large blacksnake. He froze for a moment, halting his stride in mid-air. Then, trembling all over, he slowly pulled his foot back and regained his balance. He held himself as still as possible. But the snake didn't notice him. Its eyes were fixed on those of a small brown rat that, not unlike Will himself, had frozen in the serpent's presence. The snake was slowly pulling itself into striking position. The little rodent was quivering, but apparently unable to move, paralyzed in a reflex of terror.

Will knew mice and rats lived under the church building and that the snake actually did them a favor by keeping down the vermin, but that's not what he was thinking about. The very sight of the snake sent chills up his spine. He was terrified of snakes. *I hate snakes.*

Will felt so sorry for the little rat, even if it were vermin, and in that instant he realized that he and the rat might be in the same boat. The rat's eyes conveyed a sense of unavoidable doom. Will focused on the widening white opening of the snake's mouth.

Then the snake lunged. The rat disappeared into its maw. The sudden motion freed Will of his own paralysis. Heart pounding, he leapt to the side away from the now-occupied blacksnake and ran on. The hymn was drawing to an end. The service was about to begin.

He looked up at the doors of the stark white wooden building. *What am I getting myself into?* But he had no choice. *There's nothing else to do.*

Still trembling, and wondering if he were about to suffer a fate like that of the little rat, Will entered the tall portal of the churchhouse. He saw Michael wasn't in the usual seat. He stood at the rear of the long narrow room. There were two ranks of pews on either side of the center aisle. His father was sitting in his high-backed wooden chair behind the pulpit.

In a kind of daze, Will scanned the room. He knew he'd recognize Michael's long black hair. Up and down, back and forth he looked. His friend was nowhere to be seen. Then he began to feel relieved that he wasn't there. *At least Michael had the strength of character to take action to protect himself.* That's something he knew he needed to learn from his friend. "If you don't like it," Michael used to say, "escape. There's a wide world out there that I'm just a'waitin' to see." *I doubt Michael is hiding out somewhere. He's left town. I know it.*

Whispers in the pew next to him interrupted Will's thoughts. "Why do you suppose that Halyerd boy just up and disappeared so sudden last Sunday night?" Will realized the whispers were meant for him to hear. Hell, they might as well have been meant for the whole congregation's ears.

"I dunno, but I hear tell it had *something* to do with Reverend Lee's son."

"Well, I'm not surprised," a third voice rejoined in the same loud murmur, "the way those two stayed to theirselves, so strange-like…"

"You saw how they were actin' after church last week."

"You know, the elders have been meetin' with the preacher…"

"Now what could they be planning?"

Will started to tremble. He looked around furtively. As he'd been scanning for Michael, he'd walked halfway up the center aisle. And now every eye in the church was on him. His father stood up and stepped to the pulpit. He gazed at his son sternly. Will pushed his way into the nearest pew and sat down. He leaned over and looked at the floor and wished the service would just get underway.

"Today," Reverend Lee intoned in his most sepulchral voice, "we are goin' to talk about sin." He said the last word with a kind of snap, like the sound a fisherman hears when he jerks the line and hooks the poor fish that had been nibbling carefree on the bait.

Without even hearing the next words of his father's sermon, Will knew he'd been caught—*like that poor little rat swallowed whole by the snake*. "Today, Christian brethren, I take as my text the Book of Genesis, the nineteenth chapter, from the first verse down to the twenty-ninth."

Reverend Lee looked down at his Bible. "In verse twenty-four, God says He rained down on Sodom and Gomorrah brimstone and fire out of heaven." He slammed the tome shut with a bang. "And just why did the Lord rain down brimstone and fire out of heaven?" Will could hear the glee in his father's voice as he said the words "brimstone and fire."

Reverend Lee then told about the angels coming to the city and about Lot offering his daughters to the men of Sodom. His voice rising and falling dramatically, he related how the men wanted nothing to do with Lot's daughters. "And then the Lord God rained down His fires of destruction on the city of Sodom. And all because the people of that wicked place practiced this unspeakable evil... evil so filthy we cannot even mention its nature, what with the children present here." He emphasized the word *children*. "...evil that deserves the penalty of death by stonin', the Holy Scriptures say. This is wickedness so vile it is not fit to be named among Christians. But you all know what I am talkin' about..."

Whenever Will looked up, his father was staring right at him. Every minute got worse. Finally, his father began to describe how he had personally come upon two supposedly Christian boys...

Will could stand it no more. He stood up, stepped out of the pew, turned around, and walked out of the churchhouse. Every eye was on him as he slowly strode down the aisle. It seemed as if he were never going to get out of the church. And all the while, his father continued the malediction.

His steps were uneven, but he managed to get to the back of the building and out the entrance. He carefully closed the doors behind him. He walked over to his father's buggy and climbed up to the seat. He could still hear his father preaching, though now the sounds were muffled. *This is it. I can't go back. I can't go on. The best solution would be to end it all right here—before somebody else does.*

Will had heard about the Ku Klux Klan, which had formed the previous year and had spread like wildfire through the Reconstruction South. He knew they rode out at night dressed like the ghosts of Confederate war dead. They burned crosses and strung up the freedmen they thought were acting too independent or disrespectful. He wondered if they just might come to string him up for having defiled the uniform of the Confederacy or some such charge that his father was conjuring up there in the churchhouse.

"I might as well be dead." Will reached down into the storage compartment of the buggy and fished out a rope. He fashioned a noose at one end of it. He observed that a nearby tree limb extended out at about the right height. He imagined how the congregation would react when they came out of the church and found he'd hanged himself there, right in front of their eyes.

How am I going to do this alone? If only Michael were here to help me string up the rope. Oh, Michael...

For the first time, Will stopped thinking about himself and thought about how Michael would have handled all this. *He wouldn't have let those self-righteous bastards get to him. He wouldn't punish himself. He would leave. Hell, he* did *leave.*

Will looked at the noose in his hands. *What has gotten into me?* He suddenly cast aside the rope with its nasty knot. It lay uncoiled on the grass—*like a snake,* Will thought, *a snake whose prey has escaped its fangs. Let 'em find that instead of me.* He cracked the whip and pointed the mule in the direction of town.

As the animal circled around in front of the church and headed down the lane, Will took one final look at the white church building. Remembering the slave 'Zekial's legalistically prescribed execution, he realized his father and the church elders were probably actually planning to hang him or stone him to death at the end of the service. He whipped the mule to move on faster.

15

Bosque Redondo

"Now it is your turn," Hasbaá said to Will. Each of the Diné in the sweat lodge had uttered a prayer. "Speak to Changing Woman. Say whatever is in your heart. Changing Woman will understand your language."

Will took a deep breath. "I have come here with such hopefulness in my heart, but all I can see is misery and sorrow. I pray the Diné have better lives in the future, and your people find happiness. For myself, I ask that Changing Woman help me find my purpose in life." As he completed his prayer, he added, as if by reflex, "I ask all this in Jesus' name. Amen."

As he heard the others responding in their tongue, he realized what he'd said. He hoped Changing Woman wouldn't mind. And he hoped his prayers to Changing Woman would be more effective than those prayers he'd said to Jesus in years gone by.

The others began a rhythmic chant. Will could feel the beat and began to hum, grunt and groan softly in sync with their pattern. The vibrations filled his chest and echoed inside his skull. He felt lightheaded now, no longer close to fainting but to being swept away with joy. He was surprised to see that the sweat lodge didn't seem as dark as before. The whole space became illuminated with a soft glow, like moonlight on a clear night, and it seemed to come right out of the top of his own head.

He was still very hot, but no longer uncomfortable. Rather, he felt cleansed and purified. He was amazed to see that here he was participating in a religious ritual that was being led by a man who usually dressed as a woman, chanting strange sounds, sitting naked in total darkness, and finding that from inside his mind a light was burning.

In its radiance, which was both a soft glow in the darkness and an interior illumination in his mind, Will saw that Christianity was just one set of stories about something that transcended all stories. Its God, grown old and tired through centuries of religious warfare, seemed to have become a capricious, jealous, vengeful deity obsessed with making

rules and hurling wrath and condemnation on helpless human beings—
a heavenly version of Will's own father. Changing Woman might make
a much better deity. If she were a woman, she might understand
people's frailties and be more likely to be nurturing than condemning.
If she herself were changing, she might be much more likely to adjust
her expectations to people's real situations which were always
changing.

Hasbaá sang. And somehow Will understood Hasbaá was singing
in his behalf. The music filled him and uplifted him; the heat carried
him up and exalted him. He lost all sense of time.

He thought for a while that his mother was there with him. It was
so good to feel nurtured by her presence, a presence that made itself
known to him through the heat of the sweat lodge. Then he decided
the presence was not his mother, but was rather Changing Woman.

Suddenly, the flap was thrown open, and Hasbaá clasped him on
the shoulder and instructed him to crawl out. It was dark now. The fire
outside had burned down to glowing embers. The sky was brilliant
with stars. The moon rode high and bright above.

Will felt alive in a way he had never experienced before. Everything,
even the desolation of the desert, seemed immensely beautiful. He
wondered what had happened to him there in the sweat lodge. *Maybe
I passed out.* But he didn't really think so. *I think, instead, that I passed
beyond...*

Out in the cool night air now, the little group wrapped themselves
with their blankets. Together they made their way down to the water
to wash. At Dezba's instruction, Will carried his clothes down to the
creek with him. After splashing in the shallow, slowly flowing water,
he dried himself with the blanket and dressed quickly. Few words were
exchanged. But, in a rather ceremonial way, after he had dressed,
Hasbaá took him by the shoulders. In spite of the darkness, he could
see into Hasbaá's eyes. And what he thought he saw was respect.

Then, while Will and Dezba remained sitting on rocks down near
the creek, Hasbaá and the others carried the old man back to the camp.

"Now that you have been purified by the sweat ceremony," Dezba
told him, "we may talk about what is in our hearts. Changing Woman
hears the voices of the purified more clearly. That is why Hasbaá did
the sweat this evening, so she will be prepared for the healing ceremony
tonight for those who were hurt in the flood."

It perplexed him that Dezba used a feminine pronoun to refer to Hasbaá. *Hadn't she just seen he was male? Well, there was apparently more to this than the form of Hasbaá's body or the clothes that body was dressed in. Does it have something to do with how Hasbaá, uh, makes love?* Will was thrilled and embarrassed by that thought.

"Do you mean the little man who was sitting across from me in the sweat lodge?" he decided to leave his questions about Hasbaá for another time.

"He is called Barboncito. He is my brother. And, yes, for him and for Baaneez, my mother's sister. She is too weak even for the sweat ceremony. Both their hearts are strained."

"From being stranded in the tree during the flood?"

"Not only because of the flood, but because of all the suffering that has happened to our people here. I don't know if their hearts can continue to beat..." Dezba said solemnly. "It is particularly important for Barboncito to live. He is our spokesman with the Hairy Faces. They call him the 'chief' of the Diné. Of course, we have no such thing, only a person in each outfit who is chosen to keep harmony and resolve disputes. That is my role.

"The Hairy Faces do not respect women. They would never accept me as the representative for my people. That is why Barboncito and the other men must speak for us. They should not give up asking the Hairy Faces to let us return to our homeland. Changing Woman has repeatedly given us that message, and again she communicated this to me in the sweat tonight."

Dezba took a long breath. She looked up at the sky. Will could just make out her face dimly illuminated by the moonlight. He could see pain in her expression. "You should know what your people have done to us, so that you can represent us as Indian Agent. I believe Changing Woman wants me to tell you these things."

16

NEAR CANYON DE CHELLY

"Ever since the first people came into this world our ancestors lived in *Diné Bikéyah*, the homeland that Changing Woman provided for us. Our religion teaches us that, in order to thrive, we should remain in the lands that are our birthright. Our whole survival as a people depends on following this religious instruction." Dezba looked over her shoulder toward the northwest.

"When the Spaniards first came into our homeland they called us by the name Navajo. They tried to impose themselves over us, but our ancestors resisted, and we were never conquered. Through nearly two hundred winters Diné people kept their independence, first from the Spanish Empire, and later from the Mexicans. Relations between Diné and the Mexicans were tense. Mexicans and Diné engaged in back and forth raiding.

"Though it was seven winters ago, I remember it as if it were yesterday, when some Mexican men raided our settlement and stole ten of our best horses. Our bravest young man, the one the Mexican officials called Segundo, was so mad he planned a counterraid on the nearby Mexican town.

"This one was the husband of Hasbaá, whom you know. She is my niece. Niece and I both told him to be cautious. We told him the Hairy Faces would be angered by such a counterraid. The Hairy Faces always loudly proclaim their commitment to justice, but then when they choose sides they ignore the terrible things that contributed to the problem. Thinking the Hairy Faces would side with him, my niece's husband went ahead with his plan. He and some other young Diné men rode out toward the town of the Mexicans. They had painted themselves for war in the tradition of our people. On the way, they were stopped by Hairy Face soldiers.

"When those ones called Americans came to our homeland, about fifteen winters before the time I am telling you about, the Diné welcomed them. They were very different from us. They had different customs and they looked different from us. We called them Hairy Faces.

But we believed they were allies because they, too, fought against the Mexicans in a big war.

"We had been suffering from Mexican raids for as far back as any of our families could remember. Usually they just caught a horse or two, and in response we would raid a Mexican village and steal food or supplies. It was not good, but it seemed to balance out. But then the Mexicans began to come with guns. All we had were spears and arrows. And they didn't just steal horses. Sometimes they stole our children to use as their servants or to sell as slaves. This angered and saddened our families very much. The Mexicans are our sworn enemy.

"When the Americans arrived, all we wanted with them was peaceable trade. We had no quarrel with the Great Father in Washington. This is what the soldiers said the Great Father wanted also, when we put our marks to the Hairy Faces' treaty. That treaty was supposed to mean peace. The Great Father promised to stop the raiding being done by the Mexicans.

"But the Hairy Faces signed another treaty with the Mexicans. They called these lands New Mexico Territory—as though those people were natives to this land. But this land had been the home of our ancestors long before there were any 'New Mexicans.' The Hairy Faces acted like we were lower than these people. They called us 'Indians,' a word we had never heard before. We are Diné, not like the others living around us. The Hopi, the Zuni, the Utes, the Comanches, and the Mexicans are all different from us. Our history is not like theirs, ever since we came from the other world into this world. We are not lower than any people."

Will could hear the undertone of anger and dismay in Dezba's voice.

"Hairy Face settlers moved into the Mexican towns around Santa Fe. They even intermarried with the Mexicans. Only a few intermarried with the Diné, though sometimes they forced themselves on Diné women. Segundo was born of a Diné woman who had been treated so by a Hairy Face trader. That was partly why Segundo was so upset about the way our people were treated.

"Since the soldiers would not stop the raiding as they had promised, we asked them to give us guns so we could protect ourselves and our herds. But they would not. They only repeated their promises. They built Fort Defiance on the border of our homeland, saying it was to protect us. But nothing changed. The New Mexicans still stole our horses and sheep and goats. They still enslaved our children.

"My niece's husband had shown himself to be very brave. When he went into the desert to seek a vision for his life, he was away for many days. We all feared he had tested his bravery against something too strong for him and had been killed. Hasbaá was especially sorrowful. She was younger than Segundo, but it was known from when she was very small that she was special to Changing Woman. She had already found her own vision. She hoped Segundo would return to be her husband and that their visions would be one. My niece has special powers from the spirit world. She was given to us by Changing Woman to make peace in our families, to use her powers to help husbands and wives resolve differences and heal our people's illness and unhappiness.

"He did return finally. He said he had fought with a great cat and been victorious. He believed the cat represented the invaders who were threatening our lands. He met Turquoise Boy in a vision and learned he was chosen to safeguard the Diné homeland. That is why he became angry every time there was a raid by the New Mexicans."

"And Hasbaá was, uh, involved?"

"Oh, yes. We believed Segundo's vision had showed that peace and healing would only come to the Diné if our homelands were secure. My niece joined together with her new husband to help lead our people toward that goal."

Will still wanted to know what kind of marriage Segundo and Hasbaá could have had. *Weren't they both men?*

"Segundo was very angry when the ten horses were stolen. He did not want to give in to the soldiers who stopped his counterraid. But they had more power than he and his warriors because they had guns.

"Segundo argued with the soldiers. He told them the Diné would be safe only when we had our own guns. The head soldier tried to settle Segundo and his men down by making a wager. He proposed a bet of ten guns put up by the soldiers against twenty horses put up by us. The winner of the bet would be decided by a horse race. Segundo wanted the guns so much he agreed.

"Hasbaá tried to persuade him not to do this, saying that the soldiers seldom keep their promises. But Segundo did not want to pass up the chance to get guns. And he was sure he could ride faster than any American. A few days later, we all traveled to Fort Defiance to watch this race. I will always remember that it was on the date that you call September 22, 1861.

"My people love to gamble. Everybody thought this was a good idea. We'd engage in a race with the soldiers, and this would be fun for both sides. Diné people love to watch a horse race. We didn't hate the soldiers. We just wanted them to keep their promises of stopping the raiding, or else to stay out of our way.

"Everyone was excited as Segundo and a soldier prepared their horses. We brought our families, and little children were playing all around. There was much betting going on between Diné people and the soldiers. Some of the soldiers had brought liquor, and people were enjoying drinking together. We were hopeful. We knew what a good rider Segundo was. Only Hasbaá was worried. At that time, I knew Hasbaá was special, but only since then have I come to understand how accurately Hasbaá can foresee future events.

"The officer explained the rules of the race. Rules are something the soldiers have a lot of, probably because they so often break them. The officer pointed to a soldier standing on a small ridge in the distance. Each rider was to race to that man, grab a kerchief from him, and then race back. The first one to cross the finish line next to us would be the winner.

"I saw this soldier, the one named Peak, standing by Segundo's horse. When I looked at him, he walked away quickly. I worried about what he might have done, but it was too late to say anything because the race was beginning."

Sergeant Peak, hmm? I guess I'm not surprised.

"People started cheering as Segundo and the soldier rider got on their horses. The crowd became silent as they stood at the starting line. The officer raised his pistol. He fired into the air. And the horses started to run. Everybody cheered. We were feeling happy.

"We were excited to see Segundo take the lead early. He was clearly the better rider. We cheered for him as he rode toward the ridge. The soldiers were silent. But then, just as Segundo was reining in his horse to grab the kerchief, the rein broke. His horse turned, and he was almost thrown off. Then the soldiers started to cheer. We were silent. Their rider reached the man on the ridge, grabbed the kerchief, and headed back. As he crossed the finish line, the other soldiers crowded around him. The officer proclaimed him the winner.

"By that time, the soldiers were all drinking their whiskey. Some of them carried the rider on their shoulders around the field in triumph. Others started grabbing the sheepskins and blankets we had placed as additional bets. Meanwhile Segundo returned on his horse. As he climbed down, we all ran to him. He showed us where the rein had broken. There were marks that showed it had been cut with a knife.

"Segundo went to the officer and pointed to the knife marks on the rein and demanded a rematch. But the officer was too busy claiming the horses we had put up as his prize. I shouted that I saw a soldier standing next to Segundo's horse just before the race. I pointed at Peak. 'He was probably the one who cut the rein.'

"Peak then asked, 'How do I know you didn't cut it?'

"The officer interrupted. He saluted Peak, then called him to attention. With military formality, he asked if he had cut the rein. Peak said, 'No sir.' The officer then addressed our men and ignored me, saying, 'I have to trust a man I know under my own command before I trust a squaw I don't know.' He then declared the race to have been won by the soldiers fair and square. He said it was too bad Segundo did not check his gear before the race. 'A deal is a deal,' he said.

"He then held out his hand for Segundo to give him the reins to his own horse. That would make the last one they would claim as their prize. Segundo was so angry he could not even move. Hasbaá was standing beside him, and, with a look of disgust, she took the broken rein from Segundo's hand and put it in the hand of the officer.

"Segundo started to lunge forward in anger, but Hasbaá stopped him. The officer climbed up on Segundo's horse, and he and the other soldiers rode back into the fort on our horses. They were laughing. This was our first bitter taste of Hairy Face rules."

Dezba shook her head, seething with anger. She gazed up at the distant sky. Will waited patiently for her to resume her story.

"Segundo could take no more. 'What are we going to do?' he yelled. 'Will the Diné let them steal our horses?' One of the young men, my nephew, the son of one of my sisters, who'd been part of Segundo's original war party, let out a cry and ran toward the fort. Hasbaá called for him to come back, but Nephew paid no attention. His action surprised all of us.

"By the time Nephew got to the fort, the soldiers had closed the front gate. Nephew started pounding on the gate, yelling for them to give us a rematch. He called them devils. He yelled out angrily, 'Leave our country. You are no longer our allies.' As Nephew beat on the gate with his fists, I saw Peak look over the top of the wall. He aimed his gun and fired. Nephew fell dead."

"Oh, God, no."

"We were so shocked we just stood there in silence. Then more soldiers came to the wall of the fort. They aimed their rifles at us. Peak ordered them to fire. The guns exploded in a cloud of smoke.

"I saw several children hit. Then I felt a great pain in my arm and saw blood pouring from my elbow. I remember a lot of screaming as the wounded fell. I could hear the officer inside the fort yelling to his men to stop their fire. Then I saw Hasbaá kneeling on the ground holding Segundo. I came over and saw that a bloody wound covered Segundo's chest. I sank to my knees next to Hasbaá who was crying over her fallen husband. Segundo opened his eyes and looked up at Hasbaá."

Dezba's voice was trembling with emotion.

"'The Diné homeland must be kept safe,' Segundo said. Hasbaá promised she would do as he said. Segundo's eyes were starting to close, but he kept trying to speak. 'Watch for me. Changing Woman will tell you,' he said. 'My spirit will come back to you.'

"As long as I live, I'll never forget Hasbaá's expression as she tried to keep the spirit from leaving him. Then Segundo's eyes closed, and his spirit went to the Dawn. Hasbaá collapsed, her tears mixing with Segundo's blood."

Will felt such a surge of anger at the injustice the old woman described.

"By this time, I had realized my own injury was just a flesh wound, but it still kept me from pulling Hasbaá away. I saw the danger we were all in. We were unarmed, but none of us knew if these crazy soldiers would start firing again. They were so unpredictable.

"'Come on,' I told Hasbaá. 'Get up!' Hasbaá said she could not leave Segundo. 'He's dead, Niece,' I said. 'Help the living, the wounded children. Come on, hurry. No time now for sorrow.' Hasbaá was still in shock, but she grabbed a wounded child. All of us struggled to get away, leaving the dead where they fell.

"We dragged ourselves to safety over the ridge. Hasbaá said with hatred in her eyes, 'I will never rest until Segundo's spirit returns.'"

Dezba stopped. She seemed to be looking around as though for comfort. Will felt so helpless. *What can I do about the wrong my people wrought? And are the Indians going to blame me?* Will reached out and laid his hand on Dezba's arm.

"After that day," she went on, her voice softening in response to Will's gesture, "there was no more peace between the Diné and the Hairy Faces. We had a council of all the Diné outfits. People came from all parts of our country. I had never seen so many Diné in one place. We decided anyone who would kill children was not a human being. We decided we must push the Hairy Faces out of our homeland.

"Hasbaá was a leader in this decision. She gathered all the people together and did a ritual. To make her point about the need for action, she took up the ways of a warrior, even though it is not her true nature. And she made a solemn vow to Changing Woman that she would not marry or make love again until Segundo returned to her.

"That, I think, was a foolish promise. She punished herself for the evil acts of the soldiers. But it turned all her energy and powers to the struggle. Hasbaá fought the soldiers bravely for the next two years. It is a wonder she was not killed. So many of our young men died. It is only by the protection of Changing Woman that Hasbaá lived.

"And even Changing Woman was not powerful enough to fight all the soldiers. Our bows and arrows were no match against their guns. Even when we killed some of them, they always had more to replace them. There seem to be as many of them as there are rocks on the desert.

"What really hurt us was the soldiers' campaign to destroy our food supplies. When they attacked our settlements, we had no choice but to run away. Then the soliders would rush in and burn our hogans and the food we had stored up. When winter came, we had nothing to eat and no place to live in. We were afraid even to build a fire to keep warm for fear of bringing on more attacks. We had to surrender or we would starve..."

17

Bosque Redondo

Will remembered reading in the newspapers about Kit Carson's famous "scorched earth" campaign against the Navajos in 1863 and 1864. It was just a brief sideline to the battles then being fought in Virginia. But Carson's thoroughness helped to provide an example for similar practices that Union General Philip Sheridan launched a year later against the Shenandoah Valley. Will, at least briefly, had been part of the Confederate Army that was trying to defend his state—*his* homeland—against the United States Army, just as Hasbaá had done in New Mexico Territory. Though his heart had never been in it, the way Hasbaá's was, as a Virginian and one who had seen firsthand the kind of destruction total war brings about, he could understand the pain and loss he heard in Dezba's voice as she recounted her people's tragic history with the U.S. Army.

Keeping a hand on her arm, he stared up into the night sky. The moon looked cold and the stars detached.

Will questioned what he'd heard about the Indians. He'd read that hostilities broke out between the Navajo and the Army at Fort Defiance, but he'd never heard how the hostilities started or who started them. He'd never heard about the horserace massacre. That made him wonder what other parts of the story he—and American society—had never heard.

From what Dezba told him, it looked as if the Diné had their side of the story to tell. She couldn't have made all this up. She was forthright and factual in her manner. All his intuitions told him she was speaking the truth. He thought it especially ironic that this fort to which he'd been assigned had the same name as that of the strong anti-slavery leader, Charles Sumner of Massachusetts. He wondered what Senator Sumner would think of this fort that was, in fact, a prison to keep the Diné people enslaved.

"Changing Woman, I believe, has told us you are worthy," Dezba said, "Now you are ready to know more."

Will felt a tremor in his soul as though the old woman had recognized his true self—a self he himself was only just discovering.

"I would like that very much," he answered sincerely.

"Help me up. We are going to go to the medicine lodge for the healing circle." Will stood up and held out his arm to assist Dezba. For the first time, she seemed old to him.

He wanted to ask Dezba about Hasbaá. He wanted to know how it was that the Diné had such respect for this man who dressed like a woman and who had another man for a husband. But he was hesitant to ask questions of so personal a nature. *Maybe I'm missing a simple piece to understand it all.*

They walked slowly back toward the big hogan in the center of the settlement, climbing up the bank of the river where two days ago the flood waters had splashed so fiercely.

"What did Hasbaá do after the surrender?" Will asked. He wanted to know if Hasbaá were still bound by the vow not to make love until Segundo returned. *How is that going to happen?*

"Hasbaá was never the same after that. As long as she was fighting, it was as though her grief was put aside. When we talked of surrender to the Hairy Faces, she did not want to give up. I think she would have fought till all the warriors were killed. But the hunger of the children convinced her.

"Before we surrendered and walked here to the fort, Hasbaá spoke with Changing Woman. She took off the men's clothing. From that time until now, she has always dressed as a woman. You see she still wears only the traditional woven clothes of the Diné. I've come to like these clothes the missionaries gave us," Dezba said as an aside as she flounced the oversized Boston-lady's satin dress she was wearing. "When we were made to come here, we had nothing. Our proud people had to take charity from our enemies. But these dresses, they are cool here in the desert. Hasbaá will not put on the Hairy Face fabrics.

"Until you came here, none of the Hairy Faces knew that this woman had been our bravest warrior. She was just as brave as Segundo had been.

"Oh, when Segundo was alive, they were so happy together. But since his death, Hasbaá's life has been nothing but sorrow. The people are in such need of healing. And we are so far from our homelands. Even Changing Woman's powers are weak here. Hasbaá has had no happiness."

18

The Medicine Lodge

As he and Dezba approached the settlement, Will could see several Diné clustered near the door to the big hogan and light coming from inside. "The Diné welcome you to the medicine lodge," the old woman said formally. "Hasbaá has been preparing the sand painting throughout the day."

As Dezba led him inside, Hasbaá looked up but showed no expression at all. The tall thin Indian concentrated on a large colorful design on the floor. Sitting in a circle around the design were Barboncito and the woman Dezba had said was her Aunt Baaneez along with several other Diné. Baaneez looked very frail. Will wondered how she'd survived the flashflood. She didn't appear to have the strength to hold herself up, much less to hold onto a tree in raging waters. He wondered how any of the Diné survived the hardships they'd suffered. *They must possess a deep inner strength. Maybe I can help them mobilize that strength to get back to their homelands.* And he remembered what Dezba said were Segundo's dying words.

Tallow-burning lamps illuminated the inside of the hogan. The area in the middle of the round-shaped room had been smoothed and covered with clean white sand. Atop that white sand a design had been drawn. Off to the side, near where Hasbaá knelt, were piles of different colored sand or powder.

Will followed Dezba to a place in the circle and sat down beside her. He looked at his pocketwatch. It was almost midnight. The time had gone by so fast—or had it? He wondered how long they'd been in the sweat lodge or how long he'd been listening to Dezba's disturbing account of the beginnings of the Navajo war. He wasn't at all tired in spite of the hour; in fact, he felt energized. He was beginning to understand what was really at stake in this job of his.

Intrigued, he watched as Hasbaá took a handful of one of the powders and made a fist, then expertly allowed a trickle of the grains to pour through the space between thumb and fist. Bright yellow color flowed out from Hasbaá's hand just as an artist would lay out paint with a brush.

The design showed a stylized human figure. Its head was a rectangle of reddish sand with black features drawn in: eyes, nose, and mouth. Atop the head was a colorful headdress formed of geometric feathers. Long dangling earrings hung down on either side of the face. The figure had a long thin body of blue sand. Just below the head, little arms came off the body; in each hand were something that looked like sticks or, probably, arrows. Will couldn't be sure. The ribbon of blue that represented the body came straight down from the head and then curled all the way around to encircle the face and headdress. At the end of the ribbon was drawn a short skirt in ocher sand and below that little suggestions of legs and feet.

Hasbaá drew a perfectly round circle in yellow to enclose the whole design. Will was amazed to watch that circle flow so precisely out of Hasbaá's hand.

"Now she is ready to begin the healing," Dezba whispered softly.

Will had been troubled how to refer to Hasbaá. In spite of the clothes, Hasbaá was a man. Once he had seen Hasbaá's body, he thought of the Diné as "he." But he perceived there was something deferential in the way Dezba always referred to Hasbaá as "she," as if honoring something that far transcended the form of the physical body. He decided that he, too, should think of Hasbaá as "her." Down deep inside, though he hoped there'd come a time when he could relate to Hasbaá man to man.

Hasbaá sat back from the work she'd been doing on the sandpainting. Her face relaxed a little from the concentration, but her eyes showed she was still deep in some kind of trance. She uttered a few words in Diné, and the people in the circle began to sing. While that continued, Hasbaá picked up a bowl that was on the ground near where the colored sands were piled. She handed it to Barboncito who was sitting next to her. He looked into it with an expression of disgust, but then took a drink from it. Hasbaá took the bowl back into her hands. She watched Barboncito intently. After a while a sick look came over his face. He turned away from the circle and leaned over to vomit into a clay basin one of the others held out for him.

Strangely, Hasbaá seemed pleased. Then she got up and brought the bowl to Baaneez. She raised the head of the old woman and tried to get her to drink. But Baaneez was too weak, and probably too repulsed, and kept turning her head away.

While Hasbaá held Baaneez and chanted softly to her, the bowl was then passed to the others. Each in turn took a sip and either gagged or, after several minutes, actually threw up.

When the bowl reached Dezba, she held it toward Will so he could see the putrid-looking contents. Even from a distance he could smell that it was foul. "This will help purify you and get rid of any evil within your body," she assured him. "It won't hurt you. It may make you throw up. But that is all."

When Dezba drank from the bowl and then handed it to him, he knew he had no choice. He reluctantly brought the bowl to his lips. It smelled so awful he had a hard time doing even this. *How am I going to drink this?* Will held back for a moment, mustering his courage. But even before he managed to tip the bowl to his lips, he could feel his stomach turn. He wasn't sure if he actually drank any of the liquid, though he could taste the bitterness on his lips. But uncontrollably he began to wretch. He quickly turned away from the circle and leaned over the basin.

When he recovered, Hasbaá was standing over him. She took the bowl from his still trembling hand. She looked quite pleased. *What a strange religious ceremony!*

"By doing this, you have completed the circle," Dezba whispered to him as the others continued their singing, "and all present will benefit. This ceremony is not just for the benefit of the patients, but for everyone here, including you. Healing is always for all, just as illness of any one person affects all."

Hasbaá then took up another bowl by her side. She reached in and took a small handful of the contents. She put some to her mouth and ate, then rubbed the rest over her face and neck.

As before, Hasbaá fed some to both Barboncito and Baaneez. The old woman could barely manage to eat any of it. Hasbaá rubbed some on the face and neck of the two patients. Then she passed the bowl to the other people in the circle. Each in turn ate a little and rubbed a little on his or her skin. When the bowl came to Will, he did likewise. Dezba and the others gave him an approving look.

He wasn't sure what the stuff was. It looked and smelled just like cooked cornmeal. When his mother had prepared cornmeal like this at home, they'd called it mush. They'd eaten it, but never rubbed it on their faces, though he remembered that sometimes his mother had made a paste of cornmeal to use as a facial scrub. She said it cleaned away old dead skin and made the countenance look lively. It hardly seemed that much different from what the Diné were now doing in this ritual of healing.

Hasbaá started another song and everyone but Baaneez—and Will—joined in the singing.

Several of the men stood up and lifted the elderly woman Baaneez and then carefully placed her frail body right on top of the laboriously constructed designs in the sand. Hasbaá next helped Barboncito to stand up and then sit next to Baaneez on top of the sandpainting.

It seemed to Will like a lot of effort had been put into that painting. He had just begun to appreciate its beauty when all of a sudden it was ruined. Almost as if she understood his dismay, Dezba leaned over and explained that the effort Hasbaá had put into creating the painting had focused sacred energy into it, which could now be absorbed by the patients as they sat upon the design.

He wasn't sure if that made any sense. But he recalled how doctors back home had opened his mother's veins to bleed her when it was obvious she needed life pumped into her, not drained out. That hadn't made any more sense than this. And it certainly had not produced any beauty at all if even for just a short time. At least here the patients could see the caring and involvement of their healer in the effort to help them. He could understand why the Diné showed such respect to Hasbaá. She was priest, artist, and medical doctor all in one.

Hasbaá next sprinkled a bit of each of the colored powders on the bodies of the patients. She handed some sticks with feathers attached to one end to Barboncito. Dezba told Will these were prayersticks and that they would attract the help of the spirits, while the design absorbed the evil energy in the patients that was making them ill. Barboncito took some of the sticks and held them in each hand. Will recognized that these were the same as the sticks in the hands of the figure in the design which he'd mistaken as arrows. They were not instruments of war, but of healing. Hasbaá placed the rest of the prayersticks in Baaneez's hand. They fell from her grasp. She seemed simply too weak to hold them.

The singing then stopped, and Hasbaá stood up and began to twirl a piece of carved wood on a string above her head. It made a sound like a hive of bees that grew louder and louder as it spun faster and faster. The air in the room vibrated as though everything were alive. Then suddenly Hasbaá pulled in on the string and caught the piece of wood. The sound stopped abruptly.

Next Hasbaá sprinkled some yellow powder over Barboncito and Baaneez. Dezba whispered that it was sacred pollen. Hasbaá solemnly chanted words in Diné, which Dezba interpreted: "Beauty before me, beauty behind me, beauty above me, beauty below me, beauty all around me. In beauty I walk the pollen path."

The words sounded so magical and wonderful to Will. He realized that, though there was still a bitter taste on his lips and tongue, he felt better himself, more alert, almost joyful. *Maybe this is healing, after all.*

Barboncito apparently benefitted from the healing. He looked up at Hasbaá with a smile. He had chanted the sacred words along with her. He clearly looked stronger. But Baaneez had not managed to sing the chant at all. She could barely raise her head. Her eyes looked listless. Will could see worry in Hasbaá's face.

Hasbaá once again tried to get Baaneez to drink of the cleansing potion, but she was not responding at all. Looking defeated, Hasbaá motioned for the singing to cease. She took the prayersticks from Barboncito and from where they lay near the hands of the old woman. Hasbaá held the sticks in the air and offered a final prayer. With that, the ceremony ended.

The people got up to leave. Two of the men helped Hasbaá with Baaneez. Dezba followed Will out of the hogan. Will was surprised to see the faint glow of dawn in the eastern sky. The sky was breathtaking. In the early morning, the desert seemed transformed.

"Thank you for inviting me to the ceremonies tonight," Will said. "It looked like Hasbaá was able to help the old man."

"So many of our people have died since we were brought here to this awful place. Even with Hasbaá's healing powers, more of our people continue to die. She is lonely, and her powers are weakened. It is part of our curse, since the warfare began…" Dezba paused as though considering a decision.

"I have been thinking about what Hasbaá needs for her own healing," she said.

"Yes," answered Will tentatively.

"Long years ago, Hasbaá felt great love, but she has not done so in a long time. She has the sexual needs of a young warrior, not an old widow. Hasbaá needs to experience the joy of lovemaking once again. Then she would not be so lonely. She needs a man to hold her and make love to her. Do you understand?"

Oh, I understand.

Confused but elated by Dezba's proposal that what Hasbaá needed for the sake of her role as leader and spiritual healer for the tribe was a man to make love to her, Will wandered back along the riverbank, through the screen of scruffy trees, and up to his quarters. He was surprised to see that the door had been replaced on the front of his cabin. He was sure it had been Diné who'd found it and cut new hinges of leather to hold it in place. They must have done that while he was in the ceremonies last night.

With the exciting but frightening sense that his world was changing, Will stripped off his clothes and collapsed into bed. He was exhausted, but could not calm his excitement. Sleep wouldn't come. And memories, stirred up by Dezba's suggestion, flooded his consciousness.

19

LYNCHBURG

A lone church bell rang in the distance as Will drove the mule and buggy down the main street of Lynchburg, now deserted on Sunday morning. He felt lost and confused. His father's words—"Today we are goin' to talk about sin"—echoed in his mind. *What do I do now?* His thoughts were racing. *I can never go back. Where am I going to go?*

He heard a voice call his name. He looked up and saw a familiar face smiling down from a second floor window. It was Harry Burnside, a lawyer who had his office over old Abraham Mattingly's dry goods store. Burnside had his desk situated so he could survey the street below; Will knew he lived in an apartment adjoining the office. He had often talked to Harry on the stoop in front of Mattingly's store. Harry liked to sit out there in the evenings and gab with the townsfolk. Everybody liked Harry, though everybody also thought he was a bit strange.

Will waved meekly.

"Join me for coffee," Harry gestured he should come upstairs.

"Oh, no, thank you."

"Well, why not? What do you have to lose?" Harry asked with a laugh.

What *was* the point of saying no? He had nowhere to go. He parked the buggy and hitched the mule.

Will's father had never had much to do with Burnside, claiming he was too free-thinking. When the war started, Harry refused to renounce his loyalty to the Union. "We're still brothers," he'd said. "I got friends in Washington. And they're still my friends. I've got friends in Richmond, too. They're also still my friends."

If everybody hadn't liked him and sometimes depended on his legal know-how, he might have been arrested as a Unionist and a traitor to the Confederacy. But everybody knew Harry was far enough above politics to forgive him his eccentricity. As it turned out, after the fall of the Confederacy, Harry's good connections with Washington and the Union helped a lot of local people. They needed a reputable source to vouch for them in getting qualified for taking the U.S. Loyalty Oath. Without being so qualified, it was almost impossible for any Southerner to get a job or even a contract to do business with the government of Reconstruction. Harry's good nature and his apolitical status proved a boon for the whole town. Harry Burnside was just a good man.

As Will knocked lightly on the door at the top of the stairs, he was genuinely glad Harry had invited him up. He really needed to talk to somebody.

The door swung open. "Come in, young man," Harry said cordially. Then, with a hint of tenderness, "You look like you got some worries on your mind."

Will nodded his head sheepishly.

"Well, now, maybe a cup of coffee and a little talk 'll help. It's a fine mornin'. The sun is shining. God's in his heaven; all's right with the world." Harry laughed again.

Harry Burnside looked almost ageless. His hair was white and his waist had filled out—the colorful brocade vest he was wearing stretched pretty tight about his middle—but his face was free of lines or wrinkles. Will would have placed Harry at around fifty-five or sixty, but there was something downright boyish about him.

"Mr. Burnside, do you really believe that?"

"That it's a beautiful day? Why, of course."

"No, I mean, about God being in heaven and all that." Will's voice cracked with nervousness.

"Oh, that's a line from an English poet name o' Browning." Harry ushered him into the office. "I don't think the poet believed it himself." Law books lined the wall floor to ceiling. "C'mon back to the parlor, my boy." Harry led him through the office into his living quarters. "You havin' a little problem with God?"

"Guess you might say that..."

"Well, I can see how that could be a problem for the son of the hardest-nosed preacher in town." Harry spoke in a gentle way that invited intimacy. "Just 'tween you and me, Will, I sorta got my doubts about all this God business myself." He gestured for him to sit down on a green velvet settee.

Harry poured Will a cup of coffee. "And here're some buttermilk biscuits fresh from the oven. Baked 'em myself just a little while ago. I been hopin' some nice friend might stop by to enjoy a little Sunday mornin' repast with me." Harry placed a tray on the low table in front of the settee. On the tray was a crockery bowl full of fresh butter, several little cut-glass cups brimming with colorful preserves, and an Oriental wicker basket from which Will could smell warm biscuits. Part of the charm of Harry Burnside's simple but elegant little parlor was the aroma of fresh baking. It reminded Will of his mother. And for the first time in a week, he felt himself relax.

Will had been doing all the cooking for his father and himself since Maudie left and even before that really, indeed, since the time his mother started getting sick and he had taken to caring for her. Still it had never occurred to him that a grown man could live his entire life taking care of himself the whole time, even down to the baking of buttermilk biscuits on Sunday morning.

He looked around the room. It was furnished simply, even austerely. The decor was clearly masculine, but the entire arrangement was tasteful and pleasing, not as one would imagine an unmarried man would create. A few fine oil paintings graced the walls, and several *objets d'art* were carefully showcased: a chinoise screen, a carved ivory tusk, a Persian *hookah* pipe made of shiny brass, a beautiful kerosene lamp with a shade of multi-colored glass mosaics that formed a butterfly.

"You ever had a wife? I mean, to teach you how to cook and keep house and all that, you know?"

Harry chuckled. "Can't say as I have, m' boy. Can't say as I ever missed it neither, though I've known some mighty fine women in my life. And they'd 've all made good companions. But I guess I was just always the bachelor type, if you know what I mean."

"Me, too." Will remembered Michael's declaration that he weren't never gettin' married.

Harry, who sat in a high-backed wooden chair adjacent to the sofa, reached over and patted Will's knee paternally. Will wished he'd had a father who'd patted him on the knee…

Harry sat forward on his seat and leaned in toward him, "You know, William, some of us are called to the beat of a different drummer. We have different things to do with our lives. For some of us, marriage and family just aren't part of our vocation."

"Vocation?"

"Well, maybe you could say what God has got planned for us."

"My father says God demands every man and woman be fruitful and multiply." Will responded as if by rote.

"I guess I'm not talkin' 'bout that kind of God," Harry shot back. "I don't think you are, either. Isn't that where this conversation started?" He bobbed his head and laughed gently. "Your father's God is a pretty stern and heartless fellow. But that's not the only notion of God around. You ever heard of these New England Transcendentalists? Henry David Thoreau? He's the one who said that about the different drummer. Or Mr. Walt Whitman? They talk all about God, but it's not the same notion of God your father's got."

"Father's sermon this morning was about how God rained down fire and brimstone on Sodom and Gomorrah." Will blurted out the whole story of this week's misadventure. He told Harry about his father's catching him and Michael in the barn and beating them with the horsewhip and calling them "abominations" and then recounting the whole story to the congregation in his sermon.

Harry listened attentively.

"Now, don't go basing everything on your dad, Will. He's a… well, a peculiar kind of man. There's a wide world out there waiting for you with lots of different kinds of men and lots of different kinds of ideas, 'bout God, 'bout lots o' things…" It thrilled Will to hear Harry use practically the same words Michael had used.

"You said some of us are called to the beat of a different drummer. You mean, like, like you and me?"

"Uh-huh."

"And have different things to do with our lives?"

"Uh-huh."

"But what?"

"Let me tell you a little about the world, Will." Harry began to explain about what kinds of different drum beats there were out there. He told Will how some people just aren't born for raising offspring, that they've got other talents that help all of society, not just their own little family. He said he thought these talents helped create culture and civilization, and might be more important to God even than being fruitful and multiplying. Harry talked for a long time. Will wished the talk was all a little more practical and less philosophical.

"I've never fit in here anywhere," Will finally interrupted. "How am I gonna march to a different drum in Lynchburg?"

"Then go somewhere else," Harry said, as though it were the easiest thing in the world. "Nobody's tied you down here. What do *you* want to do?"

There was the question again: What do *you* want to do? Not what do *they* want you to do?

Harry reached out and opened the Oriental wicker basket and proffered him another biscuit. While Will was fussing with the butter and preserves, Harry sprang the big question on him: "So why don't you leave now?"

Will looked up startled. Of course, that was the answer. He'd been thinking about hanging himself from that tree out in front of the churchhouse, and all he really had to do was leave town. He admitted timidly, "I guess I'm afraid. I don't know what I'd do out there for a job."

"Well, if that's all that's keepin' you, I may be able to help you. I've got some contacts in Washington. I bet one of them can get you a government post. Oh, yes, yes. Jesse McDonald. He's just the man you need to see.

"I'm going to write you a Letter of Introduction to a fellow I know in the Interior Department. I'm more than certain it'll get you an interview. You play your cards right, and this man McDonald could have you hired by the end of the week."

"Oh, this is like a dream come true," Will said. "Oh, Mr. Burnside, I could just kiss you."

Harry's eyes lit up. He leaned forward and tapped his cheek with his forefinger, indicating that Will was welcome to kiss him primly. Slightly embarrassed and laughing even more, Will did so. And they both laughed together.

"I just hope this is the start of a brand new life for you, young man. You listen for that different drummer, now, hear? Well, look, let me write you that Letter of Introduction. In the meantime, here, you look at this." He walked over to a bookshelf, took down a book, and presented it to Will.

While Harry went into his office in the next room and dipped his quill in the inkwell and wrote on his legal stationery, Will perused the volume. It was a brand new copy of a little book bound in leather, *Leaves of Grass* by Walt Whitman. This was a name Harry had mentioned earlier, one of those Harry said had a different notion of God, one that might make more sense to him.

A little later, Harry Burnside interrupted his reading, handing him an official-looking envelope sealed with red wax with Harry's professional seal. "There you are. I have no doubts this will get you a job. Can't say what kind, of course, but I assured Jesse that you were a man of many talents."

"And that's it? I take off just like that and bring this letter to Washington?"

"Just like that. The address is on the envelope. Now, listen," he cautioned, "you tell McDonald you want a good job. You might say you want one like he got when he was your age. I don't know Jesse very well anymore. But he owes me a favor. I think he'll help you. But heed my advice and don't let him, ah, take undue advantage of you. He's not the same man I used to know. You keep your distance.

"And, here, take that book. I think there're things in there that'll speak to you. You can see this copy is brand new. Why, this is the fourth or fifth copy I've bought! They make good presents for earnest young men with bright futures in their eyes. And you've sure got some beautiful bright eyes," Harry said wistfully.

"Now you better hurry, young man. The train for Washington comes through here 'bout four o'clock. It's nearly three now."

An hour! *Oh, my God.* Will grinned widely. He took Harry's hand warmly in his. "Harry, you may have just changed my life around..."

"Sounds to me like it could only get better. Hurry home and pack. Here, take the rest of these biscuits to eat on the train." He wrapped them in a napkin and handed them to Will. "Have you got train fare?"

Will assured him he had savings enough to pay for the railroad ticket. "Thanks, Harry."

Then Harry Burnside did something no man had ever done before. He threw open both his arms and embraced Will tightly and warmly.

"Now skedaddle. Remember there's another world out there. You got your future awaiting you."

20

ON THE TRAIN

Will rushed home. He saw his father wasn't there. He'd stayed for that church social in the afternoon Charlotte Franklin had been so excited about last week. *Damn Charlotte Franklin, she started all this...* Then he realized maybe he ought to be thanking her instead.

He quickly put the buggy away in the barn and unhitched the mule. He retrieved his stash of money from under the hay, then rushed into the house and clambered up the stairs to his room. He threw some clothes in an old carpetbag of his mother's.

Bounding downstairs, he stopped in front of his father's desk. Pen and paper lay waiting for him to write a farewell letter. He sat down, but then couldn't think of anything to say. The old man thought he ought to be dead. *Well, let him think whatever he wants.*

Will looked out the window and saw the neighbors driving their wagon up the road. He could see his father sitting in the front seat. The church social must've finished up. But he wasn't going to be there when his father came in the front door. He rushed out the back.

He rode off on the mule, going the back way over the river. He got to the railroad station just a few minutes before four. The train was already sitting on the tracks puffing billows of steam.

As he paid for his ticket, he noticed Japhet, the Lee family's former slave. He ran over to the man, clapped him warmly on the back and asked him if he'd do him a favor and return the mule. Japhet said he'd be happy to.

With that last bit of family responsibility properly acquitted, Will jumped on board. Even before he found his second-class seat, the train pulled out of the station with a loud long burst of its whistle. As he threw his bag into the overhead rack and took his seat, he was amazed at all the changes his life had taken in the past week. Part of him felt terribly afraid. But another part of him was thrilled and excited and glad the last few hours had happened so fast he hadn't had time for misgivings. He broke into a big smile again as he looked out the window at the countryside now beginning to speed by. *Michael had been right. There was a whole wide world out there just a'waitin'.*

Will dug into his carpetbag and pulled out the volume of poetry and the biscuits Harry Burnside had wrapped in a napkin. As he nibbled, he paged through the book, reading here and there. Harry had been right. These words spoke directly to him. He could hear the beat of the different drum.

He came across a passage that arrested him. He read it over and over again, finding new meaning with each reading. These words seemed to mark the start of a new life.

> I dreamed in a dream of a city where all men were
>   like brothers,
> O I saw them tenderly love each other—
>   I often saw them, in numbers, walking hand in
>   hand;
> I dreamed that was the city of robust friends—
>   Nothing was greater there than manly love—it
>   led the rest,
> It was seen in every hour in the actions of the men of
>   that city,
>   and in all their looks and words.
>
> Come, I will make the continent indissoluble,
> I will make the most splendid race the sun ever
>   shone upon,
> I will make divine magnetic lands,
>   With the love of comrades,
>   With the life-long love of comrades.

I will plant companionship thick as trees along all
    the rivers of America,
And along the shores of the great lakes, and all over
    the prairies,
I will make inseparable cities with their arms about
    each other's necks,
    By the love of comrades,
    By the manly dear love of comrades.

Well, if my past has been buried in the confines of family under the domination of my father, now it will be the promise of what Whitman calls "Life immense in passion, pulse, and power." This "dear love of comrades" will be the guiding value of my new life.

Will was on his way to Washington, Capital of the Union, on his way, he hoped, to the wide world.

21

WEST OF SALINA, KANSAS

The conductor came through the train, announcing the end of the line. They were truly in the middle of nowhere. Passengers would have to transfer to stagecoach to continue further. Will looked through the pouch he'd been given by the clerk at the Office of Indian Affairs. Along with some cash which he'd counted several times over during the long journey—it was the first real salary he'd ever received—and his Documents of Appointment which were in a sealed envelope he was to present to the Commanding Officer upon arrival, he confirmed he had vouchers for the next day's stage to Fort Sumner and for an overnight stay in a hotel here.

He was still baffled at how easily he'd gotten the job. He'd only been in Washington one day. It was just as Harry Burnside had promised. He was, indeed, on his way to the wide world out West. He was going to be an Indian Agent. He said the words over and over again to himself. He was proud. And he was frightened. *What have I gotten myself into?* The idea of helping the Indians become assimilated into civilized society appealed to his moral notions of virtue, but the Union was also waging a war with them. His experience of the soldiers killing the buffalo from the train the day before still rattled him. He realized that soon he was going to be living in a military fort with soldiers all around him.

As the train pulled to a stop, he could see that the town that had developed at the current end of the line of the Union-Pacific Railway was primarily an array of wooden corrals along with a hodgepodge of tents and a few makeshift buildings, the railroad depot one of them. It was here that westward travelers transferred to stagecoach or those returning east came for the train to take them home, along with the cattle. Will realized these so-called cowtowns had little to do with the human passengers, like himself, and a lot to do with the cattle to be loaded for transport back East.

This was a loading point for the cowboys driving their cattle herds north from the Texas grasslands. As Will wandered down the main street of the settlement, the cowboys he saw surprised him. Almost all of them were just that: boys. Only a few looked to be beyond their mid-twenties; some seemed no older than twelve or thirteen. Most were Negro or Mexican. Though they were covered in dust—everything was covered in dust—some of the cowboys were quite good-looking, and a couple seemed to throw friendly glances his way. But Will talked to nobody; he was tired and went directly to the hotel as instructed by the stationmaster.

It was a hardly a hotel, but rather a compound of tents set up behind the saloon which was the biggest actual wooden building in the town. Because Will was a government Agent, he got a tent all to himself. It was surprisingly well furnished with a brass bed, comfortable straw mattress, a stool, and even a small writing desk. Down the way from his tent was a public wash area and an enclosure with a bathtub inside. For an extra nickel, one could get the tub filled with hot water. Will splurged on himself. His birthday was coming up. Besides, he wanted to be fresh for the next morning's stagecoach ride.

He ate supper in the saloon and then ordered his bath drawn. While he sat in the hot water relishing the feeling of being clean for the first time in days, he was grateful for the perquisites of government service. But he felt guilty about getting such special treatment. He thought about the young cowboys sleeping crowded together in their tents; he didn't think many of them could have gotten accommodations as nice as his.

There was something exciting and forbidden about thinking of the cowboys. He pictured them, not reclining in private baths, but all standing around, stripped to the waist, washing themselves from a common tub.

He wondered what it would be like to be one of those cowboys, out on the range with only another cowboy for company. He thought fondly of Michael. He hoped he'd gotten to Norfolk safely and maybe was even now sailing the high seas.

After his bath, Will sauntered through town. There were enough cowboys around that the dancehall, and several nearby saloons were all doing brisk business. He wandered from one to another enjoying the manly camaraderie of the celebrating men. Most of them had also cleaned up and changed out of their dusty clothes. He thought they all looked ready for Sunday church, but he guessed that's not what they were thinking about.

Most of these men had been out on the trail. They were all likely to have given themselves over to celebration. Behind him, young men jostled each other to reach the bar. Will imagined they could handle a lot more beer than he. He was not a drinker, and the couple of beers he had drunk had already made him dizzy. It was time to go back to his tent and get some sleep. He downed the last swig in his glass and, with an unintentionally loud bang, set the glass on the bar.

He was just stepping back to make room when a voice spoke up out of the crowd just behind his ear, *"Perdón, señor.* Leaving so early?"

Will turned around. A Mexican man right behind him was reaching past him to get the bartender's attention. *"No vaya ahora,"* he said.

"Huh? What did you say? You want here? At the bar?"

Will was frightened by the idea of talking with a stranger. And at the same time, he was thrilled. This man's features looked so exotic to him and interesting.

"Ah… do not go," the man said. *"Buenos noches…* Er, good evening."

"Oh. Good evening."

"Me llamo Jose." Then the man corrected himself for Will's benefit, "My name is Jose Flores. I noticed the color of your eyes… "

"I'm Will, Will Lee," He was used to people remarking on his unusual eye color. With a dash of daring from the beer, he added in imitation, *"Llama Will."*

"*Me llamo,*" the Mexican cowboy corrected him, "*My* name is Will."

"No, I'm Will," he said, making a joke, "You're Jose."

"*Sí. Yo soy Jose. Tu eres Will.*" They both laughed.

Will liked the way his name sounded with the Spanish accent. "You are Mexican?"

"*Sí, señor.*"

"I've never met a Mexican before. In fact, I've never met any foreigner in my whole life."

"*Yo no soy extranjero. You* are the foreigner."

"Huh?" Will was bewildered.

Jose laughed. "I say you are the foreigner here. This land used to be Mexico."

"You live here?" Will asked.

"Oh, no. I am a *vaquero.*"

"Huh?"

"A cowboy," Jose puffed out his chest just a little. "I am driving cattle from Texas for the train." Will could see the muscles of Jose's chest under his shirt.

"And you?" Jose asked. "Is this your home?"

"I am going to Fort Sumner in New Mexico Territory. I guess I don't have a home anywhere."

"We are alike then," Jose said. His eyes cheered up. He grinned at Will and then reached out and gently ran his hand down the back of Will's neck, smoothing his hair.

Will shivered at the touch. Jose reminded him of Michael, though the *vaquero's* olive skin was much darker. He had thick black hair that fell down evenly on both sides of his face. He looked to be a couple of years younger than Will. His eyes were dark brown with long lashes. His face was round, and his nose was aquiline, giving him a kind of Indian look, but also, Will thought, a Roman handsomeness. He looked both so gentle and innocent and so manly at the same time.

"*¿Cerveza?*" Jose asked, turning to look right into his face. Will could tell Jose had seen him staring at him. He didn't seem in the least displeased.

"Huh?"

"*¿Cerveza?*" he pointed to Will's empty glass.

"Oh, no. I've had enough. I was just leaving…"

"Me too," Jose said.

They went outside together and walked up and down the short section of street that comprised the little town.

"I grew up with other *muchachos*. None of us had *familias*, so we became each others' *familia*. We learned to hunt the wild cattle. The *Americanos* want Texas beef. Us cowpokes, we round up the longhorns and drive 'em here to the railroad depot, then ride back down to Texas to hunt more longhorns."

Jose showed Will how the cattle were herded into the corrals and then into railroad cars. Will rejoined with the story of the buffalo stampede he'd seen from the train. They both agreed shooting the buffalo and leaving the bodies to rot was immoral.

Will explained about his job as apprentice to the Indian Agent at Fort Sumner. Jose was not too enthusiastic about Indians. He warned him to be careful. He admitted he'd never experienced it personally, but he said he'd heard that the Indians could be very dangerous. He said his own people frequently had to fight off Indian attacks. He added that sometimes these attacks resulted in Indians' being taken prisoner and that the prisoners were sometimes sold into slavery.

Will was not happy to hear about anybody being sold into slavery. "Slavery is stupid. How are you going to force a full-grown Indian captive to be any kind of useful servant?"

Jose answered that the Indians taken prisoner were usually children, not adults, so they could be trained.

"Indian children are riding in attacks on the settlers?"

"*Yo no sé.*"

They walked in silence. On the edge of town, Will could see tents and campfires scattered out on the plain. "You got a campsite out there?"

"The trailmaster set up camp for me and my *compadres*. I think I can find my way back there. How about you, *mi amigo*? Where are you sleeping?"

"The Indian Office arranged for me to stay back of the dancehall. Got a really nice tent that's set up almost like a room in a regular hotel."

"*Ay*, I've not ever seen a hotel."

"You've never seen a hotel? Well, you wanna see this one?" Will half knew what he'd just started. He was scared, but thrilled, and his heart was beating like mad.

"*Bueno.*"

Will didn't know if he was allowed to bring guests back to his room. So he brought Jose around to the back of the tent compound and led him through the wash area.

"This sure is a *grande* tent you got here, all *solo*," Jose looked about in wonder as he followed Will into the room.

Will said innocently, "Why don't you get one like this yourself?"

Jose's eyes widened. "*Ay*, I could never afford such a thing. But even if I could, I think perhaps the trail boss stays here. He might think I should not be in as grand a hotel as him."

Will was struck with the reality of the world, that even out here on the freewheeling frontier men were supposed to preserve the rules of social stratification that separated them. *This separation of men by class and position was exactly what Mr. Whitman was complaining about.*

Jose interrupted his thought by announcing, "Besides, I usually sleep with five other *caballeros*, all crowded together."

"Is that a hardship?" Will again felt guilty about having such affluence. He imagined poor Jose impoverished and deprived.

"On cold nights when we gotta help each other stay warm, it can be entertaining…" Jose's accent made the word "entertaining" sound so portent.

I wonder just who has been deprived, Jose or me? I've been in hotels and fancy buildings and ridden on modern trains. But I've never been with other men in a tent, at least, not men like these…

"You like that idea?"

"Oh, I dunno." Will buried his face. He couldn't bring himself to look into Jose's dark eyes.

"Or maybe just the two, *yo no sé*… like you and me. Now."

"I dunno." Will wanted to look up.

Having thought about Walt Whitman, Will rushed over to the little desk beside the bed and lit the kerosene lamp. He adjusted the flame of the lamp so it wasn't too bright. He felt funny about its casting shadows on the walls of the tent. *Maybe somebody will see there are two people in here when there's only supposed to be one!*

Out of shyness, Will changed the subject. He picked up the book on the desk and showed it Jose.

"*Un libro.*" Jose took the thin volume and flipped through the pages while holding the book upside down. "What is this?"

As Will took the book back from Jose's hand, their fingers touched. He turned the book over and pointed to the words on the cover, "It says *Leaves of Grass.*"

"*Ay,* you can read! I never met anyone who can read."

"My mother taught me, and I went to school. Didn't you?"

"How can a *Mexicano niño* in Texas go to school? I never even seen a school. I can't remember the last time I saw a book. Read me something." Jose sat down on the bed, very careful not to muss the coverlet.

Will pulled the wicker stool over close to the lamp so he could see. He paged through the book looking for something he thought Jose would appreciate. The young Mexican's desire to watch him read touched him.

Jose's eyes gleamed as he waited for Will to select something from the book. Will found one of the sections he'd read on the train and had marked so he could find it again. He looked up. He saw the light in Jose's eyes. He wasn't sure he'd picked a good passage, but he began to read.

> Clear to me now, standards not yet published,
> Clear to me that my Soul,
> That the Soul of the man I speak for,
> Feeds, rejoices only in comrades.
> Here, by myself, away from the clank of the world,
> Tallying and talked to here by tongues aromatic,
> No longer abashed… I proceed,
> For all who are, or have been, young men,
> To tell the secrets of my nights and days,
> To celebrate the need of comrades.

"*Es magnífico,*" Jose said when he had finished. "What does it mean?"

"Well," Will responded slowly, not knowing for sure how to answer, "I'm only beginning to figure it out for myself. The writer—his name is Walt Whitman—is a peaceful man. Like you, Jose. He doesn't like war or competition. He says the goal in life is to develop friendship. The highest good for everybody will come from men uniting in what he calls 'the dear love of comrades,' irrespective of their race or class or… or… whatever else. Only when we release our feelings for each other, and stop suppressing our love, will we get beyond the conflicts that divide us."

"You get all that from reading, I can't believe it. That book says it a lot better—*you* explain it a lot better—than I could, but in a way this is what us *caballeros,* us cowpokes, feel for each other, this 'dear love of comrades.' I don't know anything else. I've never been with a woman. I can count on my fingers the few times I've ever even seen a woman since I left my home. I hardly remember what a woman looks like." Jose grinned widely in exaggeration. "Have you seen any since you've been out here?"

"Nope." Will knew he'd seen women in the dancehall earlier, but he played along with Jose's jest. "Guess not."

"See what I mean? Except for the Indians, this is a country of men and boys. Sometimes whores pass through at the railroad junctions, and some of the *caballeros* buy their favors. But I don't know as I'd want to. Me, I'm just satisfied to stay with my cowpokes."

"You speak English well." Will changed the subject away again. Nonetheless, his eye was attracted to the curve of Jose's chest. The cowboy was sitting in such a way that his shirt gapped open, and the smooth surface of muscle showed taut and supple.

"Since I've been workin' for the Texans, my English is better. I'm real good at languages. Say, I can speak Navajo and Comanche and even a little French," Jose announced proudly. "You want to hear something?"

"Sure, what can you say?"

"*Tu as yeux vert.*"

"What's that?"

"*Tú tienes ojos verdes,*" Jose said. "You have green eyes. In French. There was a Frenchman worked for the trail boss. We got to be real friendly for a while, and he taught me."

"Can you say it in Navajo? I'm going to be working with the Navajos."

"Uh, that is *muy difícil,* " Jose laughed. "It is a strange language."

As Jose touted his language skills, Will could not take his eyes off the cowboy's body. He remembered the feel of Michael Halyerd's body pressed against his.

Jose held his gaze. Then very softly he repeated his sample of French; only this time it didn't sound like a language drill. *"Tu as yeux vert. Très jolie yeux vert."*

Even though Will didn't understand the second part of Jose's sentence, he blushed. He looked into Jose's dark eyes and was lost in the welcoming smile.

"I see desire in your eyes," Jose said. "If you have desires, why not do what you want to do?" He spoke very quietly as if to avoid breaking a spell. Then he leaned forward and kissed Will. It was a light kiss, but full of meaning. "The dear love of comrades." Jose reached out to Will to pull him toward the bed he was sitting on.

Will gratefully let himself be pulled into Jose's arms. Jose stood and hugged him tightly. Then he gently released his hold and, smiling widely, guided him to lie down atop the coverlet. Then he climbed up onto the bed and lay down on top of him. Jose's body pressed down along the full length of Will's, and his cheek felt warm against Will's own.

Jose pulled his face away and looked into Will's eyes, then lowered his head so his lips brushed the corners of the other's lips, then slowly wet Will's lips with his tongue. He kissed him deeply in the way that Will had been kissed only one time before, by Michael.

This time, the kiss and the lovemaking that was going to follow would not be interrupted, he knew. After a while, Will's anxiety abated, and he stopped worrying about getting caught by some raving judgmental lunatic. Relief and excitement rushed in to fill the void.

Jose unbuttoned Will's shirt and pulled at it to get it off. Will sat up a little and took over undressing himself while Jose stripped his own shirt off. Jose then kissed him on the neck, lightly biting at his skin. He had his legs astride Will's hips. He sat back on his haunches and gently, playfully slid his buttocks against Will's pelvis.

Jose unclasped the buckle of Will's belt and opened the top couple of buttons of his trousers. Then he rolled over onto the bed and undid his own pants and kicked them down.

"Let me show you what we do for fun."

"This won't hurt, will it?"

"I wouldn't hurt you, *Señor Will*. It's all for fun. The whole idea is to feel good and enjoy this lovely body you've got." He tapped Will's belly.

To get their trousers off, they both had to struggle with shoes and boots. Then Jose positioned Will in the middle of the bed and curled around so he knelt next to him. He bent down and took Will in his mouth, sucking and licking. Will lay back and let the sensations pour through him; never had he known anything like this. His boyish cuddling and humping with Michael had been wonderful, but it hadn't been as deliberate or self-aware. Jose obviously knew what he was doing. *This really is going to be making love.*

"¡Dulce!"

"Huh?"

"Sweet cock," the *Mexicano* translated. "You are a *dulce* man. A man with a *dulce* cock." He giggled at his jumble of the languages.

Will cringed at the words. A part of him was gratified to be called "sweet"; it's how he'd always wanted to think of himself. Another part of him felt frightened and repelled by the word "cock." Will knew the other boys had words like that for their sex; he'd heard them talking at school about these things that he'd learned were forbidden and reprehensible. He'd never dared think of himself with a cock.

He looked down and watched Jose suck his sweet cock. Thinking such forbidden words about himself thrilled and aroused him—and seemed to free him from that past. Seeing the length and girth of his cock disappearing into the other man's mouth sent waves of pleasure through him. These merged with the sensations of Jose's tongue caressing and stimulating the head of his penis, and his consciousness reeled with gladness.

The Mexican cowboy slid his face down between Will's legs and licked his testicles and then ran his tongue along the inside of his thighs. The pleasure surged through Will even stronger and made him groan and squirm lustily. Jose spit in his hand and rubbed the saliva over his own cock, working it deftly to full hardness. Next he crossed Will's legs at the ankles and then turned and lay down on top of him. Jose slipped himself between Will's wetted thighs. He supported his weight on outstretched arms, so he could maneuver his torso, and began to thrust in long smooth strokes.

Will hadn't understood how men would have sex with each other. He barely understood how men and women had sex. *What went where?* He had, of course, brought himself to orgasm before—and he'd had some sort of sex with his friend in the barn. But those experiences had almost always been furtive and fraught with shame. He had always kept his sexual feelings secret, almost even from himself. Now experiencing arousal like this—with another man who also enjoyed the feelings and with no worry about getting caught—abolished all the secrecy.

He knew from his experience with Michael that two men could touch and hold each other, and their arousal would bring on pleasure and orgasm, but he thought that having sex and making love was something more than that.

And this is it!

Feeling Jose's body tucked into his, he was amazed to discover that the arousal wasn't just in his genitals. Over his whole body he felt alive, tingling with energy. And, indeed, this kind of makeshift intercourse seemed so totally natural. *Of course, this is how men could have sex. It isn't a matter of connecting complementary organs as it is just giving each other pleasure.*

He strained to get closer. He ran his hands down the smooth expanse of Jose's hard-muscled back. He cupped the cowboy's buttocks in his hands and held tight, letting himself be rocked back and forth by Jose's thrusts. By now, both of them perspired freely, and their sweat-lubricated skin moved easily over each other's.

Jose quivered and trembled against him. He reared up and threw his head back; he shook his hair wildly and moaned. He thrust deep and long between Will's thighs. Then he opened his eyes and saw Will watching him. He smiled affectionately and craned his neck down to press his mouth against Will's.

As that kiss deepened, everything went out of Will's mind. He felt himself go all to jelly as his muscles began to move on their own as by reflex. His testicles contracted, and the warmth deep inside moved upward and out onto his belly against Jose's. He shuddered and convulsed in pleasure like never before. Then Jose, too, came. Will felt the hot fluid ooze against the base of his testicles and the inside of his thighs.

Jose lowered himself and clutched Will tightly. They squeezed themselves together harder and harder, trembling as pleasure continued to rush through them both. Then Jose relaxed, his breathing slowed, and he started to laugh softly.

"What are you laughing at?" Will asked self-consciously.

Jose raised up and looked into his eyes. "How wonderful bodies are." He pecked him on the lips. "How wonderful your body is, *señor.*"

They both laughed as the last echoes of orgasm surged through them, then lay together silently a long time. The young Mexican's easy wisdom of sex and love flooded into Will as though through some queer and heretofore unexperienced conjugation of souls. Will began to understand more than ever what Walt Whitman had talked about. The love of comrades took on a more concrete meaning as he lay with the cowboy. He felt such gratitude toward Jose for showing him how to feel love and pleasure. The condemnations of his father, of Lynchburg, of upstanding Christian society—all were behind him. He had, indeed, reached a new frontier, in more than one sense.

At first light, Jose roused him. He'd already slipped back into his clothes. "I'm going back to the campsite of *mis caballeros.* I think I should get out of here before all the hotel guests wake up."

Jose kissed him on the lips. "*Gracias, señor. Muchas gracias* for this dear love of comrades," he said touchingly. "*Hasta luego.* Til we meet again, Will. *Vaya con Dios.*"

Will smiled wistfully as Jose slipped out the flap of the tent and disappeared. *Will I ever see him again? What other discoveries about the dear love of comrades—and about myself—might I have in this unexpected journey?*

Part II

Discovery

22

Fort Sumner

W ill awoke in the afternoon in the little Indian Agent cabin he'd come to call home, surprisingly alert and rested. He felt he'd received some sort of healing himself last night in those ceremonies—both in his relations with the Diné and in his relations with his own past. He felt like he was still tingling all over.

A few days before, he had been despairing of ever being able to establish any significant communication with the Indians. Now he'd discovered intimate details of the Indians' lives and been invited to participate in ceremonies which he thought he might be the first white man to have ever seen. Then he recalled Dezba's story of John Blewer, the tutor who helped the Diné to speak English. He must have been included in ceremonies like this; he'd been a friend of the Diné. *And because of his friendship, Dezba seems willing to include me in her confidence.*

As he headed over to the mess hall, Will gave thanks to John Blewer. *How would I have ever managed to communicate with the Diné if it hadn't been for him? I wonder if Jesse McDonald and the Office of Indian Affairs back in Washington had known about Blewer? That missionary Pastor Benedict had said only an old lady was interested in learning English. That must have been Dezba. But then how had McDonald expected me to work with the Indians if he didn't know they spoke English and certainly must have known I couldn't speak Navajo?*

Here was another question for the list. This one didn't seem as sinister. Nonetheless, it seemed that it was he who should have to learn to speak Diné, not the Indians who should have to learn English. After all, this was their country. *When an emissary went to see the leader of another nation, like Benjamin Franklin going to the court of France, it was the emissary's responsibility to learn the language, wasn't it?*

What had Mr. McDonald thought I was going to accomplish out here with no training?

In the mess hall, Will found a pot of coffee, a couple of pieces of bread and some meat that had been left from lunch. He was famished, having eaten nothing since yesterday. Several soldiers drank coffee in the mess hall, but they ignored him. That was fine with him. He sat in a corner facing the back wall so he wouldn't be disturbed.

After eating, he headed back to the Diné settlement. He saw Gen. Carleton in the distance observing him from the porch of his headquarters, but he pretended not to notice. He thought the general ought to be pleased with his effort to learn the Diné ways, but suspected instead that he probably disapproved of his spending so much time with the Indians. Will reminded himself that as an emissary between the Hairy Faces and the Diné, he had to spend some time with his own side as well.

Carleton had offered to teach him about managing the Indians; he ought to at least talk with the man, let him know what he was learning through his own investigations. He'd observed that the general didn't pay much attention to the actual conditions of the Indians' lives; perhaps he didn't know how really oppressed they were by the conditions on the reservation. *Perhaps I can help him see and get him to do something to alleviate the hardships.*

As he neared the settlement, Will saw Hasbaá. She seemed to be preoccupied and did not notice his approach. She was carrying the bundle of feathered prayersticks from last night's ceremony. He watched her, trying to remain inconspicuous, as she held one of the prayersticks up to the sky and then deposited it at the base of a scrub tree. She then went to another location and repeated the ritual.

Will couldn't help his eyes following her every movement. He wished she'd be distracted and notice him. He wanted her to feel a similar fascination with him. But that seemed so selfish. *Here she is, trying to save and heal her people and I'm wishing she were thinking about me. Well, I hope at least she's including me in her prayers to help the people. Maybe I can help them, too, and earn her attention and affection.*

Will watched as she moved from one place to another, each time reverently placing a prayerstick before some natural object—a rock, a dead tree limb, a gulley, a bush, perhaps each the home of a spirit to whom she appealed for aid. When Hasbaá had placed all of the prayersticks, she went into the central hogan—Dezba had called it the medicine lodge. Will could see the old woman was seated near the entrance working at some project.

When Will approached, Dezba looked up and greeted him warmly. She was grinding different colors of corn with a stone pestle to make the pulverized materials that went into the sandpainting.

"Hasbaá is creating another ceremony for Baaneez for tomorrow. Barboncito is feeling much better after last night's ceremony. Baaneez is even weaker. Hasbaá distributed prayersticks to invite the spirits from all over the area to attend the ceremony."

"I saw him," Will said. Dezba did not seem to notice he'd used a masculine pronoun. Maybe they were interchangeable.

"Go inside and watch Hasbaá work on the sandpainting. The energy you put in while you watch can help the outcome."

As casually as he could manage, Will bent down and went in through the low opening. It was shadowed inside, though light came in through a smoke hole in the ceiling. His eyes took a moment to adjust.

He crouched down and watched silently while Hasbaá lay out the first elements of the design. As she completed a line that divided the painting into four quadrants, she looked up at him with a faint smile. She said nothing, but Will could feel something he valued almost as much as affection: inclusion. He felt like a participant and not an observer. He let his mind calm as he watched Hasbaá's delicate movements, though there was an undercurrent of excitement just from being in the same room with the mysteriously attractive Indian. He could remember how Hasbaá had looked in the sweat lodge without the women's clothes. And he kept thinking about Segundo. Will consciously exerted effort in his attention to add to the power of the sandpainting.

After a while, he got up and went outside. Dezba was still working with her pestle. She gestured to him to come sit with her.

"So many of our people have died. Hasbaá tries to save them. Sometimes she succeeds. But we are far from our homelands, and the spirits here are weak. Hasbaá tries so hard. It is because she did not have any chance to save her own husband, Segundo."

Seeing an opportunity to raise the question he'd been afraid to bring up last night, Will asked, "Is it acceptable to the Diné for Hasbaá to have married a man?"

"Acceptable?" she looked at him curiously.

"You know, morally right?"

Will did not know how to ask his question. He realized that how a question is phrased can already determine the answer.

"Yes. Would it be otherwise?"

"Well," he continued cautiously, "can you explain why Hasbaá dresses as a woman, when his body is that of a man?"

"She is a person with two spirits." Dezba looked down at her work. She carefully moved the pulverized corn from the stone she was working on to a small basket, then took a handful of reddish kernels and laid them on the stone. As she began to crush them, she said, "Our peoples are so different. You do not know the ways of the Diné."

He nodded agreement.

"I will tell you another story." Her voice changed tone as she began to recount the legend. "A long time ago, before my grandmother and before *her* grandmother, before the Diné even existed in our homeland, our ancestors lived in a different world. There were four worlds before this one that we are in now. In one of those worlds, there lived one of the first people, known as Turquoise Boy. The mother of Turquoise Boy was Changing Woman herself.

"You see, Changing Woman had flown up into the sky and had fallen in love with the Sun. His brightness dazzled her, and his rays warmed her body. Changing Woman became pregnant from her intercourse with the Sun. But Changing Woman was very independent, not the kind to settle down into a marriage, even with the magnificent Sun.

"After returning to the world, Changing Woman could not decide whether she wanted to have a son or a daughter. So she decided to have the best of both. The result was that Turquoise Boy was born as a combined person, a special sacred being, not either a man or a woman, but both.

"There have always been such persons, born into every generation, ever since then. It is part of the reality of the universe. We Diné believe some people are bestowed by Changing Woman with both the man's and the woman's spirits. This makes them superior to the regular man or woman who has only one spirit.

"These people are of great value. When Turquoise Boy was about twelve winters old, there was a great flood. All the people and all the animals ran to the top of the highest mountain. Still the waters kept rising.

"Back then, the animals and the people were friendly and tried to help each other. Eagle volunteered to carry everyone to safety, but it was raining so hard even powerful Eagle could not fly. Coyote gave up in despair, and cried out that they were all going to drown. But Turquoise Boy had an idea. He found a great reed which went high into the sky, higher even than the rainclouds. Turquoise Boy got Woodpecker to chop a hole in the base of the reed and Gopher to burrow a tunnel upward inside.

"Then, one by one, all the people and all the animals climbed up through the hollowed reed and came out on top. They saw they had gone far above the rainclouds, and the reed had planted roots at its crown into the dirt of another world. That is the world of our Mother Earth which we now walk on. And so that is how the Diné came into this world.

"The animals and the humans were saved, all because of Turquoise Boy. Diné feel gratitude for those with the spirits of both a man and a woman. People who are different are a special gift to us all—to help us with their talents, to open our eyes to different ways of seeing things.

"We tell many stories about Turquoise Boy: how he brought the men and women together when they'd been quarreling, how he taught us to raise sheep and goats and how to turn their hair into clothing. We tell these stories to show us about the Two-Spirit Persons in our family.

"Two-Spirit People are very creative. If Turquoise Boy had not come up with that creative idea, all the people and animals would have drowned. Even the animals respect Two-Spirit Persons like Hasbaá. She can communicate with animals, you know. Our family is very lucky to have Hasbaá with her special powers and her closeness to Changing Woman. This is how she helps the sick."

Will wondered what his father would have thought about that.

"In Diné we call people like her *nadleehí*, which means 'Those-Who-Change.' For she has had a great experience and discovered she possesses two spirits, like Turquoise Boy. The familiar name we all call her by, Hasbaá, means 'She-Comes-Out-in-Power.'"

Will thought the meaning of Hasbaá's name surprisingly appropriate. It reminded him of Michael's saying "there's a wide world out there." It was a good idea, he thought, for himself to come out into this wider world in power. *But how?*

"Two-Spirit Persons can see things from the point of view of both men and women. They see what others do not notice because most people see only as a man or as a woman.

"This word "Two-Spirit" we learned from a *nadleehí* of the Ojibway people who live far to the north. They are a great tribe. When Hasbaá was young, an Ojibway holy person was staying in our homelands through the winter. We called him Wandering Falcon because he said whenever he saw birds flying overhead, it made him want to join their migration. His vision quest had led him far from home. He told us stories about the many different peoples he visited. We learned much from him. He was very wise. When it was time for Hasbaá to undergo the Ceremony of the Bow and the Basket, Wandering Falcon explained how the Ojibway people understand the role of the *nadleehí*. He told us about the title Two-Spirit. Even as a child, Hasbaá loved these words, and we have used them ever since in this outfit."

"Ceremony of the Bow and the Basket?" Will asked quizzically.

"Two-Spirits are sometimes born into the body of a male and sometimes into the body of a female. If they are male-bodied they are called *nadleehí*, if they are female-bodied they are called *dilbaá*, which means protector," Dezba said. "But as they grow up, their character shows them to be two-spirited. If their family thinks they might be so created, then a ceremony is performed. The child is presented with the bows and arrows of a hunter and, also, with the baskets of a wife for gathering food. The spirit that Changing Woman or some other Holy Person has placed in them will show itself in their choosing which utensils to take for their own.

If a female child has been given an aggressive masculine personality, that one will likely choose the bow. Then we understand that that child is truly a *dilbaá* and will grow up to be a hunter and a warrior and a strong person in the family. If a male child has been given a nuturing feminine personality and chooses the baskets, as Hasbaá did, we say she is *nadleehí*. We Diné believe a person's spirit is more important in defining them than their physical body, so we accept them for the way they are in spirit.

"Sometimes you hear warriors tease Two-Spirit Persons, especially the *nadleehí*. You know, men are often very proud of their manliness; they think it is funny that some males are not so manly. But their teasing is only to honor the difference of the Two-Spirit. It is never done disrespectfully.

"We teach our children always to respect Two-Spirit Persons. They are sacred and holy. They are central to our whole way of life. Whenever there are no more Two-Spirit children born, that is the day there will be no more Diné. The Diné, the animals, the plants, and the beauty of our homeland would all disappear."

The approach of a soldier broke Will's rapt concentration on Dezba's words. She fell silent and looked down at her work as though to block out the presence of the Hairy Face intruder.

"Mr. Lee, General Carleton wants to see you. Immediately."

Will didn't want to leave. Not when he was just getting answers to the most important questions. But he knew he couldn't put Gen. Carleton off, especially since he'd sent a messenger to get him.

He apologized to Dezba, then jumped up and walked back to the fort with the soldier leading the way. He remembered the last time he was led to Carleton's office. But that had been before he'd discovered the self-confidence that came with learning the new perspective of the Diné.

23

Fort Sumner

When Will knocked on the door, as before, the knock was answered by a gruff response, "Permission granted. Enter."

Will opened the door to see that Carleton sat imperiously behind his desk. The general gestured impatiently for him to come in and sit down.

As he took a seat, Will couldn't help thinking the large wooden desk—piled high with papers and in-and-out boxes, two oil lamps, a couple of cigar boxes, and a huge ornate silver inkwell—served as Gen. Carleton's personal fort from which he positioned himself for battle with the outside world.

The general leaned forward in his chair. "Mr. Lee, if I may be frank… I've noticed you have spent quite a lot of time out among the Navajos the past few days."

"Yes sir," Will answered proudly. "I've finally gotten the Indians to talk with me."

"Well, that's what I'm concerned about, you see."

Will thought maybe he was being called on the carpet for taking so long to discover the leadership of the Indians. He did not want to have to admit that what he'd learned in the past days had little to do with reservation business. It had all been about his own religious and sexual questioning.

"I appreciate your concern, sir. I know it's taken me a while to get familiar with them. As you know, I've had no prior experience with Indians."

"Now here, Mr. Lee, that's what I'm concerned about—that you get the *right kind* of experience with the Indians."

"I'm trying to learn as fast as I can. I want to be a good Agent."

"Then let *me* tell you about being a good Agent..."

"Oh, yes, sir. I'm very interested in..."

"Mr. Lee," the general's voice took an edge. "Be quiet for a moment and let me speak."

"Yes, sir."

"Let me advise you it is well to keep a certain distance from the Indians. The ways of savages are not yet understood by you, and I don't want you to get drawn into something you can't later control." The general sat back in his chair and put his hands on the arms. He looked right at Will.

Not sure what to respond and not sure how since he wasn't supposed to speak, Will nodded his head. But he certainly didn't agree with Gen. Carleton about keeping distance. In his three days of contact with the Diné he'd discovered that had been the problem all along. If some of the Hairy Faces had just been listening to their side, there'd never have had to be any Navajo War at all.

"It is important that you learn about the problems of the Indians from the most authoritative source. I realize that I have been negligent in my responsibilities toward you as your commanding officer. Mind you, it is nothing personal at all, just that I have so many matters to occupy my time here. But I have decided you and I should meet more regularly. You seem like a nice young man. Perhaps an old man like myself," Carleton leaned back, opened his arms, and chuckled, "can teach you a thing or two which will be of inestimable value to you later on."

For just a moment, Gen. Carleton looked like a kindly old uncle calling for some young whippersnapper to climb into his lap. He looked at Will questioningly. There was a silence. Finally, the general said, "Well...?"

"I'm sure you could, sir. I'd be much obliged. Never can learn too much," Will felt complimented that the general had taken a personal interest in him. He'd let his memories of his father cloud how he'd perceived Gen. Carleton. Still he was wary. He didn't want to let the general's interest in him interfere with what he was learning from the Diné. "Uh, but, sir..."

"Yes, what is it, my boy?"

"I don't think you actually are my 'commanding officer,' sir. As you reminded me when I first arrived, we *both* have responsibility for the Indians' welfare, but you're answerable to the Army, and I am answerable to the Office of Indian Affairs."

Exasperation crossed Carleton's face, but then he leaned forward and put his hands together on the desk. "Yes, Mr. Lee, that's correct. I, ah, meant that only as a figure of speech, you know..."

"Well, you *are* the commanding officer around here, all right." Will had made his point. But he didn't want to alienate Carleton. "But, General, you're not an old man—like you said."

Carleton looked perplexed. It took him a moment to catch Will's reference to his earlier self-deprecating joke.

"Ah, thank you. I take that as a compliment."

"Just as it was intended, sir."

"Good. Then you go back to your quarters now and get a good night's sleep. We'll talk in the morning, say, about nine. There are some forms that require your signature. I'll have Lt. Bauer draw them up by then."

Then just as Will started to stand, "No, no," the general said, half to himself, "that won't be possible. Uh, business matters, you know. Visitors from Santa Fe coming tomorrow. Make it the next day, Lee, same time."

"Yes, sir, nine o'clock in the morning day after tomorrow. I'll be here."

The general's comment about getting a good night's sleep reminded him that though he'd only been up a few hours, it was almost sunset. He should hurry if he wanted to continue his talk with Dezba.

"Perhaps you're going down to the mess hall." Carleton apparently noticed that he'd, perhaps inadvertently, sent Will to his room without his supper. "Would you like to sit at my table?"

Will had been waiting for that invitation. But not now. "I liked your first idea, sir. Truth is I ate lunch late. I'm pretty tired. Your suggestion of a good night's sleep sure sounded fine to me."

"As you were, then," the general answered. "Perhaps another time."

"Yes, sir."

Will had no intention of going to bed. But the commanding officer had just told him to keep his distance from the Indians. He couldn't very well decline the honor of eating at the general's table because he wanted to go back to his talk with Dezba.

He went toward his cabin. Out of the corner of his eye, he glimpsed Gen. Carleton leave the office and walk toward the mess. It was getting dark, and figures were hard to make out.

Halfway to his cabin, Will changed directions, ducking behind some brush and then taking off toward the Diné settlement. Since Dezba had begun to explain the Diné way of life to him, he'd discovered all this had a direct bearing on his own life. *Maybe the other Hairy Faces don't care about the Indians and their way of life. Maybe it has no bearing on their lives. But I am not like the rest of them…*

Previously he could have imagined himself living with a loving friend, like Michael. But it would have to be behind closed doors. They couldn't have shown their true selves—not in the society in which he had grown up. But here—among the Diné—all that seemed different. The love of one man for another was recognized and respected. *Indeed, the Diné believe Two-Spirit Persons, like Hasbaá, are an advantage.*

As he made his way along the riverbank, Will wondered if what he'd felt for Michael and for Jose—and maybe now for Hasbaá—meant he was a Two-Spirit Person also. Will wasn't ready to ask Dezba yet if he could think of himself that way. Maybe she'd think that sacrilegious. But he had more questions for her.

He thought about all the religion he'd learned from his father. Most of it he thought he really believed. But some if it, he just didn't—like his father's apparent hatred for human bodies and emotional feelings. He felt torn between the truths in the Bible and the urging of his own heart. His father's religion didn't have any place for feelings like those he felt, feelings like the "dear love of comrades." He was amazed that the Navajo whom his strange flight had led him to seemed to offer just such a place for feelings of the heart.

He thought about Harry Burnside back in Lynchburg, how the old man had created his own life for himself, being both husband and wife, being an attorney *and* cooking his own biscuits, caring for people and helping them as best he could. Harry wasn't magical like Hasbaá, but he seemed like what a Two-Spirit Person might be in genteel Southern white society.

It was, after all, Harry who got Will the job and set him on the path that led him to the Bosque Redondo. *That seems pretty magical.*

24

THE MEDICINE LODGE

Coming through the screen of scrubby trees, Will could see that Dezba was still sitting where he'd left her. He hoped she'd remained because she had known he'd be returning.

"You were telling me about Turquoise Boy," he launched right into the discussion as though they hadn't been interrupted. "Don't the Diné think it is *unnatural* for Hasbaá to marry a man?"

"Unnatural?" Dezba asked. "How can following one's nature be unnatural? If Hasbaá loves someone and they live as a family, isn't that a marriage?"

"I meant how can two people of the same sex marry?"

"For a marriage, what matters are feelings of love and attraction. This happens in the spirit world. Sexual attraction is one of the ways the Holy Ones give people hints about who they should partner with. What does the sex of the people matter?"

"In my world, they say the only purpose of marriage is to have children. So men can only marry women and women can only marry men... as God ordained."

"From the missionary who came here, I saw that the Hairy Faces have strange ideas. Is this what the Hairy Face god says? What about Two-Spirit Persons? They can form a spirit marriage with a man *or* a woman. Does the Hairy Face god not know about such people?" Dezba smiled as though to acknowledge the humor in her condescension.

"For the Diné, there are many purposes of marriage. Children are one purpose. But so is spirit connection. You asked this question about Hasbaá. Maybe this is a question about yourself?"

"I guess so." Maybe he would get an answer to the question he wasn't ready to ask yet.

"Hasbaá was given to my family as a gift of Changing Woman. When Hasbaá was very young, she knew she was both a man and a woman and could love both a man or a woman. Her life came from the spirit world, not from her sex. When she married Segundo, it was because their spirits had united. Hasbaá saw it in a vision. And when she told Segundo, he, too, sought for a vision. And he saw that Changing Woman had given him Hasbaá to love for the sake of the Diné.

"Hasbaá has healing power because she is Two-Spirit. By uniting with Segundo's strength, her powers were made stronger. And Segundo was made a better leader because he had a wife who came from Changing Woman.

"Hasbaá and Segundo made love together because making love is good and pleases Changing Woman and all the spirits."

"But making love is for children. That is why my people make love."

"Is that so?" Dezba arched her eyebrow. "Making love is a wonderful gift from the spirit world. People should enjoy love. It is good for them. But I do not believe you that Hairy Faces make love only because they want children. John Blewer told us that Hairy Faces have places they call orphanages where they put unwanted children. How could there be unwanted children if Hairy Faces only make love because they want children?

"The Diné want all their children. We have no orphanages. We have no unwanted children. But we make love because we enjoy it and because it fills the longings of our spirits for other spirits."

Will thought about his mother. He'd always assumed she'd wanted him to be born. Had she? It was hard for him to imagine that either his mother or his father would have wanted sex for any other reason. His own culture seemed to have obscured these issues. Dezba's ideas seemed just right. *Where did the ideas of Hairy Face culture ever come from?* But Will had been strongly indoctrinated into those ideas. "But what if you have children before you are married? Shouldn't people wait until after marriage to have sex?"

"Why should they wait?" Dezba laughed. While she was serious, she also intentionally made fun of his questions. She sensed that he did not altogether believe what he was saying himself.

"It was Turquoise Boy who instructed our ancestors how to live, how to cultivate maize and to raise sheep and goats. This is our way of life. Turquoise Boy taught us to enjoy making love.

"Once a girl begins to bleed with the moon, she is ready to make her own choices. The spirits have shown that by preparing her body. If she wants sexual pleasure—and why not?—then she should do that. If she wishes a child, that is her choice. She should make love and give birth to a baby. Her child will be welcomed into the family of her mother. That is how we raise our children.

"We do not live as the Hairy Faces do, where men like the soldiers go off from their families and live only with other men. We would consider that very bad to live so far away from our relatives. Where are the Hairy Face women? Where are the Hairy Face families?"

Will didn't have an answer.

"Diné people always live together with lots of relatives. We do not believe married couples should live by themselves. That is not good for their children or for them. Children need lots of relatives around, and so does the wife.

"When a young man wants to marry, among the Diné, he moves in to his wife's family's home. If a marriage breaks up, either the wife tells the husband to leave her family's house or the husband simply moves out. Our ancestors decided the couple should not make it a controversy. He goes back to live in his mother's house, or into his new wife's house if he remarries. The original wife and her children stay together, as they have always lived, in the household of her mother.

"The children are raised by their mother's whole family, not just the father and mother. We all love them and help them develop. When I was a child, I certainly loved my mother and father, but I felt just as close to my mother's sisters and brothers, and to their mothers and sisters and brothers. They were all my parents.

"I pity the poor children of the Hairy Faces who have only one mother and one father to raise them. Maybe that is why they are so strange. They do not have enough love in their childhood. Or maybe it is because they do not get enough sexual pleasure. People need love and sex to develop into whole persons."

It was very dark now. Light came out of the door of the hogan. Will could hear Hasbaá chant softly inside.

Dezba struggled to get up from her seat on the ground. Her legs must have been stiff from sitting so long. Will started to jump up to assist her. But she waved to him to remain where he was.

She pulled herself up to her full height, walked over and bent down to look into the hogan. Illuminated by the golden light of the tallow lamps, her face looked ancient.

Will half-thought Dezba might have been around in the days when the Two-Spirit Turquoise Boy brought the people to this world. Of course, he knew that couldn't be possible. He also knew that the stories about Turquoise Boy weren't real history. Or at least he didn't think so. He remembered that his father had thought the story of Adam and Eve was real, that Eve really was created from one of Adam's ribs. Will thought the story of Turquoise Boy made better history anyway.

Dezba hobbled over to Will. "That is why I worry about Hasbaá. There is too much seriousness in her life these past years. She is not getting the love and sex she needs to develop. She is still so young."

Dezba took her seat on the ground again. "This morning, Hasbaá asked me about you."

His heart began to race.

"She said she does not understand you. She said she has never seen a Hairy Face spend so much time watching her. The soldiers never treat us like people. They never look at us except to gauge how much work they can make us do. I told her that you probably find her attractive." The old woman laughed. "Hasbaá turned red when I said that—just like you now."

He wondered how Dezba could see his face in the dark. *Am I blushing that much?* Will could feel how hot his cheeks were.

"I told her to try out making love with you. I told her I would like to know how the Hairy Faces have sex."

Will was so flustered he didn't know what to say. Dezba chuckled over his embarrassment.

"What did Hasbaá say?" he finally answered. He was trembling, and it was hard to talk.

"Hasbaá said she was waiting for the return of Segundo's spirit. She said she could never love another, especially a Hairy Face."

Will felt a surge of disappointment—but also relief. Dezba's indirect proposition frightened him at the same time that it excited him. *Would I know what to do if Hasbaá had said yes?*

"But I don't believe her. It is not good to hold onto the dead. Diné people are afraid of ghosts who roam the earth. We have to do our ceremonies carefully, so their spirits can be released. They need to go free to become part of the universe." Dezba waved her hand toward the sky.

"How does Hasbaá expect Segundo to come back to her except by sending her someone new to love and take care of? Would you want that to be you?"

He didn't know how to answer. "Of course" seemed like the best answer of all. But he couldn't bring himself to say that. If he were a Navajo and believed in all the things Dezba had told him about, maybe that would have been easy to answer. But he wasn't.

Feeling rejected, humiliated, vulnerable and confused, he only said, "I don't know what you mean." Then added hastily, "I have to go now. It's getting late."

"There will be another healing for Baaneez tomorrow evening. I would like you to be present. Will you come?"

"Yes, yes, of course," Will stammered. "Uh, thank you."

25

Fort Sumner

Just as Will was approaching the Agent's quarters in the last light of twilight, feeling more confused than ever and thinking that, as he'd told Gen. Carleton, he really was ready to get some sleep, he was suddenly pulled out of his emotional quandary by the approach of a rider on horseback. It was Mac McCarrie.

"Ahoy, Mr. Lee, General Carleton said to come get you. There's a detail riding out to recapture some Indians that got away this morning."

"You want me to go with you?"

"General said you should come. He told me to wake you up if you were sleeping. Said you ought to see how it is with the Injuns out on their own territory."

Will started to retort that this wasn't the Diné's territory by any stretch of the imagination, but decided to keep the remark to himself. He didn't mind being assigned a duty that would team him up with Pvt. McCarrie, though this evening hardly seemed like good scheduling. *I'm dog-tired. I'm not sure I can manage to mount a horse.*

"C'mon then, Will." McCarrie sounded friendly. "Jump up behind me, and I'll take you over to the stables so you can get mounted up. The detail's about to ride out."

"I guess I have to," Will responded, thinking that at least one bright spot was going to be riding with McCarrie. He remembered his life-changing ride with Michael. *Here I am thinking about that stuff again. Maybe Dezba had a good idea. And if Hasbaá isn't interested in me, well, maybe somebody else will be…*

When Will and McCarrie arrived at the stables, the detail commander, a lieutenant named Westerby, explained that a scout had ridden in earlier and reported seeing a camp of Indians a few miles out from Fort Sumner. Gen. Carleton's dinner had been interrupted with the news. He'd ordered the detail to ride out in the night to surprise the Indians while they were sleeping.

Will knew that just because Indians were encamped nearby didn't mean they were renegade Navajos or hostiles that belonged on the reservation. But he understood he was on this assignment as an observer and he ought to keep his mouth shut, at least for the time being.

Thirty minutes later, the detail of seven men was topping a rise in the rocky hills to the west of the reservation. It was dark, but, as Will had discovered at the stream the previous night, there was enough illumination from the moon for the riders to see where they were going and for Will to see the other men. Among them was one in particular Will kept his eye on, Pvt. Ned Johnson. This was the soldier Will had watched the morning after the flood, the one with the well-developed physique. Though Will had never talked to him, since that day he'd always paid attention whenever Johnson was around.

As they came over the rise, Will saw that, indeed, three Indians slept under the cover of a flat rock that projected from a low cliff near the ground. Smoldering embers nearby gave evidence of a fire. Some sparse branches had been pulled up to camouflage the camp. This suggested they *were* trying to avoid being seen, and that was all Lt. Westerby needed to declare the Indians escapees and order them taken into custody.

At Westerby's command, several of the soldiers lit pine-tar torches. These blazed in the night suddenly, changing the atmosphere from one of peace and serenity to one of fright and alarm.

Reminding himself to remain an observer, Will held his horse back as the detail charged the meager encampment. He watched as the Indians suddenly woke up and began running. None of them appeared armed. Will was frightened somebody was going to get hurt when he heard rifle shots and saw that a couple of the soldiers were shooting into the air to intimidate the Indians.

It wasn't long before the riflemen had ridden out past the fleeing Indians and corralled them back toward the hole they'd been hiding in. Obviously scared and defenseless, the Indians huddled together waiting for the Hairy Faces' retaliation.

McCarrie hovered near Will. It was apparent that the soldier saw his consternation and was staying close to prevent him from getting himself hurt or from interfering with the Cavalry's assignment.

"Tie 'em up," Westerby ordered. Two of the men jumped off their horses and, holding their pistols on the poor frightened captives, took rope from their saddles and started to bind the Indians tightly.

One of the Indians stood up proudly and raised his chin. *He doesn't want to be treated as a vanquished captive,* Will thought, feeling pride for the warrior. The Indian said something in his own language and then pushed the soldier away who'd come to bind him.

"He just wants to surrender without being humiliated," he said to Mac, surmising what the Indian's demeanor meant.

"Don't be so sure you can trust 'em," Mac answered. "They got different notions from us, ya know."

"I said to tie them all up," Westerby shouted.

"He don't wannabe tied up," complained the soldier, standing with the rope in his hand.

Suddenly, as if from out of nowhere, a whip flashed in the air and cut right across the proud Indian's face. The feckless soldier had to jump to get out of the way himself.

Will was startled. He looked up to see Lt. Westerby wielded the bullwhip. He pulled his arm back to hurl another assault. The gesture reminded Will of his father that Sunday afternoon in the barn.

Without thinking, he spurred his horse and galloped over to the detail commander, barely stopping in time to avoid colliding with his horse. "Stop that," he screamed at the top of his lungs.

"Hey, come back here," McCarrie shouted to Will.

"How dare you!" Westerby snarled.

"I'm the Indians' advocate. You can't mistreat them just for fun."

"Just for fun?" one of the other soldiers rejoined, sneering. "I'll show you fun." The soldier pulled his rifle to his shoulder and took aim at the Indian warrior, who remained standing proudly as the Hairy Faces fought with one another over him.

"No, no," Will shouted.

"Hey, Mr. Lee *is* the Government Indian Agent," said McCarrie.

"At ease, man," Westerby called out, and the upstart soldier lowered his rifle. Then Westerby turned to Will and said through clenched teeth. "Well, Mr. Lee, you are probably right that we shouldn't mistreat the damn Injuns without provocation, and this here man has done nothing except look proud.

"But I'll be damned if I'll let some civilian loudmouth like you interfere with my military duty. I've got my orders."

"Do your orders say to whip these men into submission?"

Westerby rolled his eyes. "As you were, men." His voice sounded tired. "Lee, you ride with McCarrie and, Johnson, you team up with Ralston there. Put the three Indians on the two horses and tie the horses together on a long lead. Let's just head back quiet-like now."

He added, "Mr. Lee, how'ze about you takin' charge of the reins there. You can lead them in all peaceable."

Westerby backing down from his aggressive stance surprised Will. It also then tossed the responsibility for the captives to him. *Well, I can handle this.*

"If they get away," Westerby inserted a warning, "I'll have to hold you accountable." He held up the coiled whip as if to punctuate the threat.

With the Indians riding flanked by soldiers, the detail headed back. With one hand Will held the lead that pulled the two horses the Indians were riding. With the other he held on to the saddlehorn by reaching around McCarrie. He tried to avoid touching the other, but now and then his arm brushed McCarrie's side. He could feel the thin red-head's rib-cage. This unnerved him, but added a welcome tinge of excitement to the late night adventure. And he couldn't keep from wishing Westerby had ordered him to ride like this behind Ned Johnson.

Lt. Westerby was not entirely able to hide his annoyance at Will behind his military politeness. After a while, he started chatting with McCarrie, but then turned the conversation in a nasty direction, talking through McCarrie to Will as though the greenhorn civilian was not there.

"Crazy how these Government Agents take the side of the damned Injuns. Why I remember takin' a detail like this out a couple of months ago to bring in the body of that damn Agent Ayers. You 'member that, don'tcha, Mac?" Westerby coaxed McCarrie for a response, it seemed, just to make sure Will took notice.

And, indeed, he did. This was something he was very interested in. *They're talking about my predecessor.*

"You know Ayers was always defending the Injuns, sayin' the Navajos were peaceable at heart. Well, you know how peaceable ol' Agent Ayers found 'em." Westerby guffawed, then explained, apparently for Will's benefit, "Ayers had hisself an Injun woman. One day, things musta got a little rough. Maybe she was resistin' his affections. Anyway, by the time, he'd finished demonstratin' to her what her damn duties were, she was dead. Had to cut her throat, he did…" Westerby laughed.

"General Carleton ordered Ayers put under arrest. But then he disappeared from the reservation," McCarrie spoke up. He seemed to Will to be as uncomfortable with Westerby's tone as he himself.

"Yeah, then," Westerby spoke louder, reclaiming his right to tell the story his way, "we found Ayers strung up on a cactus like Jesus on the damn cross. Injuns musta gone after him for rapin' and killin' their squaw. Tied him to a cactus out in the desert and left him to die…

"These were the misunderstood natives Ayers was advocatin' for," the lieutenant used a word Will had applied to himself only a short time ago, "and them's the ones that killed him. And killed him somethin' awful."

Will understood Westerby was warning him about the dangers of his role as Indian Agent. He didn't understand why the scorn behind the lieutenant's manner. But he could certainly feel the intimidation. He'd known about Ayers and the Indian woman, but he hadn't known there'd been retaliation against Ayers. His flesh crawled as he thought about the death that poor man suffered.

"Hey, Mac, you better warn your friend there not to get too friendly with the Injuns," Westerby added with a chuckle, as if to announce that he was getting the last word. Then he galloped on ahead a little.

Thirty minutes later, the detail reached the Fort. The Indians had cooperated. Will wanted to believe they understood his advocacy had prevented them from being paraded bound hand and foot.

"Look, Will, you go get some sleep." McCarrie sounded solicitous for his welfare. "I'll put the horse away for you. And Westerby there 'll take the Indians to the stockade 'til General Carleton can get one of the Mexican translators to interrogate them. I think you'd better stay out o' this."

Shaky as he dismounted, Will made a point of going over to Lt. Westerby and offering his hand. "I'm sorry about my outburst, sir. But I had my duty, too."

Apparently mollified with Will apologizing first, Westerby responded to the handshake. "Hard life out here."

It wouldn't have to be so hard if you all just thought about what you were doing to each other, Will thought as he wandered back down to his quarters.

26

Bosque Redondo

Will spent most of the next day sitting at his desk attempting to write some sort of report about what he'd learned about the source of the Indians' discontent. In fact, he stared out the window most of the time remembering what Dezba had said about Hasbaá needing to experience love again. He scolded himself for having acted so childishly when she asked if he wanted to be the one. *What Dezba said about Hasbaá is probably true about me as well.*

But Will had never experienced that kind of love at all... He thought about Mac McCarrie and about Ned Johnson. He even felt a strange pang of jealousy that maybe those two knew one another. He felt lonely and sorry for himself. He missed Michael. He missed Jose. He missed his mother's devoted, uncomplicated love.

Will ate lunch in the mess hall. Then just after sundown, when the rest of the soldiers had gone in for supper, he made his way to the medicine lodge.

Will began with a question for Dezba, one that touched other issues than Hasbaá's sexual availability. "Do the Diné believe in heaven?" He had been thinking about his mother. There was still a hollow place in his heart.

"There are many different worlds," the old woman answered, "of the Holy People and of the Earth People. When an Earth Person dies, we don't really know for sure what happens. But we think the life just ends and the spirit becomes part of the universe again."

Will hoped his mother was in heaven watching over him.

"It is sad for us to lose our loved ones, but if they have lived to old age, it is best that they pass on. This is as it should be; otherwise, there would get to be too many people, and our Mother Earth could not supply our needs."

Sadness gripped at Will's heart for his mother's untimely death.

"Sometimes, we think, the spirit of the person who has died cannot escape and becomes an unhappy ghost. Sometimes the spirit lives on for a while, watching over its loved ones. Maybe such a ghost is not so unhappy if it can manage to pass on the duties or responsibilities that were left unfinished to someone among the living. Then it can go free. The ghost of a mother who has died before her child is grown can be like that."

Will didn't want to think of his mother as an unhappy spirit.

"That is why it is important that another mother, maybe the mother's sister or her husband's new wife, watch over the child. Then she can go."

He hoped someone from among the living was watching over him for his mother so she could go free. Maybe this was Dezba.

"Dead people are not our business. The living need to get beyond sorrow and concern themselves with the living. That is Hasbaá's mistake. She is still too haunted by her memories of Segundo."

Maybe if I could help Segundo go free…

Then Dezba said something that surprised him: "It seems to me you are like Hasbaá. There is some death you also have not yet resolved."

He said nothing. But once again Dezba had seemed to see right into him.

Pain gripped his heart as he remembered coming to his mother's bedside. She was so emaciated and shrunken that she barely took up any space in the wide expanse of pillows and white bed linens. In her eyes were pain and weariness. "I just can't bear this anymore…" she'd whispered.

Tears formed in the corners of Will's eyes. "Mama, you'll be fine." He mustered all his courage and manliness to squelch the tears. He patted her on the head, as though she were a child who shouldn't know what was really happening. *Why can't we admit she's dying and I want to say goodbye? Why can't I tell her how much I love her?* He'd struggled to bring the words to his lips, but there were no words. No tears. Just a gnawing emptiness.

Even now, he still felt that emptiness…

27

THE MEDICINE LODGE

Dezba gathered up the last of the powder she'd been grinding. Several Diné men arrived, bearing Baaneez on a litter. Behind them were the rest of the Diné who'd participated in the previous healing. Among them was Barboncito. He looked fully recovered.

Will stood and followed Dezba and the others into the medicine lodge. As he settled himself in the ceremonial circle, Hasbaá looked up and gave him a faint, but slightly knowing, smile. Will wondered if Hasbaá knew Dezba had spoken with him about the elder's opinion she should make love with him. He avoided Hasbaá's eyes. He felt embarrassed that his proposal of affection had apparently already been turned down even before he got a chance to make it. His heart started pounding again. He tried to turn his attention to the ceremony.

The sandpainting was even more complicated and beautiful than the one from the other night. This time Hasbaá had created several representations of the long thin figures with ribbon bodies. Some had rectangular heads, some circular. Various animals were represented with the figures. The body of a snake encircled the whole design.

The ceremony proceeded similarly to the previous, though now Baaneez was the only patient. The old woman hardly looked to be alive at all. Hasbaá started the singing. The others all joined in. Some of the men placed Baaneez on top of the design. After she was resting comfortably, Hasbaá used the colored powders to paint several small designs on her arms and then on her legs. Then she took some fine ashes and gently blew them over the woman's body.

Hasbaá next began a prayer. She prayed a long time. Periodically, she interrupted with the shaking of a rattle. Each time the rattle grew louder and more insistent. The singers continued. Worry hung on their faces. Will guessed the patient was not showing the improvement they expected.

Hasbaá did not give up. She got out the prayersticks she had earlier placed around the area of the camp and had apparently retrieved later. She attempted to place the prayersticks in the woman's hands. But again the patient was too weak to grasp them. At last, Hasbaá stood up and began to twirl the piece of wood to make the buzzing, singing noise. She twirled it faster and faster.

Then suddenly the buzzing stopped, followed by a loud concussion from one of the walls. Will looked up to see that the cord had broken. There was a cry of alarm from the singers. Hasbaá seemed shocked. Still holding the limp cord, she bent down and placed her ear against the old woman's chest. Then she looked up with an expression of defeat and loss.

As the people in the circle also realized that the old woman had died, they started to wail and moan loudly. Dezba fell over the body of her relative and started screaming and crying.

Even though Will had seen how close to death Baaneez had been for the past several days, he was not prepared for the actual passing. He'd never seen anyone die. He'd been kept out of the room when his mother had succumbed, as though death were something private and humiliating. He'd never been allowed to feel the grief. His father had sternly insisted that his wife's death was not to be mourned because she was now with Jesus in heaven and the living should show no sorrow for her eternal gain. Reverend Lee had admonished Will that his sadness at her death was an indication of his selfishness and of the weakness of his faith.

Now, among the Diné, Will had seen incredible faith. He'd watched that faith apparently heal Barboncito. And yet even the men were mourning loudly and profusely with apparently no concern that their reaction was selfish or weak. Even Hasbaá wept uncontrollably. After Hasbaá and Dezba crawled away from the body, each of the others went individually to embrace and cry over Baaneez.

Several of the people left the hogan, only to return a few minutes later with blankets and small items which Will imagined must have been favorite possessions of the dead woman. It looked as though they were preparing the body for immediate burial and that this healing ceremony was becoming her funeral.

This was such a contrast to any Christian funeral he had ever attended. And, of course, as the son of the pastor, he'd had occasion to attend many funerals. They'd almost always been without any feeling at all. The women, the ones most likely to let emotions show, had usually had their head and faces draped with veils to keep their grief private.

Barboncito, the little man who might also have died if Will had not saved him from the flood, now came over to him and took his hand and pulled him toward the body of Baaneez. Will resisted the pull. He did not know this woman. But Barboncito was insistent. And so he let himself be led to the body. He knelt down beside Baaneez and brought his face close to hers, as he had seen the others do.

To his surprise, at least in his mind's eye, the Diné crone was transformed. Baaneez seemed to look just like his own mother, or as his mother would have looked had she been Indian. Tears began to well up in Will's eyes. He felt a hand touch him on the middle of the back. Somehow he knew this was Hasbaá who had touched him. And with that touch, he felt the permission he had never been granted before. He burst out crying, openly letting his sorrow flow.

Will could not look away from that face—which was both that of the wrinkled, brown-skinned old Diné woman and that of the dear fair-skinned Southern lady. He couldn't hold back any longer, and after a year of repressing his emotions, he wept so profusely that his body shook. He had never said goodbye to his mother. And so now he embraced the body of Baaneez as the other Indians had done. He held her to him and whispered that goodbye.

He didn't know if he was imagining things, but he was sure he heard a voice whisper back in his ear, "You were the light of my life, son. I loved you, and I know you loved me. You can make my life worthwhile by making your own future life worthwhile. Do something important with your life."

He also knew that there was a deeper message in those words. Then he heard words that his mother could never have spoken, yet he knew they, too, came from her. And, in that same whisper, he heard her add, "Bring about Segundo's return."

Will looked up. He thought Dezba must have said that. But she was nowhere near. In fact, no one but the dead woman was near enough to have spoken so intimately. He looked into her face again. This time, once again, it was the old Indian woman, lying there dead in his arms. He relaxed his embrace and knelt back on his knees.

The loud wailing had ceased. Most of the people still had tears in their eyes, but their faces were composed.

Will looked around. The people in the circle no longer seemed to him "Indians," exotic and strange. They were just Hasbaá and Dezba and Barboncito and the others—all just people, experiencing the pain and grief that goes with being human and with being alive.

Will stood up and walked back to his place in the circle. He watched as Baaneez's body was wrapped in blankets. He wiped the tears from his eyes.

As the ceremony came to a conclusion, Will began to feel embarrassed for having broken down in front of these people. *What would they think? Surely they must have thought my tears pretended. How could they know what had just happened to me?*

They had lost a relative. They had reason for tears. This person lying there dead was not my relative. What right do I have to participate in their sorrow? It was my people who were responsible for her suffering and for the suffering and death of countless of their relatives. Aren't I just a Hairy Face, intruding where I have no business, trying to weasel into their lives because I am fascinated with—and sexually attracted to—their spiritual leader? And the spiritual leader thinks I'm off-limits anyway! What am I doing here?

All of a sudden, Will was ashamed of his show of sentimentality. He looked around. Only Barboncito seemed to pay him any notice at all. He nodded perfunctorily to the old man and quickly ducked out of the hogan, leaving the Indians to their deserved grieving.

He ran most of the way back to his cabin. He remembered he had an appointment with Gen. Carleton in the morning. *Maybe the general is right that I should stay away from the Indians. I feel so confused.*

28

THE INDIAN AGENT'S QUARTERS

Will became aware of a loud knocking on his door. He pulled himself out of bed and staggered over to the door. Lt. Bauer stood there with a scowl on his face.

Oh, my God, I've overslept my appointment with Gen. Carleton.

"The general doesn't like to be kept waiting," the soldier said. "He's been expecting you all morning."

Will was still groggy. After the emotional crisis he'd gone through last night, he didn't see how he was going to be on his best behavior with the general. "Please offer my apologies to General Carleton," he answered, "I'm not feeling well. Perhaps I've come down with a fever." He didn't like lying. But the truth was he didn't feel well.

Bauer did not look sympathetic. "Is that your answer? You don't know General Carleton. He doesn't believe in missing appointments. Or in having fevers. The general's never been absent one day from his work at Fort Sumner. He doesn't expect others to miss their duties either."

Will didn't want to get on the general's bad side. Lord knows Carleton hadn't asked much of him before this. "What time is it? Should I come now?" he asked weakly.

"It's practically noon now. You missed the appointment, mister. The general's moved on to more important matters, I expect."

Just then the Fort's brass bell began to ring. The clanging just seemed to exaggerate Will's tardiness.

"Well, then. Tell him I'm very sorry. I will go up and reschedule with him myself. Now, please, Lieutenant, let me get some rest so I'll be well for General Carleton later."

"Sir," Bauer snapped to attention with a military exactitude that Will took as another insult to his civilian status.

He closed the door and collapsed back into bed.

29

Fort Sumner

The knocking on the door began again. Will pulled himself to consciousness from a wonderful dream of riding horses through a wide open meadow with his mother. Hasbaá was also there and another Indian whom he took to be Segundo, Hasbaá's husband and bravest of the Diné warriors.

The knocking was much softer than before, but just as insistent. Will grabbed for his pocketwatch. It was after 2 pm. He had slept another couple of hours. As he got up to go to the door, he feared it might be the general himself—who might be really mad if he'd expected him to come up to apologize about this morning. Will stopped at the mirror to smooth his hair so as to make a better impression. But then decided it would be better if he looked disheveled. It would support his story about being sick.

He opened the door, expecting Gen. Carleton's visage to meet his. But, to his surprise, there was a small Navajo child standing in the doorway. He looked hardly more than six or seven years old.

"Hasbaá at river. Dezba say you go now. Yes?"

Hasbaá? Why does she want to see me? Is this about what Dezba said to her?

But this is the worst of all possible times. I have to go see Gen. Carleton in person to apologize and set a time to meet with him. And I have to do that now. I am already late. What good would I be to the Diné as an Indian Agent if I get myself fired? What would I do without a job?

But Hasbaá wants to see me…

"All right. Yes," he said to the boy. "Tell her I have to do something first, that I'll be there in a short while."

Will dressed quickly, but took time to shave and comb his hair. He wanted to impress the general. As he looked at himself in his shaving mirror—*looking longer than Father would've approved of*—he thought he looked much less shy and green than when he'd fled Virginia. Indeed, he was amazed how dark his skin had turned from the desert sunlight. But more important, meeting Jose, discovering the Diné ways, and now beginning some kind of friendship with the mysterious Hasbaá had changed him. He smiled at himself. Then reminded himself to hurry. *I don't want to be late.*

On his way to Carleton's office, he began to worry that Hasbaá might be summoning him to scold him for his emotional display last night. *What if I've ruined everything?*

When he arrived at the general's office, Will saw the door was open. He knocked on the wood frame. "Who is it?" the general called out. His tone did not sound so military as usual.

"William Lee, sir."

"Oh, you. Well, ah, enter. Yes, permission granted," the general stumbled through his usual ritual.

Will started in immediately. "I'm very sorry about missing my appointment with you, sir," he said. "You know, I didn't get much sleep last night. I think I might be getting sick…"

"Enough, Mr. Lee," Carleton interrupted him. "I heard your excuse." Will could see that the general had a couple of men in his office. They were civilians. *These must be the visitors from Santa Fe the general had mentioned.* Both looked to be prosperous men with flesh on their bodies. One had a huge shock of red hair that caught Will's eye in the dim light of the office.

Carleton continued, "I make it a point myself never to get sick out here. You don't know what kind of doctor you'll get. I just refuse to take to the bed, young man. I would advise you to do likewise. But then I'm not your commanding officer…"

"I'm really very sorry, sir. Can we set another time to meet? I am truly anxious to learn from you." He knew he had to stay on the general's good side, if only so he could manage to discover the truth about the general's bad side and so, maybe, help the Indians. He'd begun to think that now it was his duty to help Segundo rest and thereby free Hasbaá from her mourning.

"Yes, yes. As you can see, I'm busy now," Carleton said. His tone was almost friendly and matter-of-fact. "Look, Mr. Lee, you will have supper with me tonight. You will sit at my table. That will be an honor."

"Yes, sir." Will was relieved.

"Come by here about an hour before sunset. We'll talk, then go down to the mess hall together. Now, let me get back to my business. You get outa here, you hear." The general laughed.

"Yes, sir, General Carleton. Thank you," Will answered excitedly. The general had actually seemed friendly. Will imagined that he must be having success in his meeting with the civilians. He wondered whether that would be good or bad for the Indians and for his objectives.

Will hurried down toward the river. He was wary of what Hasbaá wanted him for, but, he realized, he was also happy. Gen. Carleton had not seemed so threatening. *The trouble I'd feared I was in with the military just up and disappeared. Now what kind of trouble might I be in with the Indians?*

30

THE PECOS RIVER

When Will reached the banks of the Pecos River, he saw that Hasbaá sat calmly on an outcropping of rock near the stream not far from the pile of debris where Sgt. Peak had assaulted her. Will guessed she was praying to Changing Woman. He had come to think that Hasbaá was always praying.

She was dressed a little different from usual. While she still wore the long traditional woven skirt, today she had on a brightly colored shirt, and her hair was braided and tied up with colorful yarn. He thought she looked especially handsome. He could remember her body naked in the sweat lodge. He knew what flesh lay just beneath the bright-colored shirt.

Will was still wary of what she might want to talk to him about. Except to give him instructions in the sweat lodge, Hasbaá had never spoken directly with him. He wasn't sure how he should treat her. She was a sacred person. He bowed formally as he neared.

Hasbaá smiled and gestured for him to sit beside her on the smooth rock ledge. "My aunt said you wanted to see me?"

"I thought *you* wanted to see me..."

"Perhaps there was a misunderstanding." They both seemed flustered for a moment. "Even so, it is time we talked, you and I. There is something I need to say to you."

Will anticipated the scolding.

"I was convinced of your bravery when you risked your life to help us in the flood," Hasbaá began. Her voice held more of an accent than Dezba's, and her speech was a little halting, but she showed much the same fluency as the other students of John Blewer. "And I was grateful when you saved me from the Hairy Face soldier. Dezba believes you are a good man. You had... ah, qualities that impressed me. But your reaction last night to the death of our beloved elder Baaneez..."

Will's heart sank. He knew he was in trouble.

"...convinced me," Hasbaá continued, slowly and formally. "I did not believe it was possible for a Hairy Face to share feelings as we Diné have. I have never seen this before. Maybe Dezba was right when she said you told her you were not a Hairy Face."

Will felt relief beyond words. He remembered his jest to Dezba about being clean-shaven. He was grateful he had again taken time to shave before leaving his cabin a while ago.

"Your sharing your sadness shows you are interested in other things besides power. We have seldom seen this in your people. Your tears tell me you have known sorrow and that you have experienced death in your life—as I have. A person is not alive until he experiences death and knows sorrow. But he cannot stay alive if death is always with him..." Hasbaá looked down into the moving water of the creek. Her voice softened. "Dezba tells me I have not yet learned this lesson."

"Can I help you?" Will replied. "That cry last night really helped me. I feel as if I've dropped some load I'd been carrying."

He had, indeed, felt lightened somehow today. His feelings seemed closer to the surface. More than ever, he was conscious of his attraction to Hasbaá. He remembered Dezba's frightening suggestion. Today it didn't seem so frightening. In fact, he found he wanted to reach out and touch Hasbaá. He couldn't help being aware of the Indian's physique. When she moved her shoulders, the colorful shirt she wore pulled tight, hinting at the smooth, soft skin beneath.

"Dezba has told you about my husband, Segundo?"

"Yes, I'm sorry."

"Segundo would have said that if you want to help, you should arrange for the people to return to our homeland. We should leave this place. It is full of ghosts. So many people have died here. It is not good to stay at such a place. It is because of one of these ghosts our aunt died. She lost her medicine bundle in the flood. A ghost stole it."

Will wanted to talk about Dezba's suggestion that she get over Segundo by finding new love. But he certainly didn't know how to bring this up to Hasbaá. Nor was he sure he wanted to. What if she were to say no directly to him?

"What's a medicine bundle?" he asked instead.

"A leather pouch that contains sacred tobacco, stones, and, maybe, a small carving, blessed so they give spiritual protection. If you lose your medicine bundle, your life is in danger, especially from ghosts."

Will was disappointed to hear Hasbaá talk like this. It sounded so superstitious. Baaneez had died because she'd been weakened by her ordeal during the flood. Ghosts had nothing to do with it.

"Dezba told me the Diné do not believe in afterlife. How can there be ghosts?"

"It is true we do not believe, as your people do, in life after death. The Hairy Face preacher…"

"Pastor Benedict?"

"Yes. This Pastor Benedict told us that spirits go up into the sky where they live forever or else are sent down under the earth to burn in fire for all time. That sounds ridiculous. Why would the Hairy Face god want to do something like that to people? We do not believe even the Hairy Face god could be so cruel.

"No one can be sure, but we believe that a person's spirit is absorbed into the universe, into the pool of nílch'i, after they die. But, for several months, the spirit may remain near the place where they died. The spirit must be honored or else it may become unhappy waiting to become one with the universe."

Hasbaá bent down and picked up a small stone and tossed it into the slow moving water of the creek. "See, the stone goes down. But the ripples continue. The person dies, but the spirit is like the ripples. If the person died without proper respect or died unhappily, the ripples in the spirit-field may be unhappy. The purpose of our rituals is to restore harmony to the spirit-field whenever it is disrupted. The harmony of all beings in the web of life—we say *hózhó* in our language—is the reason we are alive."

"Did Baaneez die unhappy?"

"I do not think so. She died while we were having a ceremony. But even the ghost of a good person can do harm if it is not given the proper respect. In this strange place, far from our homeland, we cannot find the right plants and precious stones to offer the spirits to make them happy. That is why there are ghosts roaming here and why so many more Diné continue to die."

"But scientific knowledge is advancing every day," Will objected. "I've heard about a new discovery the doctors call 'germs.' They say these tiny things, so small we cannot see them, are the real cause of disease and death."

"That may be so. The invisible forces are the truly strong forces in the universe. These 'germs' may be invisible because they are ghosts."

Will wanted to object that Hasbaá was mixing science and superstition, but he held his tongue.

"I am distrustful of what the Hairy Face doctors think they know. They do not know about the healing powers of the plants we use. Dezba says you want to learn the ways of the Diné. Then you will have to stop thinking like a Hairy Face. Only then can you understand my people.

"The Hairy Faces know a lot about the surface of the world here." Hasbaá ran her hand across the rock they sat on. "But they do not know there are many other worlds beyond this. They do not know about the harmony of life. They think they know everything, but how can that be? They do not know about the spirit worlds. Even that Pastor Benedict, who was said to be a priest of the Hairy Face god, did not know. He insisted his god and his heaven and hell all existed in *this* world. That is silly."

"How do you know about these other worlds? Does Changing Woman tell you? Why does she speak to you more than to others?" Will hoped Hasbaá would talk about herself.

"From my earliest childhood, I was blessed with two spirits. This is why Changing Woman speaks to me. And because I listen..." Hasbaá paused for a moment.

Will heard the wind blowing; he wondered what Hasbaá heard.

Then she continued: "There are many, many other worlds out there which we cannot see. Some are too big. Some are too small. One day a Hairy Face may invent a machine to look at those worlds; then you will believe what I tell you. But Hairy Faces do not believe what they cannot see. We Diné know of these things through our faith, and we do not need to see them with our eyes. It is far beyond the human power of knowing.

Will thought Hasbaá might be right that some future scientist would invent a machine that would show these other worlds. He knew about microscopes that allowed scientists to see tiny bugs, like these things they called germs. He doubted Hasbaá had ever heard of microscopes. Who would have told her or her people about such things way out here in the New Mexico Territory? Yet she seemed to know about things too small to see, though she had it mixed up with ghosts.

In spite of his skepticism, Will was impressed that the Diné appreciated what human beings did not know. What a contrast with the all-knowing certitude of his father and the religion of the Bible that said everything humankind needed to know was there in those pages. He had discovered there was a lot the Bible said nothing about—like the existence of the Indians or of Two-Spirit Persons.

"I wonder if Changing Woman is the Diné name for the god that is in the Bible," Will said. "Did Changing Woman create the world?"

"She left creation to other spirits. She gave birth to many children. One time when she came to visit this world, she gave birth to twins whom we call Monster-Slayer and Child-of-the-Water. They are the ones who shaped our world.

"I have thought that Changing Woman might also be the mother of the Hairy Face god, but I do not know. Pastor Benedict said that the Hairy Face god created a world for the Hairy Faces. He had a book which said that. Maybe the Hairy Faces came from that world. But why did they leave that world and come here to the Diné world? Do you know about this?"

"Well, I know from that book, the Bible, that God created Adam and Eve in the Garden of Eden, but then later he threw them out as punishment."

"Why did he do that?"

"Eve ate an apple from the tree of knowledge. God had forbidden that."

Hasbaá looked quizzical. "Why? What kind of god would not want people to eat apples? Besides, I've seen Hairy Faces eating apples. Are all our problems with the Hairy Faces due to eating apples? Is this why their god made them leave their home and come here to the land of the Diné?"

"Well, actually, the first Hairy Face to come to the New World was a man named Columbus. He was trying to get to the Indies for the spice plants, but got lost. He thought he was in the Indies. That's why we call the people he met here 'Indians.'"

"Where are the Indies?"

"On the other side of the world."

Hasbaá smiled, looking playfully exasperated. "I am glad to know this Columbus was looking for spice plants. I have not heard of Hairy Faces knowing about plants and herbs. But don't the Hairy Faces understand this is not the Indies?"

"Yes, of course. But everyone still calls you Indians."

"This Hairy Face Columbus went to the Indies, but ended up on the other side of the world. And Hairy Faces call us Indians because he made a mistake. Maybe he wanted to go to the Indies for those plants because he thought your god would throw him out of his home if he ate them there, like apples." Hasbaá laughed.

Will joined in. Put that way, it did sound ludicrous. There was so much more he could tell Hasbaá about human history, but it might all sound just as foolish: the Puritans fleeing England for religious freedom then holding witchhunts to punish divergence from orthodoxy, the patriots in the American Revolution crying for liberty all the while owning slaves, the Founding Fathers' declaring all men equal but denying suffrage for women, and all those madmen in the Gold Rush ruining their lives and their families looking for shiny rocks.

Will realized that in the same way his explanation of history wouldn't make sense to Hasbaá because she didn't have enough grasp of what the world was, so Hasbaá's explanation of the spirit worlds couldn't make sense to him because he didn't have enough grasp of what spirit was.

"Tell me about Monster-Slayer and Child-of-the-Water."

"This world was created by both of them. Child-of-the-Water created everything in the seas and rivers, and Monster-Slayer everything on the land. By the time Turquoise Boy brought the people and the animals up to this world, Monster-Slayer had already brought order to the land. His efforts to defeat many monsters are told in our sacred songs. These creator gods sometimes did battle to help the people against monsters and bad luck. Their stories are exciting. But it is their mother, Changing Woman, that we turn to for blessings. She is far more important than the creator gods or the other Holy People.

"I did not understand when Pastor Benedict told us about the Hairy Face religion why he did not say anything about God's mother. I asked him about that. I remember he said only 'Papists' honor God's mother. I would like to know a Papist. They seem to know better about gods."

How am I going to explain the difference between Protestants and Catholics? "Well, the Bible does not mention God having a mother. It says God was there first."

"Ha!" Hasbaá said proudly as though she'd just won the argument. "Everybody has a mother. What kind of man would deny his mother? Your god must be very mean if he would not even tell about his own mother. That is why I think his mother is Changing Woman. She must be very mad at him for not telling the Hairy Faces about her."

"Maybe you're right."

"How did this god create the Hairy Faces?"

"He made the first man, Adam, out of dust to be just like him."

"Well, if he made Hairy Faces to be like him, that explains why they are so mean and don't respect women or the sacredness of the Earth. But how could he make the man first? How many men can make another man? Your god must really be a woman in disguise. Maybe he is a Two-Spirit and does not know it."

Will liked the suggestion that God was a Two-Spirit Person. But if so, he wondered, why was all of Christian civilization so dead-set against people like himself or Hasbaá who wanted to make love with someone of their own sex? He smiled to think how his father would react to the suggestion that God needed to make love with another man.

Maybe they got the story of Sodom and Gomorrah wrong. Maybe God had come to town looking for someone to make love with, the same way I had

come to that little town at the end of the railroad tracks and met Jose. It was
probably the church leaders that set fire to the town, not God. Maybe God
didn't stop the fire because he was too busy having sex with the handsomest
man in Sodom. Will laughed at his crazy idea, maybe he was beginning
to think like a Diné.

"If the Hairy Face god and the first man were both males, how did
they create the first woman?" Hasbaá pressed on.

"God formed Eve out of one of Adam's ribs."

"Woman came from man?" Hasbaá sounded incredulous. "No,
everybody can see man comes from woman. Perhaps the Hairy Faces
do not understand this. They must have strange ideas about sex. It is
obvious to us that no one would be here if not for our birth. Now I see
why the Hairy Faces are ignorant of women's power. Because of their
power to give birth, we honor our mothers above all. This is why
women are superior. What other Holy Persons do the Hairy Faces
worship? Maybe one of them is God's mother, and they do not know
it."

"We, uh, they," Will corrected himself, "worship only one god."

"Pastor Benedict told us that. But I did not believe him. Why would
all the other Holy Persons be ignored?"

"Well, the Bible says God is a jealous god and wants us to worship
him alone."

Hasbaá looked disgusted. "Jealousy is a very childish emotion.
Only young people are jealous. We laugh at adults who act that way.
How can the Hairy Faces worship a god like that? Everyone knows
different gods have different powers and different concerns. Our
religion allows each person to choose which Holy Person to pray to
and which ceremony to practice, depending on the particular need of
the moment. This is the way of the Diné which honors each individual."
Hasbaá's pent-up anger began to show.

"The Hairy Faces talk about liberty, but we Diné live it. We do not
have generals and presidents like you do. No one has the right to make
others go against their own wishes. This is because no one person has
all knowledge. Each of us is an imperfect being with only a tiny amount
of awareness. We do not know enough to make others do as we wish.
What if we are wrong? Each person must make his or her own choices
in life. I do not see how the Hairy Faces can talk about freedom when

they are always trying to make others do as they want. That is the opposite of freedom."

Hasbaá was so obviously right Will didn't know how to answer. There was no answer. It bothered him that their conversation was staying so philosophical. He was interested in the Diné religion. But he was more interested in Hasbaá.

He wanted to reach out to this fascinating person. He could feel an ache in his chest and arms. He wanted all this religious and cultural difference to go away. He wanted Hasbaá to stop being a sacred person. He wanted him to be just another man, like Jose Flores, with whom he could share the dear love of comrades.

But he didn't reach out.

They were interrupted by the approach of Dezba. She said to Hasbaá, "It is good that you talk with this man. I believe he can help you with your grief. I saw last night how he let go of his tears." She turned to Will, "Perhaps Niece here can learn from you how to let go of her tears."

Will blushed. He felt embarrassed by this talk, though, of course, a few minutes ago that's what he'd hoped Hasbaá would talk about. Then it occurred to him how he and Hasbaá had ended up at the river. *You set it up so we'd meet out here, didn't you, old woman? Well, thank you. I guess…*

"You are going now?" Hasbaá asked, speaking English to Dezba apparently for Will's sake.

"Barboncito and the children are waiting." Then to Will, she added, "We are going into the desert to gather sacred plants and medicine herbs. Would you come with us?"

He looked at his pocketwatch. It was just after two.

"Are you going far? I must be in General Carleton's office an hour before sunset. That gives me about three hours. Is there time?" Will was going to be sure he was on time for his appointment.

"We will not go far," Hasbaá answered. "Barboncito is still weak."

"Well, let's go then."

31

THE DESERT

The expedition consisted of Dezba, Barboncito, and Hasbaá, along with two other adult women, who apparently did not speak English because they kept to themselves away from Will. Then there were six children, two girls and four boys. One of them was the boy who'd come to Will's door.

At first, the children gathered around him. Will supposed they'd seldom seen a friendly Hairy Face. But after a short while, they ran ahead, eager to be on their way. The expedition moved slowly. Neither Dezba nor Barboncito walked fast, though both of them seemed to have more stamina than most of the older—white—people Will had known in his life.

He walked along by himself, most of the time, halfway between the adults and the children. He enjoyed the playful sounds of the boys and girls up ahead. After the several long and deep conversations with Dezba, and then with Hasbaá, the lightness of it all was refreshing.

Though they obviously did not intend to exclude him, the adults spoke in Diné among themselves. At least some of the time, he was sure, they were talking about him. He was content not to comprehend. He hoped all of the Indians would be agreeing with Dezba in urging Hasbaá to develop more of a friendship with him.

Walking along through the desert, his face shielded by a wide-brimmed hat Dezba had fished out of her hogan for him, he mused over his discoveries about the Navajo.

The Diné seemed to exist without a government, without laws, without all the trappings which his own people associate with "civilization." Yet they kept their society operating, along with a strong sense of identity as Diné. They seemed to value individual freedom above all, yet strove to cooperate with one another in order to maintain harmony among them. Will had been raised to think freedom and democracy were an invention of the Founding Fathers and the signers of the Declaration of Independence. But here were these supposedly primitive, savage people in the West actually living those ideals.

"Democracy! Near at hand to you a throat is now inflating itself and joyfully singing." He remembered words from *Leaves of Grass*. *I wonder if the poet knew about the Diné. Were the Indians the throat near at hand?*

It appeared to him that what made their society work, despite all the drastic changes affecting their lives, was their religion. The Diné seemed so different from what he had been taught about Indians. He'd never have guessed they'd be so religious.

But what a different sort of religion! The Diné religion did not appear to be one of rules but of stories and ceremonies. It was about honoring other people's freedoms.

Is it a sign of the superiority of their religious beliefs over those of European Christianity that the Diné seem to live in peace with their gods, while we Christians seemed always to be going to war in the name of ours?

They walked a long way, farther from the fort than Will had been since his arrival. Hasbaá explained the area near the fort had been stripped by previous foraging.

But then soon Dezba discovered a patch of edible plants, and the small band stopped to pick the sparse leaves and dig up the roots. Before digging, Hasbaá said a prayer in thankfulness to the spirit of each plant for allowing them to take its body for food.

One of the boys discovered a bird's nest in a bush, and the children gathered round for the eggs. There were only three eggs and six children. One of the adults intervened to distribute these three to the youngest children and to assure the older three there'd be more nests. She got them to make a game of finding eggs for everybody. Meanwhile, the three lucky ones each grabbed an egg, tipped back his or her head, expertly cracked the shell with their teeth, and then slurped down the raw contents. Will saw their enthusiasm as evidence of the lack of nutrition in their government rations.

While the children went in search of birds' nests, the adults dug up more roots. After they'd gathered a basketful, they took a break from their work. They sat down, huddled together in the shade of a huge cactus. Hasbaá handed Will a piece of root. Following the others' example, he bit into it. It tasted wet, crunchy, sweet, and only a little sandy. It quenched his thirst.

Will was musing on the simplicity of the Indians' lives, their reverence for life and for all things natural and free, when suddenly he heard screams. The adults jumped up and ran in the direction of the frightened cries. He could see the children running toward them, and behind the children, pursuing them, four horsemen.

The riders, who looked to be Mexicans dressed in light cotton pants and shirts and all wearing sombreros to shield their faces from the sun, were almost upon the children, two of them twirling lassoes.

Will ran, too. He was only a few feet from one of the children, a little girl about nine or ten, when suddenly a lasso fell over the girl's shoulders and she was whisked up into the air. Out of the corner of his eye, he saw that another of the children—it was the boy who'd come to his door—had also been lassoed.

Will remembered his own rescue by a rider with a rope. And when he looked up at the horseman who had lassoed the little girl, who was now dangling, screaming, near the horse's hooves, he could not help but think of Jose Flores. But this *Mexicano* had a very different look in his eye. This was not a rescue, and this was not a friendly cowboy.

The Diné adults had by now grabbed the other four children and shielded them as they ran from the marauders. Will could see that Hasbaá was going after the boy who, unfortunately, had already been pulled up into the rider's arms. Hasbaá grabbed hold of the *Mexicano's* leg and tried to pull him off his mount.

Will shivered to think what might happen to the little girl if the horsemen made off with her. Boys stolen like this might be enslaved as workers, but girls were more likely to be used in unthinkable ways.

Following Hasbaá's example, without allowing himself to even think, he ran for the girl. Fortunately, she still dangled from the rope and had not been pulled into the rider's grasp. Will sprinted right up to the horse and grabbed hold of the rope. He twisted it round his forearm and gave a hard jerk. The girl screamed. *The rope must be cutting into her skin.* The rider struggled to regain his balance and Will jerked again.

When he looked up at the rider this time, hoping to see him tumble from his horse, he saw instead the barrel of a pistol aimed right at his eyes. Simultaneously, he heard a shot and then one of the other horsemen yell out: "¡No! El es Americano. ¡Vámonos!"

The gun was little more than a foot away from Will's head. He jerked at the rope again, still trying to unseat the rider. The horse bucked suddenly, and the gun fired. He was shocked by the explosion, but the bullet missed him.

"¡Yo dije no!" shouted the other man whom Will took to be the leader of the raiders. Perhaps the *banditos* feared retaliation by the U.S. Cavalry which they knew would never happen so long as they only attacked Indians. But a white man was something different!

To emphasize his command not to shoot the American, the leader fired a warning shot in the direction of his henchman. The bullet hit the horn of his saddle, much too close for the rider's comfort.

Infuriated, the near victim shouted at his *compadre*, "¡Puto!" Then fired wildly at him.

The leader of the *banditos* responded abruptly, "¡Silencio!" And then—quite deliberately—he shot the man right straight in the chest. "¡Es la última vez que tu me desobedecerás!"

As the rider, who was still in the tug-of-war with Will, fell from his horse, the rope came loose from his hand. Will fell over backward, practically on top of the girl. He feared for a moment he'd been shot. But then realized it was the horseman who had been hit. Apparently, he'd been executed by his own *bandito* leader, maybe in punishment for insubordination or out of some previous animosity between them. At any rate, the man was dead, and the immediate threat to Will and the Indian child was ended.

Will rolled over and saw that the little girl was dazed and disheveled, but unhurt. In fact, she'd got to her feet and stood over him bawling at the top of her lungs and wiping at her eyes with both hands.

The other three horsemen had turned and galloped away, leaving the body of their friend behind. The Diné adults, with the children huddled about them, were clustered about ten feet from him. When he looked again, he realized they were standing over another body lying flat on the ground. It was Hasbaá.

A shock went through him. He jumped up and ran over, oblivious to the pain where he'd skinned and bruised his hands and legs in the fall.

The Diné women were weeping, one especially hard. She pulled at her hair with both hands in a gesture of desperation and grief. Will saw that the boy whom Hasbaá had run to rescue was nowhere to be seen. And Hasbaá was flat out on the ground.

Oh, my God, the first shot must've hit Hasbaá, and the raider got away with the boy.

As Will reached the cluster, he saw Hasbaá raise up on one elbow. She assured everybody she was unhurt, but he could see her skirt was torn and stained with blood. Dezba knelt beside her checking her wounds.

Will was concerned, but relieved. "What happened?" he asked Barboncito, as the little girl ran over to one of the women who was crying and laughing and exclaiming in gratitude for the child's safety.

"We are so vulnerable here in the desert. If it is not the Comanches, it is the *Mexicanos*. They attack us to take whatever we have. They steal our children for making slaves. We should not have brought the children. Since the soldiers took our weapons, we cannot defend ourselves. This is all part of our curse."

Barboncito also spoke English, but had the strongest accent. Will had to pay close attention to make out the meaning.

"The boy…" Anguish radiated through Barboncito's voice. "They took the boy."

"The boy is Barboncito's great-grandchild," Dezba said.

"I'm sorry," Will said. "I wish I could have helped."

"You did help. You saved our great-granddaughter."

Will knelt down beside Hasbaá and took her hand.

"It is only a skin wound." Hasbaá dismissed their concerns.

"She is hurt more than she admits," Dezba said. "But with Hasbaá's medicine powers, she will heal quickly." The bullet appeared to have grazed the leg just above the knee. There was lots of blood, but the wound did not look deep.

Dezba tore away a strip of cloth at the bottom of Hasbaá's skirt. She wiped away the blood, then wrapped Hasbaá's leg to stanch the bleeding. Hasbaá said something to her in Diné, and she paused to hunt through the basket of medicinal plants they'd gathered. Dezba took some of the leaves, crushed them lightly in her hand and placed them against the wound, then wound the bandage tight.

Hasbaá tried to stand up, but her face twisted in pain. Dezba said something in Diné. Will imagined she must have told her to take it easy. Will was confident that Hasbaá would not like being a patient and would certainly minimize her injury.

The children were all crying over the loss of their friend, but they rallied to Hasbaá's assistance. They gathered several long sticks and wove a travois out of the rope Will had wrested from the New Mexican rider. Dragging the litter behind them, the Indians would be able to carry Hasbaá back to the settlement without her further injuring her leg.

"We should return now," Barboncito said. "The *banditos* may come back." He held the small basket of tubers and a few bunches of leaves they'd gathered. What a meager harvest for so much effort—and at such a cost!

Will started toward the fallen *Mexicano*, but Hasbaá told him to stay away. The bandit had obviously been wounded fatally. Even if he were not dead yet, it would be only a matter of time. There was nothing the little band from the reservation could do to help him. Nor would they be inclined to. He was, after all, the aggressor. If he hadn't been shot by his own leader, no doubt it would be Will's body lying there on the desert awaiting the buzzards to clean the bones.

"Stay away from him," Hasbaá said urgently. "That ghost will be very unhappy. It could bring terrible misfortune. We must leave this place right away."

As they gathered together and prepared for the return, Dezba spoke: "Our friend Will has helped us once again. He endangered himself to save the Diné. We are in his debt."

One of the other adults translated Dezba's speech, and the whole little band buzzed in agreement. They all reached out to Will to pat and stroke his arms and shoulders in a sign of gratitude and affection. Then they spoke among themselves, and a couple of them began to wail—in grief for the loss of the boy.

Will himself felt very uneasy. He was glad to have saved the girl, but he felt so helpless now. *What can I do to help them get the boy back? How can I accept their gratitude when they've suffered such a loss?*

He was proud of himself for having acted to rescue the little girl. But he realized he only did so in imitation of Hasbaá. He was again amazed at her strength and courage. She had clearly attacked an armed man.

The little band made its way home much more slowly than they'd come out. Pulling the litter that bore Hasbaá slowed them down quite a bit. Both Barboncito and Dezba trudged dispiritedly. The group had to stop frequently to allow them to rest and to adjust Hasbaá's litter. Even Will couldn't walk as fast as usual. His hands were skinned up, and he limped with the muscle in his right buttock aching with every step. He was still emotionally shaken by his near brush with death. He had forgotten entirely about his appointment with Gen. Carleton.

Dezba complained that now another area for foraging had been contaminated. "We can never come back. The ghost of the *Mexicano* will haunt the land. Not only do they threaten our physical safety, these raiders poison the spirit-field."

Will was skeptical of the Navajos' superstitions, but he certainly recognized the hardships the raiders imposed on the Indians.

He walked along beside Hasbaá, occasionally trying to make conversation, asking how she was feeling, if this or that hurt, or if she were feeling faint. At one point, when the group had stopped to rest and change places dragging the litter, Dezba came back and lifted Hasbaá's skirt to examine the wound. Will stood over her looking on. He was distressed to see that fiery red tendrils shot out around the laceration. Will recognized that as a sign of blood poisoning. He was concerned that the plants they'd put into the wound had done this.

He felt Hasbaá's forehead. She seemed hot. He raised an alarm. But Hasbaá told him to calm down and trust Changing Woman and the spirits in the sacred plants to complete the healing. She told him she needed to close her eyes a few minutes and rest, and advised him to go talk to Barboncito.

32

THE DESERT

As they walked slowly back to the Bosque Redondo, Will took the opportunity to talk with Barboncito, the man who the whites thought was the "chief" of the Navajos. While occasionally having to interrupt his story to consult with Dezba for the proper English words to use, and even allowing Will to suggest words, Barboncito haltingly explained how the Indians had ended up at this desolate place.

"Five winters ago," he began, "the Hairy Face general, the one they call Carleton, arrived in Santa Fe. Soon after he arrived, he gave orders that our neighbors, the Mescalero, should be killed wherever they were found. Many of the Mescalero fled to the south into Mexico. Those who surrendered were brought here to Fort Sumner, like it was a prison.

"We were alarmed at Carleton's brutality. We decided to send representatives. Eighteen of our people came to meet with him. We thought he would see our sincerity and believe we wanted only peace.

"I was one of those who went to see him in Santa Fe. We told him we would forgive the Hairy Faces for what happened at the horse race the year before at Fort Defiance. We only wanted peaceful relations. But Carleton told us the Diné must leave our homeland and move to Fort Sumner.

"We were shocked. We told him we had no desire to leave our sacred lands. We told him that Fort Sumner was in the lands of the Comanches, and if we went there, the Comanches would be angry and would attack us.

"We told him that if we left our homelands, Changing Woman's power to help us would be weakened, because it was not meant for us to live elsewhere. We would not be able to locate the medicine plants which grow only in certain places. Without our sacred medicines, we would weaken and fall victim to ghosts and disease.

"We told him all these things. And each of these afflictions has befallen us just as we feared.

"General Carleton would not change his mind. He ordered the Diné to move to Fort Sumner and to learn the ways of the Hairy Faces. Or else our people would be exterminated. We could not figure him out. Why would he want to do a thing like that to our people?

"Changing Woman told Hasbaá it was because Carleton thought there would be gold in our lands, that yellow rock which makes Hairy Faces act crazy. Our homelands were given to us by Changing Woman..."

"Canyon de Chelly?" Will remembered bits of the stories Mac McCarrie had told.

"Yes, it is a magical place where we still find the traces of our ancestors. It is beautiful. We should never have left there.

"We made Carleton many promises that we would keep peaceful relations with the soldiers and that we would stop raiding the New

Mexican towns if the soldiers would stop the New Mexicans raiding us, stealing our horses and our children. But he told us he did not believe our promises.

"It was the same issue we always brought up. Which the Hairy Faces always ignored. As many times as I have talked with the Hairy Faces, I still do not understand how they can expect us to have peace as long as our children are being stolen and enslaved. There are thousands of Diné slaves held by the New Mexicans today. No one can deny it who has eyes to see.

"But Carleton refused our offer. The only choice he gave us was to go to Fort Defiance and wait to be transported to Fort Sumner.

"After having a council together, the others asked me to make a speech. I was not chosen because I have any more power than any other Diné, but because I can speak in English."

"What happened?"

"I told him we were not a violent people and had no desire to make war on the Hairy Faces. But I told him that if he continued to insist we leave our sacred lands, we would have to resist. I said, 'I will never leave my country, not even if it means I will be killed.'

"General Carleton said, 'Move or we will pursue and destroy you. We will not make peace on any other terms. Either you will move to Fort Sumner or you will cease to exist as a people. There can be no other talk on this subject.'

"Hearing his words, we got up and walked out. I cried as I went from that meeting.

"From that time onward, our settlements were attacked by the soldiers. Kit Carson, who had been our friend, turned against us and at General Carleton's command led the soldiers into our canyon. Our bows and arrows were no match for the Hairy Face guns. We felt lucky if our warriors managed to hit one or two soldiers. Our sentries warned us when an attack was coming so we could flee and hide in the rocks. The soldiers did not fight better than we did, but they destroyed our hogans and our food supplies. They burned our cornfields, cut down our orchards, and stole our sheep and horses.

"Hasbaá performed a ceremony to ask Changing Woman's advice. All we wanted was to be left alone. Changing Woman told Hasbaá we should send a raiding party to stampede the soldiers' horses. Without horses, they could not attack our settlements. This plan worked. And we felt great success. Hasbaá was honored for her vision and her bravery, along with some of the other young men and women warriors who rode in the raid.

"But afterwards, the Hairy Faces brought more horses and kept them protected inside the forts. They had so many guards. That is why we could not win. The Hairy Faces always had more horses and more soldiers to replace those who were lost. There are just too many.

"We could not believe the cruelty of the soldiers. Whenever they killed a Diné, they would rip off the hair on the top of the head. We Diné do not like to touch the body of a dead person. We would never scalp someone. The Utes and some other tribes do this, I know, but we consider such a practice barbaric.

"That the Hairy Faces did this only made us resist more strongly. However, we were weakened by the lack of food. As patrols rode into our settlements, shooting everyone in sight, we often had to leave behind the elderly people, the pregnant women, and the sick. When we returned later, we would find bodies mutilated or burned to death. One time I saw the body of a pregnant mother. Her belly had been slashed open and the little baby pulled out of her insides. It was lying there beside her with its head cut off."

Will quivered with disgust.

"It was a horrible time. Sometimes, as we would be hiding in the rocks while the soldiers searched for us, a small child would begin to cry. The mother would be forced to hold her hand over the little one's mouth so the soldiers would not discover us. I saw babies smothered to death this way. The idea of a mother having to kill her own baby is so repugnant we can never forget it.

"After two years of these kinds of attacks, we hardly had any possessions left, not even warm clothing. Many froze to death in the cold wintertime, and most others were sick. We were afraid even to build fires to warm ourselves, in fear that the soldiers would see the smoke. Those who were not already dead were slowly starving to death. Though it pained us greatly to give up our homeland, eventually we realized that we had no choice but to surrender.

"We sent a delegation to General Carleton, who promised us that if we agreed to move to the reservation he was planning, we would be fed by the government and well cared for. He promised we would have peace and plenty. We hoped our time of troubles had come to an end. Thousands of us came into the forts."

Will's mind swam with images of all these tragedies. He had no idea the Diné had undergone such hardships. He had thought their plight was having to work at Fort Sumner. Now he realized this was just the last in a long series of humiliations, injustices, and sufferings.

He understood that from the white settlers' point of view, the Indians were the enemy. The settlers had been the subject of atrocities on the part of Indians. He had read about such things in the newspapers. He realized what the papers had failed to say was that different Indian peoples behaved differently. Back East, they were all just lumped together as "Indians." He thought of Hasbaá's joking about how silly it was that Columbus called them all Indians. This had turned out to be no joke.

"Since we surrendered, everything has only gotten worse. There are diseases here that kill our people. Our medicines do not heal them. Our children are stillborn or worse…

"Others starve. You have seen how we have to search this desert to find a few edible roots. This is not a bountiful area like our homeland. General Carleton keeps telling us the Great Father in Washington will send us more food, but there is never enough and sometimes the rations the soldiers pass out to us are infested with maggots. We cannot eat such food."

"Why don't you grow your crops here? Surely that would help."

"Over and over we've tried." Barboncito's voice sounded weary. "But the soil is poison. It is the spirits' way of telling us we should not be in this place.

"We have been hungry a long time. After we surrendered to the forts, there was never enough food. General Carleton told us he had requested more rations, but day after day people starved while we waited for the food shipments. We heard some of the government officials did not agree with General Carleton's plan to move us to Fort Sumner. We did not know what would happen to us, but by this time we were so weak from hunger we could only sit and wait. Mostly, we mourned for all our dead relatives. That mourning has never ended.

"Our people spent the winter at Fort Defiance and Fort Wingate near our homelands. They were filthy, overcrowded places. Once spring arrived, General Carleton announced we must make the long walk to come to the Bosque Redondo Reservation here at Fort Sumner. He promised anyone who could not walk would ride in wagons. But when the wagons arrived, there were not enough. Many of our old and sick were forced to walk.

"Every day we marched, from dawn to dusk. I have never been in such a long walk. The weather was cold, and each night people froze to death. The next morning we would have to leave them where they lay without a burial. If a person could not keep up and stumbled and fell, he or she was left there by the roadside to die. I even saw a soldier kick an old woman to try to get her to stand up. He finally stopped kicking her only when he saw she had died. We were leaving behind us a trail of unhappy ghosts.

"After we had walked for many days, we reached the big river called the Rio Grande. I had never seen so much water. It was spring, and the river was wide and deep. The soldiers went across on horses to pull ropes from one side to the other. The current was so strong some of the horses were carried away. When they got the ropes tied on both sides, they used them as guides to float the wagons across. The old people in the wagons were terrified, since few Diné had ever seen such a river. Once the wagons were across, they told the rest of us we would have to hold onto the ropes and pull ourselves across in the water. We could not imagine doing such a thing. But we had no choice. The soldiers forced us.

"I saw several mothers trying to help their children. If the child lost its grip, the mother would let go of the rope to catch the child. Then both of them were washed away. There was nothing the rest of us could do to help. None of us knew how to swim. We could only keep pulling ourselves along the rope to try to get to the shore, our tears adding to the flowing water.

"Our troubles seemed to go on without relief. During the entire journey, New Mexican slave raiders would sneak into our campsites at night and carry off children. We could hear them screaming for help, but there was nothing we could do. The soldiers never tried to stop the raids. And we did not have the strength to fight. Sometimes when I listened to a child's screams, I thought their future as a slave might be better than what was befalling the Diné.

"By the time we finished the long walk and arrived here at Fort Sumner, over three thousand more of our people had died."

"How many of you are there now?"

"It is only a guess. I would say fewer than seven thousand," Barboncito answered after a moment's thought. "There were many more than twelve thousand before we surrendered."

"Oh, God, I had no idea things were so bad. I need to learn about this…"

"It is good that you know these stories," the old Indian said. "But my spirit is weary now. Let us talk no more of these things. We are liable to attract the ghosts that are roaming in the desert."

Will respected the old man's wish to forget about these terrible memories. He walked on in silence for a while, then let himself fall back alongside Hasbaá's litter.

33

THE DESERT

Hasbaá seemed to be sleeping. Will did not disturb her, but he noticed that now and again the travois would catch on a rock or branch. This never wakened Hasbaá, and that began to worry Will.

He reached out and felt her forehead. She seemed to be burning up with fever. He tried to rouse her, but she did not respond. He shook her shoulder, still no response. He lifted her skirt, but careful not to violate her modesty. The wound looked fiercely inflamed.

At that point, he panicked. "Stop," he shouted. "Hasbaá's unconscious. We must do something." Will felt a terrible fear Hasbaá was dying. He couldn't let that happen. "He needs water. We've got to give him water."

Everyone stopped walking. Dezba came back to look at Hasbaá. "She'll be all right. But we must get her home soon."

As Dezba spoke, Will realized he'd called Hasbaá by the masculine pronoun. "I think we should give *her* water." He corrected his choice of genders. "How about the roots? Let's squeeze some of the water out."

Dezba and the others did not seem as alarmed as Will, but Dezba agreed it would not hurt to give her some of the root, and she gently pressed a broken piece of the wet tuber to Hasbaá's lips. At first, Hasbaá did not respond.

"Please, Hasbaá, take some of the root." Will stroked her face and head.

Then, to everyone's surprise, Hasbaá opened her eyes. She chewed some of the root from Dezba's hand. Then spoke, in a very clear, strong voice.

"I have been talking with Changing Woman." She gave a piercing glance toward Will. "She told me all is well. She promised to heal my wound. It is all over now. See," she said, pulling up her skirt to expose the bandaged wound. The inflammation and red tendrils of what Will thought had been blood poisoning had subsided. The leg looked practically normal.

Will was amazed. He reached out and touched her forehead. If there'd been any fever before, it was gone now. Her skin was cool to the touch. It was a miracle.

Hasbaá reached up and took his hand in hers. "Changing Woman told me that she has sent you to us. She said your bravery in saving our daughter today was proof."

Hasbaá looked right into his eyes. The expression on her face was very soft. She looked radiant, in spite of her ordeal. "You have green eyes," she said. Indeed, under the shadow of his hat brim the light caught Will's eyes just right and they practically shone like emeralds.

Will's heart began to pound, but this time it wasn't from fear or panic.

34

Fort Sumner

As the little band trudged into the camp, with Hasbaá walking as though no bullet had ever grazed her leg, the last light of the orange sunset was fading. Will had missed his appointment with Gen. Carleton. He'd heard the bell ringing dinnertime while they were still far from the Fort.

But this time, I know, I've got a good reason.

Will bid the Indians good night. He promised to come to the settlement in the morning. Then he sprinted as fast as he could to the mess hall.

Dusty, bedraggled and out of breath, Will burst into the dining room. He went straight to the head table where Carleton was sitting. As he approached, he saw there was an empty seat at the table across from the general.

Carleton looked up at him with a scowl. "It's about time, young man. You were supposed..."

"General Carleton, I'm sorry," Will blurted out, "the New Mexicans have attacked the Indians."

"Damn. As if I didn't have enough to worry about... Well, where have you been?"

"I was with them, sir. We went on a walk out in the desert to gather sacred herbs."

"Sacred herbs!"

"Yes, sir."

Carleton looked around at his fellow officers sitting at the table. He looked back at Will who was still panting from his run. "Did they chase you in here?"

"Oh, no, sir. I ran here as soon as the Indians got back safely. I didn't want to keep you waiting."

"Well, that, indeed, is a fine sentiment, young man."

"I'm sorry, sir. But this was an emergency. Shouldn't we do something? Ring the bell?"

"Are they attacking now?" For the first time, a tone of alarm sounded in Carleton's voice.

"Oh, no. The attack was out in the desert."

"I've warned the savages not to go far from the fort. How do they think we can protect them?" Carleton made a point of sounding exasperated. "Was anyone killed?"

"Yes, sir. One of the raiders was shot..."

"Did the Indians do this?"

Will sensed the general was looking for an excuse to blame the Diné for the sins of their attackers.

"Oh, no, sir. The leader of the raid shot his own man. It looked like a quarrel between the two of them. The man who got killed tried to shoot me."

"Well, I see he didn't succeed."

"Thank God. But one of us, Hasbaá the uh,"—he had never tried identifying Hasbaá's role in the settlement before—"uh, the high priestess was wounded. And they stole an Indian boy." Will was not altogether happy with his choice of the term "high priestess," but at least it sound official and important.

"But you are safe. Well, that's good. You must be hungry."

"Sir," Will disregarded the general's concern for his appetite. "Shouldn't we organize a search party?"

"Search party?"

"Yes, sir. To rescue the boy. The New Mexicans stole one of the Navajo children."

"Oh, yes. Well, Mr. Lee, it's gotten dark outside. I'm sure the boy will survive. Maybe the New Mexicans will teach him how to work..."

"But what are we going to do, sir?"

"I think we're going to have dessert, young man," Carleton answered. "Friends of mine from Santa Fe have been visiting. They brought me a tin of chocolate. The cook's baked a cake for the officers. You know, Mr. Lee, you're not exactly an officer, and so I'm not bound to include you. But I'd invited you to sit at my table tonight. And in spite of your rudeness in being late and coming to dinner dressed like... well, like that," he said. "I see you've endured something of an ordeal out there. I'm sure you'd enjoy a piece of cake."

"No, sir," Will blurted out. "I mean yes, thank you. But, sir, what are we going to do about the Indians' being attacked and the boy stolen into slavery?"

"Well, yes, you're right. We must do something, as you say, Mr. Lee." The general beckoned to his adjutant. "Lt. Bauer, make a note of this. I am hereby issuing an order, effective immediately, that none of the Indians are to go beyond sight of the guardposts." He looked around the table. "I think that will suffice." There were titters from the officers.

Will realized he wasn't going to get a search party formed. *Of course, how could I have expected to? Hadn't I heard Barboncito's story?*

"Oh, and, Mr. Lee, that includes you. I don't want you out there either. Don't you remember what I told you? There'll be hell to pay in Washington if I have to explain how I lost another civilian Agent."

"With all due respect, sir," Will replied. "I don't think that's what's needed. The reason the Navajos go out so far is to search for food and medicinal herbs. I've seen what they're rationed. Nobody could live on that."

"Damn it, man, don't you think I'm trying?" Carleton yelled back in sudden anger. "I've spent the day negotiating with the traders and filling out extra food requisitions. You don't know how many appeals I've made for more supplies of all sorts. Those stupid politicians don't have any idea what things cost out here. They don't understand how to do business with the local traders.

"I do. I've been working with these men for years now. I've made friends with the traders. If Washington would just send me the money I need to buy supplies, we could settle all this now. But instead they're wasting their money on the salary of yet another Agent to come out here and harass me and interfere with my work."

Will was cowed by the general's vehemence. "I can understand how you must feel, sir, after all your years of hard work. But I think you've been out West so long you don't know how people think back East." He realized he was letting the general change the focus of the conversation. But he hadn't gotten anywhere with his first approach. *I've got to get on Carleton's good side.*

The general motioned to Will again, "Sit down, sit down. I'd like to know what you have to say. But I'm anxious to get to the cake…"

"Hear, hear." Several voices around the table spoke up in agreement.

Will pulled out the chair and sat down. He leaned forward and started right back in on the conversation, "There's all the troubles still going on in the South, what with the government bouncing back and forth between trying to help the Southern Unionists and the Black Republicans and trying to attract the former Rebels back into the Union. There's all the fighting going on with the Indians in the Plains. And now the talk of impeaching President Johnson…"

"Well, thank you for enlightening me, Mr. Lee." Carleton interrupted him. "It's good to have news from back East. And we all know you're a newcomer out here, fresh from the marble halls of Washington, D.C."

"Well, not the marble halls..." Will didn't know how to get around the general's wall of snide nonchalance.

The discussion was interrupted by the arrival of the chocolate cake. After Carleton cut himself the first piece and the cake was divvied up among those at the head table, including Will, the general turned back to the earnest young Indian Agent. With a forkful of cake poised at his mouth, he asked, "Well, then. You tell me what to do. Have you any ideas?"

"Yes sir. In fact, I do. Since you are probably not going to get any more rations, why not provide an armed guard to protect the Navajos when they go out foraging?"

"You must be joking, I don't even have enough troops to man the fort itself. Do you think I can send out a patrol every time a savage wants to dig up some roots?"

"Then feed them here."

"Haven't you heard a word I've said?" Carleton yelled. Then he stopped, took a deep breath, ate another bite of his cake, then moaned, "I wish I could feed them. After the Navajos gave up those valuable lands, after the great success of my campaign, I could not agree with you more. Christian charity requires us to provide them adequate food, clothing, and shelter. I've tried, believe me, I've tried."

Will tasted the cake. It was good. He hadn't had chocolate in a long time. He'd forgotten how much he missed it. But he felt guilty enjoying such a delicacy at a time like this.

"Sir, it looks to me like you have one other choice."

"And what is that?" Now Carleton's voice had lost the smugness. He actually sounded as though he were interested in Will's suggestion.

Will sensed the weight of responsibility the general must have felt on his shoulders. He could almost sympathize with him. He seemed to be a man caught between his belief in the westward expansion, his Christian ideals, and his miscalculations about how much his grand experiment would cost once the Indians surrendered. Will did not think Gen. Carleton was deliberately trying to kill off the Diné, and he did seem to feel a frustrated responsibility for them.

Yet Will could not let himself forget this was the man who was behind the subjugation of the Diné. If the things Dezba and Barboncito had told him were even half true, Carleton was ultimately responsible, however unwittingly, for thousands of deaths.

"Well, what's your idea?"

Will gulped, then said as forcefully as he could muster, "Provide the Navajos with enough arms to protect their families from attack, sir."

Carleton raised up out of his seat as though he were going to stand up and announce the suggestion to the entire mess hall. Then he sat back down. He turned his right shoulder toward Will and lay his forearm across the table casually and leaned forward as if to enter into serious discussion with him. He said, at first very softly and seriously, "Are you crazy, man? Are you addlepated from the heat?" Carleton's voice was rising in pitch and volume with each word. "Do you know what you are saying?"

Carleton sputtered, "These people want to kill every one of us. Here we are, a few white soldiers, surrounded by the fiercest fighters the Army has encountered west of the Sioux. The Navajos have run wild, causing havoc throughout the Southwest, ever since civilization reached these lands. The Spanish and the Mexicans have been fighting them for three hundred years and had never been able to subdue them. They would kill every white settler or trader or rancher or God knows who else who came near their settlements.

"For the decade and a half before I assumed command out here in '62, the savages attacked wagon trains and white settlements practically with impunity. My God, man, it was only after my campaign and my daring and heretofore untried strategies that the Navajos were removed as a threat to the white race. Now we can live in peace in these lands.

"It took the planning and leadership of James C. Carleton to bring the Indians to their knees. I had to be stern. At times I had to insist on the rules being obeyed, even when that meant being, perhaps, merciless. No matter what else happens, the Union owes me a debt."

Carleton adjusted his uniform jacket proudly. He sat back in his chair. He looked down at the medals on his breast. Then he raised a hostile stare toward Will. His eyes squinted. "And now you... you nobody... you inexperienced fool... you... you Rebel, you have the gall to sit here and tell me I should arm the Navajos!

"What on God's earth do you think we spent all the money and lives to defeat them for? They were just as surely the implacable enemies of the Union as you Rebs.

"Let me remind you of the circumstances of your appointment, young man. You were supposed to sign the damn forms and keep your mouth shut. But every time I've called you to my office to do your single duty as Indian Agent, you've had some excuse. Why do you think Jesse McDonald hired a Rebel pantywaist for this job in the first place? You and I both know why they sent you out here...

"Now don't you go ruining the hard work I've done with your lollygagging around with the damned savages. They are subdued, and they are going to stay subdued.

"Wait a minute, just wait a minute," Carleton said, interrupting himself. "*Now* I understand... What do *you* care if arming the savages will endanger our military gains? *You* don't have any loyalty to the Union. You're a damn Rebel infiltrator."

"No, sir, no, sir," Will protested strongly. "I am not a Rebel. I was just a boy who got drafted into the Southern army when it looked like there weren't going to be any more soldiers left to get killed. They made me go. I never supported secession, nor slavery. I'm a loyal supporter of the Union. I took the Loyalty Oath. You can see it in my personnel file.

"My Southern background has nothing to do with this, General. The War between the North and the South is over. I just want to relieve the sufferings of these people I was sent here to represent. Is that so wrong?"

He didn't give the general time to answer, but pressed right on. "I may be wrong about how to do it. All I can really do is apprise you of the problems and ask you to find solutions. General Carleton, please believe me, I'm not interested in fighting you, sir. I'm only interested in resolving problems the Indians are experiencing."

"Well, all right," Carleton answered. "I guess you are right about your service in the Southern Army. You can't be blamed for being born in—where was it?"

"Virginia, sir." Will was proud that his rebuttal had succeeded in countering the general's assertion.

"Yes, Virginia. Beautiful country there. Good people. I was there as a boy. I see, young man, that you just need a little educating about the problems we've got out here in the West. That's what I was telling you the other day."

"Yes, sir," Will answered, trying to sound compliant but spirited. "I'm anxious to hear your ideas. I'd like to discuss some of mine with you. Perhaps we can work together for the welfare of everyone."

"Perhaps." Carleton did not sound as sanguine as Will. "I just want you to remember that I know how you got this job. I'm willing to work with you, but I think the ideas we… er, discuss, ought to be more mine than yours."

Will was relieved Carleton's outburst had subsided. He was proud of himself for not getting hot-headed and perpetuating the animosity. But what had Gen. Carleton meant by "the circumstances of your appointment"?

"Don't I see there's another piece of cake down there?" Gen. Carleton called out in mock camaraderie. "Let Mr. Lee here have it." Will hadn't eaten the first piece yet. His stomach was too stirred up. "Let him have a little reminder of his good fortune in being a loyal white American, safely protected here by the United States Cavalry with a roof over his head, good food on the table, and protection from the savages who'd be very happy to have his scalp if they weren't afraid I'd blow their heads off if they so much as put a finger on our friend here."

What a pile of horseshit! I could tell the general a thing or two about the Diné's attitudes toward scalping. But instead Will replied graciously, "I'd be mighty obliged to you, sir. This cake is the sweetest thing I've tasted since I left ol' Virgin-ee." He hoped the general wouldn't perceive the sarcasm.

After dinner, Will went to his quarters. He was exhausted. All he'd had to eat all day had been the tubers the Indians dug up and those two pieces of chocolate cake. He lay in bed a long time. He kept reliving the episode at the general's table. What *were* the circumstances the general reminded him of? Maybe the letter from Harry Burnside? But that was just an introduction. He knew he'd been given an advantage in getting this job by that letter of recommendation. He even knew he'd dazzled McDonald and Benedict with his looks and that they'd fawned over him like mother hens. But he'd assumed those were inconsequential to his being given serious governmental duties.

But why was I sent out here so fast, with no training, and no instruction in what the job was to be?

I was supposed to be an apprentice. That had made sense. Well, no matter. It got me out here. I managed to escape Lynchburg. I couldn't have taken any more of my father.

He thought over every detail he could remember of that day he'd arrived in Washington, D.C., and, with Harry's letter in his pocket, had gone to see Jesse McDonald.

What really were "the circumstances of my appointment"?

35

WASHINGTON, DC.

The conductor announced "Washington City," as he struck his hand against the metal luggage racks above the seats to make a clanging noise. Soon Will was climbing down from the train and joining the stream of passengers still jostling each other and bumping head-to-head into departing passengers getting on another train.

Will made it down the platform and through the crowded station and out onto the front steps. The platform area had been black with soot from the engines, and the station itself was dark and close. But outside the sun was shining. There was a haze in the sky, but the air was fresh, and Will was in a brand new city. In the near distance, the newly constructed Capitol dome rose above the buildings near the station. There it was, looming over the city just like it looked in the lithographs in the newspapers.

He stopped cold, looking out at the city before him. The street was hardly less busy than inside the train station. A plethora of wagons, buggies, men on horseback, and pedestrians all competed with one another for space on the street in the direction they wanted to go. There was dust everywhere. Just to Will's right, two men tried to keep a group of pigs together in the midst of all the confusion. The pigs, as though smart enough to know they were being herded to their demise, kept separating at every opportunity, requiring the herders to race in little circles around the animals. And all the while the pigs squealed raucously. It was almost funny, if it weren't so frightening.

Well, welcome to Washington City. He felt like one of those pigs as he stepped down into the stream and joined the throng.

Will had not witnessed such confusion since the war. *Yet this is not some city under bombardment or an evacuation center for refugees. These people are just going about their daily lives. With never a word of greeting to the hundreds of faces passing them by, oblivious of the others. Each one of them might as well be a lone man walking through the middle of a cattle — or swine — herd.* Will had to snicker to himself. There was just no social interaction. Not that one could have heard any conversation anyway what with all the noise of the locomotives, the hoots of the crowd, the squealing and neighing of the animals, and the shouts of the barkers and hawkers of wares, newspapers and candies.

He wasn't sure which way to go, and tried to inquire of the man walking to his left. He turned to the well-dressed gentleman, "Excuse me, can you..." The man picked up his pace and walked on, out-distancing Will without even looking over. Will turned to the man to his right. "Excuse me, can you tell me how to get to the Department of the Interior?" The man didn't brush him off or walk away, but just looked kind of blankly at him as they moved along with the crowd, "Uh, no." "How about Constitution Avenue?" Will hastened to ask, but the man had already walked away. Will looked toward the next person coming up alongside him in the push of people down the street, but this man looked away quickly enough to communicate his refusal to get involved in whatever it was Will was up to.

It occurred to him that the newspaper hawkers on the sidewalk would probably know all the government offices. After all, they worked for the news. He walked up to the nearest hawker, shouting, "Extra, extra, read all about it... Congressional leaders talk of impeaching President Johnson." He tried to get the man's attention. But when the hawker saw Will did not have a nickel in his hand for a paper, he turned away and ran toward a customer signaling with a coin. Figuring it would be wasting a nickel to buy a paper just to get to talk to the man, Will decided he was going to have to handle this on his own.

He could see which way the Capitol was. It seemed likely that government offices would be clustered near there. And so he set out in that direction. Once he got away from the railroad station, the crowd thinned significantly. He reached into his breast pocket and extracted the envelope he'd been given by Harry Burnside. Several times during the trip, he'd pulled out the envelope and looked at it. He knew perfectly well the name and address emblazoned on it in Harry's excellent chancery hand. But he looked again just to make sure.

Indeed, the address was 214 Constitution Avenue N.W. And the street sign just above him read "Constitution Ave." His instincts had been right, and he congratulated himself for his urbane skills in getting around in this new environment. He had to walk a block to make sure he was going in the direction of the ascending numbers, then headed on toward the 200 block. He found the street numbers easily, but there was no government office building at 214 Constitution Avenue. He read the address again. Then looked at the street signs. Only then did it dawn on him that the address on the envelope had "N.W." after the name. The street signs had a little "N.E."

Will walked back the other direction for a couple of blocks and then, seeing a sidewalk vendor, stopped and purchased an apple cider to drink and a plate of grits and ham. He asked the vendor about the address and got a very complicated explanation of how the city was laid out.

"That's pretty confusing."

"Whaddya expect from government bureaucracy?"

Will enjoyed the meal which he ate in a leafy little park, but the vendor's explanation had got him more confused than ever. When he set out again, he headed the wrong way and had to double back on the other side of the Capitol. But by then he was in the "N.W." quadrant and when he got to Constitution Avenue, he came right up on the imposing building of the Interior Department.

Will was tired and dusty. But he told himself that his big chance was coming up. He shouldn't let himself procrastinate. Besides, he had nowhere else to go. At least not yet...

Will puffed up his chest, threw back his shoulders and strode down the dark hall of the Interior Department building toward the swinging doors which he'd been instructed by a clerk led to Mr. McDonald's office.

As he came to the doors, he saw etched on the glass the words: "Office of Indian Affairs." His heart skipped a beat. He'd had no idea this job Harry Burnside offered him would have anything to do with

Indians. Remembering Michael Halyerd's Cherokee heritage, he thought maybe this was just right, though he also remembered the tales he'd heard of settlers and soldiers alike being murdered and scalped by wild Indians.

He pushed through the swinging doors. Some twenty men sat around the perimeter of the large room. He walked right up to the desk in the center. His eyes roved over the highly polished surface. Just at hand was a big appointment book open to today's date. Will could see there was a long list of names on the page. Only a few of them had been checked off or crossed through. The others must all be waiting.

"I'm here to see Mr. McDonald to apply for a job."

The clerk gestured toward a pile of papers at the front of the desk. "Those are the job applications there. Fill one out."

Will picked up a form and carried it over to a vacant seat by a writing desk set up with a pen and inkwell. He noticed next to him was a man wearing a clerical collar. The man looked up and smiled warmly. Then, after Will had filled out the form which asked a long series of questions about professional experience and military service, he took it back to the clerk.

"Well, let's see." As he scanned the page, the clerk's eyes grew wide. "You served with the Army of Northern Virginia?" His voice rose with mock incredulity. "You mean to say you were a Confederate Rebel, er, Mr. Lee?"

"I was drafted. I didn't have a choice. And I never actually went to battle," he replied defensively.

"You people have caused our country all these years of war, just so you could keep your niggers to serve you hand and foot! And then you have the audacity to come in here and expect the government you tried to overthrow to give you a job." Will felt the stares of all the people in the waiting room.

"Excuse me, sir, 'cuse me," he tried to interrupt the tirade. "I never agreed with slavery. I'm the son of a preacher. My father had coloreds who worked on his farm, but we didn't have handservants, like you said."

"Ah, Charles, now don't scold the lad." The man in the clerical collar stepped up to the desk. "You say you're a preacher's son?"

"Uh, yes sir. My daddy's Reverend Joshua Lee of Lynchburg, Virginia."

"Well, son, I haven't heard of your father, but I can't believe a preacher's son would try to take unfair advantage. Perhaps you could explain to Charles here why you thought you should come to this office looking for work."

"I've got this letter of introduction." Will pulled the envelope out of his pocket.

Charles, the clerk, took the envelope and deftly opened it with a gleaming brass letter opener. He read over the contents. "Oh, I see." He folded it quickly. "Well, yes. I'll show this to Mr. McDonald." His tone was less abrasive.

"You go sit over there, Mr. Lee. This'll probably take a while," Charles added, almost kindly. "Oh, and I might suggest you would make a better impression than you have so far if you went downstairs to the washroom and cleaned your face and shaved your beard. Do keep up appearances…"

Will looked down at himself and saw his clothes were covered with dust. He rubbed his hand over his face and felt the day's growth of beard. When he looked at his hand he saw soot had rubbed off his chin onto his finger tips.

Will found the washroom easily. He took off his jacket and shook it out. He was alone in the washroom and took the liberty of stripping off his shirt. Pouring water from a pitcher into the basin, he started to wash himself using a bandana from his carpetbag. Just then the door to the washroom squeaked loudly. Will looked around, embarrassed to be caught half-dressed.

There was the man in the clerical collar.

"Did Mr. McDonald call for me?"

"Oh, no, not yet. There's still a long line ahead of both of us. It'll be a while. I, ah, came down to use the facility. Ah… I'm Pastor Sheldon Benedict, by the way."

"Will Lee."

Pastor Benedict selected one of the toilet stalls and closed the door. He remarked off-handedly, "Well, young man, you're certainly in fine condition. Good physique."

"Uh, thank you, sir." Will pulled out his razor and shaved hurriedly, then took a fresh shirt from his bag and modestly covered himself.

"Do you think Mr. McDonald will give me a job with the Indians?" he asked as the Pastor stepped out of the stall.

"Don't worry, son. Jesse McDonald's a fine man. If he likes you, he can certainly do something for you. A nice, attractive young lad like yourself shouldn't have any problems. And, besides, I'll vouch for you. I mean, here you are the son of a preacher…"

"Well, thank you, sir." Will tucked his shirt in and donned his jacket. "Shall we go up?" He wanted to get out of the washroom.

"After you, my boy." Benedict stepped aside.

As they climbed the stairs, Will allowed the clergyman to catch up with him. "Do you work for Mr. McDonald?"

"Not exactly. I have just returned from a stint of missionary work with the Navajo Indians in New Mexico. I'm just delivering a report to Jesse, ah, Mr. McDonald. We're old friends, you know." Then he added, "Thank God, I'm back to civilization and in my own parish again. My wife has missed me these many months."

When they reached the landing outside the Office of Indian Affairs, Benedict's voice dropped to a whisper, "I don't suppose I could interest you in a job here?

"Huh?"

"I mean, perhaps you'd like to become my apprentice. Stay here in Washington. You could stay with Beatrice and me. I could teach you and then, you know, after a while perhaps you could go to seminary…"

Will was surprised. He laughed as he pushed open the doors and stepped back to let Pastor Benedict precede him. "Oh, no, sir, I got a hankerin' to get out West…" He hoped that was true. At least, it was a good excuse. He wasn't interested in a job with the church. "Maybe I can help the Indians, too."

Benedict maneuvered them over to two chairs in the far corner. "Actually those savages are the vilest, most disgusting people—if I dare to call them people—I have ever had the misfortune to run across."

Now that he'd cleaned up and they were back in the waiting room, Will was getting sleepy. The excitement of the last two days had caught up with him. He struggled to focus on what Benedict was saying. His eyelids felt so heavy.

"But, my God, the Indians don't care a whit about saving their souls. Every day I patiently laid out the Lord's Word to them." Benedict droned on and on. "There was an old Indian woman, the general's maid, who seemed to want to improve her English. Why, I discussed theology with her, and I read the Scriptures to her and to the Indians daily for over a year. And you know what?"

Will startled. "What?" He feared he'd been asked a direct question.

"Not a one of them asked to be baptized," Benedict answered himself. "They just kept talking about their heathen god. Can you imagine anything so ridiculous? They worship a female god. I tried to explain to them the essence of God's nature as revealed in the Holy Bible. It is clear that the Creator could not be a woman. But they wouldn't pay any heed."

"Uh-huh," Will grunted. Benedict started talking about preaching to the Navajos about St. Paul's Epistle to the Romans, but Will didn't register a word of it.

"You look mighty sleepy, boy," Benedict finally noticed.

Will startled awake. "Oh, I guess, just tired from the train trip and all. Please go ahead. I'm really interested…"

That was the last he remembered.

The next thing Will knew the room was empty. All the men waiting to see McDonald were gone. The clerk was gone. Pastor Benedict was gone. He rubbed his eyes, then sat up and stretched. *What happened?* His heart sank. *What if I've slept through my appointment?*

"What a day, what a day."

Will could hear a booming voice coming from the inner office. The big door behind the clerk's desk stood half-open.

"First, everything is in an uproar about Congress wanting to impeach the President. And then all those people coming through here, everyone of them wanting something from me… I tell you it's just too much. And then, Shel, you come in here with your news."

"I'm sorry to be adding to your burden, Jesse."

Will recognized the second voice as that of Pastor Benedict. There were wagons rumbling by outside, and the noise drowned out most of the sound from the office.

After a bit he could make out Benedict's words again. "…handsome lad asleep out in your waiting room looking for a job."

With a shock, Will realized the minister was talking about him.

"What do we know about him," McDonald asked, "besides what you learned in the, er, waiting room?"

"He's got the prettiest eyes you can imagine."

"And, Jesse," the voice of Charles the clerk interjected, "he brought this letter of introduction from Harry Burnside..."

"Harry sent him? Well, Charles, let me see the letter."

After a moment, McDonald exclaimed, "Pshaw." Will heard him laugh. Then the sound was drowned out as another wagon rumbled by, this time accompanied by the squeals of pigs on the way to the slaughterhouse. Will wondered if those pigs he'd seen at the railway station were among them.

A moment later, Charles came out of the office and beckoned to Will. "Mr. McDonald will see you now."

The head of the Office of Indian Affairs was a heavy-set man, once handsome, but now going to fat. He was dressed in an expensive-looking three-piece suit with a brilliant-colored French silk cravat at his neck. A thick gold watch chain hung across the bulging vest, a heavy fob suspended from one pocket. He told Will that he truly appreciated the letter of recommendation from Harry Burnside and that he thought Will would make an excellent apprentice to the Indian Agent at Fort Sumner.

Will didn't raise any questions. He didn't want to jeopardize the job. He understood there was some sort of favoritism being extended toward him, perhaps because of the letter from Harry, perhaps also because of the hungry looks he spied in the faces of the government officials. He realized just how lucky he was to get the appointment. *That clerk who'd scolded me for being a former Confederate soldier certainly isn't the only bureaucrat in Washington who'd hold such a history against a job applicant.*

McDonald explained there was only one problem; they needed him to get out to Fort Sumner just as soon as possible. While McDonald and Benedict explained the expectations of the job, Charles went out and prepared the travel vouchers and official documents he'd need. By the time the job interview was over, Charles had railroad tickets, hotel vouchers, transfers to the stagecoach, and a little spending money—all in an attaché pouch ready for him. He was scheduled to depart on the morning train.

Both Mr. McDonald and Pastor Benedict offered to put him up for the night at their own homes. Will was grateful for the offers and said so. But he thought about the men's hungry looks and remembered Harry's advice and so very politely declined.

As Will was leaving the office, McDonald put his arm over his shoulder and repeated his instruction: "Be sure to send *all* your reports on the Indians directly to me. And pay attention to every single thing General Carleton tells you. And you'll do just fine in this job."

36

Bosque Redondo

So what were the circumstances? he asked himself again. It had all seemed pretty straightforward. *What had Gen. Carleton meant? Had he meant anything? Hadn't he just been treating me the same way my father did, manipulating me with vague suggestions and guilt-provoking innuendo?* Will drew a conclusion from his recollections.

"And if General Carleton is going to act like my father," he resolved aloud, "I will treat *him* like I did my father that last week in Virginia. I will simply ignore him."

Will wasn't sure how this resolution was going to work itself out in practice. But he figured Carleton didn't like him anymore than he liked Carleton. If he steered clear of the general, didn't ask him for anything for the Indians, and just groveled and flattered every time he couldn't manage to avoid the man, Carleton would probably be just as pleased to let him disappear.

As far as changing things goes, I'll write what I think needs to be done in my reports to Washington. And I'll contact Dr. Steck. Mr. McDonald had told him to send his reports straight to Washington. So far he had had no contact with Dr. Steck, his immediate superior at the Office of Indian Affairs in Santa Fe. But he would, he decided.

In fact, whenever I can figure out how to do it, I'm going to go to Santa Fe and see Steck personally.

Will's firm resolution quelled his agitation, and he drifted into the most restful sleep he'd had since arriving in New Mexico. He had a dream about what life might have been like for the Diné years ago, before their time of troubles.

As the dream began, Will found himself living among the Diné. He had been welcomed as a teacher who could help them learn English and understand the ways of the Hairy Face culture. In exchange, the Diné had provided him a place to live and taught him how to herd sheep, hunt jackrabbits with a bow and arrow, and locate water in the desert.

He was lucid enough to know he was imagining himself to be John Blewer. The time Blewer spent with the Diné outfit under Dezba's leadership had been a wonderful time. The people were living in their homeland, unaware that marauders would be coming to despoil their happiness. Their ceremonies to Changing Woman and the other Holy Persons helped them understand and participate in their proper place in the harmony of nature. They lived in warm hogans, food was abundant, the ghosts of the departed were honored and placated with offerings of herbs and sacred plants. Life was good.

Will would have liked to have known the Diné then, before his people became adversaries and before he found his own loyalties torn. Back then Hasbaá would have been only a youth, though already betrothed as a sacred mate to the tribe's bravest young man, Segundo.

But in the dream Hasbaá appeared about her age now—as Will had come to know her—and was dressed in the garments of a woman—also as he had come to know her. She opened the flap to her hogan and invited him to come inside.

As he did, he saw that inside with her was Segundo. Will recognized him immediately. He was dressed as a warrior. His face was painted. He wore only a loincloth and a beaded vest that opened to show a hard-muscled chest.

"This is my husband, Segundo," And then with a frank simplicity that surprised Will, Hasbaá added, "My aunt says you should join us."

The two Indians dropped their garments and knelt down, facing each other, on the thickly blanketed sheepskin floor. In the manner of dreams, Will discovered he was also naked now.

Segundo was tall, with broad chest and thick arms. His body was solid. He was hairless except on his head and at his crotch. From the lower patch of hair, his manhood hung full. Segundo's face was long, his nose prominent, his cheekbones high. Will was surprised to see that Segundo had green eyes, almost the color of his own.

Hasbaá was much thinner and more feminine, though she clearly had the chest of a male. But, to Will's surprise, she seemed to have the genitals of a female. He could not see a penis between her legs.

Segundo wrapped his arms around Hasbaá and pulled her to him. He entered her as a man enters a woman. Will felt the surge of sexual excitement himself as the two joined together. Segundo drove himself deep into Hasbaá. They moved rhythmically together; then both their bodies trembled. Hasbaá cried out in pleasure. Then fell back onto the sheepskin blankets.

Will saw that now Hasbaá did have a cock. He saw Hasbaá not as a woman but as a virile and strong young man. Now Segundo rose over her on his knees. He bent down and kissed her. Then he took her by the hips and pulled her up onto his lap. Again he entered her, but this time as a man enters another man.

Hasbaá looked up at Will. "Join us."

He found himself standing between Hasbaá and Segundo. They both knelt, so that their mouths were at the level of his pelvis. Hasbaá took Will's cock in her mouth—though now he understood in the dream that Hasbaá was a male and acted as a male, and so he wondered if he should use the masculine pronoun for her. Even in the dream he felt confused about pronouns.

Segundo licked at Will's testicles. His tongue teased the sensitive flesh at the base of his scrotum, while Hasbaá sucked and caressed Will's cock with her tongue.

Then Segundo rose and, to his surprise, entered Will from behind. This was something he'd never actually experienced. He didn't know what it could feel like. But he knew himself filled with the warrior's maleness and that that maleness was being pumped into him in this act.

Hasbaá pulled her mouth away and stood up. She looked deep into Will's eyes. Then looked away from Will's and into Segundo's.

Hasbaá's dream body now possessed both penis and vulva. Hasbaá reached down and lifted her testicles to guide Will's cock into the vulva down below the male parts. As he pushed inside, he could feel Hasbaá's erect cock against his belly.

Will was pressed between the two of them, penetrated and penetrating at the same time. He realized that he, too, could be both woman and man and that who he really was also somehow transcended both.

Then he felt Segundo ejaculate inside him. He felt the force of the warrior's strength drive deeper and deeper into him. And he also felt Hasbaá begin to writhe against him, and he clasped her torso with his hands and pulled himself deeper into her.

The wetness on the bedsheets roused him. The last thing Will could remember was an image of the three of them together, three men with their arms and legs intertwined on the sheepskins of the Diné hogan.

37

FORT SUMNER

Will awoke feeling more hopeful and more determined than he had since he'd arrived at Fort Sumner. After using the latrine and washing up, he sat at his desk and composed a letter to Gen. Carleton. He apologized for the two appointments he'd missed and for upsetting the general's dinner. He called his own behavior "shameful," and he flattered Carleton with flowery words of praise for his military accomplishments.

Then he offered an alternative to his previous suggestions which he thought the general would especially like. Will wrote that "we" should send a delegation to the most prominent New Mexican citizens in Santa Fe to apprise them of the situation and to explain why it was in their interests to keep the Indians peaceful. If these leaders prevailed on their own people to stop the raids, then the Navajos would be pacified, could be returned to their homeland, and would not require constant surveillance.

He volunteered to be part of the delegation, adding that this course of action would allow him to meet with Dr. Michael Steck, his superior officer in the chain of command at the Territorial Office of Indian Affairs.

He also said that he would obey the general's order not to go out on forages with the Indians or to do anything which would endanger his own safety, but added that he hoped the general's orders would not preclude his studying Indian ways and reporting this research to the bureau he was hired by.

On his way to the mess hall for breakfast, he took the letter by Carleton's office. The door to the cave-like office was closed, but in the next room Lt. Bauer sat writing at his desk.

"Did you want to see General Carleton?"

"Just want to deliver this letter."

"He'll be here shortly. You can wait."

"Oh, I don't know that General Carleton's going to want to see me of all people first thing this morning. I just thought a letter of apology for last night might be in order."

"You're probably right, mister," the lieutenant said. "On both counts."

Will placed the letter in its sealed envelope on the desk. "You'll be sure he gets this…"

"You can rest assured." The soldier seemed surprisingly amiable.

Relieved he hadn't had to talk with Carleton directly, but could let his carefully composed missive speak for him, Will went down to the mess hall. He ate ravenously, then returned to his quarters and started to draft a report about the Indians' vulnerability to slave raiders. He planned to write out two copies of it. One he would send to Jesse McDonald. The other he would take personally to Dr. Steck when he went to Santa Fe to meet with the New Mexican leaders.

Will summarized what he had learned from the Indians about their treatment by the army. While he detailed the abuses, he carefully balanced the account by noting the atrocities suffered by white settlers and soldiers alike. He emphasized the importance of distinguishing between the behavior of different Indian tribes. He remembered what Barboncito had told him. He questioned why the Navajos had been brought to live so close to the Comanche lands in nearby Texas. It seemed to be a tactical mistake to put the Navajos where their enemies would attack them and where the U.S. Cavalry would be required to protect them.

Clearly, whatever happened in the past, the treatment of these people right here and now was inhumane and counterproductive. "We're not going to bring peace to the Territory," he wrote, "by putting the Indians' safety in jeopardy, then enslaving them and subjecting them to harsh treatment. There is not enough food or shelter here for the size of their population."

Will felt good about the work he'd done. He liked his presentation and his cool-headed, reasoned arguments for treating the Indians humanely and helping them improve their situation with assistance from Washington so that they would feel grateful and indebted to the Hairy Faces. He was careful, of course, never to use that expression when referring to members of his own race. By the time he'd finished his first draft, he was proud of his persuasive writing style. *I'm certain this strategy is going to be successful!*

As Will started to edit the draft, there was a loud pounding on his door. Startled, he jumped up and threw open the door. It was Sgt. Peak.

"Letter from the gen'rl for you." There was a mean-sounding chuckle in his voice that suggested Will wasn't going to like it.

"Thank you, Sergeant."

He took the envelope and started to close the door, but Peak put out his hand to hold it. "Don't ya want me to carry your reply back for ya? Be happy t' help."

Will knew perfectly well Peak wanted to watch him read that letter. That made him all the more concerned about what was in it. But he was not going to give Peak the satisfaction. "Thank you, Sergeant," he said with feigned graciousness, "that won't be necessary."

"Well, that's up to you."

"You're quite right." Will closed the door in the soldier's face.

He sat down at the desk and carefully opened the letter from Gen. Carleton. Penned in the general's own hand, it read:

Mr. Lee,

Your suggestion is silly and naive. I will not risk my good relations with the citizens of New Mexico. Let me remind you that the New Mexicans have been loyal since we conquered this Territory twenty years ago. Which is more than I can say about you. Their loyalty saved this territory for the Union during our late bout with your Southern traitor friends.

The New Mexicans have proved themselves, resulting in my gratitude and support of them. The delegation you suggest would be an affront to their loyalty.

I will NOT cross the loyal sons of the Union for the sake of our enemies—savage or Southern.

As for you, Mr. Lee, you can go see your Dr. Steck any time you want. He is your superior. But do not expect me to waste my loyal soldiers' time giving you an escort. If you choose to go, you are on your own. I cannot and will not protect you, if you get my meaning.

And finally, Mr. Lee, you are welcome to study the Indians all you want. I don't give a damn what you do. You can go live with them for all I care. But let me remind you that you were sent out here to not cause trouble.

I promise that if you provoke unrest among the savages at the Reservation or if you incite any sort of skirmish with my men, I will have you hanged as a traitor sooner than you can say Johnny Reb.

> Loyally Yours, etc.
> J. C. Carleton
> Commander

His first reaction was that Gen. Carleton certainly liked the word "loyal," though his appreciation of its meaning was doubtful. Will felt utterly defeated. He'd thought he'd done so well. This reply simply discounted all his arguments—and all his groveling. Carleton was not going to allow anything to change.

Once again, Will noted, Carleton had made a reference to *why* he had been sent out here.

Feeling that his reports didn't matter a whit and annoyed with himself for having gotten so optimistic, Will put aside his morning's work.

He had wanted to be able to go down to the Diné settlement and announce that he'd arranged a breakthrough in relations with the Hairy Faces. Then he would have earned the Dinés' respect and, he hoped, proven to Hasbaá that he deserved the affection she'd been saving for Segundo. All those hopes now seemed dashed.

The dream of making love with Hasbaá... a stupid illusion. Why would Hasbaá care about me? I'm just another Hairy Face who can't keep a promise.

As he thought of himself as a Hairy Face, he reminded himself to shave. At least he didn't want to give any ammunition to that indictment. While he stropped his straight razor, he remembered that Peak had said his predecessor had cut the throat of an Indian woman right in this room. He'd probably sharpened the blade on this very leather strop. Will thought morosely about just cutting his own throat then and there. But it seemed he'd do better to cut the general's throat rather than his own.

He finished shaving, without cutting himself either intentionally or unintentionally. In spite of his dour mood, he decided to go over to the Diné settlement. *I need to ask Hasbaá what happened while we were dragging her back on the litter.*

38

THE PECOS RIVER

As Will walked toward the settlement a few minutes later, his mind raced. He kept restating his arguments about why something had to be done to improve the Indians' lot. He got so angry, in fact, that he was talking out loud. He made his way through the screen of trees along the riverbank. He could see Dezba with several others in front of the medicine lodge. He didn't see Hasbaá.

The sight of the old woman suddenly sent shivers through him. *What good does it do to shout at the general if nobody is listening? What good does it do to side with the Indians if I can't help them? What am I going to say to Dezba? I'd practically promised I'd get help for the Diné.*

Will had wanted to organize a search party and go rescue the boy who'd been stolen. Now he realized he'd just wanted to impress the Indians.

What am I going to say to Hasbaá?

Once again despondent and disheartened, Will detoured from his route and wandered down toward the creek. He was failing Hasbaá, failing the Indians. He felt hopeless. *What am I going to do?*

He thought about running off to be a cowboy. Maybe he could find Jose Flores. He thought about going back to Washington, D.C. Pastor Benedict had offered him a position as an apprentice. *But, my God, what would I do working for a church? And what had Benedict really wanted?*

Will wandered past the spot where he'd saved Hasbaá from Peak's assault and headed over into the pile of debris and branches that still sat there as a reminder of the flashflood. He sat down on a broken tree trunk to ruminate about his hopeless ambitions of freeing the Diné and proving himself to Hasbaá.

He had his eyes to the ground, and so he did not see that Hasbaá was coming down the riverbank in his direction.

The only person I'd felt any real closeness to back home was Michael. Then I'd felt something genuine, but so brief, for Jose the cowboy. And now there's Hasbaá. These feelings for Hasbaá are so much more complicated. Can I feel the same things for her that I'd felt for Michael and for Jose? But how am I supposed to feel those feelings for a religious visionary or for a man dressed in women's clothes?

The truth was what Will felt for Hasbaá *was* sexual. He felt pleasure just looking at her. *Was this love? Friendship? Lust?*

Hasbaá was a spiritual leader and visionary. Will could somehow accept that she'd dress in strange clothes. Religious people do that. But her strange clothes were women's clothes, and everybody called her by feminine pronouns. *How odd,* Will thought, *that what confuses my feelings is that everybody treats Hasbaá as a woman. What is wrong with me that that stands in the way of my feelings?*

Will's sexual nature had never seemed normal. Now he saw that was because what Hasbaá would call his spirit wasn't normal. Something in him had always wanted more than life was supposed to give. There was something in him that rebelled against the life he'd been expected to live and that sought other realms of existence. Not knowing what to do about that rebelliousness, he'd done the opposite: he'd given in, done what he was told, obeyed the rules, worried what other people would think. But that was all just because he hadn't known how to escape that reality.

He hoped, maybe, Hasbaá could show him how. In her, he saw the entry into other realms, where lay mystery and adventure, not rules and prohibitions. And, to his surprise, his longing for those other realms and his longing for love and the pleasures of the flesh seemed to be intertwined.

He remembered Walt Whitman's honorific devotions to human self-determination. "There is no one, not God, greater to me than myself is." A feeling of strength flowed back into him. He raised his gaze from the ground and started to get up and continue his trek to the Diné settlement.

"Don't move." Hasbaá's voice broke Will's reverie. There was the Indian standing only about ten feet from him, holding prayersticks in her hand.

"Huh?"

Hasbaá pointed to the ground between them. There a very large rattlesnake lay coiled. As Will looked, the snake raised its head and shook its rattle.

"Oh, God…" Will had always been deathly afraid of snakes. Almost in spite of himself, he panicked and jumped to his feet.

"Don't move," Hasbaá said again.

But he had already started to dart away. As he did, his foot caught in a tangle of roots. He lost his balance and fell flat on his face.

"Be still."

Will looked up, hoping to see Hasbaá with a club ready to kill the snake. But he found himself gazing right into the eyes of the snake. He had fallen inches from it. Will swore later that he could see drops of venom dripping from the long fangs.

He froze, half raised up from the ground. *How long can I hold this position?*

"Do something," he wanted to scream. But he didn't dare make a noise. In fact, he wasn't sure he could.

Will heard Hasbaá chanting. He bitterly thought she had begun the healing he'd require after the snake struck him in the face. He'd seen how much good all that chanting had done for old Baaneez.

It seemed to Will that time totally stopped, as he perched there motionlessly. The rattlesnake's fangs took on a kind of eerie prominence that made everything else go out of focus. Will imagined that this is what must be going through a cornered rat's mind as it waited for its certain death. He remembered seeing the rat and the blacksnake that day of his father's terrible sermon. He heard Hasbaa's somehow-calm chanting in the background, but everything in his being was now focused on those fangs and the piercing sound of the serpent's rattling tail. Will stopped thinking. Nothing but fear occupied his mind.

But then the rattling stopped and the snake slowly lowered its tail to the ground. Its eyes swung away from his. As Hasbaá continued to chant, the snake uncoiled and slithered away into the pile of debris.

Will relaxed. He let his head fall to the earth. He took a long, deep breath.

"Friend," Hasbaá called to him.

He had started to tremble all over. But then, sure now that the snake was gone, he jumped up. "How did you do that?"

"I did nothing," Hasbaá replied. "It was the power of Changing Woman."

"Well, I still want to thank you. Snakes and me never got along too good," Will said, laughing—more from the fear still coursing through him than from anything funny.

"Do not offend the spirit," Hasbaá scolded. "It has blessed us today by its presence."

All his muddled emotions of the morning suddenly rushed together. "Yeah," Will exploded. "I really feel blessed! First I was almost shot by some Mexican raider. Then I had an argument with the general that could cost me my job—and maybe my neck. I was trying to figure out what to do about you. And now I'm blessed outa my wits by a rattlesnake." He sat back down.

"What to do about me?" Hasbaá asked quzzically.

But Will wasn't paying attention. He just realized he'd sat back down on the pile of debris the snake had crawled into. There was no telling how many snakes were coiled up around there. Jumping away from the brush, he shouted, "I don't think I can take any more 'blessings.'"

Why am I angry at Hasbaá? For saving my life? Maybe I'm angry at myself for not being able to save the Indians. What am I supposed to do?

He looked helplessly at Hasbaá, as though she could give him an answer. He wanted her to reach out to him. He wanted to reach out to her. But for a long while they both just stood there silently. Hasbaá looked hurt, but she would not say anything. Will became anxious with the silence.

"What are *you* doing out here?"

"I am gathering prayersticks I placed earlier. I am preparing a ceremony."

"Well, I want to get outa here," Will said, feeling a shiver again. He hesitated. "I guess I'll see you later…"

He wanted to ask Hasbaá what had happened yesterday when she woke from her trance and gave him that look of affection. But he was afraid. So he let her continue on her ceremonial mission, and he continued his walk along the creek, though now staying far away from piles of debris.

He started to go back to his cabin, but he didn't want to leave things with Hasbaá like that. He thought that if he went to the settlement to see Dezba, he'd probably run into her later on.

39

THE MEDICINE LODGE

It only took Dezba a single look to see Will was troubled. "Sit down," she said.

After several false starts, he calmed down and explained about his confrontation with the general at the dinner table and about the note Carleton had dispatched to him this morning effectively eviscerating the plans he had to help the Diné. Will still had Carleton's letter stuffed in his pocket. He pulled it out and read it to her.

She did not seem to pay attention to any of it except the general's snide comment, "You can go live with them for all I care."

"Come live with us, Nephew," she said. "Join our family. We would welcome you."

"I can't do that," he answered, though he didn't know why he said it. "I am a Hairy Face. I may not be like the others, but I'm still one of them."

"You helped my people in the flood. You ran to the rescue of our daughter. Hairy Faces do not do this. You cried when Baaneez's spirit escaped the body. You drank the medicine at the healing circle. Hairy Faces do not do this…"

"Oh, I don't know."

"Come live with us," Dezba repeated the invitation. "Your skin is different. And you speak a different tongue. But your spirit is ours. I see it."

"What do you see?" Will challenged.

Dezba faced Will. "I see Segundo's spirit come back to us," she said.

"I'm not anything like Segundo."

"Segundo had green eyes. You have green eyes."

"How could Segundo have green eyes?" he asked, at the same time remembering this detail had been in his dream of Hasbaá and Segundo. "He was an Indian."

"Some of our people have green eyes," Dezba answered defensively. "Though you are right that most of us have brown, and Segundo's eyes were unusual. Do you remember I told you Segundo's mother was Diné but she was stolen from the people's outfit by a Hairy Face trapper? The members of her family were outraged that this happened. This was before the Diné had become used to the ways of Hairy Faces. A party of warriors went out into the hills and found her and the trapper. They killed that man for showing such disrespect to a woman. Nine months later, she gave birth to a son, Segundo.

"From his earliest childhood, Segundo swore he would prove that Diné blood was stronger than Hairy Face. Segundo was all Diné. We knew that. The only trace of his Hairy Face father was in his eyes. Segundo said his eyes were the color of spring.

"Hasbaá needs another spring. I know the color of your eyes reminds her of Segundo's. We Diné all need another spring. You, too... Do not give up hope. Changing Woman will lead you."

"Are you saying that Changing Woman wants me to come live with the Diné?"

"That is what Hasbaá told me," Dezba answered simply.

Will was surprised. Maybe he was right that that look in Hasbaá's eyes out in the desert had bespoken love and affection. He was mulling over what Dezba had said when Hasbaá came up from behind the hogan. In her arms were many prayersticks. In her eyes wariness.

"Tell this one what happened after you were wounded yesterday." Dezba sounded eager. She pointed at the seat next to her on the ground as if to say sit down.

Hasbaá looked hesitant.

"It is right for him to hear this," Dezba said firmly, "from your mouth, dear one." She excused herself and left the two of them sitting there together. Neither said anything about the events of the morning.

"As I was being dragged back to the settlement on the travois, I prayed for healing. Then Changing Woman reached down and picked my spirit out of my body and carried me up into the sky on the wings of a great hawk."

Will remembered seeing that hawk the day he arrived at Fort Sumner.

"We flew high into the air, up through a hole in the sky into the spirit world. There I was surrounded by many spirits and ghosts of our people. I have been carried there before, but still I was afraid. I had to calm my fear and pass beyond it, so I could see what was really happening. I listened to my heartbeat and watched my breath, and then the spirits and ghosts all changed into Holy Persons.

"Many times I have been taken up through the hole in the sky. That is how I was told I was a Two-Spirit Person when I was still very small and chose the women's gathering basket over the man's hunting bow. That time, my body was opened, and the organs of my insides were taken away and replaced by crystals and sacred plants. This was so I would have spirit powers.

"But this day no such thing happened. But Changing Woman's words were to me like being cut open. She said, 'It is time for you to leave your sorrows behind. They keep you from your work. I release you from your vow to never make love again.'

"I said, 'How can this be? Our people are still in pain. Must I not suffer with them?'

"Changing Woman answered, 'In your love is the answer to their pain.'

"I said to Changing Woman, 'It would dishonor Segundo.'

"Changing Woman said, 'You cannot help the people while your heart is downcast. By loving again, you release Segundo's spirit.'

"'Whom should I love?' I asked.

"'The Hairy Face who comes with an open heart,' Changing Woman answered. There was much talk among the other Holy Persons. They must have been as surprised as I was," Hasbaá said.

Or as I am. Will's heart began to race, and his face flushed.

"'How can this be? How can I do this thing with a Hairy Face?'

"And then Changing Woman showed me the color of your eyes. Segundo had green eyes..."

"Dezba told me."

"In those eyes, I saw his love for our people. In his eyes, I saw the sun rise over the Diné and restore us to the lands of our ancestors. In his eyes, I saw his love for me." Hasbaá's voice dropped. "Changing Woman said, 'None of this is an accident. It has a reason.'"

Hasbaá turned to Will and looked deep into his eyes. "You have a good heart." She reached out and took his hands in hers.

"I showed you how the pebble falling into the water makes ripples. I believe the ripples that went out from Segundo's life reverberated through the spirit-field and found a place in your heart."

Will felt the swirl of so many emotions. Her words thrilled him. Her touch made him shiver with excitement. He wondered if she truly loved him or if he were just a vessel for her superstitions.

"Come live with us," Hasbaá repeated Dezba's invitation, leaning forward and pulling him close to her, until their cheeks touched.

40

Dezba's Hogan

Hasbaá stood up and, wordlessly, led him to her hogan. This was not the medicine lodge, but a smaller structure nearby. They went inside and she pulled down the blanket covering the doorway. It was not unlike the place in his dream where Segundo and Hasbaá had bid him join them. There were sheepskins for laying out on the floor for sleep.

Inside, Hasbaá lay back on the sheepskin bedding and pulled Will down to kneel beside her.

"Can I just look at you?" Will was trembling with excitement. "I, uh, dreamed last night that I saw you and Segundo making love." His throat was dry, and he had to struggle to make himself get the words out. "You asked me to join you. I wanted to…"

"This will not remain a dream. I feel such feelings when I look at you, too." Hasbaá smiled sweetly. She began to unfasten her shirt. She cocked her head and, just a little coy, said tenderly, "You are pretty to me."

Seeing the expectation in her eyes, Will hastened also to unbutton his clothes. He didn't know how to speak about his feelings, but he echoed Hasbaá's words. "You are pretty to me too." His excitement surged as Hasbaá pulled off the shirt. Will trembled just looking at the Navajo's chest and shoulders. They playfully and quickly completed their undressing.

Naked, they held each other close. It seemed there was such excitement and such connection of soul and heart that they had only to hold each other. Will felt an outpouring of emotion and sensation. He had experienced sexual passion before with Jose Flores, and these sensations were like that. But there was something more, now with Hasbaá. His fascination with and attraction to Hasbaá had grown through weeks of confused emotions. He had ached with need for this unique person's touch.

He could feel warmth and energy flowing into him from Hasbaá's body. The flow of energies was strongest where their cheeks touched and where their loins pressed together. Will's cock grew full, and Hasbaá's touched his along its length. Where the heads touched lightly, a blaze of sensation blinded him to everything but his passion for Hasbaá and of Hasbaá's responding love for him.

Will wondered if the Navajos had sex like other people or if there'd be something as strange and different about their sexual behavior as there was about their religion. Hasbaá pulled her face away and looked into his eyes, and then kissed him full on the mouth. Remembering what it was like to kiss Michael and then Jose, Will realized making love with this Two-Spirit Person now would be no different, and, in fact, maybe easier, because it seemed so natural. As he kissed back, he felt himself being taken over by his desire and love for this sweet-hearted human being.

In that moment, Will realized that what he for so long had been searching for—the dear love of comrades—was not limited to those who defined themselves as a man. After all, Walt Whitman had used the word "comrades" rather than "men" to define his loving circle. Could the Eastern poet have visualized that far away in the West there were males who did not identify themselves as men? Hasbaá was both man and woman and, at the same time, neither. What Will now realized is that it was the male body, a body like his own, that he was attracted to, but that masculinity—being a man—was not a requirement.

In fact, he now saw that part of Hasbaá's attractiveness was the sweet feminine quality that made this person more like a woman than a man in character while still having the raw sexual attraction of the male body. Will reached down and felt Hasbaá's erect penis, recognizing that Hasbaá was not less than a man, but was actually more than a man. He clutched the hardness of Hasbaá's cock, feeling its heat and girth in his hand, but also being equally attracted to Hasbaá's feminine face. Will realized that in Hasbaa he had the best of both.

They rolled onto their sides and pulled away enough that each could watch as they held and stroked the other's sex. How good it felt to touch Hasbaá's body. Will turned his face again and they kissed deep as they pulled at one another, and then squeezed together again. They rolled over, kissing tighter, pressing closer.

Hasbaá pulled away and, swinging around so her mouth was to Will's loins, kissed Will's cock and then took it in her mouth. Jose had done this while Will had laid back and let himself to be made love to. Now he actively reciprocated and caressed Hasbaá's cock with his lips and tongue and then took it deep into his throat.

Will had never experienced anything like this before. It seemed so new. And yet so natural and automatic. A part of him wondered how he knew how to do this, how to make love. He'd calmed down a little by now and his heart wasn't racing anymore. He wasn't afraid. He didn't have to know what to do. His body was doing it; his mind had only to watch—and savor the pleasure he received and the pleasure he gave.

After a while they switched around again so they kissed mouth to mouth and held one another chest to chest and loins to loins. Then pulling each other tighter and tighter into their embrace, clutching hard at each other, they both were racked with the pulses of orgasm.

Hasbaá cried out. As that same cry rose in his own throat Will closed his mouth again against his beloved's. As they moaned together, they wriggled and quivered in pleasure with the rising and rising, and then gradually subsiding spasms. Finally, Will took a deep breath and sighed.

They lay together, full of feelings. "This is one of the most beautiful moments I've ever known." Will sighed again and turned his head to let his lips brush Hasbaá's.

"We live in beauty when we walk the way of Changing Woman." Hasbaá gave Will's romantic comment more mystical significance than he'd intended.

Later, when Will and Hasbaá threw back the flap and came outside, they found Dezba crouched by the cookfire near the hogan.

"I have been waiting for you to come out. Now I am going to General Carleton's office," she announced.

Will suddenly feared he'd misunderstood everything Dezba had been telling him. What if he'd committed some offense against the Indians, and now their leader was going to go turn him in?

"Uh, wh-wh-what are you going there for?"

"To clean the office," Dezba answered matter-of-factly.

"To clean the office," Will repeated in dismay. "Are you his maid?"

Dezba smiled and flashed her eyes.

"But, Dezba, you are the leader of your people. You shouldn't be doing that."

"Who else but the leader should be in the general's office?"

Not only was Dezba not angry with him, she was including him in her little joke on Gen. Carleton and the United States Army. Will laughed as the wave of anxiety that had gripped him faded away. He remembered Pastor Benedict had said the general's maid had been his recalcitrant Bible student.

"I have asked this sweet man to come to live with us," Hasbaá broke in. "He has agreed."

Dezba's face brightened. "I thought as much." She smiled. "I have prepared a meal for you. Please eat now." She gestured toward the food. "I must go." As she stood, she said to Will, "You will be welcome among our people." And to Hasbaá, "I am glad that you have finally listened to Changing Woman."

41

Dezba's Outfit

Will moved some of his clothes and personal belongings to Hasbaá's hogan. There was no official declaration, but Dezba and the other Indians began to refer to Will as "Hasbaá's husband."

"Does this make you my squaw?" Will asked.

Hasbaá spat on the ground. "Do not say such things, Husband."

"Aren't you my wife?"

"But the word you used is a bad word, disrespectful of women's place."

"I thought it was an Indian word," Will answered defensively.

"We hear this word among the Hairy Faces. That is how they talk about their women. Perhaps it once came from the speech of those you call Indians…" She said that last word as though it were strange to her. "But it is an ugly word. Do not use it."

Will was having to unlearn the few things he thought he'd known about Indians.

There was no writing desk in the hogan, so regularly he went back to his official quarters to work on the reports he was preparing for Dr. Steck. He wasn't sure how but he knew he was going to get to Santa Fe soon.

Ironically, that note from Gen. Carleton gave him all the permission he needed. He wasn't supposed to go on forays into the desert, but he'd been told he could go to Santa Fe and that he could spend all the time he wanted with the Indians. He knew he wasn't supposed to be causing trouble. *I don't think I am.*

Hasbaá was very demonstrative of Will as her partner. She insisted that he join in the daily activities of the outfit. One afternoon, while he was working on his reports, she came to get him.

"We are having a Friendship Dance. You must come and dance with me."

Will followed her down to the Diné camp. Several men who sat in the middle of the space by the medicine lodge began a drumbeat. Around them a circle formed. People of every age, from kids to elders, participated. They laughed and joked with one another as they paired up. This was apparently not a solemn ceremonial.

"We are celebrating friendship." Hasbaá took hold of Will's hand and pulled him behind her to her official place at the head of the line. "You watch my steps. It's easy."

The dear love of comrades. Of course, I'll follow.

Will stumbled a little at first, but quickly caught on. Most of the couples who joined in the dance behind him and Hasbaá were man and woman, but there were also women with women, men with men, old women carrying little children, and men with young boys. This was a celebration of friendship, after all.

Not all the Indians seemed pleased with his presence. He noticed a few men made angry scowls when Hasbaá took his hand and pulled him into the dance. These warriors, understandably still bitter toward the Hairy Faces, abandoned the circle, taking some of the women and children with them, and stalked off angrily. Will worried Hasbaá's stature in the tribe might be compromised. But most of the others seemed to welcome him. They'd heard about his efforts to help the Diné people; they must have trusted Hasbaá's intuition that this particular white-skinned man was on their side.

Will felt proud to be included. There'd been no ceremony to declare him and Hasbaá "married." From what he'd seen the Diné did not appear to celebrate marriages as such, but they did obviously acknowledge personal bonds. Women were not given to men, as they were in marriage in the Christian world. Men moved into the homes of their partner's mother. It was the mother's recognition that mattered. But now as the dance progressed, Will got a little giddy. He began to imagine he and Hasbaá were leading the people in their wedding march. *For the whole world to see...*

To Will's chagrin, he saw that one other person who watched was the obnoxious Sgt. Peak. Will had seen him occasionally surveying the Diné camp from afar, much as he had that day after the flood. He was sure Peak saw that he was living with the Diné. Now he participated in their dances, as Hasbaá's partner.

Will didn't know what difference it would make that Peak saw. The other soldiers didn't seem to notice anything he did. His friend Mac McCarrie—with that same enigmatic, knowing wink he had seen before—congratulated him, but warned him "not to be gettin' cunt-crazy." He did not know what that meant, but Will was simply grateful that McCarrie didn't seem to think there was anything wrong about his staying among the Diné. And so he felt relatively comfortable moving back and forth between the Diné camp and the soldiers' fort.

Dezba and Barboncito treated him just as if he'd always lived among them. He thought they were pleased to see that Hasbaá finally had a new husband and looked happy again. His role as Hasbaá's husband seemed almost totally accepted. It was as if this relationship gave them a way to locate him within the Diné family system and that was what they wanted.

A few of the Indians from surrounding outfits clearly disapproved. Hasbaá admitted to him that some of her people grumbled that she had no right to do this. Another of the Two-Spirit Persons on the reservation had come to her one day and complained that she dishonored Segundo's memory. But when Hasbaá explained her vision, the Two-Spirit agreed she should follow the Holy Person's instructions. It was the warriors who most disapproved, but they had no authority over Hasbaá. Some simply refused to believe a Hairy Face could be a human being.

Will worried, in spite of Hasbaá's assurances, that one of the warriors might be overcome by—perhaps, understandable—hatred for the white man and kill him in his sleep. He heard from McCarrie that the Mescaleros on the reservation had gotten wind of his camaraderie with the Navajos in Dezba's outfit and warned that this could only bring trouble. He answered McCarrie that he'd just have to take that chance, though it added to his worries.

Will and Hasbaá made love every night. At first, it seemed, both of them were racing to make up for the years of denial each had experienced. But soon the urgency passed. Once his body no longer felt so sexually deprived, Will learned to hold back his ejaculation. Hasbaá, who was remembering her own lessons about lovemaking, patiently taught him how to enjoy sex leisurely, to stretch out the experience to gain pleasure and to savor more than just physical release.

Soon Will felt confident to take a more active role. It gratified him to know he was able to evoke in his lover's body pleasures as she evoked in his. There was so much more to lovemaking than just the actions of the body. He was discovering the deep emotional roots that sex caused to grow.

Sex was more marvelous—and somehow more beneficial—than Will had ever imagined. He had once believed that having sex and spending seed robbed one of vital energy and life force. He imagined having sex would cause one to lose vigor and become dissipated and degenerate. But it seemed the truth was just the opposite.

Will was coming to life. His fearful detachment and somber introspection faded away. He lived less in his memories. He started to laugh more. The sexuality that had previously seemed so disturbing to him now seemed perfectly natural.

Hasbaá, too, was changing. While the mystical quality still surrounded her, she dropped the mournful seriousness which previously characterized her presence. She became quite voluble, in fact, with Will. They talked for hours.

42

THE MEDICINE LODGE

One evening during the second week of Will's membership in the Diné family, he and Hasbaá sat outside the medicine lodge in an area which Will had come to see as a meeting place for the Diné to talk about spiritual questions. Will presumed that was so they could easily consult with Hasbaá, clearly identified as the expert on such matters.

Several others, including Dezba and Barboncito, had joined the circle. Will was surprised, and pleased, to see their warm smiles when Hasbaá expressed her affection by resting a hand on his leg. He was sure everybody must have been able to hear them make love at night in the hogan. He was glad to see they wholeheartedly accepted it.

When a child began to cry somewhere outside the circle, Hasbaá left to attend to it. Will had noticed that Hasbaá seemed to be every child's substitute mother and nanny.

"Hasbaá is very lucky to have a family who accepts her for the way she is. My father would never accept this," he said to Dezba and Barboncito.

"On the contrary," the old man answered, "it is we who are lucky. A family which has a *nadleehí* born to them is considered by everyone to be very fortunate. A *nadleehí* brings the hogan good luck. It does good for the country to have people like Hasbaá around."

"You do not yet realize how lucky *you* are to be chosen as the husband of a *nadleehí*." Dezba ignored Will's embarrassment and went on. "You will see how well you will be treated and how happy you will be together. Your coming here was not an accident. You were sent by Changing Woman, first to save Barboncito from drowning, then to help Hasbaá find happiness. Now that you have passed the tests set before you by Changing Woman, you are destined to be of great help to the Diné. And you will find yourself at the same time."

He was moved and challenged. *What can I do to be of great help to the Diné?* Will had seen how firmly his fellow Southerners had resisted the abolition of African slavery. He decided it would be hopeless to expect the New Mexicans to give up their Indian slaves willingly. He also decided it would be useless to try to persuade Gen. Carleton to change his policies; Carleton obviously profited personally out of all this. The only thing to do was bypass him. The slave raiding seemed the greatest threat to the Diné. And it seemed obvious that as long as the Indians were enslaved by the New Mexicans, the raids would not cease. *It is my destiny to launch an attack on slavery.*

Even after Hasbaá returned to the circle and the easy banter started again, Will was caught up in plans for his frontal attack. The Indians were always good about including him, but he let them carry on in Diné, while he drafted a letter in his mind. *I will write to President Johnson. And I will write to the Secretary of the Interior and, even, to Senator Charles Sumner. Surely Sumner will want to stop the Fort's tacit approval of the New Mexicans' enslavement of the Indians, if not the army's de facto enslavement of them right here on the reservation.*

Will spent the next two entire days drafting and redrafting his letters. Then he wrote out fair copies, sealed them, and took them to the fort's tiny post office. Mail was carried back to civilization by passing stagecoaches or couriers. He knew it might take a while to get an answer. But at least he had started.

43

Fort Sumner

Meanwhile, Will wanted to do something practical to help. With thousands of Indians scattered over the reservation, there wasn't much he could do directly for most of them. But he could, at least, help those who lived in the outfit that had now become his own home.

The lack of food was the most immediate daily problem. Despite the Diné's hospitality and their willingness to share their meals with him, Will realized they had no food to spare. A practical thing he could do was to return to eating at the soldiers' mess. *At least I won't be taking food from hungry children.*

So while he spent most of his days among the Diné learning their culture, practicing their crafts, helping with farming and other household tasks, and joining Hasbaá in ceremonies, each evening he went in to Fort Sumner to eat. He did himself a favor, too. He needed to eat better. He'd lost weight during the two weeks he spent in the settlement.

Occasionally, the soldiers' rations would consist only of beans and cornbread, but most nights there were piles of smoked meats put out for them. Though the area around the reservation looked desolate, this was cattle country. Wild beef was plentiful in the nearby Texas plains, and Gen. Carleton's trader friends seemed almost always able to supply the fort with meat.

It vexed Will that if there were money sent from Washington to provide for the Indians, why was there never enough food to go around? Yet the soldiers usually ate well. He could understand why the army gave its own men first priority, but it looked to him as if the good food was squandered while the Indians starved.

One evening as he finished supper, sitting near the kitchen door, he noticed that not only were there slabs of meat left on platters on the serving table, but back in the kitchen there were even larger piles. He figured the leftover meat from tonight's dinner would probably be served again in some other form, perhaps in a stew later in the week or as hash. But still there was so much meat, a piece or two would never be missed. With such abundance, the cooks were not likely to keep track of who took what.

Partly because Will felt ostracized, he'd developed a pattern of arriving late, entering by the back door—so he didn't have to pass the head table where nightly the general held court—and eating by himself at one of the tables just outside the kitchen. And partly because of his egalitarian streak and his tendency to avoid the amenities afforded the officers, he did not leave his dishes to be picked up by the clean up crew, but carried them into the scullery off the kitchen himself.

So this evening it was simple for him to make a slight detour on his way back from the scullery to pick up a large slab of smoked beef and stash it inside his jacket. Of course, it was going to leave grease stains on his shirt and his jacket would smell like a smokehouse for days, but what did that matter compared to the hunger of his friends?

He ducked out the back of the kitchen, totally unnoticed, with his stolen treasure clutched to his ribs and headed directly for the settlement.

Fifteen or so Diné, adults and children, sat around a small campfire. They'd just finished a supper of gruel made from the cornmeal that was the one thing always allotted them in the government rations. They prepared it in clay pots over the small fire and served it with a frybread cooked in government-issue iron skillets.

As Will sat down in the circle, he grinned slyly. He opened his jacket, pulled out the large piece of meat and presented it grandly to Dezba. All the Indians, especially the children, began to jabber with excitement.

Dezba calmed everybody down, thanked Will, and then cut the slab into pieces for everyone. The children devoured the rich smoke-flavored meat. Hasbaá ate more slowly, but in her eyes Will could see her gratitude. After everyone was finished, Hasbaá led them in a song of thanksgiving. Its smooth, beautiful melody enthralled Will. He realized the song was sung to him.

"Did General Carleton give you the meat to bring to us?" Dezba asked.

"Not exactly."

"Where did it come from?" Hasbaá asked with a note of suspicion.

"Oh, it's good." Will could accept Hasbaá's concern. Everyone in the West had heard stories about how the Hairy Faces had given blankets and supplies to the Indians, gifts that turned out to be infected with disease.

"It came from the soldiers' dinner," he explained. "There was just a lot of meat out in the kitchen. So I picked this up for you."

"Thank you, thank you," Dezba exclaimed. "See how happy the children look. They smile more tonight than we have seen in many months."

"You stole this from the rations for the soldiers?" Hasbaá looked worried.

"How could I steal what was put out for anyone to take?" He tried not to sound too defensive. "There was more than enough."

"I, too, am grateful to you." Hasbaá put a hand on his arm. "But the Hairy Face soldiers would not be happy to know you did this good thing for us."

Will realized that if the Hairy Faces found out about this, it would be the Indians who'd be punished. "I will be careful," he answered softly.

The next night, he brought an old shirt tucked inside his jacket so he could wrap the meat and not spoil his clothes. Again the smoked meat was piled high both on the serving table and in the kitchen. Again he snatched up a piece as he left the dining hall. Again the children squealed with joy and anticipation when he arrived.

The third night, when he came prepared to steal another treasure of food for the Diné, he discovered supper was indeed a stew. There was no way he could bring any of this back. He especially regretted this because the stew included fresh carrots. *How long has it been since any of the children have eaten any vegetables?*

Will arrived at the campfire empty-handed that night. The adults all understood, but the children gathered round him and pulled at his clothes. They acted as though he were playing a trick on them and that, at any moment, he'd open his jacket to reveal yet another gift. This made Will all the more committed to continue bringing meat for them.

The next two nights he was again successful. One night, he came with several thick slices of roast pork dripping with sweet fat.

After the pilfered treasures had been consumed and the Indian families had led their children away for another night of sleeping without hunger, Hasbaá announced very solemnly for the elders left in the circle to hear, "You should not do this anymore."

Will looked at her baffled. "Why not? Your family is hungry."

"You should not steal."

"How can you care about my stealing meat from the soldiers? They stole your homeland from you."

"Changing Woman warned me you must stop this."

"Well, thanks for your concern. But I've got this down pat. The cooks'll never miss the meat. I'll be extra careful. Stop worrying. And you can tell Changing Woman not to worry either."

Will's little joke did not sit well with Hasbaá. "Don't think you can tell Changing Woman what to do. We Earth People must respect the spirit world. If Changing Woman tells us to do something, we accept her wisdom as best. We must trust her. You have not yet learned how to be fully civilized."

"Well, thanks for the gratitude," he shot back. He wanted Hasbaá to take him in her arms and hug him and make love to him for his efforts to help her people. But instead she was preaching this superstitious religion of hers.

"Well, at least the children's stomachs have been full this week. What has Changing Woman ever done better than that? Seems to me that Changing Woman has not paid much attention to the problems of your people." Will took out his frustration and confusion on Hasbaá.

"You must *never* speak such words about Changing Woman. Faith in her is the only strength we have left. If we lose faith, we have no hope. We will then be truly abandoned."

Will regretted his sacrilegious remark.

"You must be patient with Changing Woman." Hasbaá's tone softened. "Her powers to help us are weak since the Diné were never meant to live here. We must return to our homeland in order for her to be able to make us strong again. Still, even here, her powers can help us if we keep faith. I fear your doubt and disrespect will bring harm upon you.

"Husband," she said imploringly but firmly, "you must promise me you will not steal any more meat. I worry about your safety."

"All right, all right. If it will make you stop worrying so much, I'll think about it. But I'm still concerned about food for the children."

Hasbaá looked back at Will with piercing eyes. "I'm concerned about food for *all* the children. There are thousands of hungry children here. Can you hide enough meat under your coat for all of them? It is more important for you to remain free and use your authority to get the Hairy Faces to let us return home.

"You spend your efforts trying to protect us from the raids of the New Mexicans or to bring us a little extra food. We don't want more army rations. We don't want more guards to protect us. Haven't you heard a word we have said? We don't want the improvements you've tried to make. We want to go home."

Dejected, Will went back to the Indian Agent's quarters that night and to his lonely little cot. He did not sleep in Hasbaá's arms.

He did not sleep much at all, in fact. He lay awake for a long time and fussed at himself, at Hasbaá, at the impossible circumstances he was in. *I'm just one person. How am I supposed to save the Navajos? It's not my fault they're on this goddamn reservation. If that damned Segundo hadn't made that stupid bet and then gone and got himself killed, they wouldn't be in this situation.*

First he—she—Oh, I don't know what the hell Hasbaá is... First, she says she loves me, then she tells me I haven't listened to a word she's said since I came out here. Hey, I'm the one that's kept trying to help... Hasbaá would never have spoken to me if I hadn't kept after them. My God, I risked my life for them. Yeah, I was risking my neck for them every time I brought them a goddamn piece of meat.

In the morning, he felt a little calmer. He realized Hasbaá had been right. Making things better for the prisoners in a hell-hole isn't nearly as important as getting them out of the hole. The Northern abolitionists had been right. They had not worked to make conditions better for the slaves in the South; they had declared that slavery was evil to its core and needed to be abolished entirely. President Lincoln had not written a proclamation to improve the situation for slaves; he had freed them. Will had to take the same approach to free the Diné from their imprisonment at the Bosque Redondo.

After breakfast, Will wrote another round of letters to the officials in Washington. This time he stressed the importance of allowing the Diné to exercise self-determination in where and how they would live. He felt especially proud of this set of letters. *This is what I should have said in the first place.*

Will turned the letters in to the post office, then went back to his quarters and napped for a while to make up for his sleepless night. He woke up a little before suppertime and made a decision. As he had done today, he would start working for the Diné's release from the reservation. *But in the meantime, I will continue to take them food. Maybe not every night, but at least occasionally. I'm sure that when I come to the campfire tonight with another slab of meat and the children squeal and laugh, Hasbaá will see I am right about this. It doesn't have to be one or the other.*

That evening, confident in his resolution though worried about crossing Hasbaá, Will went to supper. He took his customary seat near the kitchen. As usual, there was meat out for the soldiers—and more meat than they could eat. He ate slowly, giving most of the others time to finish and leave the mess hall. The clean-up crew was gathering the dishes from the officers' tables. Everything was as usual.

No, one thing is different, Will told himself as he nervously looked around and began to fight with himself about whether he should stick to his hard-headed decision. The cook, who had usually disappeared from the kitchen by this time, stood behind the serving table. Occasionally, it seemed, he glanced over at Will.

Well, no matter. I'll grab a piece from the kitchen. Nobody's in there.

Will picked up his dishes and carried them to the scullery. He started to walk back over to the table in the kitchen where the meat was laid out when he recalled Hasbaá's words: "Changing Woman warned me you must stop this." Will felt his determination wither. *What if I get to camp and Hasbaá is angry because I disobeyed her?* He didn't want to cross her. Even the one night sleeping by himself, he felt bereft. And he wondered if he dared cross Changing Woman. He remembered the presence he'd felt in the sweat lodge. He remembered the rattlesnake looking him in the eye.

Thinking better of his earlier resolution, Will did not reach for the meat, but turned and headed out of the kitchen.

There, to his surprise, was the cook standing in the doorway. In one hand he wielded a large fork. Will had an image of the cook suddenly descending upon him with that fork and stabbing him in the hand if he had reached for a piece of the meat.

Will started to tremble. "What are you lookin' at?" He feigned innocence. "That sure is a big pile o' meat. 'Nuff for an army." He laughed nervously, then turned on his heel and headed out the back door. Empty-handed but free.

He headed down toward the circle he knew sat around the fire. Halfway through the darkness, he stopped and looked up into the star-filled night. *Thank you, Changing Woman,* he proclaimed. *Pardon my impatience and disrespect. I'll find another way to help.*

Hasbaá was waiting for him. He opened his jacket to show he had not brought any meat. Hasbaá smiled and embraced him affectionately. He felt such a relief. He hadn't got caught. And he had been welcomed back into his beloved's arms.

He did not tell the Diné about how he almost got caught. Or about his amazement that Changing Woman's warning had come just in time. But Hasbaá seemed to know. None of the Diné, even the children, complained that he came empty-handed. They were all glad just that he came.

After the children had gone to bed, Dezba said to Will, "I have something to tell you you will not like."

Fearing she was going to tell him that for some reason he would have to break off his relationship with Hasbaá, Will felt his stomach turn. "What is it?"

"I was cleaning the general's office this afternoon. I heard somebody in Lt. Bauer's office next door. A soldier came to Bauer. He said he had some more letters from the Indian Agent. He wanted to know if he should leave them in the general's office. The lieutenant said to give them to him and he'd take care of putting them in the file. Do you know what this means?"

"Oh, God. What that means is that General Carleton is intercepting my letters. Damn, damn, damn. And putting them in a file! I bet nothing I've written has been sent anywhere. None of my reports. None of my requests for more food or better conditions.

"I've been writing them to document the problems here: the lack of shelter, the slave raids, the inhumane treatment, all the unnecessary deaths. I'll bet none of it got through."

Hasbaá sat down beside him and put her arm over his shoulder sympathetically. Then she sat back and turned to him and asked, not at all sympathetically, "When are you going to give up on these reports? Don't you understand? Your Washington *does not care* what happens to starving Diné on the frontier. You seem to think if you simply tell them what is happening, they will act to correct things. But you are wrong. This Great Father of yours in Washington does not care. It does not matter whether your reports were sent or not. Even if they had been, all they would do is sit and gather dust."

"Thanks a lot," Will muttered.

The circle, Dezba, Barboncito, Hasbaá, Will, and several other adults sat in morose silence. Then Hasbaá stood and raised her hands toward the sky, almost as Will had a little while before.

"Oh, Changing Woman," she prayed, "give guidance to this man. He has a good heart, but he does not think well. Tell him what he should do." She stood staring up toward the stars. Will wondered how long this was going to go on. Then a wind blew up suddenly, and an owl screeched.

Hasbaá announced, "Changing Woman says you have been trying to persuade the government by talking about the Dinés' needs. Even if your letters had been sent, they have heard talk like that for years about many tribes. They have never acted. Changing Woman says you must forget the needs of the Diné and appeal to the needs of the government. That is what they will act on."

"What does that mean?" Will inquired, a little testy.

"Changing Woman means you must show that General Carleton's policies are bad for the Great White Father."

"How do I do that?"

Hasbaá laughed scornfully, "How should Changing Woman know? *You* are the Hairy Face. You are part of the government. We Diné do not even have such a thing."

Will felt betrayed by Changing Woman's obtuse advice, but he began to scheme. "Hasbaá," he said, "ask Changing Woman to help. I think what I must do is go to Santa Fe and see Dr. Steck."

That night, Will slept again in Hasbaá's hogan. They made love for a long time. Will kept remembering his dream of sex with Hasbaá and Segundo. He recalled how in the dream Segundo had entered him and he'd felt the brave's strength injected into him. He knew now he needed strength and luck. Perhaps Hasbaá's powers could strengthen him. He asked Hasbaá to put aside her role as wife and be husband to him as Segundo had in the dream.

Hasbaá seemed to sense the connection with Segundo also. Will had noticed her sometimes look at him inquisitively and smile to herself as if she beheld some part of her long lost love return to her. As they made love—and Hasbaá initiated him into a kind of sex he had not known before—he imagined Segundo's spirit actually completing the sexual bond between the three of them. When Hasbaá came inside him, Will felt as if the spirit of Segundo had entered him and was now part of the person who was William Lee.

Hasbaá lowered herself so she lay against the muscles of his back. They stayed together like this for a long time, with Hasbaá remaining inside him. Will felt so safe and secure. Now that fate had brought them together, was it possible for anything to come between them?

I hope not.

44

DEZBA'S HOGAN

Will woke in the morning loosely cuddled in Hasbaá's arms. He rolled over on the sheepskin, pulled away a little, and gazed into her face. Without the characteristically feminine shirt and skirt, Hasbaá was simply a soft and fine-featured young male. The Navajo looks presented a kind of austere handsomeness.

Will was in a state of absolute wonderment. It seemed a lifetime, but it was, in fact, only just over six weeks ago that he fled his father's wrath. Then he was a farmboy, barely even aware of the power of love and sex, still only occasionally touching himself in secret and suffering guilt and self-recriminations and making firm resolves never to do it again. Now he was the chosen husband of the spiritual leader of the Diné people, freely making love with this beautiful and powerful person, routinely sharing affection openly in view of all his family and reveling in their love and acceptance. And *now* he was making resolves to wage battle with the U.S. Army—at least on paper—and thereby to save this wonderful human being, this welcoming family, and this ancient culture.

Hasbaá lay bare atop the creamy white fleece. Will marveled in the look of her rich brown flesh and dark black hair. Indians, he had discovered, generally possessed a thicker, oilier skin than whites. This made them practically hairless, protected them from sunburn, prevented wrinkles, but allowed deep creases to form with age in their faces, and gave them a smooth well-fed look, even when they were starving. Hasbaá's flesh was typically Indian, but because she was so tall and thin, her skin pulled tighter around her body and defined her musculature more than in most.

Will's own flesh was white. Where it was exposed to sun, it had reddened and dried. His skin was very thin and showed every muscle and sinew and vein beneath it. He thought he looked as if he were starving, even when he was well-fed.

Recalling his close call last night, Will once again thanked Changing Woman, surprised that he seemed to be getting religious again. He roused Hasbaá.

"Good morning."

Hasbaá answered in Diné. Will recognized the words. He felt proud of himself for beginning to pick up Hasbaá's language. That was how it was supposed to be.

"I'm going to the fort for breakfast. I don't want the cook to think I'm acting guilty after last night. If I show up for breakfast, everything'll seem normal."

45

Fort Sumner

As Will came through the screen of trees, he noticed there were rolls of cloth lying around on the ground in front of his official quarters. *Was this some kind of trap set by the cook or by Sgt. Peak? What could it be?*

Will went over toward the cabin. As he neared, he spied several horses tied at the back of the building. At that moment, one of the rolls of cloth moved. Will startled, then called out. "Hello?"

"*Buenos días, señor,*" said an unfamiliar, heavily accented voice.

It's the New Mexican raiders. Will started to panic.

"*Ah, Guillermo Lee, mi amigo,*" another voice spoke up. This one was familiar.

Will scolded himself for being so skittish. *Have faith in Changing Woman. It is none other than Jose Flores.* He'd learned enough Spanish in his weeks at Fort Sumner to appreciate what a pretty and appropriate name this man had—Jose of the Flowers.

"What are you doing here?" He rushed over and bent down to his friend who was struggling with the bedroll.

"*Ay, es muy caliente,*" Jose complained. "What are *you* doing here? I thought you were going to live with Indians. This is a desert here. No Indian in his right mind would live here."

"There's a story to that. What are *you* doing here?" he repeated.

"Me and *mis amigos* arrived late last night. The sentry sent us over here. But you weren't in your cabin."

"How come you're here at all?"

"We came to visit you."

"But you were in Kansas..."

"Oh, *yo comprendo*. After that trail drive to Kansas, when we met, *Señor Will*, us guys worked around there for a while hunting strays that had gotten out of the corrals. Then we heard about a job in El Paso with a trail drive coming up from Mexico.

"So you were not so far out of the way. I said to *mis amigos*, 'I have a friend on the Navajo Reservation at Fort Sumner on the Pecos River.' They all agreed we would come to see you." Jose looked around again at the desolate countryside. "I did not realize what I was getting us into."

"It is pretty hot and dry round here. But, hey, Jose, I'm very glad to see you. I think of you often."

"I think of you, too…" Jose's voice held lascivious inflection.

"Oh, yes." Will began to wonder how he was going to deal with this new wrinkle in the fabric of his life.

Will took Jose and his *amigos* down to the Sutler's Store for breakfast. This was a privately operated business just outside the compound of Fort Sumner. Here a wide variety of supplies and goods were available for purchase. Will showed the visitors around the fort, though he stayed away from the officers' quarters lest they run into Gen. Carleton. Then, leaving the four *amigos* back down at the store, he led Jose over to the Diné settlement.

"I'm husband of a Navajo," he said to Jose as they walked.

"Congratulations, *mi amigo*. So now you will settle down and raise a family of Indian *niños*."

"Not exactly. It's different from that, Jose. The person I am husband of is, uh, not a woman. But he looks and dresses like a woman."

"Ah, I know of such things," Jose said. "You are the husband of a *berdache*, yes?"

"*Berdache?*"

"That is what my friend the Frenchman called the Indian men that live like women. You remember," Jose added proudly, "I know French."

"I remember," Will answered. "I don't know about *berdache*, though I know the Navajo believe there are people who are both man and woman, Two-Spirit Persons."

"Aye, that is *berdache*." Jose's words seemed timid for a man always full of self-confidence and gusto. "Does this mean you aren't playing with the *amigos* in the tent?"

Will was grateful Jose asked. He hadn't known how to bring up the subject. "Guess so."

"*Que lastima.* I was looking forward to…"

"I know," Will interrupted. He didn't actually know if Hasbaá expected sexual exclusivity of him, but he'd been brought up to believe one can be married to only one person. Besides, he realized, for all that he frequently remembered the night with Jose, his emotions and affections had become so focused on Hasbaá and his life so obsessed with helping the Indians, he didn't feel the urge to have sex again with Jose. At least, not now.

This surprised him, since his memories of Jose were so frankly sexual. He remembered his dream of making love with *both* Hasbaá and Segundo. He knew Jose could play the third role in something like that. In fact, he thought that would be nice. *Maybe someday.*

When he first saw Jose that morning, his reactions had been a mixture of excitement and fear. He felt his love for Hasbaá challenged as though he would have to make a choice between the Indian and the cowboy. Jose's easy acknowledgment allayed that fear. There was no choice asked.

When Will and Jose arrived at the settlement, several of the Indians immediately hid. They, just as Will had earlier, mistook Jose for a slave raider. Will, therefore, went right to the hogan where he and Hasbaá lived.

"This is the man I told you about," he said to Hasbaá. "He's a cowboy from Texas. He first showed me how men can make love with each other. He's a friend."

Hasbaá took to the young cowboy right away. Perhaps she saw in him, too, a little of the blend of maleness and femaleness that was the essence of her own personality. At any rate, she did not seem at all threatened. In fact, after they'd talked awhile, she suggested Will team up with Jose.

"My husband wants to go to Santa Fe to see the officials of the government there. We Diné have been ordered not to leave the reservation. We cannot escort him. I believe Changing Woman brought him a friend to help him with this journey."

"You want me to go with Will to Santa Fe?"

"I cannot go by myself," Will admitted. "I'd get lost in the desert."

"Ay, you are right, *Americano*." Jose laughed and slapped him on the back. "You need a cowpoke, like me, who knows the range."

Will was a little embarrassed. But, of course, this was true. "Do you know how to get to Santa Fe?"

"Why, of course, just follow the river. In fact, my friend Jesse lives in Santa Fe. I haven't seen him in three years."

"What about your job in El Paso?"

"Who needs that job? There are jobs in Santa Fe. I will go there and visit Jesse and his wife Thanya."

46

THE NEW MEXICO DESERT

Jose's four *amigos* would continue on to El Paso, it was decided. But Jose would go with Will to visit his friend in Santa Fe and to act as Will's guide. Jose, ever the free spirit, seemed to rejoice in changing his plans and going off to do something totally spontaneous. Will envied him. *If I were as free, I wouldn't need to seek an escort.*

Will spent the day completing the report he would present to Dr. Steck. That night, after seeing to the needs of Jose and his friends who slept at the Indian Agent's quarters, he went back to the Diné settlement and stayed the night with Hasbaá.

He didn't really fear that anything would happen to him. He knew he'd be back soon. Though he warned Hasbaá that if he had to wait for an exchange of correspondence with Washington, he could be gone for weeks. Will cried at the prospect of being parted from Hasbaá that long.

They both agreed this was the best chance for bypassing Carleton and the best chance of changing the plight of the Diné people. Barboncito arranged for Will to ride one of the Navajo horses.

Just before dawn, in hopes of getting away without being noticed, Will and Jose rode out toward the northwest along the Pecos River. They decided to avoid the trail, known euphemistically as The Avenue, that ran north toward the settlement of Las Vegas, New Mexico, crossing the trail to Santa Fe on the way. This was the road the stagecoach had brought Will to Fort Sumner by not so long ago. Away from The Avenue, they were less likely to run into soldiers or traders. It was a 150-mile journey they were beginning. It would take them three or four days.

Will had become so much more emotional and talkative since he'd developed his relationship with Hasbaá. It changed how he related to Jose. He spent long stretches of their time together describing what the Diné were like and what their problems were and, most of all, what a strange but appealing character Hasbaá was.

Jose carried on with his characteristic sexual bravado, yet there developed in his voice such a sweetness when he spoke of Will and Hasbaá together.

On the way, Jose told Will about his friend in Santa Fe.

"Jesse was a slave in Louisiana. He escaped a long time ago—long before there was any talk about freeing the slaves. He crossed the border into Texas and headed west. I met him in San Antonio. We had all gone there to the mission to see the holy ceremonies at Christmas time and to enjoy the feasting. The *padres* at the mission give out *pan dulces* during the procession of Mary and Joseph to find a place to give birth to the Christ child. Ah, Will, it is a wonderful time. There are candles burning on the roofs of houses all along *la posada*. You should come with me to San Antonio to see…"

"I'm not very religious any more," Will interrupted, deflecting the invitation to join in another journey. Already his thighs and buttocks ached after only the first day of this ride.

"Not religious!" Jose joked, "you are married to the *sacerdote alto* of the Navajos."

"The what?"

"The high priest—the Pope—of the Indians." Jose laughed heartily.

"It's not exactly the same thing…" Will remembered he'd once described Hasbaá to Gen. Carleton as high priestess.

"Oh, isn't it?

"So my boss, Luis Solis, hired Jesse to work the next trail drive with us. Luis's sister, Thanya, had come with us to see the Christmas pageant. She was *muy bonita* in those days. She and Jesse ran off from the procession and found a barn—just like Mary and Joseph," he joked. "Only it was many months later that their baby was born, but they named him Jesus in honor of the way they met.

"After Thanya had the baby, Jesse decided he didn't want to be a cowboy anymore. Thanya's uncle had a store in Santa Fe, so Jesse and Thanya and *poco Jesus* all went up there to work for the uncle.

"My boss, Luis, loved his sister. So whenever he heard about a trail drive coming out of North Texas or New Mexico, he'd always take us up there with him and we'd all go visit Jesse and Thanya.

"You will like them, *Señor Will*. They love me and *mis amigos* like we were their own family. Me especially. Only, see, I have not gone up there for such a long time 'cause I don't work for Luis anymore. But I will show you. We will have a great time in Santa Fe."

47

Santa Fe

By the time they got to the capital city of the New Mexico Territory, Will was convinced he'd never make it as a cowboy. Life on horseback didn't agree with his buttocks.

Jose had been right about Jesse and Thanya. Jesse, the ex-slave, had taken his wife's last name and had inherited her uncle's prosperous business, the Solis General Store in the bustling frontier metropolis of Santa Fe, a few blocks from the cathedral on the town square. The Solises lived in an adobe building behind the store.

The family had recently had an addition. Thanya had given birth to a daughter less than a week before Will and Jose arrived. Will worried they had come at an inconvenient time and would be imposing. But, to his surprise, Thanya insisted they stay with them, even though their adobe dwelling was small and now overcrowded with the new baby.

"You must be the godfather for *mi niña Maria*," Thanya exclaimed. "That will make you part of the family, Jose. Then you will have to visit us more often."

"How can I stand up for Maria's baptism? I have no wife to be the *madrina*. The *padre* would not allow this."

Jesse clasped Jose's shoulder in a half-embrace. "Hey, *amigo*, maybe you be the *madrina*. Your friend here can be *padrino*."

"Jesse, Thanya, this is my friend Will. From Virginia," Jose formally introduced his traveling companion. "*Ay*, but he cannot be godparent to Maria. He is already married. To a handsome Navajo warrior."

"A warrior," Jesse said, obviously joining into the humor, "Lucky you. He must keep you satisfied."

"Well, actually, she's not a warrior exactly."

"A *berdache*," Jose interjected.

"Ah, I see, a holy one."

Will was pleased Jesse knew about such personages among the Indians.

"Thanya," Jesse said, "I think Jose is right. Padre Quintana at the Cathedral would not allow such a choice to be godparents at our Maria's baptism." He laughed as though their priest's conventional-mindedness were a regular item of humor in the family.

"Jose," Thanya scolded with the same ribald humor, "you must find yourself a bride then, before it is time for our Maria to be baptized. Now, both of you, sit down, sit down. Jose, tell us all about yourself. Are you on the trail? Or have you come to settle down in Santa Fe?"

Will sat back and listened while the three old friends caught up with one another. After a while, they fell into Spanish, and he could not follow the conversation. He marveled that this black slave had succeeded in shedding his previous life and making such happiness for himself. How fortunate he'd been to escape the oppression of the South!

They'd arrived late in the afternoon. Jesse went back up front to the General Store for a while, then closed and returned to assist Thanya prepare supper. Will felt totally welcomed. These people were friendly and accepting.

As he sat at the little wooden table near the fireplace of the adobe house and ate cabrito and beans and tortillas, he realized he'd come with a bias against the New Mexican people. So far, the only New Mexicans he'd had any contact with had been the raiders who nearly killed him. That experience, and the Dinés' understandable hostility toward this other race of invaders in their homelands, had turned him against them.

Now he saw that just as there were good and bad people among his own white race, and good and bad people among the diverse population called the Indians, so there were good and bad people among the *mestizo* Mexicans who had colonized this part of the Southwest.

After dinner, Jesse went back to the store and got a bottle of tequila. Thanya did not take any of the bitter alcohol; she was nursing Maria and said it would taint her milk. But Jose and Jesse imbibed enthusiastically. Having been raised by a strict preacher, Will had little experience drinking spirits. He tasted the drink, but the harsh tequila was too much for him. Nonetheless, by the end of the evening, just from a few sips now and then, he was mildly intoxicated and quite jovial.

When it came time for sleep, Thanya insisted Jose and Will take the bed. She rolled blankets out on the floor between the bed and the dining table for herself, Jesse, and little Jesus. Baby Maria was in a wooden crib that Jesse proudly announced he had carved himself.

Will was embarrassed by this show of hospitality. *Why should these people give up their comfortable bed for me?* But as tipsy as he was he was in no shape to argue with them. Besides, he figured, it was Jose's place to accept or decline the hospitality.

After they were all tucked away, the boy Jesus demanded to sleep in the bed with *Tío Jose*. Thanya apologized, but then explained the boy usually slept with them in the bed.

"Besides," she said, "you are his favorite uncle, Jose."

Jose agreed.

Will was relieved. The presence of the *niño* in the bed cooled his acute awareness of Jose's bare flesh next to him under the sheet.

48

The Territorial Superintendent's Office

In the morning, Will set out to find Dr. Steck and the Office of Indian Affairs. In fact, he had only to walk a block from the Solis Store. There, facing the plaza in the center of Santa Fe, was the building that housed the government offices.

The clerk in the lobby asked Will to take a seat and then disappeared through a door. In a few minutes, a big man with a full head of hair and a beard trimmed away from his chin strode into the room and exuberantly introduced himself as Michael Steck.

"William Lee, Indian Agent at Fort Sumner, New Mexico Territory," Will responded, thinking that, though this man carried more weight and his face was fuller, Michael Steck looked just like the martyred President Abraham Lincoln. He made a good first impression.

Steck led him back to the small office assigned to the Territorial Indian Superintendent. Then said frankly that he'd never heard of William Lee, Indian Agent. "I thought we were still waiting for those damned bureaucrats in Washington to assign someone."

"Didn't Mr. McDonald write to tell you I'd been assigned?"

"Jesse McDonald stopped writing to me about the time Jim Carleton was put in charge of Fort Sumner. I didn't like Carleton then and objected to the appointment. But, son," he asked paternally, "if you're the new Agent, why haven't you sent any reports to this office?"

"Mr. McDonald instructed me to send my reports directly to him. But I've recently discovered that mail I've tried to send has been intercepted by General Carleton. I'm not sure anything I've written has gone anywhere." He held up the sheath of papers in his hand. "But, here, I have a report to present to you."

Steck took the papers, invited Will to take a seat, then sat down himself behind his desk and quickly looked through the pages.

"This is very good," he murmured a few times. "Very interesting... Hmm, just as I suspected..." After a while, he closed the report and looked up at Will. "Tell me, young man, just how *did* you get assigned to this job?"

"Well, sir, that's one of the things I came to see you about. Recently General Carleton said something to me about 'the circumstances of my appointment.' I don't know what he meant. I thought you might."

"What was the reason he made the comment?"

"The general, sir, reprimanded me for urging him to send a rescue party for a young Indian boy who'd been stolen by slave raiders."

"Slave raiders?"

"Don't you know, sir? It's there in my report. General Carleton objected to my asking that something be done to stop the raids on the Indians. He said those words, 'the circumstances of my appointment,' as though I was supposed to know what it meant."

"What does it mean?"

"I don't know, but I think the general meant I was supposed to know I was not sent out here to help the Indians."

"But if you're the Indian Agent, then, of course, you're supposed to help them."

"Well, as my report indicates, they have serious problems, sir. But I don't think their problems are reported properly. I mean, there's very little food, no housing, and no protection given them. They are practically starving out there. I personally had to save several of them from drowning when there was a flashflood. And then..."

"All right, son. I'm very interested in this. You know, we send quite a bit of money to Carleton. Where's it going?"

"Money for the Indians?"

"A million a year for the last three years."

"Well, it's not going to the Indians."

"What's happened to Mr. Ayers?"

"Ayers?" Will asked.

"Your predecessor. I'd heard he'd been accused of a heinous crime. But I knew the man and didn't think it was possible."

"They say the Indians killed him. I heard the soldiers talking, but nobody would tell me, sir." Will feared he sounded like a feckless fool. "One of the soldiers told me my predecessor had raped and killed an Indian woman. General Carleton said something about the previous Agent wanting to receive rewards of some sort..."

"The second part sounds like Ayers. He was always scheming to get rich the easy way. But I can't believe he'd rape or murder anybody."

"Sergeant Peak said the Indian had her throat cut in the Agent's quarters. I guess it looked pretty suspicious."

"Your quarters?" Steck exclaimed. "That must be disturbing to your sleep."

"I'm living among the Indians now, sir. But I guess it was not so bad. I mean, I didn't know about it at first."

"You are living among the Indians?"

Will didn't mention the sexual nature of his relationship with Hasbaá. Jesse and Thanya Solis had been accepting, but this Dr. Steck was a white man. He seemed open and friendly, but Will had no way to know just how much truth he could take. But Steck's question gave him the opportunity to explain the problems he'd delineated in his written report.

Steck listened attentively till Will finished. "I never liked Carleton. He's a pompous horse's ass as far as I am concerned. All so cocksure he's right about eliminating the Indians from the Territory. I admit this job would be easier if there were no Indians around. But there are…"

"And they are human beings, too, just like us," Will interjected.

"Some years ago I made a personal inspection of the Bosque Redondo area. I did not see how that barren land could support any more than two thousand people. Carleton tried to move in twelve thousand."

"According to Agent Ayers' count in '65, there were nine thousand. The Navajos estimate there are less than seven now."

"Well, there are still Navajos attacking settlers. So I know a lot of them never got to the Bosque Redondo. Carleton was wrong about his original estimates. But there should be more than seven thousand down there. Where did the others go?"

"They died, sir. What did you think?"

"Died? Oh, my God. Well, I see there is a problem here."

"Yes sir." Remembering Hasbaá's message from Changing Woman about how to present the accusations against Carleton, he asked a suggestive question. "Is General Carleton still requisitioning food and supplies for twelve thousand Indians?"

"That's a good question, son. That's a very good question." Steck appeared to have hit on a thought. Will was pleased.

"Let me study your report, then do a little investigating. We've got a telegraph here now, you know. I will contact Washington and see what I can learn. I think I've been kept in the dark about what's going on down there. I'd thought my friend Ayers was handling everything. Now I see I've been mistaken about that." Steck stood signaling the end of the meeting.

"Where are you staying?"

"Last night with Jesse and Thanya Solis. They are friends of this cowboy who rode up here with me."

"Oh, yes. I know Jesse Solis. Good man. Say, haven't they just had a baby?"

"Yes, sir."

"Then it must be crowded at their house."

"Yes, sir."

"Well, well. Let's get you out of their way and into a hotel. We're spending a lot of money on this Bosque Redondo experiment of Carleton's. You just might be able to save the government some of that expenditure. I'm sure we can afford to put you up comfortably. Besides, you may be around here a while. I may need to put you to work drawing up some more reports for me on the conditions there."

At Steck's instruction, Will took a room for himself at the Sangre de Cristo Hotel. Jesse and Thanya told him he was welcome to remain with them, but they were also obviously relieved that he was moving elsewhere. Jose said he'd decided to give them back their bed and to move his bedroll out behind their adobe house so he could sleep under the stars as he was used to. As before, he didn't want to spend time in a hotel, especially not one paid for by the government.

Will was also relieved. He'd been very glad to see Jose again. He was grateful for his help in getting to Santa Fe. He wanted to maintain a friendship. But at least for the time being, as long as he was a new husband to Hasbaá and potential savior of the Diné people, he didn't want to confuse his emotions by moving the Mexican cowboy in with him.

49

THE SANGRE DE CRISTO HOTEL

The Sangre de Cristo Hotel, named for the range of mountains rising just north of Santa Fe, was a thick-walled Spanish hacienda with cool, shaded gardens all around. The hotel and the gardens were staffed with Indian laborers. While Will liked seeing that the Indians, some of which must have been of Diné origin, were well fed and happy, he thought it a shame that they or their parents had been taken from a life of freedom out in their native homelands. *What is civilization going to do to this land?*

The hotel offered amenities such as Will had never imagined. Steck had told him to put anything he wanted on the bill. In fact, he instructed him to be lavish. "After all, you're not on the reservation now."

So the first night Will ate a huge meal in the luxurious dining room and then ordered a bath. The clerk at the front desk asked if he'd like a rubdown as well. This was something he had never experienced before. It sounded to him almost sinfully indulgent. But in the interest of discovering all that this new life of his had to offer, he agreed to the clerk's suggestion.

Will went for a short walk in the early evening. It was much cooler here than in the desert. *How delightful to stroll through the gardens and watch the stars come out!*

When he arrived back in his room, he found that a tin tub had been carried in and placed right in the middle of the spacious chamber along with a narrow table draped with soft white towels. A short, well-muscled Indian, clad only in a woven loincloth, stood over the tub, pouring steaming hot water from a bucket. His manner was docile but commanding.

The Indian never spoke a word but communicated through simple gestures that Will should take off his clothes and climb into the tub. The water was hot. At Fort Sumner, he was only able to wash from a basin or occasionally to bathe in the creek. This was the first hot bath he had had since his railroad stop in Kansas.

The Indian took soap and lathered it in his hands and then stroked the rich suds through Will's hair. He massaged his scalp and then poured fresh water from the bucket to rinse away the shampoo. He handed Will a cloth and gestured to him to use it to wash his face. Then he took the cloth and scrubbed Will's back and arms, then underarms, sides and chest. He motioned for him to stand up and then carefully and innocently washed his lower body.

The whole experience unnerved and titilated Will. He'd never had anything even vaguely like this done to him, he supposed, since he'd been an infant and his mother bathed him. But, of course, this was altogether different. The Indian was always gentle but thorough, even in washing his private parts. He did not avert his gaze, though he also did not seem any more interested than in any other part of Will's body. Though at first Will had become aroused, the Indian's conscientious indifference allowed him to relax and enjoy the sensuality of the moment without getting caught in sexual tensions.

After allowing him to soak in the warm water, the Indian helped him to stand up again and rinsed him with more warm water from the bucket. Finally, he dried him with a soft towel, then helped him out of the tub by lifting him right up out of the water. Will steadied himself with a hand on the man's thick shoulders. He marveled at the ease with which the Indian picked up him.

The Indian dried his legs and feet, then bid him lie down on the towel-draped table. Starting with his shoulders and back then, he massaged and kneaded every muscle in Will's body. Finally, he briskly rubbed him down, back and front, with a spicy-scented ointment that made his skin tingle. Then he covered him with a sheet. While Will drifted in and out of light sleep, the masseur carried the tub away and straightened up the room. After that, he gently woke him and helped him move into the bed.

As the Indian masseur was leaving, Will spoke up to say thank you and goodnight. Believing he'd been right in thinking this man a Navajo, Will used words in Diné that he'd learned from Hasbaá. The Indian replied in similar sounding words, but Will didn't understand them. But he was glad he'd shown respect for the masseur's cultural identity.

Later in the night, Will awoke and lay for a while feeling guilty that he was here in all this luxury while Hasbaá and the others suffered such hardship back at the reservation. A part of him wanted to flee the New Mexico Territory altogether and wash his hands of the responsibilities for the thousands of Indians out there in the desert. *How can I possibly help them? It's all beyond my powers.*

Another part of him resolved to turn this self-indulgent luxury toward service to those who needed help. *As much pleasure as all this gives me, that much effort and struggle will I devote to the cause to undo the Dinés' suffering.* Will made a prayer to Changing Woman. He pledged himself to her service. Then he rolled over and slept soundly throughout the night.

50

THE YELLOW ROSE CANTINA

Will spent the next day with Dr. Steck going over his written report. He learned that the Superintendent also disapproved of Carleton's policies and felt the Indians were treated far more harshly than necessary. Steck said he didn't like the high-handed way, as he called it, Carleton treated him. Steck explained that James Carleton was a familiar sight in Santa Fe. But he was known around town not as a strictly disciplined military man, but as a rich dandy who flaunted his money and his connections.

"Santa Fe is an old city with a Spanish heritage and blue-blooded aristocracy. These people resent an American soldier coming into their community and behaving toward them as though they were the foreigners or, worse, his servants. A couple of the Spanish aristocrats are part of his circle, but most of the upper class of Santa Fe thoroughly dislike him and think him crass.

"Carleton's buddies, with whom he sits around in the dining room at the Sangre de Cristo smoking cigars and drinking brandy, playing poker and lording it over the other diners, are traders and land speculators."

Steck's mention of the Sangre de Cristo Hotel as Carleton's playground sent shivers of guilt through Will. He imagined the general ordering himself a massage like the one he got last night.

"It makes sense for him to be friends with purveyors to the government and the military," Steck mused aloud, "but why the speculators?"

That evening, Will felt misgivings about eating in the dining room of the Sangre de Cristo. Instead, he decided he'd find a place less aristocratic. He wandered out into the town square. He went by the Solis Store and looked in a window, but the store was closed. He didn't want to impose on Thanya and Jesse. And he was already feeling guilty about the amenities of urban life; he didn't want to tempt himself further by socializing with Jose—at least not when he had a plush bed in a hotel room for Jose to get him to take him to.

A little way from the town square and out from under the shadow of the Cathedral, he came upon The Yellow Rose Cantina. The name sounded like something right out of a Western penny novel. He pushed through the swinging doors and walked in.

Will swaggered up to the bar, trying to look like he belonged, and ordered himself a beer. Then he leaned on one elbow and surveyed the room. In one corner, he could see several tables of diners. He could smell the rich spicy aroma of Mexican cooking. In the opposite corner were large round tables that appeared to be for poker games. No one was over there at this time of evening. Most of the room was occupied by a large dance floor surrounded with chairs and small tables for drinks. Five or ten men sat in those chairs, as though waiting for entertainment to begin. Along the bar sat another five or ten men. Some faced the bar; others were turned so they, too, faced the dance floor. Most of the men in the place looked like the cowboys Will had seen in the saloons at the railroad stop in Kansas.

He was just finishing his beer and thinking that he ought to see about getting something to eat, when a burly fellow with a big droopy mustache and a guitar came out to the center of the dance floor. After a few words in Spanish, he started to play. Then a young boy came out with a taper in his hand and carefully lighted kerosene lanterns set behind reflectors in a ring near the back of the dance floor to create a stage.

As the guitarist started in on another melody, a young Hispanic girl in a ruffled red dress with a long flowing train came prancing out onto the stage singing in a high-pitched but strained soprano voice. She carried a fan in one hand, and she waved and opened and closed the fan with great verve as she strode back and forth. At the end of each transit of the stage, when she'd turn, she'd reach back with her free hand and toss the train of her dress with a dramatic flourish.

Will ordered himself another beer, climbed up onto a stool along the bar, and settled back to enjoy the show. After a while, the singer somehow detached the train of the dress with one of those dramatic gestures and threw it offstage. She flounced the skirt a little, pulling here and there, and somehow transformed it into a French dancehall dress. The guitarist made a valiant effort at the can-can while the singer struggled by herself to do high kicks in time with the music. It was all a little hilarious, even as it was amateurish—even to one as inexperienced with nightclub life as Will Lee.

He was thoroughly taken with the young singer. She was so pretty and so delicate. He had not seen a woman like this since he'd left the Eastern seaboard. He wondered how she managed out here in the rough and manly West. In a way, he felt a kinship with her: a young innocent amidst all these crude men.

He felt embarrassed for her when, after she finished her act and took a bow, one of the customers drunkenly called out, "Show us your cunt."

"Who's the singer?" Will asked the bartender as the man was drawing him another glass of beer.

"Joelle," the bartender laughed. "That's what he calls himself. Real name's Joel."

Joel, Will thought. And the bartender used a masculine pronoun. *Is this young singer at The Yellow Rose Cantina also a Two-Spirit Person like Hasbaá?*

To Will's dismay, when he turned back with his beer in hand, he saw that the lovely young Joelle had gone over to the man who'd made the rude call and was even now leading him offstage with her by the hand. With the other hand, the man dug in his pants pocket.

Little Will, innocent amidst all these crude men, was not so dumb as to miss what was going on. Indeed, before this oddly matched couple disappeared into rooms in the saloon behind the bar, he saw that Joelle stopped, took the thin wad of bills from the man's hand, counted them, and then stuffed them into her bodice. *A common prostitute.*

But is she a male?

Will was troubled, but intrigued. He decided he'd better get something to eat before he got drunk. He staggered over to one of the tables and told the waiter he'd take the special, whatever it was. He was more intoxicated than he'd ever been before.

The hot, piquant Mexican food that was soon placed before him helped clear his head. The unusual and unfamiliar but delicious flavors reminded him he was in a world he knew nothing about. *Better not to make any rash judgments.*

About ten minutes later, the man who'd followed Joelle came back out and sat down hard in his seat, doffed off the rest of the beer in his glass, and then lay across the little table next to the chair and fell asleep.

Joelle, in a slinky low-cut dress of dark blue satin, strolled out into the cantina. She walked around from table to table, joking and flirting with the customers. Several of the men patted her on the behind or stroked her shoulder when she bent down at their table. Will was surprised. *If Joelle really is a male, all these sexual gestures seem out of place.*

Joelle made it over to Will's table. Instead of just bending over to exchange a word or two, she pulled out a chair opposite him and sat down.

"*Hola, amigo,*" she said, her Mexican accent thick. She boldly reached across the table and stuck her finger into the mashed beans on

Will's dinner plate. Then she sensually and lasciviously licked the beans off her finger. "You like the *frijoles refritos?*"

He didn't know how to answer. He nodded in affirmation.

"It is strange to see an *Americano* like you in here. Did you come to hear me singing?"

"Actually, I enjoyed your singing very much. You have a beautiful voice."

Joelle batted her eyelids. "*Me llamo Joelle*. It sounds French, *¿sí?* You will enjoy my other talents as well. I have a cunt to make your cock feel good. Your *huevos* too can release all their tension."

Will was taken aback. He was drunk enough to just ask, "I heard your name is Joel. Are you a boy?"

"Well, sure, *amigo*," Joelle was undaunted, "but I'll make your cock feel better than a woman."

"Well, actually," Will slurred the word into something closer to "egg-jewelry," "I wouldn't know. I've never been with a woman."

"Then you make love with other men?" she said enthusiastically. "You are so handsome and strong. Look, your eyes, they are beautiful. Don't you want Joelle?"

To deflect her forceful proposition, he answered her first question directly, "I've made love with two, maybe three men."

"Oh, just a baby," Joelle teased. "I bet you are older than me. I have gone with hundreds of men."

"I'm twenty-one."

"I, I am only *trece*, ah, thirteen."

"You're just a boy."

"I am so pretty." Joelle turned her profile to him. "I like being a girl. Besides, it pays the bills."

"Are you a Two-Spirit Person?"

"*No comprendo.*"

Will tried to remember the word Jesse and Jose had used. "*Berdache?*"

Joelle shook her head, not understanding. As if answering some other question of her own devising, she went on, "I only go with *machos hombres*. They want a *femenino*. And I want a real man, one who fucks women. I only want them if they are virile. They should have a bunch of *niños* running around and keep their wife pregnant."

"Why be a whore to married men?" Will thought the word "whore" sounded more biblical than "prostitute." His father had often spit the word from his pulpit.

"I take care of them when their wives are in their time of the month or not in the mood. Among us *Mexicanos*, after a wife has a *niño*, she's not interested in more fucking with her man for a while. It's unlucky for the little one. That's when the man comes to me. And I make sure he goes back to his wife. I keep those marriages together, because he has no energy left for another woman by the time I'm through with him. A little *loca* like me, I can always bring the big *hombre* down. Don't you want to see?"

"I don't think so, Joelle, uh, Joel. I think you're too *loca* for me." He didn't know what that meant. But it seemed to follow from Joelle's words.

"Then you will be my sister," Joelle declared gleefully.

Will wasn't sure what that meant either, but it seemed to allay Joelle's sexual come-on. She relaxed and then signaled to the waiter. In a moment, he brought her a drink. "You will buy me a whisky?"

Will nodded to the waiter. He didn't want to get bamboozled by this strange character. But he was curious. He'd managed to understand that the Diné spiritualized sex in a way that made sense of Hasbaá's sexual identity. But this was something different.

"May I ask you a question? Don't your customers object to your being a boy?"

"Why should they?"

Will didn't quite know how to ask this, so he just blurted out the words his father would have used. "Because it makes them sodomites, doesn't it?"

Joelle laughed. She turned to a man at the next table. "Manuel is a satisfied customer, as you say. Let's ask him? Manuel," she called out, "are you a sodomite, a *maricón*?"

"What's *maricón*?" Will interrupted.

"I'm no *maricón*," Manuel slurred testily. "Nobody gets in my ass."

"A *maricón* is a boy who likes to get fucked," Joelle answered.

"She is the *maricón*." Manuel leaned back in his chair and pointed with his beer glass toward Joelle. "*Es femenino y una puta.* She's no better than a woman. That's why we call her 'she,' 'cause she lost her manhood when she started getting fucked."

"But if *you* have sex with her..." Will said logically.

"Can't you see I'm not like her? I have a wife and many *niños*. I've proved my manhood." Manuel was getting agitated. "As long as I use my *verga* to stick it in the hole, what difference does it make if it's a girl or boy who gets it? The one who does the fucking—he is the man. Don't you *Americanos* understand nothin'?"

"I'm sorry, sir."

Joelle turned toward Manuel and sat up tall in her chair and arched her eyebrows. "Manuel..."

Before she could say another word, Manuel stumbled over and hugged Joelle. He looked sheepishly at Will. "But we all love her..."

Joelle pecked Manuel on the cheek, then gestured at her bodice and rubbed her thumb and forefinger together. Swaying on his feet, Manuel struggled with his pocket. In a moment, he found a bill and held it up for Joelle to see, then stuck it into the top of her dress.

"I have them all by the *huevos*," she proudly whispered to Will as Manuel sat back down and returned his attention to his plate of *arroz y frijoles*. "I make them happy as no woman can. And with me they don't need to worry about having more *niños* to feed."

There was a certain logic to all this. But still it seemed inequitable. Reverend Lee would certainly have declared Manuel at least as much the sodomite as Joelle. In fact, maybe more so, since he would be in the more responsible role. Apparently, Mexican culture turned these issues on their head. As he had so often in the last few weeks, Will again marveled at how different the world was from what he'd been led to believe in provincial Lynchburg.

"But are *you* happy?"

"Who is happy?" Joelle answered sarcastically. "I'm eating breakfast and supper. That's all that matters." She downed the rest of her drink and got up. "Perhaps I will see you again. Come back tomorrow to hear me sing."

Will finished his plate of food, then headed straight back to the hotel and went to sleep, troubled by his discovery of the Yellow Rose Cantina.

51

The Territorial Superintendent's Office

In the morning, bleary from the beer he'd consumed at the cantina, Will returned to the Superintendent's office. He spent most of the morning by himself in an adjoining room carefully rewriting his report on the Bosque Redondo according to Dr. Steck's suggestions.

Just before noon, Steck called him to come have lunch in the larger office. He had a picnic basket sitting on his desk.

"My wife fixed fried chicken," he announced proudly as he opened the basket. "When I told her about you, she insisted on making lunch. She said it was the least we could do. You're a lucky young man, Will." Steck chortled. "Agnes never fixes lunch for me. She says I eat too much anyway."

"Please give Mrs. Steck my regards then." Will asked curiously, "Is your wife out here in New Mexico with you? I don't see many women around. This seems like a man's world."

"Agnes is a remarkable woman. When I got assigned to this post, she insisted on following me out here. We don't have children, you know, so there was a certain freedom…"

"It must be hard on the married men. I mean, being out here so far from home and having to leave their wives and families."

"Are you married?"

"Oh, no, sir," Will lied. He wasn't going to explain why that wasn't entirely true.

"Well, you seem like a nice young man. I'm sure you'll find the right girl. Though probably not out here in New Mexico," Steck added with a grimace. "So, tell me, Will, how are you liking Santa Fe? Where do you spend your time when you're not in there working for me?" He pointed into the little office where Will was penning the report.

"Oh, the hotel is beautiful. Most luxurious place I've ever seen in my life. Thank you."

"You're certainly welcome. Is that all you've seen of our fair city?"

"Oh no, sir. Last night I ate my supper at The Yellow Rose Cantina. It was very, uh, entertaining."

"The Yellow Rose, hmm. I don't mean to sound prudish, but may I give you a piece of advice?"

"Of course, sir." *Now I've said too much and am going to get reprimanded.*

"You understand I was a physician before I took this assignment. I was a field surgeon at the start of the war. Saw a little too much. That's why I retired from my medical practice and came out here with Agnes to get away from all that. But never mind my story. I just want to give you a little warning. I know how it is to be a young man. And I, ah, know what kind of place The Yellow Rose is."

"Sir?"

"Well, there are prostitutes there, I understand."

"I don't know about that," Will fibbed.

"That's good. But you may find out. And I think you have to know about the dangers."

"My father's a preacher. I've heard him preaching about sin…"

"Oh, no. I'm not worried about your sinning. You can take that up with your father. I'm talking about your health. There are certain diseases, like syphilis, that spread among the prostitutes."

"Yes, sir." Will answered.

"I get consulted now and then, 'specially by folks around here who don't want their case brought to the attention of the local physicians. You understand, people are embarrassed by the diseases of the reproductive organs. Why, not long ago, one of the *padres* from the mission, passing through here on his way back to Mexico City, came to see me for 'the drip.'"

"'The drip'?"

While he and the doctor ate Agnes Steck's fried chicken, Will was introduced to a branch of medicine which he'd previously heard nothing about. This subject had always been left to the priests and preachers. They had never done a very good job of communicating this knowledge, Dr. Steck pointed out, as the case of his recent patient, the *padre*, demonstrated.

"You know what the name Yellow Rose means?" Steck asked, chuckling, as he finished the medical lecture.

"No, sir, I don't suppose I do."

"It's a joke in these parts that there are so few women for all the men and some of these cowboys are so hard up that they'll go with practically anything. Rose is a kind of mythical prostitute who has turned yellow with the jaundice."

"Liver disease?"

"Exactly. And it's probably contagious."

"That's not a very funny joke."

"Right, young man. It is not a very funny joke."

52

THE YELLOW ROSE CANTINA

By late afternoon Will's hand ached from holding the quill. He left the office and stopped again by The Yellow Rose Cantina.

The bartender was sweeping. Will asked about Joelle.

"She's not ready yet. You come back later."

"That's all right. I only want to talk. She, uh, invited me to come see her." Once again, he fudged the truth just a little, but with good intention.

The bartender pointed to the back door and grunted. Will headed backstage. The door led to a hallway with several doors off both sides. The hall was dark.

"Joelle?" he called out.

"In here," came a muffled answer.

He followed the sound about halfway down the hall. To his left, he saw one of the doors open just a little.

"Joelle?"

"Come in. I am almost done."

Will let himself into the dimly lit room. A candle provided all the light there was. He discovered he had entered a bathroom. A young man was standing up in the tub. The bather reached out daintily, apparently for assistance in climbing out of the tin basin. "Ah, the *Americano*."

"My name's Will, Will Lee."

"*Sí*, and I am Joel Sarria. Joelle," he added with a demure smile. "I remember you from last night. *Buenos días, señor*. But you are early."

Will couldn't help looking at Joel's body. He was thin and, save for a sparse patch of pubic hair, smooth and hairless. Without the dress and makeup he'd worn last night, Joel looked delicate, but clearly masculine. *In fact, he's quite handsome.*

"I came by to apologize. I didn't mean to insult you."

"But you didn't..." Joel reached for a towel hanging on the hook by the tub.

"Well, I mean, by asking, you know, about your being a sodomite and all..."

"*No importa.* I know what I am," Joel answered matter-of-factly.

While Joel dried himself, Will stood by watching. Though he enjoyed Joel's ease with his nakedness, he was becoming increasingly uncomfortable himself. "I really liked your performance," he finally said. "Thanks for coming over and talking to me."

"You were a new face—*y una cara bonito.*" Joel wrapped the towel around himself, tucked up under the arms as a woman would.

"I don't speak enough Spanish to know what you just said."

"I said you have a pretty face."

"Oh, well, thank you." Will was embarrassed, though flattered. He changed the subject. "I wish I could speak Spanish. I feel like a foreigner."

"If you live in Santa Fe, *señor*, you should speak *español.*"

"*Sí, español.*" Will almost got the pronunciation right.

Joel laughed. He walked past Will and led him out of the bathroom, through the hall, and into what appeared to be a dressing room and bedroom. He stopped in the doorway and—letting the character of Joelle show through—did a curtsy and gestured archly with his right hand, "*Mi boudoir,*" he said, mixing Spanish and French to Will's confusion.

Will stepped into the room. There were a couple of gowns like the ones Joel wore last night hanging from pegs in the wall; there was a small dressing stool and table strewn with vials and boxes of makeup; and there was a bed. Will was conscious of what that bed was used for.

"I will teach you," Joel exclaimed dramatically. "I have a great tongue."

"Teach me what?" Will had started to sit on the corner of the bed, but decided instead to stand.

"*Español.*"

"You know, I don't live in Santa Fe. I'm just visiting. I'm the Indian Agent to the Navajos down at the Bosque Redondo Reservation."

"Ah, I think I have heard of this place." Joel pulled off the towel and began to dress himself in ordinary male attire. "There is a fort there? Some of the soldiers from there have been to see me," he said suggestively.

"Fort Sumner." Will supplied the name, amazed and amused to learn something about the soldiers he would not have expected.

"So. How are the Navajos?"

Will started answering that question. He had a lot to say about the subject. After all, he'd spent the day writing all this out for his report. At first, Joel seemed only to half-listen. He busied himself around the room; then he invited Will to follow him to another room along the same little hallway. This one had a couple of chairs in it. Will kept talking. After a bit, Joel actually seemed to get interested. When he was describing Hasbaá, Joel was sitting on the edge of his seat.

"The Navajos consider people like you to be special," Will said earnestly. "They are looked up to as sacred people. They are healers and religious leaders. The person I love—her name is Hasbaá—is what you called a '*maricón*' like you. But among her people, rather than being an entertainer in a cabaret and a prostitute, she uses her talents to make many contributions to her community and to her family."

"I have no *familia*," Joel answered, downcast. "*Mi padre* never liked that I was *feminino*. I stayed with *mi madre* in the kitchen. Ever since I was seven years old, the older boys all wanted to fuck me. They treated me like a girl. But when I finally let them have it—I was eleven—they bragged about it, and *mi padre* heard. He threw me out. *Mi madre* cried, but I had to leave.

"I hitched up with some cowboys. I did the cooking for them. They fucked me, too. But they were nice about it. It was with the cowboys I really learned to like sex. But I didn't like living on the range..."

"I can sympathize..."

"It was hard work. So when we came to Santa Fe one time, I met this guitar player. He liked my voice and showed me how to dance and sing for him. The cantina owner lets me have these rooms if I will just sing for the customers and give them sex when they want. I miss *mi madre*. I think sometimes I am very lonely. But this is my life."

"Joel," Will said hesitantly, "I was talking with a doctor today. He was telling me about the diseases that come with sex..."

"*Ay*, I know. I worry about this. In fact though, it is not so bad. I really don't let most of the men fuck me. They think they do. But they are usually so drunk. Some of them, I think, never know I am really a boy. I squeeze my legs together real hard, and they think they are fucking a woman."

Will recalled Jose Flores' technique.

"They don't know any better. They usually can't squirt. So I have to take them in my hand anyway. See, I know about these things. Men are such fools." Joel laughed hard. Will could hear pain behind the laughter.

Will found Joel easy to talk with, at least in the identity of Joel. Joelle was more of a strain. Though as they talked, Joel led them back to the dressing room and applied his makeup for the evening performance. Will wished there were something he could do for his new friend. He felt as though this boy were like a younger sister who needed protection.

"I have an idea," Joel said. "If I could get me a horse, I could go out and become a trader, taking supplies to trade with the cowboys. I don't want to be a cowboy, but I would like to visit them now and then. I don't like being in town all the time. Working in the cantina here is fun. But it is not enough for my future. I need a profession. Maybe I could even visit *mi madre*. If I return as a prosperous trader, *mi padre* would have to accept me. But how would I buy a horse? I can never save any money. Working at the cantina I always spend everything in my pocket."

In response to Joelle's talk about her strapped financial situation, Will offered to buy her supper. The business in the cantina was beginning to pick up. Then, after two plates of tamales and beans had been placed before them on the table, he said, "I have a business proposition for you."

"*Now* you want to fuck me?"

"Oh, no, not like that," Will hastened to say. "Earlier, when I first got here today, you said you could teach me to speak Spanish. Maybe it was just a joke. But I haven't got much to do during the day. Tomorrow I'll finish my job for Dr. Steck. I may be in Santa Fe another week or two. What if I paid you to teach me? I've been getting a paycheck from the government, and I don't have much to spend it on. I'd like to spend it on you, Joel. I mean, so I could learn the language. I'll pay you by the hour, however much you have time for."

"I have to sing at the cantina."

"Of course."

"And you will pay me cash, just like my other customers…"

"No, I don't want to pay you cash. I want to set up an account for you at the bank. Then you can save up to buy a horse."

"*Bueno*," Joelle exclaimed.

"I don't know if I can guarantee you prosperity. But if you will work hard to help me learn, I promise I will help you save some money. One other thing, I want you to come to my hotel, and I want you to dress as a boy. I don't think the hotel would approve if they thought I was bringing in a whore every day."

"*Yo tampoco*. And you will call me Joel?"

"Right."

"You need to give me a quarter now as an advance."

"All right," Will agreed, handing the boy the coin and wondering why he would require an advance. Did Will have to guarantee a reservation for Joel's time?

He stayed to hear Joelle's first song. But then after only one beer this night, he went home. *I want my mind clear for my Spanish lesson.*

53

Santa Fe

Joel arrived, as planned, just after lunch. They would only work a half day this first lesson. Will had had reports to write at the Indian Affairs office in the morning.

Will waited in the shaded garden in front of the lobby. When he saw Joel coming up the front walk, he went out to meet him. Joel immediately handed him a brand new little booklet printed in Spanish.

"This is what the quarter was for, isn't it?" Will was proud of the boy for having the good sense to purchase the book in advance. It made the first lesson much easier for Will.

After an hour, he was comfortably greeting everybody they passed with "*Buenos días*" or "*¿Cómo está usted?*"

The second day of lessons went even better. Will enjoyed the challenge, and Joel seemed to enjoy the legitimate employment.

They spent the morning in the hotel, then went for a walk. They headed to the bank to open Joel's account. Joel talked on and on in Spanish while Will struggled to understand.

Confident of the boy's intention and determined to make a real difference in his life, Will put down what amounted to a full week's salary for the opening deposit. Joel's eyes lit up when he saw the amount in the passbook.

"I'm not going to touch this money until I have saved enough for a horse and some saddle blankets. Then I will trade the blankets to the cowboys for a cow. Then I will bring the cow back to Santa Fe to sell it and buy more blankets. Soon I will be rich."

"I have a friend who is a cowboy. His name is Jose. I will introduce you."

As they left the bank, Joel offered to show Will around Santa Fe. They would continue their lessons while they strolled. It was a lovely day. In spite of being surrounded by desert, Santa Fe, because it was situated in the mountains, had a relatively temperate climate. Will imagined the Diné homelands must have been similarly blessed. *No wonder the Indians want to go home.*

When they came by the U.S. Government Land Office, Joel stopped. He called Will's attention to a map of the New Mexico Territory in the window. Joel found a list of geographical expressions in the little Spanish booklet. As they went over the words, they searched for examples on the map.

This exercise got them talking about the location of Fort Sumner and, in turn, the distance from there to the Navajo homelands. Will found the Canyon de Chelly, far to the west of Santa Fe. He had never seen these locations on a map. Barboncito's story of the suffering of the Long Walk now made much more sense to him. He was beginning to get an appreciation for the expanse of what was called the West. The 325 miles that the Navajos were forced to march, Will realized, was longer than trying to walk from Lynchburg to Philadelphia. The thought of General Carleton ordering elderly people, and those who were ill, to do this in freezing weather was, Will concluded, beyond irresponsible. *It was evil.*

"A couple of weeks ago I was looking at this map with a customer of mine from the cantina. He had offered to buy me lunch if I would meet him in the morning. That is when he liked it.

"He told me he worked as a foreman for a rich man who was buying mineral rights to the land out there." Joel pointed to the places on the map, in the northwest corner of the Territory where Will had said the Navajos came from. "He boasted he would bring me a gold nugget some day, and he could buy my services for a whole week. You say that is Indian land. My friend—he may get his scalp cut off."

"Well, first of all, Joel, the Navajos do not practice scalping. So your friend is safe. Besides, the Indians all got moved out of there by the army."

"Was that so the army could get the gold?" Joel asked innocently.

"Well, I wonder. Can you remember anything else your customer said?"

"I don't know. He was bragging about how much gold and silver his boss thought there was out there. The boss was apparently buying shares in the operation. My friend was also bragging about how rich his boss was. He was paying a lot of money for his share."

"Do you know who this man was buying the shares from?"

"*Yo no sé.* He probably said the name. I don't remember. I am a whore. I am not a spy."

Will wanted to be a spy.

He directed their stroll so they would pass the Solis Store. Through the window he could see Jesse standing at the counter. Behind him, placing merchandise on the shelves, was Jose Flores.

"Joel, let's go in here. This is the cowboy I want you to meet."

After making introductions, and seeing that the store had momentarily emptied out of customers, Will asked Jesse if perchance he'd heard rumors of a mining operation in the lands to the west.

"We sell all kinds of supplies for prospectors, you know. Now it's supposed to be secret, but I been hearin' some rich investors are planning to bring gold and silver out of there. To tell you the truth, Will, since you're a friend of Jose's, I'd thought about stocking up on gold pans and prospectin' equipment. Seemed like it'd be a great opportunity for business if they started a gold rush round here. But Thanya talked me out of it. She said we ain't seen no gold nuggets yet, and it wouldn't be fair to get people's hopes up. There's enough disappointment out here as it is."

While Jesse was talking, Thanya came up behind him from the back. She was carrying little Maria at her breast.

"Besides," Thanya broke in, "I heard this land is not going to be opened up for prospecting. They say some army generals have got the land all tied up. And soldiers might be sent out to shoot trespassers."

"Thanya's got a good point," Jesse said. "If the generals and the land speculators around here are trying to get first claim on this land, they might not take too kindly to anybody round here announcin' a gold rush. We got a good enough business right here. Some of those land speculators are regular customers. I don't want to make any enemies."

"That seems fair enough," Will observed. But he pressed his questions a little further. "Thanya, do you know who these generals might be that've got the land tied up?"

"*Yo no sé,*" Thanya answered. Will felt proud of himself for understanding every word.

"Well, you know who occasionally comes to town and wines and dines with the speculators," Jesse said, "is that Indian fighter name o' James C. Carleton."

"Will," Joel, who'd been talking with Jose, broke in, "You asked me earlier who was selling the shares in the mining operation. That is it, the name my customer said. Carleton. I am almost sure. I remember he said the man was an Indian fighter…"

"Isn't he the commander of that fort where you're stationed?" Jesse asked.

"Yes, he is." Will couldn't help thinking of the old nursery rhyme about the boy who stuck his thumb in the pie, came up with a plum, and said, "Oh, what a good boy am I."

Joel had been telling Jose all about his plans to sell supplies to the cowboys. Jose thought it was a great idea and said he'd like to help. In fact, while Will was fishing unsuccessfully for more information on Gen. Carleton, Jose interrupted to ask Jesse if he could act as a traveling salesman for the Solis Store. Echoing a comment Joel had made to Will yesterday, Jose said he liked working for the Solises, but that he missed his life on the open range. If he went in with Joel, maybe they could both enjoy the best of both situations.

Will hoped introducing his two friends to each other might help both of them. But he was really too preoccupied with his discoveries to think about that now. Indeed, when Jesse got pulled into trade negotiations with Joel and Jose, he excused himself. He told Joel he'd see him in the morning. In the meantime, he wanted to pay a visit to Dr. Steck.

54

THE TERRITORIAL SUPERINTENDENT'S OFFICE

"Sir, you expressed curiosity about why General Carleton would associate with land speculators. Well, I think I know. I've learned that Carleton is selling mineral rights to the Indian lands and gathering investors to finance a mining operation there."

"Oh, you have...?" Steck asked leadingly.

"Uh," Will hesitated—he wasn't sure how to state this— "wouldn't that be against the law?"

"It certainly could be, young man. At least, I would think it would be unethical for Carleton to profit personally from his role as military commander. Do you have something in mind?"

"Well, I was just thinking that maybe we could notify his superiors in the War Office of this rumor..."

"Carleton's a powerful man. I doubt a rumor is going to threaten his job."

"But it doesn't seem fair for Carleton to take the Indian lands and profit from it himself. If there's gold and silver, doesn't it belong to the Indians?"

"Well, son, I don't know that I can rightly agree with that. The land's been claimed for the United States of America. I think the mineral rights probably belong to the federal government."

"But the government stole it from the Indians."

"That's one way of looking at it, but I don't think that's such a popular way."

"Well," Will argued, "it certainly isn't right for General Carleton to take the Indian lands for himself and then starve the Indians to death out in the desert."

"I could agree with you about that. The Union is spending a lot of money for the Indians' care. Probably this gold—if there is any, mind you—ought to go back to the government to reimburse expenses."

"But Carleton's not spending the money on the Indians," Will practically shouted.

"Yes, I know that's what your reports indicate."

"Do you believe me?"

"Yes," Steck hesitated. "Yes, yes. I do."

"So where is the money going? Into General Carleton's private bank accounts?"

"Now, now, son, we don't have any evidence..."

"Please, Dr. Steck, I'm not asking this for myself. I'm trying to do something for those poor Navajos out there dying in the desert."

"I understand. And, I suppose, I agree with you. I don't like Jim Carleton. He's a high-handed son of a bitch and a pompous ass. But, Will, he's got political support."

"What does that mean?"

"Look here," Steck went over to his desk and searched through a pile of papers. "I was going to show you these..."

"What is it?"

"I got back a reply on the telegraph. You know, I'd sent a message to Senator Sumner, as you suggested. And I sent a message to a friend of mine in the Interior Department. I thought it a good idea to bypass Jesse McDonald."

"Yes, sir." Will was glad to see that the Superintendent had trusted his perceptions. He was anxious to hear.

"Sumner replied: 'I abhor slavery in every form. But cannot side with Indians. Send more information.' Well, at least we've got his ear. And I'll send him that report you wrote."

"And the other reply?" Will asked. He was disappointed Senator Sumner hadn't immediately called for an investigation and had Carleton removed.

"My friend Jack Osborne says, 'Budgeted for 8577 Indians. From 1865 census. Carleton has powerful allies. If evidence of wrongdoing available, send me. But won't risk my neck. Sorry, Mike. Yours truly, Jack.'"

"That doesn't sound very helpful. But, look, sir, it's not the whole twelve thousand, but it's still a lot more than there are real Indians. The figures are two years old."

"It looks like he hasn't accounted for attrition all right. But, Will, I think that was your responsibility as Agent to correct..."

"My reports weren't being sent, sir," Will snapped back. "And what you call 'attrition' is people's lives."

"So it is. Well, Osborne says he'll look at evidence. You've got to understand, son, that you need solid evidence. You can't expect the government to remove a military commander just on your word."

"But, it's not my word. It's as clear as day that the Indians are being mistreated."

"That won't get a lot of sympathy from Washington."

"How about from you?" Will challenged.

"I want to see them kept peaceful so they can finally be incorporated into civilized society."

Will was once again reminded of Changing Woman's advice for how to fight this cause.

"If General Carleton is defrauding the government..."

"I would be the first to call for his removal. But, Will, you heard Jack Osborne's words. Carleton has powerful allies."

"You mean the men he's selling the mineral rights to?"

"Those are certainly among them."

"Would you be willing to help, shall we say, eliminate some of his powerful allies? You know some of these men, don't you?"

Steck sat down in his chair. He peered out the window a moment. Will thought he was probably wrestling with his conscience.

"Yes, I do know some of them. Socially anyway. And yes I guess I would be willing to help. So long as it's nothing illegal."

"Oh, no, sir. But, look, I've got an idea."

55

The Home of the Territorial Superintendent

The next Sunday evening, Will arrived promptly at seven-thirty p.m. at the adobe hacienda about two miles from the middle of town that was the home of Michael and Agnes Steck. It was simple, but—save for the Sangre de Cristo Hotel—the most comfortable place he had been in since he left home. Except for the uniform whiteness of the walls and the unusual construction demanded by the building materials, this house might well have been that of a high-ranking government official back in Virginia.

Already a few of the guests had arrived. The Stecks were hosting an elegant dinner party for some of the prominent citizens of Santa Fe. Michael Steck, Will discovered, had been welcomed by the upper crust of the city not because he was Superintendent of Indian Affairs but because he was a physician. Doctors were rare. Though Steck was no longer practicing, just as he had helped the missionary with an embarrassing ailment, so he sometimes attended members of the city's upper-class society.

In preparation for the evening, Will had devised a disguise for himself. He let his beard grow for several days—now he really was a Hairy Face, he joked with himself—and he found a pair of weak spectacles for sale at the Solis Store. He was not sure a disguise was necessary. But when the trader with the shock of red hair, whom he'd seen in Gen. Carleton's office, turned up among the dinner guests, he was glad he decided on it.

He was introduced as Agent Lee Williams, a surveyor, metallurgist, and geologist sent out from Washington to evaluate various sites in the New Mexico Territory. According to the story Dr. Steck told so well, this Mr. Williams from the Department of the Interior happened to be passing through Santa Fe after a visit to the northwestern parts of the Territory. The host of the party let it seem a last-minute invitation that brought Mr. Williams to this august gathering.

Will was a little nervous, but excited. Worried that he'd forget to answer to a fictitious name, he'd chosen a pseudonym based on his real name. He was also worried he'd be asked something specific or scientific about prospecting or metal extraction. He knew nothing about the subject.

But at every opportunity Dr. Steck insisted that the dinner guests not discuss business. Steck did not let himself get too far from Will throughout the evening, so he was almost always there to deflect any question about gold and silver prospects in the Territory. And, of course, the more Steck prevented questions, the more the guests wanted answers.

Then dinner was served: wild turkey roasted on a spit out in back of the house with several unusual vegetables that looked like cactus and roots, prepared by Agnes Steck's housekeeper, an Indian woman who reminded Will of Dezba. This was not an Easterner's turkey dinner. But it came close. Will imagined this was the cuisine the Diné would have enjoyed back home.

After a dessert of fresh strawberries and cream, the ladies who'd come with their husbands went with Mrs. Steck to the back parlor to gossip, while the men moved out to the wide veranda across the front of the house to smoke cigars and sip brandy.

When Dr. Steck offered a toast to welcome their visitor, one of the men spoke up finally, "I understand you want to rest after your expedition, sir. But can you just tell us briefly what you will conclude in your report to Washington?"

"I'm not at liberty to discuss my findings before I make my report," Will temporized one last time just to whet the curiosity to a keen edge. "But I understand some of you may have interests in the financial prospects of this Territory. It's beautiful land you have here…"

"Yes, yes." The heavy-set man with a brandy snifter in one hand and a cigar in the other tried to hurry him to answer his question.

"Well, if I may speak confidentially, just for the present company…"

Steck interrupted. "I must insist everyone here make their solemn oath, as gentlemen, that whatever Mr. Williams says will not go beyond this gathering. Perhaps the future of the Territory is at stake."

"Here, here," spoke up several of the onlookers.

"In actual fact," Will got to the meat of his plan, "I have to say there is not much to report. My team looked for potential geological excavation sites, and we saw only a few locations which gave any evidence of possible silver or gold deposits. Preliminary surveys at each of these sites proved to be unproductive. You understand we were looking at the lands previously controlled by the Navajo Indians, so I can only speak for those lands. But I would have to say, gentlemen, that I see very little hope for success with precious metal speculation."

There was an audible gasp among the men.

"But General Carleton has spoken of great likelihood of both gold and silver deposits there," protested one of the men.

Perhaps pushing the ruse too far, but unable to help himself, Will looked quizzical. "General Carleton? Can't say I know his name." He turned to their host. "Dr. Steck, perhaps you can enlighten me?"

"Carleton's at Fort Sumner, down south of here."

"Oh, yes," Will said. "Perhaps I do recognize the name…"

"But Jim Carleton owns all that land out there you said you were surveying…" someone said.

"Is that so?" Will replied. "That's odd. I am certain that land belongs to the federal government, if not to the Navajos."

"I've paid Carleton for mineral rights out there," another spoke up.

"Well, sir, I'm sorry to question the general. Perhaps there's been a misunderstanding. I am speaking as a scientist, not a businessman. But frankly, if I were you, *I* would not put one penny on the chance of getting it back in mining profits from those lands. I hope none of you have placed significant sums into such purchases. Those Navajo lands out around Fort Defiance are good for nothing better than to give back to the Indians."

Will gathered up all his integrity and innocence for the final climax. "In all honesty, I can tell you gentlemen, I have never found one single speck of gold or silver on any of the Navajo lands."

There was a hubbub throughout the gathering. "I'll be damned," someone said, "Carleton took me for a fool." From another: "I always suspected Carleton was a crook."

The big man with red hair rebutted the accusations. "Jim's always been fair with me. I can't complain. The commissary officer's been overstating the size of the beef rations for the damned Indians, and Jim's been fairly splitting the difference with me every month. He's no crook as far as I'm concerned."

No wonder Carleton had been in a good mood that day I saw the red-haired trader in the office.

Another spoke up: "I bet he thought there were riches out there. That's why he cleared the redskins out. But when he discovered there was nothing, he tried to sell it to us!"

"Tried to?" an angry voice responded, "Damn it, he did."

Dr. Steck put up his hands and gestured to the group to quiet down. "I must insist we have imposed too much already on Mr. Williams.

You are asking him to go beyond the bounds of what a geologist can say. I think we should let him retire..."

Will couldn't resist one more comment. "I'm very sorry to be the bringer of bad news. I had no idea you would have been expecting a different report. Haven't you seen the land out there? It's very beautiful, especially the Canyon. I thought you merchants here would be pleased with my findings that there are some lands in that sector for grazing cattle and spacious areas for sheep and goat herding. Why, Santa Fe could become the wool capital of the country..."

"Wool," somebody spat. "Who wants wool?"

"The Indians seem very good at weaving it..." Will said. But the men had lost interest in his comments and were animatedly talking among themselves.

"Good night, gentlemen," Dr. Steck announced. "Thank you for coming."

After the party, both Will and Steck believed they had successfully undercut Gen. James Carleton's political and economic power. His previous allies were not so likely to exert influence to defend him if any evidence of real wrongdoing could be found against him now.

"You understand, Will," Dr. Steck reiterated, "it isn't enough to get some people mad at him. You may only have gotten yourself in trouble tonight. If you say Carleton's defrauding the government and abusing the Indians, then you've got to be able to prove it in a court of law."

"Well, how am I going to be able to do that?"

"We need something in writing, something from Carleton's own hand. If you could get a receipt signed by him showing he took money for Indian services and, say, deposited it into his own bank account..."

"Isn't the suffering of the Diné proof he isn't serving them?"

"Diné? Oh, the Navajos. Well, how are you going to take that into a courtroom?"

"What are we going to do?" Will pleaded.

"Son, I think *you* are going to have to go back down there to Fort Sumner and find evidence. There's bound to be records around there."

"But how am I going to get to see them?"

"Marshal your resources. You're a clever young man. You did well tonight. Tell them you're doing a report for me..."

He wanted to object that Gen. Carleton wasn't going to cooperate with any kind of investigation he might say he'd been instructed to do, especially by the Territorial Superintendent. But what was the point? He knew what he had to get for Steck. He thought about the man's advice to marshal his resources. *I don't have any idea how Hasbaá and the Diné can help, but they are certainly my resources. And I've seen Hasbaá can come up with some unexpected resources of her own.*

56

THE DESERT

The next morning, Will cancelled his Spanish lesson. He thanked Joel and gave him a receipt showing he'd put another week's pay into the bank account. "I promise I'll be back to collect on the lessons."

He went over to the Solis Store to ask Jose to consider accompanying him back to Fort Sumner. Jose urged him to go on his own. "You can do it, *Señor Will,* you did real good coming up here. Me? I got duties now here at the store. And Joel and me are going into the trading business together. I have no reason to leave Santa Fe."

Jose was right that there was no reason for him to go with Will. He would then have to go on to El Paso or return to Santa Fe alone. *Why shouldn't I be the one to travel the distance by myself? I'm not the incompetent fool I'd been when I first arrived in the West.*

So, after he collected his things and bought a few supplies from Thanya, Will retrieved Barboncito's horse from the Sangre de Cristo's stables. The horse had eaten well during their two-week stay in Santa Fe. Will thought it probably looked healthier than it ever had. He felt proud he'd be returning the steed in such good condition. The horse seemed eager to get underway. *It probably felt cooped up in all this civilization.*

By mid-morning, Will was on his way back to Fort Sumner and Hasbaá. The three and a half day journey was one of the most intense experiences of his life.

By the afternoon of the third day of constant riding during all his waking hours, Will was in a kind of daze. There was a hawk that flew above him, high in the sky, for many hours. The bird was obviously tracking him. At first he feared it had mistaken him for prey. Then it occurred to him that, from the bird's point of view, that might not have been a mistake. Finally, though, he realized, the bird protected him.

He'd passed beyond his early fears of being alone in the desert to an almost delirious joyfulness in being out there splendidly free and buoyed up by nature. Soon it was easy to see how the bird overhead protected and guided him. For a while, Will began to fancy seeing from the hawk's point of view. In his imagination he flew over the strange landscape. It reminded him of the vision he'd had his first day at Fort Sumner.

The horse, too, seemed to possess a personality all of its own. Most of the time, it acted simply like a well-trained mount; in fact, it seemed to sense Will's inexperience and to accommodate him. But occasionally the animal seemed preoccupied with other exigencies than Will's comfort. Once it abruptly stopped in the middle of nowhere. It peaked its ears and slowly scanned the horizon back and forth. For well over ten minutes it stood, oblivious to Will's efforts to spur it on, but then, as if satisfied, the horse resumed the journey. Will wondered if they had come upon wandering ghosts which the horse knew to let pass undisturbed. On the afternoon of the second day, the horse, unbidden, broke into a headlong gallop. Will clung to the horse's strong neck, finally himself moving from fear to exhilaration, as the animal careened, occasionally neighing triumphantly, as fast as it could run for what seemed like hours.

The Indians had talked to Will about the coming-of-age rituals in their culture in which they went out alone into the desert or the mountains to seek the presence of their guiding spirit. Will imagined they did Indian religious practices, chanting and drumming. *I don't suppose they just ride all day, but this journey is certainly proving to be a coming-of-age for me.*

Will had never seen landscapes like these. The stark and barren mountains around him looked as if their skeletons were showing through. Rock formations were carved out of the sandstone by wind and water. In these formations, Will began to see faces. He knew it was just imagination, but the vision became very powerful. He saw these were the faces of the dead, crying out in their anguish. At first, he saw the dead among the Diné and sensed the pain and anger of the restless ghosts. Then he also saw the dead among the white settlers and the Hispanics who'd colonized the territory under the direction of the Spanish Conquistadors and the Franciscan missionaries. He saw hooded and helmeted figures brooding in the ravaged shapes of the rocks. They, too, cried out that there had been too much death.

There were so many unhappy ripples in the spirit-field. Will understood that he somehow could be loyal to both sides. He remembered the stories of Turquoise Boy. He recalled one in particular about Turquoise Boy bringing the men and the women back together after a quarrel. He hoped he could bring the Indians and the white men together.

Will rode as late as he could each day. But after nightfall even the horse had a difficult time finding its way. Without a moon overhead, the nights were darker than anything Will had ever seen in Virginia. Here the skies were not blue at night, but black as pitch. There were more stars than he'd ever imagined possible.

Sometimes he sang. He did all the hymns he could remember from his father's church. In his spiritual deliriousness, the songs all took on new meaning to him. Now those songs about God and Jesus and about loving your neighbor and receiving blessing seemed to be about Changing Woman and Turquoise Boy and about achieving an historic victory and saving a people from extinction. The God that had seemed so distant to him as a child, a white-bearded ruler on a great golden throne, now seemed as present to him as the brilliant sun that filled the sky over his head during the day.

How have I ever failed to realize the sun is God?

It's from the warmth of the bright burning star overhead that all life grows on earth. Even in this blazing heat, that's obvious. The lush woods back home, the grassy prairies, this barren desert—the plants, the birds in the air, the fishes in the sea, and animals on the land—all are incarnations of the light pouring down from heaven. And, in us human beings, somehow, that life has become conscious of itself and has begun to imagine the source of life is personal, like a parent. But it's not. The personality is in us. Not out there.

Will felt a wonderful relief that the sun was not personal. This God he glimpsed had no opinions, didn't care a whit about what he did, didn't judge or condemn. God just radiated life. *The sun is the source of* life. *The earth is life's creation and nuturing. That is why the Diné see the sun as Father Sky and the earth as Mother Earth.*

That's what Changing Woman is. Not some personal goddess out there somewhere, but nature itself. Mother Nature. That's why she's "changing," Nature is always in flux. The days go by. The seasons roll past.

When Hasbaá says Changing Woman speaks to her, she means she sees in the round of nature the clues for how to live the right life, the life that honors and participates in Mother Nature's ongoing life.

I'm always in the presence of God, Will rejoiced, weary with travel and dazed by the heat and brightness. *Beauty before me, beauty behind me, beauty above me and beauty below me. All around me is beauty*

57

Bosque Redondo

When Will arrived at the Bosque Redondo Reservation, just at twilight, he skirted the fort. He didn't want Carleton or any of the soldiers to see him. Perhaps they'd never missed him. At any rate, what he'd been doing was none of their business.

He went right to Hasbaá's hogan. He was hungry and wanted to eat more than anything. But there was another part of him that hoped Hasbaá would be waiting for him with the sheepskins laid out on the floor, ready to take him in her arms.

When he entered, however, he found Hasbaá was not alone. With her were Dezba and Barboncito and several of the adult Navajos he'd come to know as part of this family.

"We've been waiting for you." Hasbaá embraced him in the stooped way possible inside the low-ceilinged hogan. Will wondered how they could have known he'd arrive this evening, if that's what Hasbaá meant by "waiting for you." In his state of mind, he explained to himself that the hawk that had followed him must have told the Indians he was coming.

"Tell us what happened," Dezba and Barboncito asked almost simultaneously.

Dezba gave him a piece of jerky to chew on and water in an earthen cup. Without a pause, Will started in on the story.

A half hour later, he finished his tale. "So I did not learn anything about 'the circumstances of my appointment.' *And* we somehow have to get physical evidence that Carleton is a crook. I don't know how we'll do that."

There was a period of awkward silence. Then Hasbaá smiled comfortably. "You have done well, my husband."

Will relaxed. He felt such affection from her. It made all his hardship worthwhile. "We have prepared the sweat lodge for your return. Let us go now."

"Oh, Hasbaá, I don't think I can do that. I'm exhausted."

"You are weak from your travels. You need purification. The sweat will take all the poison from you from being around the Hairy Faces."

Will felt his cheeks. He'd grown a beard for disguise and now had another four days' growth. He was pleased to think that Hasbaá saw beyond this fact.

"Changing Woman awaits you in the sweat lodge. She will reward you and give you comfort. She will help you fulfill your mission."

He could not resist Hasbaá. If he had paid just a little more attention, in Hasbaá's last sentence he might have perceived a hint as to what was about to happen—sooner than he'd expected. But he had not, and so, becoming almost joyful in his exhaustion, he followed the Indians to the sweat lodge.

58

The Sweat Lodge

It was dark now. The sky was brilliant with stars. Near the lodge, a fire blazed yellow and orange. Will marveled how the colors of the flame flickered across the shell of the lodge and across the bodies of the Indians. His senses seemed particularly acute.

Before they entered the sweat, the people formed a circle around the firepit. Hasbaá drummed and chanted. After a while, a bowl was passed around, and they all drank from it. Will recognized it as the bitter potion they'd sipped before to make them purge poisons from their bodies. He wondered what was in it, but then decided it didn't really matter. He trusted Hasbaá's medicine. Tonight, in spite of its familiar bitterness, he did not find it offensive and drank deeply. The vomiting that followed felt good to him. He did not gag at all, but simply opened his throat and allowed his body to empty itself. Soon his head cleared. He felt awake, fully alive. He was no longer tired. He no longer wanted food. He was still hungry, but the hunger was for knowledge and for victory.

Hasbaá sprinkled water on the participants, as before, as they entered the lodge. Will took his place in the circle. He was naked now, and the nakedness felt good. For two weeks, he'd been dressed up like a city dweller all the time. *What a relief to shed the artificial skin and be myself again!*

The hot rocks were pushed into the lodge. Sacred herbs burned fragrant. Water sizzled on the rocks and filled the lodge with steam. The people sang and chanted and prayed. Now beyond his control, Will's consciousness moved out of his body to encompass the whole space of the lodge. He couldn't tell where his body began or ended. It didn't seem to matter. Soon he felt the presence of Changing Woman in the heat.

Then the flap flew open, and cool air rushed in. It brought him back to his senses just a bit. He felt the night outside. It thrilled him to remember the past few nights sleeping alone in the desert with the huge sky above him. The stars were icy cold in their distance. Will shivered. When the flap closed and the heat surrounded him again, the caress of the cleansing steam was Changing Woman's presence.

"We must make a journey of discovery, Will," Hasbaá said. "We must go out into the darkness. Can you cleanse your inner vision until you see only the Light?"

Soon the cleansing powers of the sweat lodge overtook him. He began to observe the pale white light he'd seen before. Though it was pitch dark, save for the rocks in the pit glowing dully, an ethereal light came to fill the lodge. *Maybe this light is only in my mind, but for the first time, I can really see.*

In the strange mystical state generated by the heat of the sweat lodge, Will felt he could see to a god beyond God, to a meaning behind religion. He glimpsed an important truth—that to do God's will, to do what's good and right, isn't to do what *other* people expect of you, but to do what *you* expect of yourself.

Then the flap opened the second time, and white hot light poured through the opening. Will was surprised to see that a strange character outside the lodge stooped down, looked in, and beckoned to him to follow him out. The character seemed clearly to be Turquoise Boy, the round-faced, blue-bodied figure Hasbaá had painted in the sand. But now the character was man-sized. Its body was tall and thin. Will thought perhaps this was Hasbaá wearing a mask with her body painted blue. But he was sure he could still see Hasbaá across from him inside the lodge. *Another Indian then in a ritual costume.*

Will followed Turquoise Boy out of the lodge. He quickly dressed himself in Navajo garments he found laid out on the earth beside the lodge. Then he followed the figure dressed as Turquoise Boy. There was light outside now, perhaps the wan light of early morning. If so, he was surprised the sweat lasted so long. Turquoise Boy led him around behind the lodge to a ladder that stood straight up. Will's eye followed the ladder up, up into the sky. *I wonder why I never noticed that was there before.*

Following Turquoise Boy, he began to climb. As he got farther and farther from the ground and the little sweat lodge dwindled to a tiny speck below, he could see the ladder led up to a hole in the sky. And he climbed on up through the opening right in the center of that blue abyss.

Will hoisted himself up through the hole in the sky and found he was standing on solid ground. Turquoise Boy was there waiting for him. The masked figure never spoke, but Will understood that he was to follow and that no danger could befall him in Turquoise Boy's presence.

They were on a red plain that stretched out in all directions. Overhead a blue-green sun shone down. As they walked, Will noticed that to his right and left stood huge figures, like the sandpaintings of the Holy Persons. He thought he recognized Monster-Slayer as one of these figures that towered above the red plain as high as a mountain. And there was Child-of-the-Water.

Then they came to a lone hogan. Turquoise Boy pulled back the woolen rug that covered the opening and bid him enter. Inside he found there were corn cakes set out for him to eat. He was very hungry and ate ravenously. Then he looked up and saw that Hasbaá crouched next to him with a drinking gourd in her hand. She offered him water from the rawhide bucket slung over her shoulder. He drank the water gratefully. *I wonder where we are.*

"You ask why Changing Woman brought you to this place," Hasbaá said gently and compassionately. "You seek to learn the circumstances of your appointment?"

"I do," Will answered as though he were participating in a ritual.

"Rest here." Hasbaá gestured toward the sheepskin rugs on the floor. Will felt a great rush of sexual excitement and thought that Hasbaá was going to make love to him in this spirit-realm hogan right now. But he reminded himself they had work to do first.

"Sleep," Hasbaá said, "We will journey together in your dreams."

59

Washington, DC.

William stretched out on the soft fleece and closed his eyes. He was grateful finally to be allowed to rest. Then he heard Hasbaá calling.

He roused himself and was startled to see he was in the waiting room outside Jesse McDonald's office in Washington, D.C. He told himself he must still be dreaming. But he certainly felt wide awake.

Hasbaá was in the room with him, not dressed as a woman today, but in the loincloth and vest of a warrior. Hasbaá's face was painted for battle. She beckoned to Will to get out of his seat in the back corner of the room and to come over to the half-open door into McDonald's office.

Will remembered that this is what had happened to him before. He'd awakened to find that the waiting room was empty and that he could hear voices in the adjoining office.

He got up and walked over toward Hasbaá at the half-open door. When he looked back, Will was surprised to see that his body was still sleeping soundly in the chair and that he was now a kind of transparent image of himself. He realized Hasbaá was also transparent. He could see through her to the wall and tall-backed wooden chairs behind.

Hasbaá spoke softly to him. "You are free to enter now and listen. You will not disturb them."

Will walked past Hasbaá into the office. Behind the desk was Jesse McDonald. Across from him Pastor Benedict. The secretary, Charles, stood at McDonald's side, methodically handing him page after page of a thick pile of papers he held.

While McDonald gave a cursory glance to each sheet, Pastor Benedict talked. "So Ayers started recording how much money Carleton was getting for the Indians' housing expenses. That's what he noticed first."

"I was always generous in recommending disbursements to the Congressional committee," McDonald said. "Carleton's done a fine job out there of settling down the Navajos. If there was a little extra cream in the milk, he certainly deserved it. Besides, keeping Carleton happy keeps the Indians pacified. And that's my job."

"Oh, Jesse, I'm not questioning you. I'm pointing out that Ayers noticed the discrepancy between what was allocated and what was actually spent. He saw Carleton was paying local contractors for work the Indians were having to do themselves.

"Now I thought this was not a bad strategy myself. The general was certainly good to me. He understood the hardships I suffered out there so far from home—such a sacrifice being away from Beatrice!" Benedict winked. Will wondered what that meant.

"And, of course, Jim knew that you and I were friends..."

McDonald gestured at the pastor to get on with the story. "Carleton kept the Indians occupied and managed to channel a little prosperity into the region. I think even Ayers saw the wisdom. But he also saw a certain, shall we say, vulnerability in Carleton's position. I guess he wasn't satisfied with the gratuities he was receiving and expected more.

"Now, you understand, Jesse, that I'm presupposing all this. I didn't pry into Jim Carleton's business. But I did keep my eyes open. I think Ayers threatened to expose the whole deal if he didn't get cut in..."

"And just who was he going to expose it to?"

"I suppose to you."

McDonald chortled under his breath. "And so...?"

"Well, all I know is that Ayers then ended up in trouble. Carleton's old sidekick from way back, Sergeant Peak, went out to Ayers' quarters and found an Indian woman with her throat cut in the bed. Looked like she'd been raped and murdered. Or maybe the other way round."

Will shivered to hear the details. *Will I ever be able to sleep in that bed again?*

"Did Ayers do it?"

"That was the accusation. Didn't really seem in character for the man. But Carleton ordered him put under arrest. Then he disappeared. Some soldiers found him dead a few days later out in the desert strung up to a cactus. It looked like the Indians had taken revenge. Carleton said he didn't like it. Threatened to hang some Indians. He didn't want the soldiers to worry something like that might happen to them, too. But then he laughed and said it served Ayers right, anyway. Never did punish the Indians. I always thought maybe Peak was behind it all. But it's not my place to judge," Pastor Benedict said sanctimoniously. "As a man of God, I must remain neutral."

"Well, Sheldon, that is mighty fine of you. But let me ask you a simple question. Just for my information."

"Certainly, Jesse."

"How much is Carleton making out of this for himself?"

"I have no idea. Honestly."

Charles had stood by silently. "We know he's laid claim to some of the Indian lands up around Fort Defiance."

"I'm not objecting," McDonald answered defensively. "But, look, if I'm going to cover for him, he can't be robbing the agency blind. Why should he be the only one profiting? He has a right to his due, and to a little cream on the side, but he shouldn't be overdoing it. We had enough controversy over Carleton's ideas in the Indian Wars."

"You'll have to take that up with Carleton yourself, Jesse," Benedict shot back. "When I told him I'd had enough of trying to convert those damned heathens and wanted a transfer back to Washington, Carleton asked me to come see you and explain why he didn't want a Congressional investigation."

"Appointing a new Agent could certainly raise suspicions in Congress," Charles said. "They're all looking for excuses to indict the Administration."

"Now, Charles, I appreciate your political perspicacity. But what difference is one Agent getting himself killed for philandering with an Indian going to make?"

"Well, sir, there's this last report you've got from him in your hands. Have you been reading it?"

"Not exactly."

"Well, now, if you read between the lines, you see Ayers was already setting Carleton up for a fall."

McDonald handed the pages of the report back to his secretary. "Then why don't you just get rid of this?"

"Say," Benedict spoke up, "I carried that all this way. It's got some glowing words about my efforts to convert the Indians to Christianity."

"I'm sorry, Sheldon, but you'll just have to be satisfied with knowing somebody appreciated your efforts. But it won't be Congress."

"But then there's no Agent, and there've been no reports," Charles whined. "If some Radical Republican Congressman hears about this, he can use it as evidence that Johnson is neglecting his duties while he's mollycoddling the South and trying to undo the Acts of Reconstruction."

"This doesn't have anything to do with the impeachment," McDonald retorted.

"Then keep it quiet. Don't forward any reports to Congress that say anything but that Carleton's policy at the Bosque Redondo is a great success."

"I guess, you're right, Charles. What a day, what a day," McDonald exclaimed. "First, everything is in an uproar about Congress wanting to impeach the President. And then all those people coming through here, every one of them wanting something from me. I tell you, Shel, it's just too much. And then you come in here with your news."

Will recognized this part of the conversation as something he'd heard before. He imagined that if he went back outside to the waiting room, he'd discover he was just waking up and was about to eavesdrop on this conversation. He could hear so much better in the room this time.

"I'm sorry to add to your burden, Jesse."

"I know it's not your fault. And I'm always happy to see you, you know that, Sheldon."

"We go back a long ways."

"Why do I put myself through this?" McDonald groaned in a kind of mock complaint.

Charles answered, "Because, Mr. McDonald, you like power. And you like the money that goes with it..."

"Once again, Charles, you've hit the nail on the head." McDonald sounded jovial. "No wonder you and I get on so well. So, let's quit the belly-aching. We got a problem here to deal with."

"Appoint an apprentice to the Agent. Nobody'll know the difference. When the apprentice gets there, he just takes over 'cause his predecessor's gone."

"There's a handsome lad asleep out in your waiting room looking for a job," Benedict said. "Says he wants to help the Indians."

"You think he can be trusted?"

"I've been talking with him out there in the waiting room."

"I thought you two were in the washroom," Charles interrupted.

"The washroom…" McDonald guffawed.

"As I was sayin', Jesse, I was talking with him in the waiting room."

"Imagine that!" Charles chimed in again.

"Oh, Charles. He's just a little boy. Give him a chance. Carleton can write the reports. This youngster will just sign them. He won't know the difference. He'll take instruction from Carleton and, I'll bet, he'll do fine."

So that's what Benedict really meant. He was recommending me because he thought I'd be a dupe.

"Are you sure, Shel?" McDonald asked. "What do we know about him besides what you learned in the, er, waiting room?"

"He's got the prettiest eyes you can imagine." Benedict answered as though that were reason enough to hire him.

"And, Jesse," Charles interjected, "he brought this letter of introduction from Harry Burnside…"

"Harry sent him? Well, Charles, why didn't you say so? Let me see the letter."

"But he's a Confederate Rebel."

"All the better. He'll have no political allies in the Congress."

"He'll be just right for appointment as an apprentice." Benedict's voice dropped to a conspiratorial whisper. "And, Jesse, I can certainly sympathize with his plight. You and me, we oughta help him, just for old times' sake. He needs a job. He's bright-eyed and bushy-tailed. Just your sort o' young man."

"Ah-hem." McDonald audibly cleared his throat.

"I mean, he's like you were as a lad. Why I remember when you and I first met…"

"But is he going to be just another problem?" McDonald cut short Benedict's nostalgia. "You said he wanted to help the Indians."

"I said he was handsome, Jesse, and had pretty eyes. I think he's kind of simple. He looked dopey and he fell asleep while I was talking to him. I don't think he knows a thing about Indians except that they're somewhere out West. "

"I'm not sure you'll like this." Charles handed McDonald the letter from Harry Burnside.

McDonald began to read the letter. "Pshaw," he said.

Will walked up to the desk and looked over Mr. McDonald's shoulder. He could plainly read the letter from his patron and friend.

Dear Jesse,

The bearer of this letter, Mr. William Lee of Lynchburg, is a fine young man, the possessor of many talents.

I remember, Jesse, that you were once such a fine young man. When you were Will's age, I was glad to take you into my home and my heart and to teach you how to be a cultured adult and to give you your first job in government.

I have heard that you have used your position for personal gain and that political power has gone to your head. I am ashamed of the things I've heard. I once cared for you greatly.

I urge you to redeem yourself in my eyes by giving William Lee an appointment in your department. Give him a hand as I gave you one when you needed it.

Those of us who march to the beat of the different drummer had best maintain our ranks. You understand what I mean.

Sincerely,

Harry Burnside, Esquire

As he finished reading the letter, McDonald burst out laughing. "Well, I'll certainly have to redeem myself in ol' Harry Burnside's eyes," he said scornfully. "Charles, go wake the boy up."

Charles went out to the waiting room. "Mr. McDonald will see you now."

60

Dine Bikeyah

Will found himself back in the lone hogan in the spirit realm. Hasbaá was calling his name. "Husband, do you now understand the circumstances of your appointment?"

"I was sent out here to help hide Carleton's crimes. But I will not cooperate. I'm going to expose him."

"Let us get the evidence to stop the Hairy Face." Still dressed as a warrior, Hasbaá stood and gestured to Will to follow her out of the hogan.

In a reflex to Hasbaá's reference to Carleton, Will felt his face. To his surprise, he was clean-shaven, not a Hairy Face. *But when did I shave?*

Outside on the red plain, Segundo waited with three magnificent horses. Will thought it odd that Segundo was with them, but he had seen so much that was odd he'd become accustomed to it.

Segundo handed him the reins to one of the horses. Though, Indian style, there was a blanket but no saddle, Will somehow jumped up onto the horse and straddled its girth easily.

In a moment, the other two were also mounted, and the three began to ride fast across the plain. As they rode at a breakneck pace that reminded Will of galloping like this on Barboncito's horse, he saw that the sky was filling with dark billowing thunderclouds. Lightning flashed all around them. Then to Will's amazement, the ground seemed to drop away, and the horses hurdled forward, their hooves pounding into the very substance of the clouds. It was as if they had become the lightning itself and raced across the sky.

There was rain pouring down around them, but it created no discomfort. It seemed to Will to cleanse and purify him after the experience in the office in Washington. He felt so used, so dirtied. He was grateful to Harry Burnside for the assistance, but he thought Jesse McDonald had hardly fulfilled Harry's wishes. He hadn't given Will a hand. He had sent him out to be another victim of his own and Carleton's greed. *What about the different drummer?*

Will imagined himself a cloud blown through the sky on the rush of wind. The storm carried the three riders far. Then it began to subside.

The rain dwindled to a fine sprinkle. There were trees around them: aspens, pines, junipers and piñons. The horses slowed to a walk. Segundo held up his right hand in a signal to halt. The three descended from their mounts and began to climb a gentle slope.

The ground all around was a sandy yellow clay. In the rain, it had turned to sticky mud that clung to their feet as they padded through it.

Then there spread out before them a deep valley. Through the middle of it ran a clear blue stream. Will stood between Hasbaá and Segundo and looked out over the countryside. He recognized this as the canyon he'd seen in his vision the first day.

This was *Diné Bikéyah*, as the Navajo homelands were called in their native language. This was the labyrinthine Canyon de Chelly. All through these canyons and ravines, the Diné people had made their settlements. Here they'd raised their children for generations. Here they herded their sheep and goats and grew their food and gathered sacred herbs. Here they worshipped their gods, in the land Turquoise Boy had led them to through the reed ladder.

Will felt great joy. He looked at the other two and saw the same joy in their faces. Hasbaá and Segundo spoke to each other in their native language. And, to Will's surprise, he understood. Then simultaneously, spontaneously, they began to laugh together. The laughter rang through the valley. Will realized they were rejoicing in their return to their homeland. They were rejoicing in Segundo's return to life. He had, indeed, come back to Hasbaá as he had promised.

And as they laughed, the three men rejoiced in their manhood together. In the way of dreams, Will saw that they now stood naked. They were showing their bodies to one another, reveling in the love and admiration of the others. The sun was warm on their chests. Will saw how strong and beautiful was Segundo's body. He marveled as Segundo presented his manhood for all to see. And he saw how lithe and beautiful was Hasbaá's body. He marveled at Hasbaá's manhood and at this Two-Spirit Person's ability to comprise both manhood and womanhood.

Will felt how strong and lithe and beautiful his own body was. He marveled at how he had become a man and could now present himself to these other men for their respect and admiration.

A torrent of energy engulfed them. Like a fire shooting up from earth and rising high into the sky, life force coursed through them. Their laughter rang out like a lover's cry at the moment of climax.

Again as in the way of dreams, Will realized he now wore the loincloth and beaded vest that Segundo had worn. And now Segundo was gone. It was only Will and Hasbaá. Hasbaá looked deep into his eyes with such love and respect. "Welcome home, my husband," she said in Diné. "I love you," she added in English.

Then Hasbaá directed him back to the horses. "Come, we have a mission to complete." Hasbaá spurred her mount.

Will followed Hasbaá away from *Diné Bikéyah*. Soon the sun set, and the clouds closed behind them. Again they raced through the stormy night. Lightning struck at the horses' hooves behind them, and spurred them to frenzied pace. The horses neighed jubilantly, exultant in their power.

Will hung onto the reins, sometimes clinging to the horse's great neck. The mane smelled musky-rich and wild.

Then they left the storm behind them. Will thought he heard the toll of the Fort Sumner bell echoing across the desert. They rode through the night, down the wide rut of the Pecos River along the boundary of the Bosque Redondo. In the distance, he saw a few gleams of yellowish light—fires or lanterns at the fort.

Hasbaá reined in her horse near the Diné settlement. They jumped down from the great steeds and climbed up the rocky walls of the wash. Will looked back to see the horses, milky white and shadowy roan in the darkness, canter off proudly to the spirit realm whence they'd come.

61

Fort Sumner

Will knew he was dreaming and that his physical body still sat in the little sweat lodge, the shadow of which he could just make out as they passed. In the dream, he noticed, he and Hasbaá were still garbed as Diné warriors. They went up through the screen of trees, on beyond his quarters, and right up to the gate of Fort Sumner.

They crept stealthily and avoided the sentries who, in any case, did not seem to take any notice of them even when they slipped right behind one of them and into the officer's compound. By now, Will had realized where they were headed. *Of course, where else but to Gen. Carleton's office? Dr. Steck had said to get written evidence. That is where that evidence would be found.*

But what's the good of getting it in a dream vision?

They walked right up to the door of the office. It was locked. Hasbaá stepped away and went quickly into an unlocked office nearby. In a moment, she returned with a key.

"From Lt. Bauer's desk," she whispered.

Will unlocked the door and went inside. At first, the room was pitch dark. But he soon began to see well enough to make out the desk and the filing cabinets behind it. The same ethereal light that had filled the sweat lodge now began to illuminate the military office. Soon it was bright enough to read.

Heavy curtains were drawn across the window. Will hoped that the mysterious light could not be seen from the parade ground outside. It was the middle of the night, and he and Hasbaá had no business in the general's office.

Hasbaá suggested he look first in the filing cabinet. Opening the top drawer, Will read the titles printed on the folders. They were not in alphabetical order. He riffled through them. He hoped one or another of the titles would mean something. The first such folder he came to caused him to sputter angrily. He pulled the folder out of the drawer, turned around, and set it on the desk. It was titled "Reports of William Lee, Indian Agent—unacceptable."

He looked quickly through the pages. He saw all the reports he'd carefully penned and posted to the Office of Indian Affairs. In the back of the folder were the letters he'd written appealing for aid. They had never been sent. Dezba had been right.

He saw the next folder in the drawer was titled "Reports of Indian Agent—to be sent." Inside was a single page with a few short paragraphs. He did not bother to read it. He knew what it must say: "Everything's fine here. Gen. Carleton is great." Folded over it was a half sheet of paper with the note: "Awaiting signature."

In another drawer, toward the back where the files were probably never looked at anymore, he found a report titled: "Soil Conditions at

Fort Sumner." He looked through it. It indicated that as early as 1863, before the Indians were moved to this area, a government assayer had determined that the soil was too alkaline for food crops. *Even before the whole Bosque Redondo experiment started, Carleton must have known it would fail. The Indians could never have become self-sufficient here.*

Another folder in the back of the drawer held a report titled: "Comanche Activity along Texas-New Mexico Border." It was also dated 1863. It argued that settlers in the most habitable areas in the central and northern portions of the New Mexico Territory could be protected from attack by the belligerent and already inflamed Comanche tribes in west Texas by placing docile or vanquished Indian settlements on reservations along the border to create a buffer zone. *This was the real reason for putting the Diné at Bosque Redondo!*

In a more recent set of files, Will found a folder labeled: "Cost Reports on Indian Housing." In it were receipts showing large government disbursements for building materials. Some of the receipts actually had attached to them breakdowns of how the monies were supposedly used: lumber, tools, carpenter supplies, even roof tiles. But there were no buildings on the reservation made of lumber and roofed with tiles. There was practically no housing provided for the Indians at all. And one of the receipts was for that damn brass bell from St. Louis. Carleton had charged the cost against the Indians' housing allowance.

He showed Hasbaá what he found. "Is that what you need for your Dr. Steck?" the specter asked. Will could see right through Hasbaá; she seemed to glow from an inner light. She was obviously an apparition, just as she'd appeared in Jesse McDonald's waiting room.

"Well, by itself this doesn't prove the buildings weren't built. We need something that shows where the money actually went. I wonder if Carleton keeps his personal records here."

"In the desk," Hasbaá suggested. "See, this drawer is locked." She pulled on one of the brass knobs.

"How are we going to get in?"

"The key is behind the nib drawer in the inkwell."

"How do you know that?"

"My aunt is the general's maid."

Will was just thinking that if Dezba had access to this office, then perhaps tomorrow they could get her to get these files in reality. The dream quality of his experience had faded a little. He no longer flew through the sky on a magical steed. But he was sure this was all still a dream. *What would I be doing in the general's office in the middle of the night?*

Will found the key secreted in the inkwell. As he opened the drawer in hopes of finding Carleton's personal records, it occurred to him that even if Dezba could get into the files unnoticed, in spite of her ability to speak English, she probably couldn't read the Hairy Face language. *Who else but he could possibly retrieve these documents?* He had a sinking feeling. In a way, he hoped the dream investigation would prove nothing. *I'd hate to have to do this kind of espionage in reality.*

In the drawer was a small canvas-covered ledger. Will checked back to find the date for one of the receipts for housing expenditures. Then he scanned through the ledger to find that date.

And here's the evidence I need!

In what looked like the general's own handwriting were notations that showed how the expenses were to be reported alongside a record of deposits to various bank accounts. In the back of the ledger was a loose sheet of note paper that listed a series of bank account names, all under the officially penned rubric: "Accounts of James C. Carleton, General." Some of the accounts were styled Carleton, but others had apparently unrelated names: St. Vrain, Romero, Cantrill, Maxwell, Baca, Winthrop—fictitious names the general used to hide his embezzlement.

In the bottom of the drawer, Will found several hand-drawn copies of a map of the New Mexico Territory. If he understood what he saw, it looked as if vast tracts of land in the *Diné Bikéyah* were labeled with the names from that list of accounts. The general must have put in claims using those same fictitious names.

He showed Hasbaá what he'd found. "Pull these out and bring them with you."

Will didn't believe they'd be able to bring the documents back from the dream, but this was Hasbaá's medicine at work. He did as instructed.

"I will watch for the sentry while you collect the evidence you need." The spectral warrior slipped out the office door and closed it behind her.

Will replaced the folders in their respective drawers. He took the page about soil conditions and one of the materiel receipts that matched a breakdown of deposits to Carleton's own pocket. Everything else went back into the file cabinet where it had come from, except the folder of Will's "unacceptable" reports. He did not notice that he'd left that on the corner of the desk.

He put away the ledger, minus a couple of pages, and determined that everything in the desk drawer was back in place. He folded the pages Hasbaá told him to take, along with one of the copies of the map and the list of accounts, and tucked them under his warrior's vest. He was beginning to get nervous about this whole thing. *This is a dream, of course, but it seems so real.*

He locked the drawer and slipped the brass key into its hiding place in the inkwell. Just then he noticed the folder of his reports that had to go back in the file cabinet. As he grabbed it up, his eye was caught by the ornate desk set. The silver gleamed softly in the pale light that filled the room. Will found he couldn't take his eyes off the gleam. He stood there transfixed.

The pale light faded out. The gleam from the polished silver waned. The room became pitch dark. Will was still paralyzed. He tried to call out to Hasbaá. But he couldn't get his mouth or throat to work. *I must be waking up.*

Just then a light flashed under the door to the office. Then the door swung open and the room filled with brilliant illumination from a lantern. Will could just make out Gen. Carleton's enraged countenance in the glare. Carleton was holding the lantern at arm's length just above his face. In his other hand was his shiny silver pistol.

Suddenly there was an explosion that rocked Will's consciousness. Then another. Gen. Carleton had fired his pistol into the air to summon help.

Will realized he was awake. And he could move. *But how did I get here?* He'd expected to awaken in the sweat lodge. *What am I supposed to do now? Hasbaá had been my guide. And now she's gone. What's happened?*

"You little bastard, how dare you enter my office!" The general shouted as he strode into the room. "How dare you defile my desk with your Injun-loving hands!" His eyes blazed in the light from the lantern. "I will not tolerate *anyone* in my office without permission. Much less you, Mr. Lee."

Will's sight was dazzled, but now he could move. He cringed under Carleton's threatening glare. To defend himself, he held up the sheath of papers. "These were supposed to have been sent to Washington. What are they doing here?"

"I am the Commanding Officer," the general thundered. "I decide what gets sent where. What you wrote demonstrates total disregard for my policies. That is tantamount to insubordination. Who do you think you are to question me? I've been in New Mexico since '63, when you Southerners were waging war against the Union. You rebels should have all been executed as traitors."

Gen. Carleton came around the back of the desk. He pushed Will out of the way and knocked the sheath of reports out of his hand. As Carleton noticed the pages scatter onto the floor, he lowered the lantern and exclaimed, "Look at the mud you've tracked in here. God damn your soul."

There was dried and caked yellow mud all over the floor.

Setting the still-smoking pistol down, the general tugged at the locked drawer of his desk. He found it secure and appeared satisfied that the young Agent had not gotten into his private papers.

Will stood still half paralyzed. He watched helplessly as a sardonic grin spread across the general's face.

"You seem so concerned about your reports. As though anybody really cared what you have to say. Well, now you'll get your reward for your diligence. You have just committed a crime against a general officer of the United States Army, Mr. Lee. Considering your background with the Confederacy, I believe this is an act of treason.

"Since coming to Fort Sumner, you have repeatedly ignored my advice. You have flouted my instructions about your duties. God damn you, man, you have even failed to appear for one scheduled appointment after another. You may be a civilian, but you are going to pay for this, you bastard, just like the Rebel infiltrator I believe you really are."

Will felt threatened. But more than anything he felt abandoned and betrayed. By Hasbaá? Yes, but more by his inability to distinguish dream from reality. For the first time in his life, he couldn't tell the difference.

Will felt relieved he'd got everything back in place and that drawer locked. He wanted to feel for the papers inside his shirt, but didn't want to give away the hidden evidence. He hoped he really did have them.

He discovered he wore his own clothes again, not the beadwork vest of Segundo. He touched his cheek and felt that he was clean-shaven. Before any of the dream had started, he'd been sporting seven days' growth of beard. He was still in a daze.

"Maybe I should just shoot you, but I guess we'll do this by the book." Carleton held the pistol on Will while several sentries, brought by the gunshots, the light and the commotion, showed up at the door, among them J.F. Peak.

"Sergeant Peak, take the traitor to the guardhouse and lock him up," he heard Carleton say to his aide and felt himself hustled out of the room.

In his rage, Carleton did not instruct Sgt. Peak to search Will. And so, obedient to the letter of his command, without a word, the big sergeant grabbed the young civilian by the upper arm and dragged him out of the office, across the parade ground and over to the guardhouse at the far end. He laughed mockingly as he threw Will into the cell and pulled the heavy wooden door shut with a bang and locked it.

Though Will was mortified at being caught, he realized he had discovered the crucial documents with which to challenge Carleton's control, and as he lay sprawled on the bare floor he felt for the precious papers inside his shirt.

Part III

Home

62

The Guardhouse

There was no furniture in the small cell: no chair; no bed, mattress or pillow; only a bucket, which stank of excrement, and a rough woolen blanket for bedding. As upset as he was about being discovered and jailed—and desperate to know what had happened to Hasbaá—Will felt that the secret papers made the whole effort worthwhile. And, indeed, he *did* have the papers. He was amazed that he'd actually managed to get hold of them.

He tried to sleep. He hadn't slept in several days and needed to rest. But he had had such a perplexing adventure leading up to his incarceration, his mind was racing. He wondered and worried about Hasbaá. *Why hadn't Hasbaá alerted me? Was I mistaken that she'd accompanied me? Where is Hasbaá now?*

He kept falling into fitful dreams in which a guard would come upon him suddenly in the dark and demand to search the cell. If they found the incriminating documents on him, Carleton would kill him for sure and the evidence would be lost. He knew he had to get it to the Diné before the general discovered the papers missing.

During the night, he began to hope that his capture and incarceration were all just another part of the strange dream that had started several hours ago in the sweat lodge. But, in the morning, he awoke to find himself still in the cell. The first thing he did was to feel for the documents hidden in his shirt. Finding them there, he knew that everything he remembered had actually happened. *But how?*

Soon after sun-up, the temperature began to rise, and with it the stench in the cell. It was hard to breathe. To cope with the heat Will stripped off his shirt and trousers. He'd been wearing the same clothes for six days; at least, he thought so, though he also remembered being dressed as a Navajo warrior.

Now, in only his muslin underdrawers, he hunched over the small iron-barred window of the cell. He had tucked the pilfered documents into the folds of the blanket. He kept vigil at the window because he couldn't bear the stink of excrement in the cell, but also because he hoped to spy one of the Navajos come by. If he could pass the papers to one of them, he or she could deliver them to Hasbaá. Will was sure the Diné could use these documents to prove their grievances, but it all depended on getting them to Dr. Steck in Santa Fe.

Will knew it was not likely for an Indian to be in this area of Fort Sumner. But he hoped maybe luck—and Hasbaá's powers—would be with him. He understood that in some way Hasbaá was able to exercise influence over things like luck and coincidence. This is how Hasbaá was a healer and guide for the Diné—and for him.

He was proud of himself for having accomplished his task last night in getting the evidence on Gen. Carleton. But he knew it had been as much Hasbaá's accomplishment as his own. And, at least until that last moment, it had seemed luck had been with him. Maybe his arrest was going to turn out also to be part of that good luck, though for the time being he was scared. From his cell window he could see the gallows erected in the parade grounds.

Will's thoughts were interrupted by the sudden clank of the cell door. Sgt. Peak came into the room, bringing a cup of cold coffee and a dry biscuit. The sergeant took one look at him and spat on the dirt floor. "Look at you, not a stitch on you but them drawers. Ain't you got no decency? You look like one o' them goddamn savages you been runnin' with."

"It's hot in here," Will retorted.

It occurred to him as he ate the meager breakfast that if Sgt. Peak saw him practically naked, he wasn't too likely to worry about his carrying concealed documents.

The morning passed uneasily. Will kept expecting to be hauled off to be harangued again by Gen. Carleton or even to be put in front of a firing squad. He remembered that Carleton had used the word "treason." *Treason is a capital offense.*

As the time dragged by, his mind swirled with images of suffering and death. He thought about the previous Agent's gruesome demise. His heart reeled at the horrifying ways a person might be gotten rid of out here in the desert. *How ironic that I might die at the hands of a Yankee general two years after the War for Southern Independence had ended and clear on the other side of the continent! But if Dr. Steck succeeds in convincing the government to remove Carleton,* Will thought, *at least my death will not be in vain.*

Just then an old Diné woman cautiously came up to the window of the cell. "Dezba!" Will's mood changed abruptly.

She came close enough to whisper, "The general sent for me. The Hairy Face soldier said mud had been tracked into his office. So they ordered this old woman to clean it up for them." She sounded sarcastic.

"Is Hasbaá safe?"

Dezba nodded calmly. He felt a great sense of relief to know his Indian spouse was not chained up to a wall somewhere or lying dead outside the fort.

"Hasbaá spoke with Changing Woman. She said I should come to you."

"I have the papers that prove what Carleton's doing," Will whispered. "You and Hasbaá and Barboncito must get these to Dr. Steck." He looked around to make sure no one was watching, then retrieved the packet and passed it through the window.

"I will protect these papers, Nephew. You need not fear. We are grateful to you. Hasbaá speaks to Changing Woman on your behalf."

"Tell Hasbaá I'll be all right."

As Dezba left, with the documents tucked into her wool skirt, Will wondered if there were any basis for his assurance to Hasbaá. He'd seen enough of Hasbaá's mystical powers to believe that if he were really going to be all right, it would have to be because of Hasbaá's doing, not his own.

63

The Guardhouse

William languished in the cell for two more days. He was given very little to eat, a couple of biscuits, a bowl of beans, occasionally a cup of water when the soldier in charge of the guardhouse happened to stop through to check on him. But otherwise no punishment was imposed. No civilian charges or military court marshal were pressed. The general did not come to harangue or interrogate him. Sgt. Peak did not come to torture or beat him up.

Lt. Bauer did stop by the second afternoon.

"Look, Mister, you're in deep trouble. You better come clean with me."

"Yes sir."

"Do you have any papers from the general's desk?"

"No, sir," Will answered quite truthfully. The papers were safely in Dezba's hands. He gestured around the cell. He tossed the blanket into the air to show there was nothing in it. He shook out his clothes.

"Damn, I was hoping you had it. The general's blamed me for losing it."

"Something's missing?" Will feigned sympathy.

"It was his own damn fault. It was a loose sheet of paper," Bauer fussed. "Look, Lee, you're telling the god's own truth that you did not get into the general's desk?"

"On my word of honor," he said—truthfully, but fudging just a little, "I would never in my right mind have gone into General Carleton's desk."

"I guess you're correct about that. But that didn't stop you from getting into the office and rummaging in the file cabinet."

"Those were *my* reports."

"Say, Lee, how *did* you get into that office? I'm sure I'd locked the door. The general said the office was open, and there weren't no key in the door. My key was... well, where it belongs." Bauer seemed to realize maybe he'd already told Will too much.

"Perhaps you'd forgotten to lock the door," Will suggested innocently. He didn't have any idea how he'd gotten into that room. Had Hasbaá actually been there to bring him the key? *But she'd been only an apparition.*

"I never forget." Bauer was firm. "Well, Lee, you'll get blamed for the whole thing just the same. Carleton can be a hard man. I'm sure not taking the responsibility."

That evening, just after supper, Mac McCarrie came to visit. He stood at the window and chatted through the bars.

"You know what your problem is? You let yourself get emotionally involved with the Indians. Hey, I understand 'bout gettin' sex."

"Huh?"

"Sure, I got me an Indian squaw over in the Mescalero camp. Hell, what's a guy to do 'round here? Too many of the men are havin' it out with each other in the bunkhouse for my taste. I ain't like that. Guess I can't blame 'em tho'."

Will was so surprised at Mac's announcement he didn't take time to admonish him about the word "squaw." He was hurt by the soldier's saying, "I ain't like that."

"But, damn it, man, you gotta keep all this outa sight. Everybody can see you're livin' with that Navajo. That riles some folks up. Look, the women are for fuckin', but that's all.

"You show 'em a little kindness now and then. Buy 'em some trinkets from the Sutler's. Or take 'em some grub from the mess hall. That keeps 'em happy and everybody stays quiet. You don't want to go angerin' the Indians none. They can be pretty dangerous."

"You took food from the mess hall?"

"Sure, there's more meat than the men can eat…" Mac tossed off.

"Weren't you worried about the cook catching you?"

"Catchin' me?" Mac laughed. "Hey, I take him a bottle of whisky now and then. He gives me anything I ask for. Wraps it like a butcher shop. All's he wants is his tip."

Will almost laughed himself. *How ironic! I thought I'd been endangering the safety of the Diné by stealing the leftover meat for them. All the cook wanted was a tip. Changing Woman didn't seem to understand the ways of the white man any better than I did!*

"It's the Indians you need to be afraid of, not chef. They been beat down so bad, they're angry. Can't blame, but ya gotta be careful.

"You know that first day you and me met, Mr. Lee, it was over that Indian who I'd said tripped me, 'member? He was cousin to my Mescalero woman. He'd been in on a feast I brought over one time. He threatened to get me in trouble with my ladyfriend if I didn't bring vittles special for him. I was just tryin' to make friendly with 'im that day, when he went 'n kicked me in the nuts. I told myself I shoulda known better…

"I was pretty embarrassed when the Sarge came along escortin' you and caught me."

Have I ever understood what's really going on around here?

Pvt. McCarrie's visit was interrupted by the arrival of Sgt. Peak. Mac ducked away from the window.

"The general's decided to release you, Lee," Peak announced. "He apologizes. Don't want to overstep his authority by arrestin' a civilian.

That'll just mean more forms for him to fill out. Believe me, he don't need no more controversies."

Will did not understand. *Is Carleton going to let me go that easily?*

"The general said he understood why you might be peeved your reports weren't sent. In fact, he told me to tell you he'd be happy to go over those reports with you and show you just where your errors were. Then maybe you'd wanna do 'em over again. Right, this time."

"I'd certainly discuss the reports with General Carleton." Will didn't want to screw up his chance of getting out of this cell. He needed to talk to Hasbaá. He felt very confused about what was and wasn't real.

"Look," Peak said, as though taking him into his confidence, "we all know what's going on around here. I mean anybody can see the requisitions aren't going to feed the damn Injuns. But the general's got a reputation to protect. He was one of the great Injun fighters. He don't want no problems here.

"Now Gen'rl Carleton's been known to be generous with his friends. He ain't done so bad for hisself out here. You know, there's pretty good money flowing through this reservation. That Agent 'fore you, Ayers—he'd 've been happy with a cut. You think about it."

"Sergeant, all I want is to do my job of looking out for the Indians' welfare as best I can. I don't want any cuts."

"If Ayers had been satisfied with the general's offer, he wouldn't 've got himself strung up on that cactus. Just remember, the general can be generous. Or he can be merciless. It's up to you. Anyway, for now, you're a free man." Peak opened the door of the cell. Will didn't think the way he said "free man" very convincing. But he got out from behind bars just as fast as he could.

Outside, he looked around for Pvt. McCarrie, but the fellow had apparently run off. He wondered how much he'd heard and what he'd understood. He felt so in the dark himself.

Will wondered how much Carleton knew he knew. Maybe not much. From the way Bauer and Peak talked, it sounded as if they thought he had sneaked into the office just to find out what had happened to his reports. But Bauer had revealed that Carleton had noticed that that page of phony accounts was missing.

The first thing Will wanted to determine was if those documents had really been real and if Dezba and Hasbaá actually had them in their possession.

64

Dezba's Hogan

Hasbaá was waiting outside her hogan. She greeted Will warmly and held him in her arms, then bade him enter. Dezba and Barboncito were seated inside. They looked delighted. Dezba held out the packet of documents for him to see.

How in the world?

"I had quite an adventure," Will commented with magnificent understatement.

"We are all proud of you," Hasbaá said. "Changing Woman is proud of you. You have done well."

"We have to get these papers to Santa Fe as soon as possible."

"My horse will be waiting for you in the morning," Barboncito said.

"Can you make the journey back?" Hasbaá asked.

Will started to ask that someone accompany him. But he knew an Indian risked punishment if he or she left the reservation. *Besides, I've done it once already by myself.*

"I'll leave before sunrise."

He explained to the Diné leaders what the evidence they had gathered meant. They were appalled to learn how they'd intentionally been put in harm's way to create a safety buffer for the settlers and angered to hear how Carleton had turned their misfortune and suffering to his own profit. Will talked with them about what he expected to happen. Steck would telegraph the report of Carleton's misdeeds. Then they'd have to wait to hear from the War Department. He'd probably be away another two or three weeks. He hoped he'd return with news that Washington was going to send investigators.

Hasbaá urged him rest before his arduous journey. Once Carleton realized he had disappeared from the reservation the next day, he was bound to catch on. Perhaps he'd send a posse out. Will would have to ride swift and sure.

The others left. Hasbaá and Will lay together on the sheepskins and held each other. Hasbaá's touch was comforting.

"What really happened?"

"What do you mean?" Hasbaá replied. Perhaps she was being coy.

Will described the whole series of events as best he could recall: seeing Turquoise Boy come into the sweat lodge, then following the mysterious Holy Person up the ladder through the hole in the sky, their walking in on the conversation in Washington, then riding the horses through the storm, and going up to Carleton's office. "What really happened?"

"What happened is what you experienced."

"Well," Will shot back, "what did *you* experience?"

Hasbaá was silent a moment as if composing an answer. "You fainted in the sweat lodge. We brought you out and carried you here. You slept for several hours; then some time in the night you got up and left. That is when you went to General Carleton's office?" She added the last as a question.

"Weren't you with me?"

"I lay beside you and prayed to Changing Woman for you. In my dreams, I went with you to *Diné Bikéyah*, the homelands of our people. Segundo was there."

"Yes, I remember."

Will rolled over and laid his head on Hasbaá's chest. It didn't matter what really happened. What mattered is that they got the evidence they needed. He'd done something quite risky, he realized, something foolishly valiant. He didn't think of himself as heroic exactly. He apparently had done it all as if sleepwalking. He'd never had a chance to be heroic. He hadn't believed it had been happening.

What was heroic, he told himself, was that he'd let himself feel his affection for Hasbaá. He'd overcome the barriers of race and culture, and in so doing entered into another realm of existence where heroism was natural and a matter of course for being human, where the universe helped every well-intentioned effort to abide in harmony.

Now those feelings of affection began again to overwhelm him. He clung tight to Hasbaá and then raised his eyes to hers and felt the deep human connection that transcended all the armies of differences between them. They made passionate love. Will was husband to Hasbaá; he entered her deep and strong, and she bucked against him to rouse him higher and harder. Their bodies were hot where they touched. Will felt such bodily love for her. Then they changed positions and Will opened himself to Hasbaá and she was husband to him. He felt himself filled with the Indian's strength and exotic vision. It was all so intensely sexual, yet also mystical. When they came, Will felt that inner, ethereal light that had guided him in the general's office explode from the depths of his body and surge into his head. As the waves of pleasure subsided and he came back to himself, he wondered if Hasbaá had seen his emerald eyes light up in the darkness.

Afterwards, Will thought about the spirit orgasm he shared with Hasbaá and Segundo on the bluff above *Diné Bikéyah*.

"I remember, too," Hasbaá whispered.

Afterward, Will rolled over and tried to sleep. He clutched the packet of documents to his chest for safekeeping. In spite of his exhaustion, he couldn't rest. He kept waking up with dreams of danger.

How come Carleton let me out of jail? And what did Peak mean about accepting the general's generosity? Had he been offering a bribe?

Will knew he couldn't betray the Diné for money. But he worried the Diné might betray him—not Dezba and Barboncito. But there were certainly Navajos who did not like his joining Dezba's outfit. He remembered what Mac had told him about the Mescaleros. What if Mac wittingly or unwittingly betrayed him? What if he told his Mescalero woman about the bribe Peak had offered?

Will thought he heard sounds outside the hogan. Was it attackers coming to get him? He tried to go back to sleep. He told himself it was just normal activity in the camp. But then something familiar burned at his nostrils: the pungent oily scent of kerosene.

He heard the gurgle and splash of the flammable fluid being poured around the outside of the hogan. This wasn't a mystical dream. This was a down-to-earth attack. He was suddenly struck with the fear that tonight's dreams of danger were also coming true.

"Hasbaá, wake up. We've got to get out of here quick."

In a moment, they were both out of the hogan. It was pitch dark. They ran stealthily to a spot where they could hunker down behind the sweat lodge and watch. Will still held the packet tight.

Soon a light sputtered in the darkness as a match lit. Flames flickered along a trail of kerosene toward the hogan. They quickly spread all around the base. The fire looked particularly intense near the door flap, which must have been doused especially generously. Fire ran up the sides of the hogan in fingers where the flammable liquid had been splashed. And then the whole thing suddenly burst into a raging blaze as fumes inside exploded.

The figure that set the fire had backed away. But in the sudden bright light, Will recognized Sgt. Peak's weathered and embittered features just before he turned and disappeared into the darkness. *No wonder they let me out. They planned to kill me.*

"My god, they almost burned us alive."

"Changing Woman has work for you to do. That is why she woke you up."

"Well, I'm sure glad she did." Will was starting to tremble in recognition of what a close call they'd had. "Well, maybe this works in our favor. If they think they killed us, they won't come after me. We've got to let them think they burned me up."

Indians began to swarm from the huts and hogans around the settlement to see what the ruckus was. "Hasbaá." "Hasbaá!" One after another, the people began to call out as they saw what had happened. Keening and wailing filled the night.

Hasbaá and Will still hid behind the sweat lodge. They were both naked. Dezba came up behind Hasbaá. "It will soon be dawn," she said to Will. "You should eat something to prepare for your journey."

"I should put on some clothes."

"Aunt, you must let the people know I am safe," said Hasbaá. "I hear such grief in their cries."

"Will you show yourself to reassure them?"

"We must stay hidden." Hasbaá's voice sounded conspiratorial. "Will must leave the settlement, and I must perform a mission for Changing Woman before the Hairy Faces come to investigate."

"I will reassure them, but protect your secret." Dezba excused herself.

65

THE DESERT

Will would have liked to have slept a little longer. He would have liked to have held Hasbaá and shared her touch before having to leave. He thought wistfully and lustfully of their lovemaking earlier. But, indeed, a faint glow lit the eastern sky, and it was time to get underway.

Soon the settlement calmed. There was still a sense of tension in the air, but the wailing and grieving had stopped. Dezba sent one of the young boys over to the Agent's quarters to get Will some clothes. Will ate a little to prepare himself. He collected the few supplies he'd need. When he was ready to go, he looked around for Hasbaá. But she had already gone off on her mission. He felt sad that he hadn't got to say goodbye. He wondered what she was doing.

As he rode away, he remembered his last sight of Michael Halyerd. "Save yourself," he had called out to him as Michael fled his father. He never saw his friend again. Now as he fled from Fort Sumner—to save himself—he wondered if he would ever see Hasbaá again. *What if Carleton is not removed? I certainly have no place on this reservation otherwise.*

Barboncito's horse seemed to understand the importance and urgency of this journey and bore him swiftly. They made the distance in under three days.

The trip was not so exhausting this time. Will rode, the crucial evidence at his heart, with ease and expectation. He was thrilled to realize what had happened to his life. He wondered how it had happened and what it was that really had happened.

How had he returned to Washington, D.C. to that fateful moment when he'd been given his appointment? Of course, he had actually been in that waiting room sleeping a couple of months ago. And so somewhere in his mind, perhaps, he'd heard the telltale conversation. So maybe, in some way, Hasbaá had rekindled his memories so that he was able to recall what he had unconsciously overheard.

The European magician Anton Mesmer had used animal magnetism to induce strange trances in people. *Perhaps Hasbaá had used such animal magnetism on me.* Once a Mesmerist had come through Lynchburg with a carnival and used this animal magnetism to cause volunteers to do odd things, such as quack like a duck or stand on their heads, while in deep trance. His father preached against the carnival and said, especially, that the Mesmerism demonstrations were the work of the devil. Will felt sorry for his father; the old man's narrow view of life prevented him from perceiving so many marvels.

It was a marvel that had somehow brought these papers into his possession. How had that happened? The door unlocked, the mud tracked in, his face clean shaven—these he explained away as coincidence and amnesia. After all, he'd been exhausted and punchy and famished from days of traveling even before going into the sweat lodge. Who knew what state his mind was in?

Maybe all of it has obvious explanations. Maybe Lt. Bauer forgot to lock the door. Maybe I came up by way of the creek and got my shoes muddy there—but it was yellow mud I tracked in, not the red clay around Fort Sumner. How was that? Maybe I stopped at my quarters in my delirious state and shaved and just forgot. But how could I have done that? How did I know to find the key in the inkwell? Had Dezba or Hasbaá told me in my sleep? But then how did I see in the dark?

Will had seen it in his own mother's eyes and in the eyes of soldiers back in his father's congregation who'd been wounded in the war: anodynes they were given for pain or nervous conditions, like laudanum or stramonium, caused their pupils to constrict or dilate. *Maybe if my eyes were dilated more light would get in and I could see better. Maybe it was that potion the Indians gave me. I wonder what was in that. Whatever it was, it was like a miracle…*

Will remembered childhood hopes of working miracles. In fact, these events were closer to that than he'd ever really expected. He used to believe the power to work miracles would come from being obedient to God's law. Now he realized it was the natural outcome of good intentions and a will for the harmony of life. *Perhaps that's what God's law really is.*

Maybe miracles are always a combination of such things as coincidence, forgetfulness, and misperception—like sleight of hand. Perhaps the real miracle isn't the event, but that the coincidence happened at just the right moment and that the mind perceived it as a miracle. *That was certainly miracle enough.*

Will scried a hawk again in the sky. He felt its presence a comforting omen.

66

THE TERRITORIAL SUPERINTENDENT'S OFFICE

Dr. Steck was delighted. "I hadn't expected you back so soon. This is exactly what we need. I'll go to the telegraph office with this right away. You've done a great job."

"Well, thank you, sir. I really had the Indians' help getting these. Can't say I can take all the credit."

"How's that?"

"I'll tell you the whole story sometime," Will promised. "But now I'd like to get some sleep."

Dr. Steck accompanied him to the Sangre de Cristo to get him set up in a room. "I'll order you a bath and a rubdown," Steck said as they were waiting at the front desk. "You deserve it, young man."

"Thank you, sir." Yes, Will looked forward to a repeat of that luxurious experience. He, too, thought he had earned it.

That evening, he went down to the Yellow Rose Cantina to let Joel know he was back in town and have a bite to eat, then enjoyed another sensuous massage. Clean, and with all the tension worked out of him, he slept soundly for the first time in days.

In the morning, Joel was there to resume the language lessons. Later Will went to see Dr. Steck and learned that the messages had been sent. The Superintendent had already heard back from his friend Jack Osborne that the news that Carleton had been defrauding the government and keeping much of the Indian money for himself had infuriated Osborne's contacts in Congress and in the War Department.

"The federal envoy to the Territory dispatched a military courier to Fort Sumner this morning to order Carleton to report back here immediately for an investigation of the sale of Indian lands. The envoy thought that was more within his jurisdiction than the fraud charges."

"It also looks like a charge that could have arisen here in Santa Fe," Will observed. He'd begun to realize that if Carleton knew what had really happened, he might retaliate against the Diné. "Thank God, Carleton thinks I'm dead."

"Well, young man, that's another charge perhaps we should levy against him—attempted murder."

"Let's just get him out of Fort Sumner. And get the Diné back to their homeland."

"I doubt this action will have much effect on the Indians. Though maybe a new commander at the Bosque Redondo may be better at caring for their needs."

"But, please sir, the reason for all this is to get the Diné back home." Will worried that his efforts might come to naught after all. "That's what'll bring peace. You've got to see that!"

"Perhaps you're right, young man. I'll certainly convey that message. You did a yeoman's job, you deserve to have your say."

"It's not my say, sir. The Indians deserve to have their lives."

"Well, yes." Steck dropped his eyes. "Well, not much for you to do now. You can take a rest. It's all in the hands of federal prosecutors."

Afraid the white government just wasn't going to understand, but hopeful Changing Woman's advice about strategy had been right, Will did take the opportunity to rest. The second night of his stay at the hotel, he again got a massage. He was beginning to feel a bond with the Indian masseur. The man, who was called Ganado Mucho, was indeed a Navajo. He spoke no English and only a little Spanish. Will used the small vocabulary of Diné words he now knew. Ganado Mucho smiled, but didn't respond and Will decided to respect the man's silence. He was in awe of his strength and his awareness of the human body. Ganado Mucho was certainly not a Two-Spirit *berdache*. If anything, he was overly masculine. But there was a deep spiritual calm about him. Will imagined he, like Hasbaá, must be dear to the Holy Persons.

During the first week, Will took his Spanish lessons, did a little work for Dr. Steck at the federal offices, filing and recopying documents, and helped out at the Solis General Store. He was pleased to see that Joel and Jose had continued their partnership in the trading business. Joel also helped out at the store to acquaint himself with good business practices and to make extra money to deposit to his bank account.

By the end of a week, Will had grown used to the pattern of living in the hotel and working at his couple of jobs. During the second week, however, everything changed again.

67

THE SANGRE DE CRISTO HOTEL

One evening he had eaten, as usual, at the Yellow Rose. After he watched Joelle's first show, he went back to the hotel. He tried to read a book Steck had loaned him about the Indian Wars, but got restless. *Why haven't we heard from Washington? Why isn't Gen. Carleton behind bars? Why hasn't the federal envoy sent marshals to arrest the man? What's happening to Hasbaá?*

That last question kept gnawing at him. *What's happening to Hasbaá?*

It wasn't very late, so Will decided to take a stroll through the gardens. Stretching his legs might help the agitation. He left his room, locked the door behind himself and headed down the dimly lit corridor. As he came around a corner, he walked right into an army officer in full-dress uniform. The officer had a pocket flask in hand. He'd apparently stopped in the corridor to swig from the flask, just a few steps too close to the corner. The officer had his head tilted back and hadn't seen anybody coming. When Will bumped into him, the flask spilled, and whisky went all down the front of his uniform.

"Excuse me," Will said perfunctorily and kept walking.

"Damn you, man," the officer shouted a little drunkenly. "Don't you walk away from me." He screwed the top on the flask, put it into his breast pocket, and pulled out a handkerchief to wipe at the whisky. "Why don't you watch where you're going?"

Will turned back. "I'm sorry, sir," he answered civilly. Just then, the army officer looked right at him. And he looked back at the officer.

"What the hell? It's you, Lee. I thought you were dead."

"Oh, General Carleton, what a surprise to run into you here."

"I saw your bones in the ashes of that burnt-out Indian hut."

"It's called a hogan."

"I don't care what the damn things are called, you idiot," Carleton spat out. Will could hear slurring in the general's speech; he started backing slowly down the hall.

The general followed him. "I've been ordered to report to the federal envoy to the Territory. They put Bauer in charge and ordered me off my own command." The general's voice rose. "And then I get up here and discover my financial backers have double-crossed me."

"I'm sorry, sir."

"They said a surveyor name of Williams had come through here. And said my land was worthless. What a damn lie!" Suddenly, a light seemed to dawn in the general's eye. "Williams? That was you, William Lee, wasn't it? You pretended to be a surveyor and turned my backers against me." Carleton pulled the pistol from the holster at his side. "You goddamn son of a bitch. Damn Peak. That fool can't do anything right."

Carleton was clearly intoxicated. Will imagined the man had reason to be drunk. He must have just arrived here in Santa Fe to discover his empire had fallen apart.

Carleton started to laugh. "Well, Lee. Looks like I'm gonna get the last laugh anyway." He cocked the pistol.

Will felt his stomach sink. He said a prayer to Changing Woman.

"You'll be pleased to learn, I'm sure," Carleton said sarcastically, "that I had those Indians you run with arrested for your murder. That skinny squaw you seem so fond of, and the old lady, and that damn Chief Barboncito. Here was a chance to get rid of a pack of troublemakers all at once."

Carleton waved the gun. "I don't know what you're doing here. But you sure look like you just tried to rob me. I can't be blamed for defending my person." Carleton steadied himself. He raised the pistol and held it at arm's length, aimed right at Will's face.

Will thought about Changing Woman. He thought about all he'd accomplished. He thought about his dreams of going off to the Navajo lands. *Now's the time I need a miracle. Where is Turquoise Boy now?*

Just then, Ganado Mucho came noiselessly around the bend in the corridor behind Carleton. He carried a wooden water bucket in each hand. Ganado took in the scene, then looked straight at Will. Something unspoken passed between them.

"Goodbye, Mr. Lee. And good riddance." Carleton fired.

Ganado swung one of the buckets. It struck Carleton on the arm just as he pulled the trigger.

Will was blinded by the flash. He felt the bullet whiz by his head. But it missed him. A large clay pot full of flowers hanging behind him exploded.

Ganado swung the other bucket. This one struck Carleton powerfully on the head. The general crumpled and fell to the floor unconscious.

Will thanked Ganado profusely for coming around the corner at just the right moment. Silently, he also thanked Changing Woman.

He and Ganado carried the unconscious general into Will's room. They used the decorative tie-backs from the curtains to bind him securely to the bed. Ganado kept guard while Will rushed to Dr. Steck's house. It struck Will as poetic justice that a Navajo now guarded

Carleton, keeping him a prisoner, just as, for the last four years, Carleton kept the Navajos prisoner.

He arrived out of breath. Panting, he explained what had happened. Steck was delighted. "Carleton sealed his own fate by attacking a U.S. Government official. Now we really do have a case of attempted murder. I'll get the sheriff right now."

Will also explained to Dr. Steck what Carleton had said about the Diné leaders' being charged with his murder. He said he had to get to the Fort as soon as possible.

"We'll have Carleton behind bars tomorrow, Will." Dr. Steck promised. "He won't be a threat to you anymore. Godspeed on your journey. I pray you'll be in time."

68

Fort Sumner

Will rode into the night. He slept for a while in the early morning. Then, soon after sunrise, he started in again. He didn't know if he could get there in time. *What if the military already executed Hasbaá, Dezba and Barboncito for my murder?* His only hope was that Carleton's ploy had been to make his scheme look legitimate by doing his violence through the law. That probably meant there would be some kind of trial. But two weeks have passed already...

One question he couldn't answer was how Carleton had seen his bones in the ashes of the hogan. *Had someone else been in the hogan, someone who did burn to death?*

Day passed into night and then into day again. He lost track of time. He rose with firm purpose. He slept a little while he allowed the horse to rest and eat, but both horse and rider seemed propelled by urgency.

Will woke from a short nap, moaning from a dream in which he came back too late and arrived to find Hasbaá, Dezba and Barboncito hanged on the gallows in the parade grounds of Fort Sumner, their bodies left in the blazing sun as a warning to the Indians of the power of white man's wrath. He vowed he would not rest till he reached home.

Hasbaá will not die by my fault, he swore. His heart seethed with anger and helplessness. All he do could was hurry as fast as possible.

Will felt carried by the wind at his back. *I'm sure Changing Woman won't desert me now. She's brought me half way across the continent to help her people.*

When he arrived at Fort Sumner late in the afternoon, he went straight to Lt. Bauer's office. He knocked hard on the door.

"Come in."

"The Indians?" Will shouted as he threw open the door. "What about the Indians? Are they all right?"

"Lee?" Bauer showed great surprise. "We thought you were burned up."

"Well, obviously I wasn't. I'm alive and well, and I pray to God you haven't done anything to the Navajo leaders."

"I saw the bones in the ashes."

"What about Hasbaá and Dezba and Barboncito?"

"It's okay, mister. But I guess you got here just in time. We thought they'd murdered you."

"What happened?" Will asked urgently.

"There was a trial. Pvt. McCarrie testified that he'd heard Peak offer you money for cooperating. Mac said it didn't seem like you. But he admitted he told a Mescalero female about it and said somehow the Navajos must've got wind of it. 'Tell one Injuns, and ya tell 'em all,' Sgt. Peak testified."

"It looked pretty obvious that the Indians killed you for betraying them and set fire to the hogan to destroy the evidence. The three Navajos you mentioned were sentenced to be hanged. We were waiting for General Carleton to return. I thought he'd want to oversee the executions himself. He's apparently been delayed in…"

"Carleton's not coming back," Will interrupted peremptorily. "He's in jail in Santa Fe for attempted murder and defrauding the U.S. Government."

"The general's in jail?"

"What about the Indians?"

"They're in the guardhouse. I guess there's no case now. I'll let them go. But, Mr. Lee, this is all very strange. Did the Indians know you were alive? They never said a word in their own defense. The tall woman just kept saying you were dead."

My God, the three of them were going to sacrifice themselves.

"What about the bones?" Bauer asked. "We all saw human bones in the ashes of the burned hogan. General Carleton ordered the pit filled as your grave. We even stuck a cross with your name on it, right there in the middle of the Indian outfit."

"It was Peak who set the fire." Will tried to sound assured so Bauer wouldn't guess he didn't have the slightest idea himself. "Ask him."

69

The Talking Circle

Later, as Will sat with Hasbaá, Dezba, and Barboncito in the talking circle near the medicine lodge, he asked Hasbaá to explain.

"When you left to go to Santa Fe, you said we should make them think you were dead. I knew it had to appear you died in the fire.

"Changing Woman told me where to find the bones of a dead man. I did not want to do this, because I would never want to disturb a ghost, but I knew I had to. So I went out and brought the bones back and carefully placed them in the ashes.

"I hated doing that, touching the remains of a dead body. A Diné would never do such a thing. I prayed constantly to Changing Woman for protection. I told the ghost that he had died because he endangered the Diné and that this was a chance to make it up. The ghost obviously forgave me, and went to his rest. Otherwise the ghost would have stopped you from reaching Fort Sumner, and we would have been hanged.

"In the morning, the Hairy Faces came to investigate. General Carleton ordered the hogan buried, bones and all. He said the dead man was obviously you. "

"But whose bones were they?" Will asked.

When Dezba told him, Will burst out laughing. *How absolutely perfect!*

"But you were going to let yourselves be hanged?"

"We will all die, Nephew," Dezba replied. "It is the young who are important. So many have died. We believed your efforts would bring the young ones back to *Diné Bikéyah,* so the Diné way of life can continue in the future. That was all that mattered."

It took Will a while to calm down. This was all so amazing to him. After a bit, he explained that Gen. Carleton had been called to Santa Fe to answer accusations of wrong-doing, mismanagement, and embezzlement. Lieutenant—now Captain—Bauer had been put in temporary charge of the Fort. Investigators would come from the War Department and from the Office of Indian Affairs. Will said he was sure the Diné could make a strong case for why they should be allowed to leave this god-forsaken reservation.

70

Fort Sumner

In the morning, he went to see Captain Bauer.

"Well, Mr. Lee, you sure seem to have shook up things 'round here." Bauer took his seat behind the desk and gestured for Will to take one of the other chairs.

"That's not what I intended. I just wanted to see some problems fixed."

"Look, man, I'm not sure how to say this… It's not like I haven't known what's been going on. When I first started to work for General Carleton, I saw he was too sure of himself even when he was totally wrong. I saw the power go to his head. I knew he was defrauding the government. I know I should have turned him in myself. You wouldn't believe how many times I told myself today is the day I do something about the general. But, Mr. Lee, I just never got up the guts to do it." Bauer half stood and leaned across the desk and put out his hand. "You're a better man than me."

Will shook the Captain's hand. *What a turn of events! This guy was scolding me for not cooperating only two weeks ago; now he's congratulating me.*

"Thought you might want this." Bauer handed him a sheet of paper.

He saw it was a Certificate of Death. It declared William Lee had been killed in a fire in the Indian settlement while exercising his duties as civilian Agent. Will folded the paper and tucked it into his breast pocket.

"Say, Lee, I believe you that Sgt. Peak set the fire. But who did die in that fire?"

"Nobody, sir," Will answered. "Those were the bones of the Mexican raider that was killed in the attack that day I had the argument with General Carleton at the dinner table."

"That was the night of the chocolate cake?"

"Right! The Indians knew it was important that Carleton believe he'd killed me so I could get the necessary evidence to Santa Fe. They put the bones in the ashes to trick the Hairy Faces."

"Hairy Faces?"

"That's what they call you soldiers."

"Really?" Bauer said. "I didn't know that. I bet there's a lot you could teach us about the Indians. They must really like you. It seems those three were willing to let themselves be executed to protect you."

"I guess they do like me, sir. But that's just because I showed I knew they were human beings with feelings. I don't know that they were exactly sacrificing themselves for me, Captain. They were sacrificing themselves for the future of their people."

71

FORT SUMNER

Under Captain Bauer's administration, conditions at Fort Sumner improved. More food was rationed for the Indians. Strict orders came down that none of the soldiers, especially Sgt. Peak, harass either the Indians or Agent Lee. Captain Bauer, it turned out, despised Peak almost as much as Will did. Peak and some other troublemakers were assigned to tents on the eastern edge of the reservation, where they were to protect against attacks on the Navajos from Comanche or *Mexicano* raiders. Will thought of Peak spending the rest of the sweltering summer in the desert as suitable punishment.

Meanwhile, word came that the Army appointed General William Tecumseh Sherman himself to come to Fort Sumner to examine the state of the Bosque Redondo experiment. Sherman had been sent out west to look over the reservations in Indian Territory in what would later be known as Oklahoma. He was nearby and was empowered to negotiate a new treaty with the Indians of New Mexico.

Will was told he'd be called upon to brief Sherman. He could hardly believe it. Who would have ever thought a Southern boy would be briefing the Yankee general who devastated the South so badly just three years before? Weeks passed. The summer heat abated. Autumn rains began to fall. As the dust of summer was washed from the trees and brush, the land turned less forboding. As if in celebration, many of the cactus even put out brightly colored flowers. The Pecos River began to widen and run deep. Now what had been but a slow-moving creek in the summer had become by fall a fast-flowing river.

72

Bosque Redondo

Hearing that the Peace Commissioners, as they were called, under Gen. Sherman's leadership would arrive soon, the Navajos held a coyote ceremony at Fort Sumner. Following Hasbaá's instructions, Barboncito led the ceremony. First, he sent a sizeable number of Navajos out in various directions until they encountered a coyote, an animal sacred in the Diné tradition for its wiliness. That was a trait the Indians had to learn to negotiate with the Hairy Faces. Next, the animal was encircled. Frightened by all the people, it crouched down to the ground. Barboncito slowly approached, then daringly placed a shell bead in the coyote's mouth. The circle widened, and the coyote rose slowly and then walked away. The direction the coyote chose to escape was to the west.

By this ceremony, Barboncito was given the power to speak convincingly to the white leaders, and the sign was given that the Holy Persons would now accompany the Diné to return to their homeland in the west. Hasbaá was overjoyed with the outcome of the coyote ceremony.

After Sherman's entourage arrived a few days later, Will reported to the general about the New Mexicans' enslaving Navajos, Carleton's uncompromising attitude, the starvations, and other problems that the Navajos experienced at Bosque Redondo.

The first order Sherman gave was that the Indians be fed a hearty meal. The cooks were told to take the supplies from the storehouse for the troops. In the future, Sherman ordered, the soldiers and the Indians would all share the same food. The soldiers would not feast while Diné starved.

Sherman then called for a meeting with representatives of the tribe. In the parade grounds of Fort Sumner, a table was set up. Sherman sat on a chair behind the table in the middle, all splendid in his blue dress uniform. Clearly, he represented the Great Father in Washington. With him, also in chairs, sat the four other members of the commission: two military officers, two civilians. Two more chairs were placed to the side of the table, where Will and Captain Bauer were seated. Will was anxious to be as close as possible to Sherman in case the general had any questions. In contrast to the white officials in chairs, the Diné representatives were sitting on the ground in front of the table. A crowd of Diné people behind them eagerly listened to Dezba as she translated the proceedings for them.

After a few opening words, Gen. Sherman called on Barboncito. The Diné spokesman welcomed the commission politely. "I know you are great war leaders of the Hairy Face army. I honor you for coming here, to this place far away from your homes." Barboncito spoke eloquently. "I beg for you to open your hearts to our words. I beg for you to take our true thoughts back to the Great Father in Washington.

"We Diné, the people whom the Mexicans call Navajo, are also far from our home. Since we were brought to this place, a great many of us have died. This ground is cursed with thousands of ghosts of our relatives. Their spirits tell us, and we know ourselves, it is not right for us to live here.

"We plant the ground, but it does not yield. The animals we have brought here have nearly all died. Our enemies, the Comanches and the *Mexicanos,* have stolen our herds, our belongings and even our children. We have done all we could possibly do. Yet, we who were once well off, now sleep on the bare dirt. My mouth is dry. My head hangs in sorrow to see my people so poor and miserable. Whatever we do here causes death. I hope you will do all you can for us. This hope goes in at my feet and out at my mouth."

Barboncito sat down. There was silence throughout the meeting ground. The commissioners whispered among themselves. Then Sherman addressed the gathering.

"All of us are agreed the evidence shows what you say to be true. We do not think we need to hear more testimony. It is obvious the soil conditions at Fort Sumner do not afford an opportunity for the Navajos to become self-supporting. To have each tribe of Indians become self-sufficient farmers is something the government and the Great Father in Washington desire greatly.

"Therefore, this commission is in unanimous agreement: the reservation at Fort Sumner should be abandoned. This is a failed experiment, the closing of which is long overdue."

Barboncito stood and bowed to Gen. Sherman. A look of pride glowed on his weathered face.

"But," Sherman continued after the hubbub among the Indians subsided, "there is still another issue. The question remaining before us is where the Navajos should be relocated.

"We commissioners have just come from the Great Plains, in the area set aside by the government as the Indian Territory, between Kansas and Texas. We were quite impressed with this area. Those lands are much better than this desert. I recommend the Navajos should be moved there, to the east, to become a part of Indian Territory along with the other tribes."

Barboncito and the other Diné looked crushed. Hadn't Sherman understood their petition?

"But, General Sherman, what the Navajos want is to return to their homeland in the west," Will shouted out.

"The government policy is to concentrate all Indians into one territory. The Navajos will be much better off there. They can adapt to the plains easily."

Without another word, Barboncito got up and walked away. The other Diné rose and followed him out of the parade grounds. The commissioners looked uncomfortable and whispered among themselves. Sherman asked rhetorically, "Why did they leave?"

"To show displeasure with your proposal." Will walked up to the table.

Sherman urged, "Let us follow them. We must resolve this question now."

73

The Pecos River

By the time the commissioners reached the Diné settlement along the banks of the Pecos River, Barboncito was addressing the assembled people in Diné. As he spoke, a shrill wail went up. The people started crying loudly.

Will led the commissioners right into the middle of the crowd. The five white men were ill-at-ease, surrounded by a host of the brown-skinned people they warred against. But they followed Will's lead.

"Why are they crying?" Sherman asked.

"We are afraid we will be moved to still another strange place," Dezba answered him. "We only want to go back to our homeland."

Several women rushed to Sherman's feet and fell weeping and begging in Diné. Others did likewise before the other commissioners. The white men looked at one another in bewilderment.

What happened next was even more surprising. Hasbaá turned and, without a word, started to walk toward the river. Suddenly all the women rose, grabbed the hands of their children and, as if by some silent signal between them, followed Hasbaá to the riverbank. They were crying as they reached the now swollen Pecos.

"What now?" Sherman asked.

Barboncito answered. "The women say that if you don't let them return to our homeland, they will lead the children into the river."

Will rushed to Sherman's side. "General, the Navajos cannot swim. They will all drown."

"Order them to stop," Sherman shouted excitedly at the Diné leaders.

"We men cannot order the women," Barboncito answered. "It is not the Diné way. They are resolved. After these many years of suffering, they will die rather than take one more step farther away from our homeland. This day will mark the end of the Diné people. We cannot endure any more."

"A mass drowning?" one of the commissioners exclaimed. "We can't allow that."

"Why won't you consider another place?" Sherman asked Barboncito.

"When the Diné first came to this world, First Woman declared that our lands were bounded by the four sacred mountains and that we should never move east of the river you called the Rio Grande or west of the river called San Juan or disaster would befall our people. Our life here at Bosque Redondo has fulfilled that legend.

"It has been several winters since we were taken away from our home at gunpoint. The graves of our ancestors are lonely. Our children have no connection to their past. Outside the area of our mountains and canyons our medicine has no power. We sicken and die. Our sheep sicken and die. The Diné were not meant to live in any other land than the one of our ancestors, the *Diné Bikéyah* given to us by Changing Woman."

Barboncito drew his knife. The Peace Commissioners gasped. But before anyone had a chance to move, Barboncito hurled the knife into the dirt right between Sherman's feet. "If you cannot agree for us to return to our homeland, I ask you to take this knife and plunge it into my heart right now. Since we left our homes, I have already seen too much sorrow, enough for ten lifetimes. My heart cannot stand the pain any more. I will not move from this spot alive unless it is westward toward my home."

Sherman and the other commissioners were shaken by this demonstration of Navajo resolve. The women and children remained poised by the river's edge. "We have to have time to think about this." Sherman stalked away nervously. The other commissioners followed.

The group of white men walked a little way toward the Fort. Will ran after them, begging Gen. Sherman to reconsider. "General, the Navajos are not making an idle threat. They *will* drown themselves." He looked nervously for Hasbaá among the crowd of women, who had now begun a dirge-like chant.

It was obvious the Indians were not going to disperse after their departure. Sherman stopped and spoke with the other commissioners. Finally, they turned and walked back down to where Barboncito and the other Diné "chiefs" now sat on the sand.

When Sherman approached, the Diné did not get up. Following Will's example, Sherman and his commission awkwardly sat down on the ground. There were now no tables or chairs to signify status difference.

"If the Great Father allowed your people to return to your homeland, would you guarantee never to wage war again?" Sherman asked straightaway.

"We have had enough of war these last ten years," Barboncito replied. "Our young men are dead. Our children cry from bad dreams of the fighting. If only you will agree for us to go home, we will pledge ourselves to peace forever more."

One of the commissioners asked, "Will you be an expense to the government?"

"We desire nothing more strongly than to support ourselves by our own labor. Our women want to farm and weave wool. Our men want to rebuild our sheep and horse herds. All we ask is that the *Mexicanos* not attack our settlements and steal our animals and enslave our children. If we will be left alone, we know we can become prosperous again. All we want is peace in our own homeland."

"This much we can guarantee," Sherman replied. "We have a powerful leader in Washington whose name is the same name as the fort here. Senator Sumner is a committed abolitionist. He has learned of the enslavement of the Navajos in the New Mexico Territory and has dedicated himself to stop all such enslavement."

Will wondered if Sherman understood the irony he'd noticed earlier himself in Sen. Sumner's name.

"The Government of the United States to which I have devoted my life has just completed a great crusade against human slavery. All of us are committed to wiping out the last vestiges of this wretched practice from our reunited country. Anyone who raids the Navajos will be severely punished, by my personal order."

"If this is as you say," Barboncito said, "then we pledge our loyalty to the Great Father in Washington, so that we can live in peace. This is all we were asking many winters ago when the warfare started between the Diné and the soldiers."

Sherman looked around at the commissioners. They all nodded their agreement. He reached across to Barboncito and grasped the Indian's hand. "Very well, then, we have a treaty. You can leave this place and go back to your homeland with the blessing of the Great Father."

A look of relief finally appeared on Barboncito's face. He clasped Sherman's hand for a long time. He had not been sure he would live to see this time. "My knife will go back into its case. Never again in the future will it be drawn in anger against the Hairy Faces. The Diné will live in peace always with the soldiers. The Great Father in Washington can smile once again as well."

Barboncito then stood up and yelled in Diné to the crowd of women and children. A great cheer went up from them, and they began running back away from the water.

Will's and Barboncito's eyes made contact. They both burst into tears. They did not try to suppress their joy. Will noticed that even the hardened eyes of Gen. Sherman grew misty. Will dismissed his fears about what might have happened if the decision had not gone that way. He tried not to think of Hasbaá in the waves of that rushing river.

74

THE RIVERBANK

That evening, the Diné settlement was abuzz with excitement. Drummers beat out a triumphant rhythm. The people sang and danced, jubilant in the turn of events. Will saw an aliveness, a spirit of almost trance-like serenity in the dancers that he had never observed before.

With the flush of success enlivening both of them, Will and Hasbaá walked out away from the camp to be alone. They wandered south along the riverbank, past the spot where Will helped the Diné trapped in the flood, and past the crook in the river where Sgt. Peak had tried to rape Hasbaá. The piles of debris had now been carried away by the river.

The sun had set. The sky glowed blue; great fingers of orange shot up from the west. A breeze blew across the face of the desert and wafted gently into the faces of the lovers. They laughed quietly together. They'd both tired of the struggle to talk. And even to think. They simply longed to relax in each other's presence—certainly one of the joys of romantic love, Will had discovered.

And so he did not notice that he and Hasbaá were followed. He did not see that Sgt. Peak kept pace with them about fifty feet to the left and a little ways behind.

When they came upon a patch of unusually prolific vegetation, Hasbaá paused to look for medicinal herbs. Will was pleased to just stand and wait. With Hasbaá nearby, he was satisfied just to stare into the twilight sky.

Suddenly, a shot rang out. A chip flew from a rock along the waterline a few inches from Will's foot. He jumped, then spun around. There was his nemesis waving a pistol at them.

"Well, well, well," Peak said drunkenly, "what have we got here? Just think, Mister Lee, you was gonna blackmail Sgt. J.F. Peak 'cause I saw the male parts on this Injun woman o' yours. Well, la-di-da, look who's taken up with the freak.

"It's just as I thought. I told the gen'rl, after I seen you'd moved in with the Injun. Told 'im you was doin' unspeakable things down there. Gen'rl Carleton—now he was a gentleman—he said he'd believe you was a traitor, Lee, 'cause you was a Rebel and all. But he said he would not believe that even you would be guilty of such abomination." Peak laughed menacingly. "Well, I was right. Now I think mebbe I'll just shoot me two sodomites. I'll send your private parts in a box to the general to prove ol' J.F. Peak knew whereof he spoke, just like them Injuns scalped my daddy."

"No, Sergeant, you won't get away with this."

"Say, you done told on me 'bout settin' the fire in the Injun camp. That damn Bauer's figured out it was me killed that squaw in Ayers' cabin and then made it look like the Injuns took revenge. Bauer ain't never liked me much nohow. Who's gonna stand up for me? You got my damn boss fired. Sgt. Peak ain't so popular round here, mister. I don't think I got anything to lose. So what if I shoot an Injun freak and a lily-livered, Injun-sympathizin' grayback Rebel! They can only hang me once."

"You are an angry man," Hasbaá said.

"You bet I'm angry. I been cornholed by life. When I was a kid livin' wit' my ma and pa in Nebraska, life was just fine. Then the Injuns came. They burned our house. They killed my pop and my brother right there. Shot arrows in 'em, then scalped 'em while they're still alive. They carried off my mom. God knows what heathen things they did to her 'fore they killed her. One of 'em cut my throat and left me to bleed to death, a seven-year-old boy. Neighbors saw the smoke and come to investigate and found me. I got put in a foundlin' home. The day the Injuns came was the last day o' happiness in my life. I ain't got nothin' better to do than kill Injuns."

"It was not my people who did this to you," Hasbaá said firmly but softly.

Will imagined the Hairy Faces had taken the land from the Indians in Nebraska, just like they had taken it from the Diné. He could see why those Indians reacted so violently and tried to scare the settlers away. But in Hasbaá's voice Will could hear that she understood the emotion and pain in Peak's story.

"There has been too much killing on both sides. It must stop," she said.

"Not 'fore I kill me the two o' you."

"You are a wicked man. You started the shooting that killed my husband, Segundo. You do not belong in the lands of my people. It is unfortunate your life has been so sorrowful. But it is not the fault of the Diné."

"Damn you," Peaked shouted and raised the pistol.

Though Will felt panic, Hasbaá remained calm. She said to Peak, "You bring all this on yourself because you have no love in your heart. Your anger makes you prey to other beings who kill blindly. It is you yourself your anger will attack."

With that, a loud whirring sound suddenly rose up from the ground. Four large rattlesnakes had surrounded Peak and were coiled, with their heads up ready to strike and their rattles going like crazy. They must have slithered out of the nearby brush while the soldier told his story.

Peak reacted. He fired his pistol first in Hasbaá's direction, and then at one of the snakes. Both bullets missed their marks, but the concussion startled the already agitated reptiles. One of them struck Peak's ankle. Its fangs pierced right through his boots. Peak suddenly froze, then began to scream in agony.

The pistol fired again and again. Peak tried to shoot the snake as it pumped its venom into his leg. He failed to hit the snake every time, but did succeed in shooting himself in the other foot. As the bullet blasted the top of his boot away, he fell to the ground. He landed on top of another of the rattling serpents. The snake struck right at his throat.

Within seconds, Peak's neck began to swell, and his windpipe was squeezed closed by the inflammation around the poisonous bite. He struggled to scream, but nothing came out. His back arched in pain. His eyes bulged. And then his whole body went limp.

As if satisfied, the four snakes uncoiled and slithered away into the brush.

In a mixture of triumph, relief, fear, and uncontrollable loathing, Will started to scream. Hasbaá tried to calm him. "Show respect for the snakes. They will not harm us."

Will finally managed to recover his composure. *What a burden had been lifted! Carleton in prison in Santa Fe. Peak dead. The threat is gone. The Navajos are going home.*

Will had accomplished his heroic deeds and saved the people. But there was still one more question to answer: *What is going to happen to me?*

75

The Indian Agent's Quarters

Agent William Lee, formerly of Fort Sumner, was authorized under joint orders of Gen. William T. Sherman and Dr. Michael Steck to oversee the Dinés' homeward journey. Soldiers were assigned to accompany the Indians and to protect them. Will was authorized to dismiss or discipline any soldier who mistreated the Indians.

One of the soldiers who was assigned to Will's authority was his buddy, Mac McCarrie. Will arranged for a promotion for Mac to Sergeant and put him in charge of instructing the men in respecting the ways of the Indians. Even though his testimony had been used to indict the Diné leaders, the red-headed private with the big grin proved to be a good friend. Will regretted that at the end of the journey Mac would return with the rest of the soldiers for a new assignment. But he was happy to know there would be soldiers sensitive to Indian concerns. *If only there had been such sensitivity from the start...*

The other soldier Will had been fascinated with, Pvt. Ned Johnson, was about to finish his tour of duty when Fort Sumner was being closed down. He was granted an early discharge. He'd stopped by the Agent's cabin—and happened to catch Will at his desk—as he was leaving for Santa Fe. He said he wanted to say goodbye. He told Will he was planning on settling there outside Santa Fe. He had a buddy in town. Will saw the twinkle in his eye as he said the word "buddy." They were going to try ranching together. Will's heart skipped a beat. He thanked Ned for stopping by.

"Maybe we'll run into one another some day," Will said, "in the Solis General Store. It's owned by friends of mine."

"I know the establishment well. So it's a date." Johnson laughed and gave Will a tight embrace before he headed off to catch the stage in front of the Sutler's.

76

The Trail Home

There was a bustle of activity around the Bosque Redondo as the Diné got ready to go. The camp quartermaster wanted them to wait a bit longer to accumulate more supplies for the journey. But the Diné were so eager to depart that Gen. Sherman approved an early march. Before his own departure, Sherman ordered that the excess rifles in the military armory be distributed among the Diné. The return journey would not be like the Long Walk eastward. Sherman coordinated carefully with Dr. Steck in Santa Fe to make sure adequate protections and supplies were offered at every stage of the journey.

The migration went amazingly smooth. Considering how many people had to be moved and the weakened conditions of the Diné, it was surprising that only a few deaths occurred in the month-long trek back to *Diné Bikéyah*. The people truly had a new strength, and though they took a slow pace in consideration for those who were too old or too weak to walk fast, every Diné person on the journey seemed to have a longing pulling them. With every step, they seemed more hopeful.

Will was thrilled by the Diné people's apparent lack of hatred for the government. *They really seem to want bygones to be bygones and to get on with their lives without complaint.* And he, in turn, did everything possible to insure against complaints. He joked that he must have requisitioned every available wagon in New Mexico to allow at least the old people and the children to ride in comfort. Of course, some of the Indians had horses and rode proudly. With the soldiers protecting them and with some of the Diné themselves armed with U.S. Springfield rifles, there were no attacks from raiders.

Dr. Steck kept his word about supplying the Diné for the journey. Every day, traders arrived with wagons full of food, blankets, and medicines. This trek was a boon to the shopkeepers and merchants throughout the Territory. The government expenditures improved the local economy and lessened the resentments which might otherwise have come from Carleton's previous provisioners and vendors.

Some traders showed up from Santa Fe. One of them was the big red-haired man. He never seemed to notice that Will's face should have been familiar to him. Was it simply the absence of spectacles and facial hair? He proudly told Will the newspapers were filled with sympathetic articles covering the problems faced by the Navajos during the previous years. There was a wave of support building among the residents of the Territory for the Indians.

Strong anti-slavery proclamations were publicized by the local government and at last there was a general recognition among the New Mexicans that peaceful relations would not last unless Indian slavery was ended. Most owners emancipated Indians held in servitude. Only a reactionary minority resisted. But with the government now actively under the influence of the abolitionists, they could do nothing about it. With every passing nightfall, more slaves escaped, and no sheriff's posses were organized to recapture them.

On the contrary, as they passed south of Santa Fe, the local sheriff brought ten wagonloads filled with Diné children who had earlier been captured and held by New Mexicans. Barboncito was dumbfounded when he realized that one of these children was his great grandson who had been stolen by the horsemen on that day they went looking for food in the desert. The boy ran into the old man's arms, and they stood there holding each other for a long time. Dezba, Hasbaá and so many others surrounded the two of them, and all held each other tightly. Tears flowed freely, but now they were tears of joy at the safe return of a member of the family. Will saw other families doing the same thing as they were reunited with their little ones.

One day, when the great band was about half way home, Hasbaá pointed out a lone burro approaching the camp. The poor burro was packed so high with trade goods, the rider was hidden. But as it got closer, Will could see that the rider was a small young man. And in an instant he realized who it was.

Will introduced Joel to Hasbaá who, not surprisingly, took an immediate liking to him. Hasbaá seemed to sense that Joel was a kind of kindred spirit. Joel was not dressed as a girl, but neither did he wear regular male attire. His clothes seemed to be his own unique creation, with pants so big they looked almost like a lady's riding outfit. The whole style, somewhere between masculine and feminine, reflected Joel's personality.

"I didn't have enough money for a horse, but Jose loaned me enough to add to what I had from you, *Señor Will*, for this burro. I named her Monique. It sounds continental, *n' est-ce pas*? Jose is teaching me French, just as I was teaching you *Español*.

"*Ay*, all of New Mexico knows about your journey. After you left Santa Fe, Jesse and Thanya heard the Navajos would be walking home. The shopkeepers all said there was money to be made selling supplies.

"I bought lots of cigars to sell. As soon as I heard they came from Virginia, where *mi amigo* William came from, I knew this was a good trade for me. I bet your troops haven't had a good smoke in a while. Let me peddle them, yes?"

"Of course."

"I also brought some new saddle blankets to make the ride easier."

"Well, I'll buy one for myself," Will declared, laughing.

"Little sister," Hasbaá said, "I will help you sell these to the Hairy Faces, but I am not happy with these saddle blankets. Back in our country, before the time of warfare, I used to weave saddle blankets from sheep's wool which were much superior."

Hasbaá accompanied Joel on his peddling. Within an hour, they had sold all his cigars and saddle blankets to the soldiers. Will noticed that some of the young Navajo men kidded with Hasbaá and Joel.

The young men teased Hasbaá. "I hear she has the cock of a donkey," one of them shouted. "But takes it like a man."

"'Cause her asshole's as big as a canyon," another one rejoined.

"You two must have *poco vergas*," Joel shouted back, "since you crave Hasbaá's."

"Oh, we hear she is the best sex in the whole countryside," one of the men replied, laughing.

For a moment, Will wondered if he'd heard the words correctly. He felt his anger rise. *What right do those men have to say such things?* But then he saw that all of them were smiling and laughing, Hasbaá included. He remembered Dezba said such teasing was meant in respect and not ridicule. *How different this culture still seems to me.* He was glad to have discovered its innocent ways. He also was happy to see Hasbaá laughing and joking. This was a new side of Hasbaá Will had not seen before. He liked it, partly because it reminded Will of his first love, Michael.

As Hasbaá passed him on her way back to camp with Joel, she reached out and touched his hand affectionately and rolled her eyes. Will could imagine her saying with a sigh of reconciled petulance: "Men...!"

For the rest of the evening, Joel and Hasbaá gossiped and laughed together. Will hoped they said nice things about him. He had seldom seen Hasbaá so carefree.

The next morning, Joel took off early, to ride briskly back to Santa Fe on his little burro, now all unburdened except for the roll of bills in the rider's pocket. He intended to buy another load of cigars. Hasbaá persuaded him not to bring any more of the inferior saddle blankets. Joel expected to catch up with the march once again before they reached Fort Defiance and make another tidy profit. Perhaps he would soon reach his goal of being a respectable merchant.

77

The Diné Homeland

Once the Diné saw their sacred mountains on the horizon and the spidery arms of the canyons shadowed across the plain, they practically ran into the territories that had been their homes. The government wisely provided each family with a horse, several sheep and crop seeds. This allowed them to start to rebuild their economy.

As Government Agent, Will oversaw the distribution of goods. There were a number of sickly horses and sheep which he prevailed on the purveyors to give to him rather than destroy. He presented these to Dezba; she and Hasbaá tenderly nursed each one back to full health. Barboncito had relatives farther west who had retreated into inaccessible canyons or hid as far as the Grand Canyon to escape the 1864 removal. They now returned and brought additional stocks of sheep. Within a couple of months, Dezba's outfit had the beginnings to build a small herd.

Back in their native land, the Navajos daily fanned out into the countryside to gather familiar species of wild plantfoods, nuts, berries, and roots. The prized fruit orchards and fertile farmlands along the floor of the Canyon de Chelly had been destroyed in the warring, but they were able to reestablish winter gardens of corn, beans, squash, and other vegetables. Everyone worked together to prepare for the cold weather to come. The boys made bows and arrows to hunt jackrabbits for fresh meat. The girls helped the women in farming and caring for the sheep.

Before it got too cold and the sheep would need their fleece themselves, Dezba and Hasbaá and several of the other women used heavy scissors to cut the matted wool off the bleating animals. Then later, after the temperature dropped, they brought the wool inside and prepared it on carding tools, pulling out the tangles and stretching the fibers into thread for weaving. They made dyes from various wild berries and soaked the wool to give it brilliant colors. Hasbaá set up a loom and every day worked to transform the wool into beautiful colored fabric.

One day, Hasbaá presented Will with a woven mat. "This is how a saddle blanket should be woven. Now you can ride in comfort." Hasbaá was right; the weave did make a difference.

Besides herding, weaving, and searching for wild foods, Hasbaá and the others constructed new hogans in the traditional style. They built brush arbors next to the hogans, where they could lounge comfortably in the shade. The thick packed earth walls of the dwellings absorbed the daylight warmth so that even during the hottest part of

the mid-afternoon the dark interior remained cool and comfortable. At
night, when the high desert air chilled, the interior of the hogan stayed
warm. Barboncito said the hogans would retain heat through the coldest
winter nights with only a small fire. This prediction proved true as the
chilly winds began to blow.

Will told Hasbaá he was surprised. "How well they hold heat and
yet stay cool when it's warm outside."

Hasbaá gave him a look of exasperation. "You are still surprised at
the wisdom of our ways. Our ancestors developed the best methods
for living in this climate over centuries. You Hairy Faces always think
your ways are superior. Our hogans are much better than those wood
boxes you people live in."

"Tell that to the government." Will felt properly corrected. "They
are the ones upset about me living in a hogan."

That was true, Will knew. Dr. Steck would certainly defend his
right to live according to the Diné way, but he had learned that
bureaucrats and missionaries who also had a say in Indian affairs had
heard tales of him and his turning Navajo. They disapproved.

Will worried that some of them would discover that he was married
to an Indian male and that there really was something going on they
would want to disapprove of. As far as the soldiers and the other whites
knew—even Dr. Steck—Hasbaá was Will's wife and that was that.
White men on the frontier sometimes took Indian women as common-
law wives. The government generally looked the other way if an Agent
was "living in sin" with a native woman. *But what would they do if they
found out I am living in sin with a native man?* He dreaded to think.

Will remembered that Sgt. Peak said he had voiced his suspicions
to Gen. Carleton. From what he had learned of Jesse McDonald's own
past from his dream visit back to the office in Washington, Will imagined
that if Carleton and McDonald ever compared notes, he might easily
be exposed.

Now that they were home and there was no reason for pretense,
Hasbaá sometimes dressed as a woman and sometimes as a man. Will
was learning the wisdom of not using pronouns. Hasbaá began to follow
the style of so many of the Diné women who'd adapted the castoff
clothing of the Hairy Faces, pulling the hoops out of the white ladies'
hoop skirts and decorating the fabric to make regal-looking gowns. In
the satins and velvets, the Diné women all appeared particularly

dignified. Will bought Hasbaá a blue velvet frock from one of the traders. She tore out some of the seams and redesigned the dress to suit herself and Diné styles. Hasbaá had come across a crude religious painting of the Blessed Virgin Mary among the wares of a Mexican trader. The Madonna was clad in the same shade of blue. Hasbaá joked with Will that now in her blue velvet dress she looked like God's mother. She kept the dress for ritual occasions and for special times with Will.

Most of the time, it seemed, Hasbaá was a partner and equal to Will and Will was a partner and equal to Hasbaá.

Outside Diné culture, Will knew, such arrangements wouldn't be tolerated. And so he seldom went to the trading posts and even less often to Fort Defiance. He kept his reports short and to the point. He stressed that the Diné were readjusting to their homeland quite well, and there was no need for any further government intervention.

In the Navajo homeland, Will seldom heard English spoken. His absorption of Diné came much faster. It was still difficult for him to express complex thoughts, but he improved his skills daily. He learned to herd sheep, locate water, and live in the desert.

78

DEZBA'S HOGAN

One day after the hard freezes of January and February had passed and the days were lengthening, Barboncito returned to the camp with a pair of horsemen. It was Joel and Jose.

"We had to search all over Navajoland for you," Joel exclaimed. "I've been missing you and Hasbaá. Jose and I wanted to see your new home. So here we are. And we want to introduce you to these *niños*."

Jose jumped down, shook Will's hand in a formal but affectionate way, then turned back to the horses and helped down two Indian children who had ridden, one with each of the adults. There was a girl and a boy, both about seven or eight years old. They allowed themselves to be introduced to Will and Hasbaá and Dezba and Barboncito, then ran off to play with the other Diné children whom they saw laughing and running around the settlement.

"I found them wandering the streets in Santa Fe. Their parents had died, and they had no relatives. I took them to the cantina and fed them. Jesse and Thanya took care of them for a while. But then Jose said we should bring them to you. They are Navajo *niños*. We do not know their names. We thought you should give them proper Diné names.

"And see the boy is so gentle and the girl is so determined to be her own person. I think we will discover one day that they are both Two-Spirit Persons. Like *us*," Joel proudly proclaimed.

"We will adopt them," Hasbaá announced.

Will shook his head in disbelief. "Wait a minute; would this be the best thing for them?"

"Of course, it would," said Jose. "There's no one in Santa Fe for them. They would have to go to the Catholic orphanage."

"You will make a wonderful *padre*," Joel chirped. "And who could make a better *madre* than Hasbaá?"

"And I will be grandmother," Dezba added her approval. "It's time you and Hasbaá got some children. You are a married couple now."

"But why not a man and woman who already have children?" Will suggested. "They would know better how to raise them."

"But why?" Hasbaá asked. "We have no children. Why should they go to adults who already have others to take care of?"

"It only makes sense for you to take them," Dezba said. "The Diné believe those without any children of their own should be first to adopt. Niece will give them all the mothering they could want. And you, Nephew, will make a better father than you realize."

Will had to admit Dezba was probably right. Even though he had seen how naturally the Diné had accepted him and Hasbaá as a couple, down deep inside he had thought two males could not provide as good a family as a male and a female. *But perhaps Changing Woman has brought these children to us for a reason. Perhaps ripples from early lives reverberating through the spirit-field have brought them here, just as the ripples from Segundo's life had apparently brought me to Hasbaá and to Diné Bikéyah.*

Hasbaá called to the children. Within moments, they sat comfortably and unafraid in her lap. Dezba was right. Hasbaá was a natural mother. Will recalled how much he'd liked mentoring Joel. *Maybe I can be a father after all.*

These children needed a home. Will shuddered to think what would happen to them in an orphanage. *Maybe Joel is right about them. What if either or both of them grow up to be Two-Spirited?* Will would not want them raised by guilt-ridden Christians. *Wouldn't they be better with good exemplars like me and Hasbaá? And if they are not Two-Spirit Persons, wouldn't they still be better off to grow up in a household where their own choices about their lives will be respected?*

Will bent down and asked the boy, "How would you like to stay here and live with us?" He kissed the girl on the cheek. "We can teach you how to herd sheep, farm, and weave beautiful blankets. We can laugh and play and help each other. I can teach you how to read."

The youngsters shyly hid their faces, but giggled in anticipation. They jumped out of Hasbaá's lap and ran back to the other children who stood around to see if these newcomers would be welcomed into Dezba's family.

Will looked at Hasbaá, then nodded solemnly in agreement. Hasbaá had tears in her eyes. The other children all saw and began to jump up and down in glee.

"Let us name them Segundo and Baaneez," Will suggested.

Dezba and Barboncito began to cry tears of joy.

"See how they laugh." Hasbaá smiled widely. "Among the Diné, we celebrate when a child first laughs. It is a very special and holy sign."

"Probably the parents of little Segundo and little Baaneez were not able to celebrate this event with their people," Dezba said. "Hasbaá, you will have to arrange such a ceremony now."

"It will be an honor. We are creating a family."

Will felt a pang of joy well up in his heart. Hasbaá seemed so handsome to him and so desirable.

"Don't you two want a family?" Will teased Joel and Jose.

"We are the godparents of Maria, Thanya's little girl," Jose answered. He pointed at Joel. "We told the *padre* this is *mi esposa* Joelle." He laughed heartily.

"But now we have a great business enterprise to launch," Joel said proudly. "We are not yet ready to be parents."

"But after you are rich…"

"Then, *señor Will*, we will free all the children in the orphanage," Jose said in grand exaggeration. "And make the most *grande familia* the West has ever seen." They all laughed.

"Speaking of business, let me show you what I have here." Joel reached into one of the saddlebags on his horse and brought out a streamlined metal instrument. He held it up for all to see.

"What is it?" Hasbaá asked.

"A sheepshear?" Dezba suggested.

"*Sí*. It is the newest design. See how easily it fits the hand." He passed it to Dezba.

Barboncito, who had been watching all this from his horse, jumped down and went over and brought a sheep from the flock. It had been sheared already, but the fleece was already growing out. Hasbaá and Dezba took turns with the newfangled instrument. It was clearly easier to use than their old heavy scissors.

Joel offered a deal. He would leave several of the shears for free if Hasbaá would weave some saddle blankets in exchange. Joel said he wanted to establish commerce with the Diné. He would bring manufactured goods to barter for Diné weavings and blankets and other goods the Indians produced. He said he would sell the blankets to the cowboys on the range and trade what he had gathered for cows. Then he could sell the cows in Santa Fe. The cowboys would have better blankets and ride more comfortably. The Diné would prosper. And he and Jose would get rich.

Will smiled. With ironic humor no one would appreciate but himself, he declared, "Why Santa Fe could become the wool capital of the country..."

Dezba thought the plan would be good for everybody all around and agreed wholeheartedly. She invited the two visitors to come up to the brush arbor and rest. Hasbaá said she would prepare supper.

As the business dealing ended, Joel reached into his saddlebag again. "Will, Dr. Steck asked me to deliver this letter to you. He said it was *muy importante*."

"Oh." Will took the envelope and tore it open. Inside was a note in Steck's handwriting. Also a formal letter on Indian Agency stationery. He read it first.

Dear Agent Lee,

On the advice of the Commissioner of Indian Affairs, Mr. Jesse McDonald, this office has concluded that you may be setting a bad example for the civilization of the Navajo Indians. It has come to the attention of the agency that you are intimately involved with a Navajo Indian of scurrilous reputation. The government of the United States cannot condone the commission—or even the hint of commission—of such offenses as we understand these savages are capable of.

We are concerned that you may be endangering the salvation of your soul by continued residence among the savages. Think of your Christian heritage.

You are hereby ordered to return for reassignment to a clerkship in the Washington office. Residence in a civilized city will bring you to realize the error of your ways. Pastor Sheldon Benedict, also an associate of the agency, has offered to assist you in your reconversion to the Christianity of your upbringing. Your employers are sure you will be pleased to benefit from the Pastor's kind offer.

You are to report to the Indian Office in Santa Fe as soon as possible. A ticket will be awaiting you. If you do not report for reassignment, we will be forced to dispatch federal marshals.

Will was stunned, though, he had to admit, not really surprised. He had expected something like this. He had made enemies in the Indian Office with his attacks on Gen. Carleton. *It is just as I feared; now Carleton and his buddies are going to get the last laugh after all. It's as clear as can be. After a decent interval has passed, my exposé of the Fort Sumner fiasco is going to subject me to bureaucratic punishment.*

He looked at the note from Steck.

My friend,

I am sorry about this. There is little I can do. You may soon learn that I have retired from the Office of Indian Affairs. Now that the Diné are resettled in their homeland, I believe my work is completed here. Agnes and I are returning to Ohio, where I hope to reestablish my practice as a physician.

If you come to Santa Fe soon I look forward to seeing you. You are a good man. If I can help in any way, you may certainly call on me.

Your friend,
Michael

Will followed the others over to the brush arbor. A cool wind was coming up, and Hasbaá was preparing a tea made from native plants. Will was trembling. He read the letter from Washington to his friends. After he finished, Hasbaá asked quietly, as if preparing herself for a difficult and painful emotion, "What will you do?"

"What else can I do? They're going to come after me. That could endanger all of you." He was afraid of what he was about to say. "Let me think about this." He excused himself and started to walk away. When Hasbaá jumped up to follow, Will gestured to her to stay where she was. "I need to be alone."

79

The Diné Homeland

He walked away from the settlement and stood among the trees. He gazed out into the valley that had now become his home.

I would never have come west, but for the machinations of Jesse McDonald. Can I stay in the West, especially without the government job? Will recalled that he'd discovered he could make a living as a sales clerk in Santa Fe, but that was not a life he wanted. *Can I give up my employment, my security? Can I really give up my identity as a civilized human being? Can I give up being a white person, with a long Virginia heritage?*

Will knew he couldn't hide out here for long. *If Carleton and McDonald and the others are going to get their revenge, won't they soon send the soldiers here to arrest me and take me back by force? Won't they use that as an excuse to abrogate the peace?*

Am I going to do once again what they tell me to do? Or wait for them to come for me? Do I have any real choice?

Of course, he told himself, *the answer is obvious. The officials are right: Mr. William Lee of Lynchburg, Virginia cannot remain in the West living like an Indian wildman.*

Will turned and headed back toward the Diné settlement. As he approached the brush arbor where his friends waited, he worried over his decision one last time and then detoured over to the hogan he shared with Hasbaá.

He rummaged around to find his mother's worn carpetbag. Here were the few personal belongings he'd kept from civilization. He found what he was looking for. He opened the folded sheet of paper and then took a quill and ink and quickly scratched a new date on the top of the page, then carefully tore off the signature penned at the bottom. There would be room for Dr. Steck to sign it over again and make it official.

When Will returned to the brush arbor, everyone was waiting in silence. A look of sadness hung over the little group of friends.

Will held up the paper for them to see. "Joel, when you return to Santa Fe, please take this to Dr. Steck. Tell him it requires his signature."

"What is it?" Joel asked timidly. He hated to see Will leave the frontier.

"It's my death certificate," Will answered. "It says here Agent William Lee was killed in a fire in the Indian settlement. It doesn't say where the settlement was. Let it be here." He grinned. He "died" once before in the buggy in front of his father's church, and it had started him on a new life. Now he would "die" again and win that new life for good.

"You are my dearest friends, my family. I've learned from you the meaning of the dear love of comrades. I have found a reason to live. As far as the United States Government is concerned, William Lee is dead. They will not come for me." He turned to Hasbaá, "Will you prepare a ceremony? I too want to be called by a name that belonged to an honored member of the Diné family. And ask Changing Woman to see that our needs are provided for. After all, we've now got two children to support. The future of our family depends on it."

"And now it is time you two had a proper wedding ceremony as well," declared Dezba. "You now have a new hogan together; you will bless that as your marriage hogan by sharing maize from the wedding basket together. Our whole outfit will join together to bless your family. Your love for one another gives blessings to us all."

Will bent down and kissed Hasbaá on the forehead. She wept openly. Will, too, started to cry. These were tears of happiness and joy, tears for a life that had passed beyond, tears for a new beginning.

Will looked back wistfully seeing how far he had come, both in geographical space and personal growth, in such a short time. Like the heroes of old he had read about, his journey began when he made the decision to leave the strangling confines of his father's world, and by the happenstance of Harry Burnside's job referral, to take off on a mythic quest. Now he wondered if indeed that meeting with Harry Burnside was happenstance; maybe it was the work of Changing Woman even as far away from *Diné Bikéyah* as Lynchburg.

Once he had arrived in New Mexico Territory, he'd begun a process of discovery, as he learned about the Diné way of life. His vision expanded as he discovered that all the world was not as it was in Virginia. But more than that, he also went through a process of discovery about himself. He had grown from a feckless adolescent who let events control him, who thought that the only choice was to conform to social expectations or to commit suicide. Now he had become a confident adult who learned to take charge of life and direct change to the benefit of others as well as himself.

And in the process of this journey of discovery, in Hasbaá Will had found a love and a family and a society that had taken him in wholeheartedly. Hasbaá was a Two-Spirit Person, but in a larger sense Will and Hasbaá had become Two Spirits, two individuals, united by their love to protect the Diné people, this ancient culture and the Two-Spirit wisdom.

By realizing that he did indeed march to the beat of a different drummer, Will had opened himself to finding a new home. As he gazed lovingly on Hasbaá, Will knew in his heart that *Diné Bikéyah* had become his real home. He committed to living his life in appreciation for the spiritual power of Changing Woman and for the intimacies of the dear love of comrades.

Will also sent back with Joel a short letter to Harry Burnside. It said simply that he was very grateful for all the help he had received. He told Harry that he would probably hear rumors that he had died out in the West. He said he couldn't confirm or deny the rumors. There seemed to be truth on both sides.

He asked Harry to drop a note to the Reverend Joshua Lee. He wanted the old man to know his son had lived and died well, that in dying as he had, he had done something heroic. He said he wasn't sure the Reverend Lee would understand it if he knew the details, so it was better for him just to know that one of the last things the boy said before his identity passed out of the world of civilized men was that he thanked his father for starting him on this adventure and forgave him for not knowing what he had done.

Epilogue

80

DINE BIKEYAH

One beautiful spring morning, the white-skinned Diné herdsman, who was called Manuelito after one of the great leaders of The People, rode up to the top of the fertile valley where he and his family lived. He rode high to the summit of a bluff where he could see out into the whole canyon.

He could spy the hogans of the outfit; the gardens glowed green even from this far away. In the distance, he could see the two tall pinnacles of red-orange sandstone that stood at the mouth of the canyon. He understood why the legends of the Hairy Faces called this the Navajo fortress. With its steep walls, branching canyons, rocky prominences and lookouts, it made a stronghold and safe haven. It was as though the Earth itself had opened up a fold in her body to provide a home for The People.

This place looked familiar to him. He had been here before, he remembered. Manuelito felt the sun on his face and chest. In the lowlands, the air had been balmy, and he'd gone out riding bare-chested. But it was cool in the high reaches. The warmth of the sun felt good.

He wondered if anyone he'd known during his childhood would ever hear of him again. He thought not. As far as that world was concerned, he had disappeared forever. He looked out at the land. He thought about the cities of the Hairy Faces. He remembered the crowded and unfriendly streets of Washington, D.C.

He knew how powerful were the ways of the Hairy Faces. He knew these white-skinned people had crossed a wide sea to come to this land and then plodded across the continent to settle in every fertile and habitable part of it. He wondered if someday they would bring their cities to this very valley.

Manuelito saddened to think what those people might do. He prayed to Changing Woman that human beings never forget about her and about the sacredness of the Earth. Still, he thought it was inevitable that the Hairy Faces would come but he hoped that the strength of Changing Woman would keep the Diné from forgetting their sacred wisdom.

Reverently, he repeated the sacred Diné phrase *"Sa'ah Naagháii Bik'eh Hózhó"* he'd heard many times in ceremonials. Hasbaá said that restoring *hózhó*—beauty and harmony—is the purpose of human life.

Manuelito had come to believe his Beloved's explanation that each person's life makes ripples in the spirit-field. *Everyone of us lives on the crest of a wave. That wave comprises the ripples of every life that went before. We are all always living out the unlived lives of our ancestors. They live on in us as we live on in those who will come after us. That is why we should choose the best and most vital parts of their dreams, aspirations, and intentions, so that that is what will live on of us.*

Through the help of old Harry Burnside, through the wisdom of Walt Whitman and his loving comrades, and through his own willingness to look beneath the surface of race and culture and find his own Two-Spirit nature in his love for Hasbaá the Two-Spirit Person, he had discovered a new life. Somehow the ripples of the life of the brave warrior who died at the gate of Fort Defiance had reverberated in his spirit, and in him Segundo had lived on to help his people and free Hasbaá from her mourning. Manuelito was grateful for all the ripples that had passed through him and made him who he was. He hoped his own life would reverberate so well in other souls someday. He hoped the ripples would help restore *hózhó*.

Manuelito wondered if the Hairy Face culture of that future when they had overrun these lands would understand the nature of Two-Spirit Persons. He wondered if someday in that strange, unimaginable future other Two-Spirit Persons would arise to help bring the human race back to its true homeland, to remind people that the rigid, legalistic, guilt-ridden, nature-defiling ways of the white culture are but one way to perceive and treat the world, and that a new time will dawn when those ways too will fade in a whole new awakening of Earth's spirit.

"For every atom belonging to me as good belongs to you"—words of the poet, whose leather-bound copy of *Leaves of Grass* was the only book still in his possession, reminded him that somehow he'd be part of whatever future came to be.

He recited a Diné chant Hasbaá had taught him:

> *The mountains, I become part of it.*
> *The herbs, the fir tree, I become part of it.*
> *The morning mists, the clouds, the gathering waters,*
>   *I become part of it.*
> *The wilderness, the dew drops, the pollen,*
>   *I become part of it.*

He looked out into the valley and felt himself but a tiny ripple in the vast cosmos that stretched back into the four worlds before this one and out into the stars. As a single individual he was insignificant, and yet all of this beauty, this *hózhó*—and all the success he'd helped Hasbaá achieve for the Diné and for the future—it had happened to him. He was so grateful for his life.

He hoped that someday Two-Spirit Persons of that future might hear of and remember him and Hasbaá and reverberate to the ripples created by their lives.

Perhaps someday Two-Spirit Persons will hear tales of their predecessors and remember their own deepest identity and heritage as spirit guides and leaders in recreating a religious attitude that honors the human body and honors the Earth. The Diné herdsman who had once been called Will Lee hoped so.

The spring breezes in the high places of the *Diné Bikéyah* were sharp and cold on his skin. And presently Manuelito turned his horse and headed back down into the valley.

About the Historical Accuracy
of This Novel

Today, Fort Sumner itself is nothing more than ruins. The Chamber of Commerce for the village of Fort Sumner has a web site that practically ignores the national and international significance of the fort's role as a prison for Native Americans. Instead, this website invites the public to visit a museum honoring the white pioneer families who settled in the area in the 1880s, to go fishing at the new Bosque Redondo Lake and campground, to "take a pleasant stroll along the historic Pecos River, or take your kids to the grave of outlaw Billy the Kid."

The biggest tourist draw in Fort Sumner is the Billy the Kid Museum. Though thousands of tourists trek to the gunfighter's gravesite each year, few know that in 1881 Billy Bonny was shot in the building that had once been the officers' quarters of Fort Sumner. By then the old fort had been remodeled into the private home of Lucien Maxwell, a successful land speculator.

The main commemoration of the fort itself is an annual four-day "Ole Fort Days," billed as a celebration, that features such western pioneer events as a rodeo, horseshoe pitching, goat roping, art show, western dancing and musicfest, along with "The Billy the Kid Tombstone Race, Wild West Shootout, and The Great American Cow Plop Contest." And every year, a few Navajos are hired to come in and do a performance of "Indian Dancing."

The presence of these few Navajo dancers at this annual celebration of white frontier culture must seem incongruous even to the casual tourist. A visitor who knows the truth about what happened at Fort

Sumner in the 1860s might think this would be like Germans holding an annual "Ole Auschwitz Days" celebration of German culture, complete with Jewish folk dancers, at the site of the Nazi concentration camp. But until 2004, when a New Mexico State Monument was finally erected at the ruins of the old fort, a visitor would have been hard pressed to find any evidence at all that Fort Sumner is seen by many Native people as an American concentration camp.

Though this novel is fiction, the story is based on historical fact. General James Carleton was, in fact, the deeply religious and moralistic commanding officer in New Mexico Territory. He was filled with zealous righteous certainty, and allowed himself no change of mind or admissions of error. After being removed from command at Fort Sumner, he spent his last years trying to justify his record by publishing books on his campaigns. He died in uniform at age 59 in San Antonio in 1873, never having taken responsibility for the thousands of deaths that occurred due to his policies. Carleton was obsessed with discovering a gold and silver fortune on Diné lands, and he predicted that the lands he had taken from the Indians in New Mexico would prove to be "richer in mineral wealth than California." That Carleton did not think the Diné people themselves deserved to be the beneficiaries of this wealth can be seen by this racist characterization in which he claimed: "An Indian is more watchful and a more wary animal than a deer. He must be hunted with skill."

In contrast to General Carleton, Colonel Kit Carson, the second in command, preferred to negotiate a diplomatic solution with the Diné. He protested to Carleton that he had joined the U.S. Army to fight against the proslavery Southern secessionists, and his heart was not in dispossessing Indians from their lands. Nevertheless, Carleton threatened Carson with court martial and forced him to pursue a policy of total war against the Diné. The scorched earth policies pursued against the Indians were not any less extreme than anything done against civilians in recent wars. Carson's troops destroyed millions of pounds of Diné crops, killed thousands of livestock, dismantled and burned Diné housing, and shot fleeing civilians on sight. Murder, mass starvation, and multitudes freezing to death was the direct result.

General Carleton ignored New Mexicans' raiding of Diné outfits to steal women and children as slaves, and under his jurisdiction about

5,000 Diné (close to one-third of their entire population) were held as slaves by New Mexicans long after the Thirteenth Amendment to the Constitution declared slavery to be unconstitutional.

During the 325 mile Long Walk to Fort Sumner about 3,000 died out of 11,500 who embarked on the journey. Many elderly and infirm Diné who could not keep up were left on the roadside to starve. Another 2,000 people died (one-fourth of their population) during the next three years at Fort Sumner.

Dr. Michael Steck, Superintendent of Indian Affairs for New Mexico Territory, strongly opposed the Bosque Redondo Reservation. He estimated that the poor land would support no more than 2,000 people. Carleton stubbornly insisted that there were no more than 5,000 Navajos, and when almost 12,000 surrendered by 1864, Carleton was left with too few supplies to feed them. Many more Diné starved to death as a result of Carleton's miscalculations and rigidity. Dr. Steck doggedly pursued the removal of Carleton, for incompetence, malfeasance, and wastefulness. Steck accused Carleton of mishandling over three million dollars in government funds, which would be the equivalent in consumer purchasing power in today's dollars to over $38 million. What a waste of money!

By the actual time of Carleton's fall the Territorial Indian Superintendent was Steck's successor the New Mexican Felipe Delgado, whose family actually ran the dry goods store in Santa Fe and whose complaint with Carleton's policies was that the Navajos had not been subdued *enough*. What a waste of lives!

General William Tecumseh Sherman did allow the Navajos to leave the Bosque Redondo in 1868 and return to their homeland after negotiating with the Navajo spokesperson Barboncito. Though the timeframe in the novel is dramatically compressed: the Dinés' liberation actually took nearly two years, not one summer.

The horserace that led to a massacre on September 22, 1861 resulted in the deaths of fifteen Diné people, mostly women and children. Another fifteen were seriously wounded. The Diné rider whose bridle broke was in reality named Manuelito, but unlike in this text he did not die in this massacre and he later went on to become a respected Diné negotiator with government officials.

The characters of Dezba and Barboncito are based on real people with those names who actually lived the ordeal of the Long Walk and the Bosque Redondo experiment recounted here and helped their people return to their ancestral homelands around the Canyon de Chelly in what is now northeastern Arizona. Segundo and Ganado Mucho are fictional characters but their names were those of real individuals. Though these names, of course, show Spanish colonial influence; they are not Diné language names. These are the names that have come down historically for the real people, but they are not the names the characters would have actually used for one another. In fact, the Diné generally do not address each other by name or use another's name in that person's presence. Hence the occasional construction that may sound odd to English speakers in Dezba's and Hasbaá's dialogue to show their reverence for personal names.

Photographs of these very individuals, as well as of the conditions at the Bosque Redondo, are preserved in the book *The Army and the Navajo: The Bosque Redondo Reservation Experiment 1863-1868* by Gerald Thompson (University of Arizona Press, 1976) which describes the whole period in detail and served as a primary source for this novel. Many of these same photos are accessible through an Internet search on "Bosque Redondo."

The character of the English teacher John Blewer is entirely fictional. Few Diné spoke English at that time. But had the Diné characters been unable to speak English, Will (and the reader) would have had a much more difficult time learning the Native American Two-Spirit wisdom.

The character of Will is also entirely fictional, though there was an Indian Agent at Fort Sumner in the 1860s who did help the Navajos get home. His name was Theodore Dodd. We have no way to know his sexual orientation or his motives. Dodd's motivations for helping the Navajo might have been just as this novel imagines Will's—born out of compassion and human decency, but also out of personal drive and longing for intimacy.

Some of the events in the story—the murder of Agent Ayers, Steck's easy access to the telegraph, Will's alienating Carleton's allies, etc.—are fiction, devised to support the plot and wisdom-message of the novel. Hasbaá's willingness to violate the taboo around the body of the dead *Mexicano*, for instance, may not be historically accurate, but does convey the important spiritual message that goodness and right action can sometimes require abrogation of religious rules and social conventions.

Nadleehí—"Changing Ones"—is the Diné term for Two-Spirit Persons. While this particular *nadleehí* is fictional, there were undoubtedly Two-Spirit healers like Hasbaá among the captives at Bosque Redondo. Such androgynous, gender variant, Two-Spirit Persons were highly respected not only among the Navajos, but also among many other Native American cultures.

As Diné scholar Wesley K. Thomas, who graciously provided a commentary for inclusion with this novel, points out, *nadleehí* is the actual word Dezba would have used, not "Two-Spirit." The term "Two-Spirit" comes from an Anishinabe/Ojibway term, *nizh manitoag*, which was officially embraced by contemporary lesbian, gay, bisexual and transgendered Native Americans to describe the gender variant persons of Indian cultures at an international gathering in Winnipeg, Manitoba in 1990.

The character of the very far-traveling Wandering Falcon was invented to allow the Navajo protagonists to follow the modern (Ojibway-based) usage—*and* also to exemplify the reality that Two-Spirit Persons were often diplomats and emissaries and that there was lively interaction, communication and trade between the various Native American peoples.

The fictional relationship between Will and Hasbaá is based on a certainty that, just as in our day same-sex relationships cut across races and social classes, so some white men on the Western frontier must have formed loving relationships with Native American males. It makes sense that those we today would call homosexually oriented were encouraged by Native Americans' supportive attitudes toward same-sex marriage and acceptance of same-sex eroticism. Homosexual unions are not new in America; there was "gay marriage" on the North American continent long before European immigration.

The reader may have noticed that Will never wondered if he were "homosexual" or "gay." That is because those words—and concepts—did not yet exist. "Homosexual" did not become widely used until the end of the 1800s. Gay consciousness did not develop until the twentieth century, though it did grow partly out of the ideals of Democracy and "the dear love of comrades" expressed in Walt Whitman's *Leaves of Grass*.

Will would not have had the sophistication about things gay that we now have nor an appreciation of the nuances of sexuality conveyed in such categorical terms as homosexual, bisexual, transsexual, transgender, transvestite, etc. Will would actually have been wrong to have thought of himself as being a Two-Spirit in the same way Hasbaá was. In fact, generally Two-Spirit Navajo *nadleehí* bonded as secondary wives or consorts to married men or as marriage partners with masculine-identified men, often Chiefs; Two-Spirits generally didn't bond with other Two-Spirits in the way modern gay men bond with like partners. But Will would have been right in understanding that his same-sex orientation came down through time in a long line of men who comfortably blended masculinity and femininity and maleness and femaleness and who seemed to transcend conventional gender roles. Homosexual orientation has always bestowed liberation from gender.

Some readers will recognize in the name of Harry Burnside a commingled homage to Harry Hay and John Burnside, men of our own day who helped create the modern Gay Movement and articulated, especially, its claim of a special and socially-contributing spiritual identity as part of homosexual orientation. Similarly, "Pastor Sheldon Benedict" combines the names of contemporary gay rights opponents who confuse religion with cultural bias and, like the well-meaning but wrong-headed missionary in this novel, do no good for anyone with their well-intentioned but misguided notions of family values and moral virtue.

Native American traditions of respect for Two-Spirit Persons go back to ancient times and the discovery of such traditions has struck a positive chord among self-identified gay, lesbian, transgender and queer people of the twentieth and twenty-first centuries. Many modern queerfolk have found in these traditions evidence of a spiritual identity that they have felt strongly burning in their own souls, but for which they found little support in Christianity or mainstream American society—or pop gay culture, for that matter.

"Native American culture" comprises a huge number of different societies and different cultures. Not all of these societies honored Two-Spirit Persons. The vision of Navajo culture portrayed in this novel is based in Walter Williams' personal experiences in living among a variety of these societies. The authors have taken liberties in portraying life on the Bosque Redondo. Dezba's outfit's sophistication about other tribes and about political theory, their ease with nudity, even mixed-sex nudity, their positive attitudes about sex, their use of mind-altering plant medicines—these certainly represent aspects of Native American wisdom that modern gay people resonate with, but they're not necessarily specifically Diné. The term for the Union soldiers, "Hairy Faces," was actually an expression in the Lakota language. It exemplifies the possibility of categorizing people by traits other than skin color. The Lakota, by the way, called their Two-Spirits *winkte* and *wapetokeca* which means "people with special powers."

The quotations of chants and descriptions of Navajo ceremonies were taken from accounts already published and do not reveal any sacred secrets. The descriptions of the ceremonies and sandpaintings have been intentionally simplified and fictionalized in reverence for actual practices.

Indeed, the spiritual wisdom of this story is presented in the imagery of Navajo religion but does not necessarily accord with Navajo orthodoxy. The tales from Diné myth are actual folklore however their particular interpretation and application in this story, which is itself a mythologization, necessarily reflect the issues and values of modern life out of which the authors'—and readers'—own mythologizations arise.

The notion of "ripples in the spirit field" was conceived by the authors to explain the place of sexual variance in the evolution of consciousness. This is a concern of 21st Century thinkers, but not inconsistent with the trans-temporal worldviews of Native American traditions.

The sacred Diné phrase Will meditated on *Sa'ah Naagháii Bik'eh Hózhó* in its simplicity means "Continuing, Re-occurring Long Life in an Environment of Beauty and Harmony."

This sacred phrase alludes to the Diné sense of being connected to all of one's relatives all the way back to the beginnings of The People and all the way into the future. All life is interconnected. *Sa'ah Naagháii Bik'eh Hózhó* is the life force itself creating the world. Symbolically, *Sa'ah Naagháii* [continuing, re-occurring long life] is the semen of First Man, identified with the Sun, and *Bik'eh Hózhó* [beauty and harmony] the reproductive egg of Changing Woman, identified with the Earth. Individuals manifest the marvelous generativity of all life by passing the life force down through time from generation to generation in offspring. But the life force is more than just the animation of the individual person in an individuated and apparently separate body. For at death, one's life force "returns to the Dawn" and becomes part of the "undifferentiated pool of *nilch'i* [animation, breath]" out of which future living beings will arise. Thus *Sa'ah Naagháii Bik'eh Hózhó* is the dynamic by which kinship is both biological and spiritual. The life force is in all things and it connects all things. We are all part of *Sa'ah Naagháii Bik'eh Hózhó*. We all resonate with the spirit-field. That is why how we live our lives matters.

A major need in the creation of contemporary gay culture is to place variant sexuality and "gay identity" directly in the line of the transformation of humankind through evolution, to restore harmony for ourselves and our way of seeing the world. Gay people need to know their place in the scheme of things (as Diné culture admirably demonstrated). Non-gay people need to accord them their rightful place (as 21st Century global culture is just beginning—hesitantly—to do). Establishing the claim to one's place in evolution is a function of mythology.

The very nature of myth is to blur history and culture into meaningfulness, and to weave unconnected, disparate, but loosely historically-based memories into a web of societal meaning. For example, the familiar Christmas story of the Magi and the massacre of the Holy Innocents merged unconnected, but culturally powerful and newsworthy, events—the appearance of a comet, the arrival in Jerusalem of missionaries from India, and apparently some horrendous act of military infanticide—to dramatize the universality of Jesus' message. The point of the story wasn't to relate history, but meaning. So it is with all myth.

The mystical phenomena Will experienced—whether induced by sacred plant medicines or just by exposure to a totally new worldview— were introduced for dramatic purpose. They signify the expansion of consciousness that comes from being exposed to an alternative world. In Will's case, that alternative was Diné culture. For many gay people the alternative is modern gay culture. There is a "mystical" and "magical" experience in coming out and discovering enlightened liberated gay consciousness.

For some of those gay people and many others in the modern world, mind-altering drugs provided that exposure to alternate realities. Mind-altering substances have long been part of shamanic religious experience. Trance, or ecstasy, is inherent to the shamanic spiritualities of the Americas. The current day Native American Church, which includes many Navajos, ritually uses peyote, the cactus containing the psychoactive alkaloid mescaline, to induce enlightening experience. Peyote was not known among the Navajo in the 1860s, and at that time its use appears limited to tribes living further south in Mexico. It is not inappropriate though to weave some sort of sacred drug use into the story of Will and Hasbaá.

Drugs have become a highly contentious and problematic issue in modern life. Drugs have been part of the liberation of some gay people, and the ruination of others. Modern society lacks a framework for understanding mind-altering substances. Native American shamanism offers a good example of how these powerful substances should be used properly for spiritual insight, not just mind-numbed recreation.

In the novel, the mystical phenomena move the story into mythological realms: this isn't just an adventure or a history, it's a story of discovery about the sacred and the eternal.

In the past, people who today would be called gay or queer were the seers, shamans, soothsayers, wizards, witches, mystics, oracles, wise old men and wise old women of legend. While some of these individuals were persecuted by the institutions of religion, and sometimes *because* of the persecution, they have been centered in the driving force of the evolution of consciousness. These queer forebears created ripples in the spirit field to which modern lesbians and gay men resonate. Understanding this allows a mythical way of describing gay identity that places us clearly in the line of responsibility for the Great Work of "saving the world" and "perfecting Humankind." As Hasbaá and Will were messengers of Changing Woman, so today their spiritual descendents are messengers of Gaia the World Soul to an overcrowded, ecologically imbalanced, sexually neurotic, and mythologically bereft modern world.

The aspiration of this book is to offer an entertaining and appealing reminder of that age-old identity.

A Commentary

Wesley K. Thomas

Though most people know us as Navajo, our traditional name for ourselves in our own language is Diné, which means "The People." Ethnohistorian Walter L. Williams has at last broken his silence and exactly twenty years after the publication of his award-winning book, *The Spirit and the Flesh*, has published another book on gender variance in Native American cultures. But unlike the academically-written non-fiction book that he is most famous for, he decided this time to aim for a wider audience by conveying his ideas in fictional form. He chose as his collaborator experienced award-winning fiction writer Toby Johnson, and together they have produced an historical novel that presents another picture of America's history.

This novel is more than just an exciting story of Native Americans in the Civil War era. Drawing upon Diné philosophy, it presents a positive way to approach life. It calls for acknowledging and respecting the important role that eroticism plays in a person's existence. It provides a sense of humanity in its recognition that people, who would today be identified as transgendered or gay, were always part of the Diné way of life. Above all, this book—I hope—will provide the means for Americans to look at, if not re-look at, the Native population which has been pushed into the cracks between the pages of American history textbooks.

Professor Williams has taught both Native American Ethnohistory and Civil War History classes for many years. Having done much research and publication on Diné people's role in the Civil War years, he decided to make the setting of the novel in the 1860s. The Civil War was as devastating for the Diné as it was for any group of people in

North America, North or South. The Civil War was as central to the Diné people as World War II was to the Jewish people; both groups experienced a holocaust. Survivors of Germany's concentration camps vowed to never let it happen again and they still remind and educate us. America distanced itself from its own holocaust since it rubs open the scab wounds. The survivors from America's concentration camps have completely died off and are no longer living. We do not have any reminders.

Though Williams' and Johnson's book is written in fictional form, many of the things that are recounted in the plot were actually done by real historical persons like General James Carleton, Barboncito, Dezba, Dr. Michael Steck, and General William Tecumseh Sherman. Barboncito's skilled work as a negotiator with U.S. government officials has been particularly well documented. The fictional character William Lee is similar to a U.S. government Indian Agent in the 1860s who was unusually sympathetic to the Diné. In studying Diné history, I always wondered why this agent had such different attitudes than his contemporaries; Williams and Johnson provide a more plausible explanation than any other I have considered.

Though the timeframe has been compressed, to keep the plot moving quickly, this book includes many real events that actually happened: the massacre of Diné women and children following a horse race in 1861, the genocidal campaign of total war that General Carleton waged against the Diné people in 1862 to 1864, the Long Walk in 1864, and the imprisonment at Fort Sumner from 1864 to 1868.

Also accurate is the novel's depiction of conditions at Fort Sumner and the Bosque Redondo, in the desolate lands of eastern New Mexico Territory. The central point of the book is correct: Under the command of General Carleton, Fort Sumner was a scene of unparalleled death, misery, and despair. Fort Sumner is known among my people, even today, as a "place of suffering" and a place where "death was perfected by colonialism." It is a place where our people and our way of life almost disappeared.

Recently, due to the historical importance of Fort Sumner in my own research work, I mentioned to my relatives that "I planned to visit America's concentration camp in eastern New Mexico." Among my relatives, I heard only silence. I was instructed by my family members and relatives that I should not go there as it is a place of dishonor; a place of death, a place of wrongs the country has bestowed upon its own human beings. It is still believed that the ghosts of many are "stuck" there and are unable to leave. No action of any form has been taken to resolve this matter, so those ghosts continue to linger there.

Just as the Fort Sumner years almost resulted in the disappearance of the Diné way of life, today also, our traditional Diné values are in danger of disappearing. This novel reminds us how much those values have changed since the 1860s. The current pressures that are destroying our traditional values are not coming at the point of a bayonet, but are due to years of indoctrination by mainstream Euro-American culture.

For nearly a century, the avowed purpose of the United States Bureau of Indian Affairs school system was to wipe out Diné culture. Generations of Christian missionaries flocked to convert our people away from their ancestral Indigenous religions. For the last half-century television has had an insidious impact on our young people. As a result of all these pressures, we are now experiencing the beginnings, if not more, of a period of cultural loss. Today the majority of Diné people below the age of fifty cannot even speak the Diné language.

Specifically, this novel records the high level of respect that was given by our ancestors toward *nadleehí* and *dilbaá*. *Nadleehí* means "one who is in a constant state of changing." This refers to morphological males (and also intersexed persons) who have a feminine gender status that is between a man and a woman. *Dilbaá* applies to morphological females who have a masculine gender status that is also between a man and a woman. Be mindful that these are not alternative genders. Diné was a multi-gendered society that recognized four genders of equal status. "Alternative" suggests that a space has to be carved out to find another place for an additional gender.

Nadleehí are more inclined to be feminine and are most likely to settle on the woman side of gender identity, whereas *dilbaás'* name derived from their participation in the war battles of years ago: *-baá* is the root word for "conflict/aggression." Due to the form of aggressiveness, this term is associated with masculinity. Therefore, *dilbaá* are more inclined to be aggressive and are most likely to settle on the man side of gender identity. In addition, the term *-baá* is culturally connected to the need to raise one's arm for protection, in defending one's children and family. It is a name that makes claim for control over a matter relating to conflict.

When early anthropologists came into our homelands, they recorded our high level of respect for *nadleehí* and *dilbaá*. They called it by words like "hermaphrodite" and "berdache." By the 1960s and 1970s, as a result of the growth of gay rights movement, some young Diné adopted gay, lesbian, bisexual and transgender identities. Most of the *nadleehí* and *dilbaá* by this time had been eliminated from the Diné culture through acculturation and assimilation. In the 1990s, there was a reaction of young queer native people against merging into the general GLBT population. They turned back toward Indigenous traditions of respect as their model, and adopted a term "Two-Spirit" suggesting a person who has both the spirit of a man and the spirit of a woman united into one unique androgynous individual. They saw, if not taught by their tribal culture, such a person as being twice as spiritual as the average person, and that is why so many Native American cultures provided them a venerated spiritual role as religious leaders.

While Two-Spirit is an accurate and appropriate term for some tribes, it is problematic for many Diné people. In the first place, referring to a "spirit" reminds Diné of ghosts. There are two concepts of "spirits" within Diné culture. One is associated with the living and the other with the dead. For this particular reason, the term "Two-Spirit" cannot be translated into Diné language. Diné people even today do not like to be connected in any way with deceased people's spirits or ghosts. Secondly, many Diné see Two-Spirit as a recently created identity to encompass a once tribal way of life with Western forms of marginalized identity. Many Diné still resist the term Two-Spirit because they long to connect culturally with the tribal past identity of *nadleehí* or *dilbaá*.

The struggle for a sense of place is difficult for young Diné people in light of western education, Christian missionization, lack of exposure to the practice of oral tradition, or downright shame for being Diné. This shame led many Diné people to drop their prior respect for *nadleehí*. Because so many Diné young people go into the United States Armed Forces, for example, they see the ridicule and condemnation that are so prevalent in the non-Indian population toward androgynous, queer, and transgender people, and they adopt these negative attitudes.

The ignorance of their own cultural traditions, if not arrogance toward those who are different from the norm, led many young Diné to embrace homophobia. Many Diné now do not have access to their cultural knowledge. Due to this deprivation, homophobia has become part of the culture. The Diné way of life once had great wisdom, an emphasis on freedom and individualism, on being inclusive and accepting of differences.

Today, the traditional roles and duties of *nadleehí* and *dilbaá* are close to disappearing from Diné reality. For some, we learn of these once important people through Western culture and by means of an alien form of communication, such as reading of *nadleehí* and *dilbaá* in English (as in this novel). This sorely indicates we no longer have ownership of our intellectual cultural knowledge.

Publication of this novel informs us how far we have stepped out of Diné cultural boundaries in reference to inclusion. Acceptance and tolerance are marginalizing terms. Why is there a need to practice acceptance or tolerance when it is (was?) normative in Diné life? Not owning the great wisdom of our past as Diné means that in the future we will be in danger of becoming Diné in name only with no cultural practicality. It is time for Diné people to learn about their ancestors' ways of thinking, and to take ownership of our traditional values of inclusion and acceptance of peoples' differences so that we ourselves can produce our own novels and education of our young people.

In the meantime, I am grateful to Walter Williams and Toby Johnson for producing this book that is as much of benefit as any form of writing about Diné culture. It not only informs the reading audiences of the importance of Diné history, their way of life, their sufferings, and their desires, but it also reminds us about the importance of accepting all types of people, in spite of their differences. This book conveys the wisdom of my ancestors that all human beings are important and essential, especially for their contributions to help us all in clearly defining what diversity is all about.

Wesley K. Thomas, Ph.D. (Diné)
Assistant Professor of Anthropology,
Gender Studies & International Studies
Department of Anthropology
Indiana University

About the Authors

Walter L. Williams, Ph.D has been one of the people primarily responsible for bringing to light Native American Two-Spirit traditions. He is professor of anthropology, history and gender studies at the University of Southern California, where he teaches gay, lesbian, bisexual and transgender studies, and also American Indian Studies. He was president of ONE National Gay and Lesbian Archives, founding editor of the *International Gay & Lesbian Review*, co-founder and chair of the Committee on Lesbian and Gay History for the American Historical Association, and an officer of the Society of Lesbian and Gay Anthropologists. His award-winning non-fiction book *The Spirit and the Flesh: Sexual Diversity in American Indian Culture* carefully and inspirationally recounts the respected place many Native American cultures accord to persons who combine both the spirit of man and the spirit of woman into their personality and sexual behavior.

Based on his own experience talking with Diné people on the Navajo reservation and on his wide reading in Navajo history, Walter Williams conceived and crafted the story of this book. Out of the real historical events of the tragic 1860s Bosque Redondo experiment, he wove a plausible story showing how same-sex relationships in the past might have helped bring disparate kinds of people together, at least to accord each other respect, freedom, and love. These are traits needed in the contemporary multicultural society.

Toby Johnson, Ph.D., novelist and spiritual writer, joined the project to give texture and style to Walter's story. His mystical gay-positive storytelling is exemplified in his novels *Getting Life in Perspective, Plague* and the Lammy-winning science fiction novel *Secret Matter* (now in an updated second edition). From 1996 to 2003, he was editor of the quarterly journal of gay men's spirituality, *White Crane*. Johnson is author also of several non-fiction titles about spirituality and religion in modern consciousness, including *Gay Spirituality: The Role of Gay Identity in the Transformation of Human Consciousness*. Johnson was a student of the renowned comparative religions scholar Joseph Campbell.

Toby Johnson and Kip Dollar, partners since 1984, ran Liberty Books, the lesbian and gay community bookstore in Austin, and gay B&Bs in the Rocky Mountains and the Texas Hill Country. Dollar and Johnson are champions and models of successful longterm gay relationship. In 1993 they were the first male couple registered as Domestic Partners in Texas.

Walter Williams and Toby Johnson discovered in each other parallel interests in communicating Earth-based Native American wisdom to contemporary readers. Combining the strengths of both the scholar and the novelist, their collaboration provides a model of a way to reach readers that either alone could not accomplish.

Williams is profiled on the Internet at <www.livefully.info> which also includes several essays written by him.

Johnson at <www.tobyjohnson.com>

Contact information is available there.

CPSIA information can be obtained at www.ICGtesting.com
Printed in the USA
LVOW08s0854061213

364160LV00001B/151/P